THE MASKED VICTOR

FATE'S INMATE

BOOK 2

L. BLAISE HUES

Stag Beetle Books

To Natalie, *who cares deeply about fictional characters*

and

To my GB San Antonio Fam;
You made this place my home and I'm a better person for my friendship, training, and association with you. Thank you for teaching Victor-27 how to fight!
Obrigada! OSS!

CONTENTS

THE MASKED VICTOR

HOPE AND FEAR ARE EQUALLY DANGEROUS

CHAPTER 1
THE ROAD TO KHIZMIT

My life hadn't flashed before my eyes. It had faded. Everything became muted and stale and quiet.

My blood, hot and sticky, had spread across the snow and melted a vicious red hole as if the earth itself had a gaping wound. The pain had been searing and all-consuming, and for a long, sharp moment, it seemed as if my soul had plunged its fingernails into my bleeding corpse, clinging to the last shreds of my life, begging to stay.

Roman had buried his blade clear up to the hilt, once in my stomach, just below my lungs, and again in my side.

Even as I relived the moment, my sides pinched.

I should be sunk deep into the snow with my insides trailing out a gaping hole in the left side of my body, or half-eaten by the wild wolves that roam these woods. I'd robbed them of their reward. I'd defied death. The beasts howled a promise to the skies that they would find me and kill me themselves.

Their threats, as real as the blood on my torn prison clothes, pushed me forward. I had no reason to believe any guards pursued me. But the wild animals, who'd undoubtedly smelled the metallic tang of my should-be execution? They hunted me now.

The wind bit at the back of my neck as I ran south, fueled by fear of the wolves and the adrenaline rush of my sudden freedom. The air was so cold it seemed to freeze my entire chest as I breathed. Swallowing and digesting the truth that I had lived, that I was able to survive those lethal wounds, was even more chilling than tramping through the icy snow.

With the truth of my ability to block pain and heal myself came other revelations—why Roman had forced me—trained me—to run long distances without rest. Wild how I could suddenly be grateful for something I'd resented so bitterly. Pieces of our final conversation replayed in my head as I took step after step away from Predvoi Prison, my predators in pursuit.

"You're going to help me?"

Roman had seemed almost annoyed when he answered me. *"What the skudge do you think I've been doing for you this entire time?"*

I'd believed I'd been alone, left for execution at the hands of the firing squad. After they'd taken Lockbox from me, what else could I have assumed?

Just as Roman had said, the gap beneath the fence was big enough for me to crawl beneath. Beyond it, I found a road. *The road.*

The sun glinted through the trees at my right as it made its descent beyond the far mountains. Thick black shadows striped the ground ahead of me. The frozen snow was difficult to walk through, but my boots at least kept my shins safe. The beauty of the scene was minimized as the wind howled along with the wolves—cold and angry.

I wished I could have brought my sweater. I wish I'd done a lot of things differently. Night was coming soon and with it, more threats. Biting wind. And plummeting temperatures.

During certain times of the year, Rhosivi had daylight for twenty hours. Other times, the outside was just as dark as the rat holes. Come nightfall, the wolves would catch me, and dangerous as I was, I had no desire to fight an entire pack of wolves.

I'd been following the road south toward Khizmit, ears alert for any approaching vehicles or people. I didn't know if I'd find camps or small towns en route, but there was nothing as far as I could see. My eyelashes threatened to freeze together each time I blinked.

The trees thinned as I continued, leaving me open to prying eyes, if there were any looking for me. The only other living things around were the few birds of prey I'd seen far above. And they didn't care about my trespassing, just the remains I'd leave behind if my predators finally caught up to me.

The road stretched directly ahead in the distance, appearing to drop off the earth. I followed it to the edge, where the land sloped downward and began to zig-zag down the steep, rocky terrain on this side of the mountain. I could walk it, adding distance to my trip, or scramble straight down the side, crossing over the road at least eight times in the process. Climbing was out of the question—far too danger-ous. Out here, there wouldn't be anyone to help me if I broke a leg.

Then I laughed at myself, my warm breath billowing around me like the puffy clouds that had begun to sink lower in the sky. I had nothing to fear.

My head ached as if someone was inside, chiseling away for coal within the depths of my skull. If I continued to use my abilities to heal and block pain, the headache might drive me to insanity. Even now, its rhythmic thudding made it hard to think. Hard to reason.

I stopped running after what I had to assume was between five and seven kilometers south of Predvoi to gather and swallow some snow. I drew a hand to my cheek where, for five years, a thick scar had blanketed my dimple, erasing the innocent look I'd been born with and replacing it with a savage mark. My tongue explored the smooth inside of my cheek as my fingers ran along the stubble. No scar. No visible lasting damage of Flak's attack.

If only the tattoo on my wrist had disappeared the same way. I tried once to erase the tattoo while resting from running. But it wasn't a proper injury, so no amount of focusing or hoping dulled the black letters designating me as a prisoner.

If anyone took note of the mark on my wrist, they'd either faint or shoot me outright, depending on their fight-or-flight response. My scar was too prominent and identifiable. And whoever found out or knew I was a Victor would want me dead. They always had. A wrist tattoo could be easily hidden. A facial scar could not.

And so, I'd erased it.

V-27 had been inked onto my wrist on my 8th birthday, the same day they sent me from the Children's Academy for Prisoners, CAP, to begin labor in the Rhosivi Mine.

To think I'd wondered if I was dangerous. The fear surrounding my title of Victor was, in fact, well-founded. Dangerous didn't even begin to cover it.

Most of my abilities had lain dormant until Lockbox pulled me aside and told me what I really was. The knowledge had been like unlocking a key in my mind. Same as Roman had done when he told me to heal myself. We were incarcerated not because of what our parents did, but because of what Khizmit had done to *them*. Experimentation. Super soldier serum. *Should it have been any surprise that their entire group of prisoners used their new abilities—speed, strength, enhanced senses—to escape?*

How many Victors had there been initially? How many had escaped?

My father was an X-ray. My mother, a Victor. I hated the fact that I'd reduced them to those titles. I never knew their names, never understood what crimes they had been accused of that landed them in prison. *Who were they before they'd become unwilling test subjects for their twisted tormentors, the scientists of Khizmit, concocting new serums to win the war against Latvani Enclave?*

Being a Victor alone gave anyone with an understanding of the Test Criminals reason to fear me. In reality I was much worse than a Victor. As a hybrid of two dangerous criminals, I likely possessed their most deadly and impressive traits. For years, I'd wondered what my prison tag meant. Wondered why I didn't see more Victors in my life.

Lockbox had been the one to shed light on so many of my questions. Lockbox had shown me compassion, sharing his knowledge and his vyco. The incessant drumming in my head left me wishing I had some with me now to ease the pain.

My friend was alive, and while I didn't know where he was, I assumed it wasn't at Predvoi Prison. Someone, some inmate, would have seen him. I wished Roman would have told me if Lockbox was still there.

The Chancellor Supreme's threat echoed in my head. *"What are you? Tell me the truth or Oscar-17's conditions will worsen significantly."*

I'll find him, I swore to myself. *I'll find Lockbox and keep him safe.* An insane part of my brain took that thought further. I'll save the lurpers. It wasn't fair that I should escape and taste freedom when so many of the other inmates faced death.

We all had abilities and unique skills that corresponded to each of our titles. Alphas, Bravos, and Charlies were all compliant, with Charlies being most obedient. Deltas, Echoes, and Foxtrots were fast, but Echoes were the fastest. Golfs, Hotels, and Indias were strong, but Hotels were always the strongest. Juliets, Kilos, and Limas were fighters, gifted with a premonition of how battles would end, combined with a rage to fuel each fight to its victory. Yet, of the three, Juliets were the ones to fear the most.

Mikes, Novembers, and Oscars had photographic memories, and their skills with strategy left the rest of us in the dust. The Oscars were the best. Lockbox had told me that Papas, Quebecs, and Romeos had quick reflexes and violent tendencies that resulted in early termination for most of them. I didn't need him to tell me how Romeos were the most violent and gifted of the bunch, mostly because I'd thought of R-22, Flak, almost daily since he gave me that scar. I wondered if he ever thought of me. A twisted part of me wished I'd scarred him too.

Sierras, Tangos, and Uniforms were almost unheard of, and once I learned they had the ability to heal themselves *and* block pain, it became obvious why. Either they'd been killed for knowing what they were capable of, or they'd unconsciously blocked their pain to the point that they died of their injuries, never aware their lives were in danger until it was too late. Uniforms were deemed the most gifted of that group.

But Victors were something else entirely. Victors were a Romeo/Uniform hybrid. And X-rays were a Hotel/Juliet hybrid.

If all the Test Criminals and their offspring were considered freaks, then I was a skudging monster. If they'd understood the truth when I was just a child, they wouldn't have stopped at simply tattooing me, they'd have killed me on sight.

With good reason. I was everything they feared, neatly packaged inside the body of a reckless teenage boy.

They didn't know I would have helped them in the war against Latvani if they'd asked. I'd tried to help Khizmit by mining. For my whole life, I'd tried to prove to them that I was more than my tattoo, and all it had gotten me was near-death experiences, malicious threats, and a head full of doubt and self-loathing.

The sun disappeared behind the mountains, and while the sky remained lit in purple hues, I had to decide what to do for the night. I could tell from the increasing howling that the wolves were getting closer, waiting for the cover of darkness to attack me. Every shift in the snow left me picturing Head Warden Velky at my back or Bolest creeping through the trees with a razor and syringe.

Either I could find shelter and some means of keeping warm, or I could push on—walk through the night, keep my blood running hot through my extremities—and hopefully arrive at Khizmit by morning before the wolves caught me.

Rest called my name, but I didn't want to take the chance of lying down in some outcropping of rock or a cave and finding myself frozen solid or half-eaten come morning. Could I even heal myself back from that? I didn't feel like finding out.

Not daring to wander far from the road, since it afforded me a wider view of an impending attack from the wolves, I continued walking. If it became essential, I'd stop on the side of the road for a brief rest, careful to keep my senses alert and my pain in full force. Anything to avoid falling asleep, numbing the pain, and drifting off into death as unsuspecting as a baby bird scrambling from its nest into the frozen snow below.

I imagined my parents in the chaos of the Test Criminal breakout, dodging bullets with super speed, or perhaps bending bars as they made their escape. Somehow meeting in the melee, helping one another, connecting. *Was it so wrong that I wanted my parents to have simply been misunderstood?*

Maybe my father had been imprisoned for stealing food. I had no idea what the laws were in Khizmit, but I wanted to give my parents the best backstory I could think of. Maybe they'd been heroes misread by their government, imprisoned and separated, before finally meeting back up after receiving their heightened abilities. They'd run off, hid together in Khizmit, only to be discovered later. I wanted a reason to mourn them in their death, because if I saw them as the serial killers they were branded, then I also had to mourn my own existence.

I refused to believe my mother would have ever hurt me, despite what the wardens from CAP had told me time and time again. And Khizmit, with its Preemptive Initiative, had chosen to punish me for just existing. They said they locked us up for the crimes of our parents, but Lockbox had shown me what they'd really done was punish us for the crimes they themselves had committed. They'd been the ones to turn criminals into super-soldiers, and for almost eighteen years, I'd suffered relentlessly as a result.

What I really wanted to know was who had been keeping the truth from me, the truth about my past. Lockbox had explained to me that us lurpers got our abilities because one of our parents—and I wasn't sure it mattered which one—had been experimented on at Zalar Correctional Facility. *One* of our parents.

Both of mine had been altered by a powerful serum. It was no wonder everyone feared me. As Roman had once told me, it wasn't just because of what I could do to others, but what I could do to myself that set me apart, the lone wolf, nearly invincible.

The hues along the distant mountains faded darker until they turned black, and millions of stars now opened their eyes to watch me. I had the heavy sense they weren't the only eyes on me. My head hammered as I walked, a constant reminder of the cost of having healed myself. At times, it became so intense that I had to sit down and take a few deep breaths. I sucked on some snow, and while it almost froze my mouth, I was grateful for it.

A slight shift to my right sent my heart racing. I straightened. The wolf had found me. I would have been able to hear the scrape of his claws against the ice much earlier if my headache hadn't been hammering so intensely.

I'd imagined the animal would be brown, so the flash of

white threw me. By a macabre twist, it was the blood on its snout that made it visible against the snow. Was it mine? Had it lapped up the blood I'd spilled back at Predvoi?

If it had, I should thank it. If any guards went back to check for my body, they'd find pawprints in the snow.

The wolf wasted no time charging me. I pulled out my blade and slashed through the air. My arm went high, missing the wolf entirely. *This skudging headache!*

The wind blew up small flurries of flakes, and the wolf disappeared into them. I growled, inviting it back. I knew in an instant that it was behind me, and I whipped around just as the wolf launched itself toward my head.

I pulled my arm back to drive the blade into its stomach just as it locked its teeth around my wrist. My hand went limp as he dragged me across the snow. I blocked the pain and used the wolf's grip on my arm to swing myself up and onto its back. I wrapped my free arm around its neck, gripping tightly to try and strangle it.

It twisted, throwing me over its head, when a snap and a tingle of numbness announced that it had broken my arm.

Disoriented by rage, I fought it, giving into every animalistic urge I'd ever felt. Without my headache, I became alert, tuned in to the wolf's every move.

I didn't need the dagger.

I was weapon enough.

My vision tinged with crimson as I wrestled my prey. My fingers dug in its fur, our bodies tumbling through the snow, and with a dull crack, I snapped the wolf's neck. It fell limp to the ground, atop my legs, and I let it sit there as I caught my breath.

My vision returned to normal, and I caught sight of my arm. In haste, I healed it, half-mesmerized, half-mortified by my ability.

A sense of self swam back as I dropped the block to the pain, intensifying my headache and my confusion. The ice and snow beneath my hands and knees grew colder as I propped myself upright, staring at the dead beast.

The wolf was bigger than I'd expected it to be. I crawled beside it now that the body was still. It was nearly two meters in length, not including the tail. Had it come in a pack, it would have succeeded in killing me. But I got lucky.

It was, like me, a lone wolf.

Reasoning that wolves couldn't be all that different from rabbits, I crawled over to the dagger and brought it back to the carcass. Using Roman's knife and gloves, I worked to remove the coat. Not only would it keep me warm, but it provided better camouflage in this tundra than the stripes of my prison clothes.

Warm blood entered my right glove through the holes the wolf's teeth had torn as I slipped the coat off and draped it over my shoulders. I cleaned the blade and stood.

It wasn't a rabbit.

I looked at the naked wolf, its bold red body in stark contrast to the snow. I felt I almost owed it to the wolf to eat some of its meat. The strong gamey aroma was sure to draw other wolves. Maybe by leaving its body here, I could get some distance from the rest of the threats.

I scraped the skin off the coat, cut off a few pieces of the meat to chew on, and cleaned my knife in the snow.

If more wolves watched from the trees, I didn't hear them. I couldn't see them. The drumming in my head was so loud, I couldn't even hear my own feet crunch through the snow. Then, dizzy as I was, I hurried away from the warm and inviting carcass.

Until the sun came back up, I'd have to walk rather than run. It had taken a toll, but I'd slain a beast with my bare hands. As I navigated the treacherous road, I imagined what my abilities would look like in someone who was truly predisposed to violence. Someone who wanted to rape, maim, and murder for pleasure or power. They'd be unstoppable. More dangerous than Warden Velky, Bolest, or Riah Dulka could ever know. Proving my innocence or good nature had done nothing to win them over. Even Warden Markos—Commander Pedrick Markos—had chosen to betray me in the end.

My mind kept me company as I walked, for better or worse, as it was the only thing that could slightly distract me from the pain. My steps became synchronized with the beating within my pounding head. I felt myself slip into something of a daze.

It had been dark for at least two hours by the time I saw an unnatural shape over the edge of the sharp turn in the road. The sides of the shadowy thing were too angular to be a rock. Cautiously, I stepped off the road and peered closer at the bulky dark shape that sat at the bottom of the drop-off.

The thing wasn't alive; I knew that much. Which was also why I felt no fear as I approached it. Initially, I wondered if it was some kind of shack or guard post. Glass glinted, reflecting dots of starlight in its fractured face.

I climbed down the side of the cliff slowly, unearthing a few loose rocks, which tumbled down and crashed into the shape below. The clang of rocks upon metal told me all I needed to know.

A truck. I'd usually seen them from behind at Rhosivi as I loaded them with coal. This one had evidently never made it to its destination, having driven right over the edge of the road. The truck bed held no bags of coal, and no bodies in the crushed cab. I had a hunch that if I'd dug around in the drifts, I could have found some coal, as the bags had likely burst open upon impact. With no sign of Khizmit in the distance, I didn't have to worry about someone seeing the light of glowing coals. But I waved the idea away, envisioning my hands becoming so frozen and stiff, as there'd be no way for me to light it.

Maybe I could take shelter inside the truck for the night.

My legs would have been fine running or walking till the sun rose, but my headache had become so severe even the minimal moonlight reflecting off the snow from above caused piercing pain.

I couldn't heal my head—I'd tried. I could block the pain, but when I eventually had to remove the numbing, the pain grew far worse.

At this point, worse might kill me.

I narrowed my eyes and examined the vehicle.

The entire front portion of the truck was in shambles, smashed like a soda can. They apparently hadn't taken the bodies out from the driver's door since it had all but melded into the side of the mountain. The bodies had likely been dragged elsewhere by wolves, maybe even the one whose coat I had wrapped around my shoulders. That sort of image should have disgusted me, and maybe, if I hadn't grown up in prison, it would have. I imagine a lot of things would be different if I hadn't grown up in prison.

I skirted my way around the truck, careful of the icy rocks beneath my smooth boots. I tugged on the passenger door. It creaked and protested before opening, breaking free of the snow and ice.

The upholstered seats groaned as I pulled myself into the cab and willed my body to relax. Although the windows of the vehicle had been smashed, the subsequent snow, rain and freezing temperatures had erected something of an ice cocoon around the car. I wrapped the wolf's coat tighter around myself and blew hot air into my hands so it would warm my nose and cheeks.

My head pounded, the pain beating like a pickaxe, sharp and invasive.

The few visible holes in the windows that hadn't sealed over with ice, especially in the door that I'd disturbed, were going to let out too much air. Digging around me, I stuffed fistfuls of the powdery snow and blocks of ice into the holes before reclining the seat as far back as possible and curling into a ball.

I shut my eyes, hoping my own body heat would be contained enough in this small space to keep me alive through the night.

Within seconds, darkness claimed me.

CHAPTER 2
THE SKUDGING WALL

Morning came too soon. The light didn't hammer at my head through my eyelids as it had before, so I dared to open them and assess my extremities. The inside of the ice wall surrounding me shone as though it'd melted during the night.

I smiled. It worked. I'd made it through the night. My first night as a free man, and I hadn't died.

I hoped other wolves had eaten the one I'd killed so there wouldn't be a trail to follow. But if they thought I was dead back at Predvoi, they wouldn't be looking for my tracks.

Hunger compelled me to leave the shielded sanctuary of the truck and continue toward Khizmit. And the raw wolf meat hadn't settled well. With my stomach clenching, I climbed back up to the road.

The day had barely begun. Not even the sun had shown its face yet, but the world celebrated its arrival with vibrant orange and peach strokes scattered along the mountains. Dazzling pastels in shades of purple, blue, and yellow streaked through the thin clouds, and I stared, unsure if this was the first time the sun and sky had orchestrated such a stunning display, or if I'd just been ignorant of its brilliance before this day.

The burst of color brought warmth to more than just the distant hills. The white and grey of the snow all around seemed to absorb the color and reflect it around the icy world. The overwhelming beauty of it fueled my hope for the future.

Hope. Fear. Turns out there is a difference. And glimmers of hope were beginning to brighten my vision.

Since it hadn't snowed last night, the road remained clear of ice. With anticipation sparking my adrenaline, I took off running, careful to watch my footing.

It couldn't have been more than an hour when I thought I heard something ahead of me. The run had been mostly downhill, leading me to the valley where Khizmit awaited. The sounds were distant, and I only heard them when I consciously amplified my hearing. All around me, coniferous bushes grew tall, their shadows introducing a new chill when I passed through them, but I remained veiled by their covering as I crept to the edge of the hill toward the sounds.

It was there, nestled among the frosted needles, that I caught the first glimpse of my new home.

The lights of Khizmit began to wink out between the trees as they thinned, and then I saw it. The city rested at the bottom of a valley, protected on three sides by mountains, one of which I'd just hiked. I stood there, leaning against a tree trunk as the sun rose. The few lights that remained on until now began to dim and turn off. Sunlight jumped across the red roofs of the smaller buildings where I assumed the residents lived.

A giant tower rose above all the other buildings, topped with a bulbous green spire that seemed to glow in the morning light. The sun sparkled on the city for a moment before it rose high enough to hide behind a collection of thick, grey clouds. A giant cemetery spread from one side of the city toward the smaller houses, awash in the dimmed light. *How appropriate,* I thought, looking at the clouds, *that the city should become shrouded upon my arrival.*

Roman's comment about Khizmit came back to me, and I smiled. *Did I expect it to be a utopia? Did I think they'd welcome me, embrace me? That they would serve me a warm, hearty meal out of the kindness of their hearts?* I had to remember—these are the ones who voted on the Preemptive Initiative. They were culpable for my captivity.

Could I blame them? If I knew someone possessed the abilities I did but knew nothing of their character, would I not also vote for their incarceration?

I frowned. I had to believe I wouldn't, but do any of us ever know what we will or won't do given someone else's circumstances? With their unique hopes and hurts, their history of losses or dreams?

Lockbox once told me that Khizmit was at war, so it shouldn't have been a surprise to see such an enormous wall around the city. All the buildings and citizens were protected by thick stones, piled wide and high. It was shocking to think I hadn't been brought down earlier from Rhosivi to help build it. Would they have let me so near to their children, though?

The numerous day trips from my more compliant inmates finally made some sense. Inmate hands had to have built this colossal shield, just not mine. Hands they could trust built it, or at least entrusted with as much as was necessary. Alphas, Bravos, and Charlies must have done this work, and they'd done a skudging good job of it!

From my vantage point, I could see two entrances to the city, both of which were accompanied by a small but occupied guard shack. A checkpoint. Pillars of smoke drifted out of the small chimneys all around the city.

A short distance, a couple kilometers or so outside of the back entrance to Khizmit where the cemetery lay, great vapors rose from huge circular columns reaching higher than any building or tree I'd ever seen. The chimneys belched out plumes of thick smoke, mingling seamlessly with the dark clouds above as they ascended until I wasn't sure which was which.

I'd seen, and helped run, the small coal factory at Rhosivi which was responsible for powering the prison and making the frigid wasteland habitable. For obvious reasons, I had little desire to follow the trail of black boot prints dredged in coal dust clear to the factory.

My gaze traveled around the outside of the building and then back along the path which wove around the short black fence enclosing the cemetery. I could step into the factory and get warm within its walls, but it would take me further from my destination: the heart of Khizmit.

Without food or shelter, along with the constant threat of guards on my tail, I had to get into the city as fast as possible if I was going to survive.

But the walls left me feeling a little uneasy. *Was I trading one prison for another?* Roman had said to go to Khizmit, and I had no one else to trust. A few more instructions and a change of clothes would have been welcome, but I suppose there were only so many syllables one could utter while stabbing you between the ribs.

Staying outside in the woods indefinitely was out of the question. Besides all the threats that lay outside these walls, my headache was returning and still threatened to split my skull wide open. My toes and fingers already tingled in the cold, and my empty stomach nudged me forward, too tired to even roar anymore.

The full branches of the pines and spruces kept most of the snow's burden off the ground, but below, between the gravestones and the open spaces around the city, white patches piled several centimeters deep.

I stepped through the shallow snow on the hill toward the entrance at the far end near the cemetery, moving slowly. They hadn't built the wall to include it, but there wasn't anything helpful to me among the dead. No reason for me to go there.

Frozen clusters of ice crunched beneath my boots, and I moved slowly, not because I thought anyone could hear me but because I had little doubt they would be eager to check my wrist for a tattoo if I were to be spotted. Actually, they wouldn't even need to see the tattoo. I still wore the striped linens from Predvoi Prison, practically announcing to anyone who saw me and knew slag from silver that I didn't belong anywhere *near* Khizmit.

My main objective was to get within the city's stone walls. Once there, I could decide what to do with my life. I could determine if there was any way to find out what had happened to Lockbox. Roman said there were other prisoners who'd been released from Predvoi, others who had graduated. *If I could locate them and explain my situation, would they have sympathy for me? Help me? Or would they be more likely to turn me in, knowing what a Victor was capable of?*

Again, these were problems for the future. First, I had a decision to make. I could either try to get in through the entrance near the cemetery, which provided me a wide-open space and a single checkpoint station—the entrance in the front that faced away from all the mountains to which the road led. Or I could try to scale the outer wall composed of rocks with scant handholds.

My hands and fingers weren't hurting anymore, but my head drummed so intensely, I considered numbing some of the pain just to help me concentrate.

This side of the valley had no roads and no guards, and from what I observed, they didn't need them. At least, not with the well-constructed wall protecting them from anything that might approach from this side. *Everything except for me,* I hoped. I could climb the wall and find some new clothes. While I didn't expect I'd find some in my size just dangling from a clothesline, there had to be other options. Like stores. I could break into a store.

I sighed, my breath visible in the frosty air. Already, I was considering criminal activity. *What did that say about me? That I was becoming exactly what everyone feared I was? Or that the Chancellors and Wardens had successfully left me with no other option?*

Audacious as it was, I approached the wall and looked around. Now that I stood beside it, it was much taller than it had appeared from afar. It rose at least four, maybe five meters above my head.

I reached up, grateful my gloves were on tight, and tried to get a decent grip on the rocks.

"Skudge," I muttered as my fingers slipped. Whether from freezing rain or some defensive devising on the part of the commander over Khizmit, the wall was coated in a slick sheet of ice.

Removing my gloves, I tried again, hoping my bare hands might make a difference. They didn't. My body heat only seemed to melt the ice beneath my fingers. Although I found a few hand-holds, the longer my hands hovered, the ice would melt, and I would slide away, falling on my ass, time and time again.

I reached up once more, fingers clamped on the slick stone above me, tension spreading down my wrists. Focusing my entire attention on the wall, I heaved myself up with as much determination as I could conjure.

And failed. Again.

The gloves had worked better, so I dug them out of my pockets and tried again.

At one point, I was almost two meters high when my boot slipped from beneath me. I plummeted to the frozen ground, landing hard on my back. It was as if I'd been hit with a thirty-kilogram sack of coal launched at me by a catapult. Defeated and out of breath, I lay on the hard earth for a minute, staring up at the unforgiving sky swirling above. My head throbbed, my fingers ached, and now my back hurt, too.

Stupid. My whole plan was idiotic! I'd wasted hours trying to scale the wall, but the sun, which barely touched the upper half of the wall, only melted the ice on the rocks enough to make them slicker. I had one option now: checkpoints. *Guarded* checkpoints, at that. One in front, one in back. I'd have flipped a coin if I had one, for all the difference it would have made.

I could no longer see the front entrance, but since it had a road leading to it, I wasn't convinced anyone approaching on foot would even be seen as a threat. The back side led to the cemetery, and while I wasn't sure what business anyone had in a cemetery, I'd read books where characters sometimes returned to visit the bones of the dead.

Maybe I shouldn't say it like that, but that's what it is, isn't it? The person you know isn't there. All that remains is skin and bones. I haven't decided if I believe in life after death, but either way, I wasn't in any rush to find out for certain by joining them in the ground. If I didn't step carefully around the armed guards outside Khizmit, I just might end up shot in a cemetery.

There are worse places to die, I reminded myself.

Like the rat holes in Rhosivi.

A painful memory surfaced.

While digging through the rat holes at age fourteen, I'd found an inmate half-buried in rocks, only he'd done it to himself. The thirteen-year-old kid had gotten lost, and then trapped himself with no will to get out. He seemed to have no strength either, until he saw that I'd intended to return him to the surface. A small bit of light had shown me the D-14 on his wrist. I'd dragged the Delta out by his ankle, and he had fought me the whole way, swinging his pickaxe with the rage of a wild wolf until I'd taken it from him.

When I'd reached sunlight, I'd imagined calling the

guards over and having them finally look at me without seething hatred. But when I'd emerged from the hole, triumphant, with the half-dead inmate in tow, the guards had surrounded me, drew their palkas and sidearms, and had them all pointed at me.

The guards had stood there, seething with palpable hatred, their furs wrapped around their necks and wool uniforms buttoned over layers of clothing, while my arms and ankles took the biting wind and bitter cold. Just my luck, Warden Velky had been out patrolling. He'd seen the commotion from atop his guard tower and had taken his time walking over to me.

"Drop the weapon, Victor-27," he'd snarled.

Weapon? I'd thought, before looking back at the axe. I'd dropped it, and it'd hit the ground with a hollow thud. The rest of the topside inmates had frozen in place, staring at me. I didn't mind when guards pulled out their palkas. That happened regularly. Granted, the metal palkas left bruises so deep I swear they could scar your bone marrow. The metal batons, a little more than half a meter long, usually served their purpose of ensuring compliance without being used.

It was the guns that worried me.

We'd seen guns pulled out before. I'd heard them fired every time an older inmate didn't pass his Judgement Board and seen firsthand what they did to inmates who tried to scramble over the huge fences surrounding the whole of our prison-mine. Never before had I seen so many guards with their attention, and muzzles, fixated on a single prisoner.

And I'd done nothing.

"I found him," I'd explained, gesturing to the Delta who I could now see had lost his helmet somewhere in the hole.

Velky had strode over to me as soon as one of the guards pulled the boy away. The words that came from him next were a threat. A promise. "The next time you pick up a weapon, no one will hesitate to fire."

"But Mr. Chief Preemptive Officer, I wasn't holding it as a weapon. I took it to–"

"That's enough from you, lurper," he'd hissed.

The captains and second lieutenants had still kept their sidearms aimed at me; sergeants, junior sergeants, and privates had their steel batons in hand, no doubt because Velky hadn't said to lower them. Up in the towers, silhouettes of men had their rifles directed at me.

"I helped him!" I'd insisted, gesturing wildly to the Delta who still hadn't sat up.

"For all we know, you did this to him," Velky had said.

"I found him half-buried, and I helped him."

A snarl had come from Velky's lips. "You help the Enclave. You do your job. That's why you're alive. Or do you need to be reminded of the conditions of your survival?"

"No, Sir," I'd hissed through my teeth.

"You get back in the rat hole, and you bring back enough ore for both his daily quota and your own."

I'd glanced back at the pickaxe sitting on the dark earth. A bitter gust of wind had picked up and frosted my nose and ears.

"Without the pickaxe, Sir?" I'd asked, not daring to move. You'd have thought he'd found a reason to kill me by now, but he hadn't. I think he had too much fun toying with me to end my life.

"You're a skudging Victor. No weapons." He'd smiled and reached a gloved hand up to pull his black ushanka down over the tips of his ears.

"Yes, Sir." I'd rubbed my arms, attempting to warm them against the wind. No matter what I did, these guards would see me as the enemy, except for the few who, despite their best efforts, hadn't successfully masked their fear of me with malice.

Many had lowered their weapons at this point, but not all. I'd glanced at the faces of the men and then back to the hole in the ground. It'd never looked more inviting. The jagged opening in the earth was like a tomb—a dark spot among many that speckled the landscape here in the heart of the mine. And yet, I'd be more likely to survive another trip into the hole than I was to survive a conversation with Velky. I'd walked back to the hole, dropped to my knees, and scrambled in.

A distant scraping emanating from the cemetery pulled me back to the present. Back to my spot beneath the trees outside Khizmit.

I was a prisoner no longer, and I wasn't going back to Rhosivi or Predvoi. I'd find a way into Khizmit. I wasn't going back to Velky.

Newly motivated, I slunk around the side of the wall and looked toward the sun. Despite being hidden, it illuminated a group of clouds brightly enough that I could discern where it was. Judging by its position, I'd spent all morning on that skudging wall. By now my hunger pangs had returned, reminding me that if I didn't eat soon, I'd be reduced to skin and bones as well.

Every moment is full of decisions, each one presenting a different route that breaks off in front of us like paths in the woods, though some roads lead to the same destination. I wondered, *why did so many of mine end with death?*

I supposed all of our paths end with death, but at seventeen, this truth was hardly encouraging.

The scrape of a shovel on the ground broke through the air as I crept closer to the cemetery. A bit more than a hundred meters from where I stopped, two men were busy fighting the frozen ground beneath them. The area where they were working stood out like a lantern in the mines, since it was the only patch not covered with thick white snow. Rather, it was brown from dirt and trampled by their boots. The harsh scraping sound carried across the still air, assaulting my ears.

From my position behind a large tree trunk, my gaze

returned to the factory in the distance. It had no wall of protection. Some men moved to and from the place in groups now, at what appeared to be a shift change. Men trickled out of Khizmit in a steady line, each one stopping to talk with the guards at the exit before stomping their way along the path.

Despite my aversion to the coal factory, maybe one of these inmates—*no, that was wrong.* No one here was a prisoner. Not even me. Not anymore. Never again.

Maybe one of these crusters—

They weren't crusters. They didn't have uniforms. They weren't inmates either. They were just, men. Maybe one of them would lend me a coat and some pants. As my toes tingled painfully beneath me, I decided I wouldn't say no to a pair of socks either.

Begging for clothes was going to be even more laughable than my attempts at climbing the wall. No, I'd have to take what I needed by force, as unpleasant as that might be for everyone involved.

I could jump a group of them easily enough, knock or choke them out, stealing only a few articles of clothing from each so they wouldn't freeze before regaining consciousness. The actual act of assaulting them would be easy, but I didn't like it. Needless violence didn't settle with me. Besides, no one out here knew an escaped prisoner was roaming the streets. If a random stranger attacked a bunch of men and left them alive, they'd go back to Khizmit with a story to tell, and it wouldn't be hard for someone to figure out a lurper had done it.

I could wait until the cover of night and sneak into the factory when there was sure to be a smaller staff at work, throw a piece of ore at one's head, and strip him down in the shadows. At least that way no one would see me. I could even leave his body near the furnaces so he wouldn't get cold. He'd likely be punished later, but was that really my problem? *No.* My problem was these slaggy, striped prison clothes.

Another option flew into my mind. If I used the coal to darken my clothes, they wouldn't stand out like I'd been a prisoner, at least not at first glance. Still, wearing clothing coated in slag wasn't going to be a good look for uniformity as an upstanding citizen in Khizmit.

I sighed, blowing out a burst of air as my stomach grumbled again.

I had to eat. I had to change my appearance. I had to get into Khizmit. I needed to do all these things as soon as possible, or I was going to skudging die out here in the cold. And on top of all that, I had to take care of this impossibly persistent headache.

Think! I had to get the clothes before I could enter the city, but I also had to anticipate what they'd ask or do if I tried to enter Khizmit.

Step one was to sneak into the cemetery and use the headstones as cover while I got close enough to the soldiers at the checkpoint. I needed to observe their procedure, hear what they were asking, and see what they were checking for.

I waited until the group of men from the factory was far behind me, then moved down the mountainside and across the path they'd made in the snow, to the short fence surrounding the cemetery. Clearing it easily, I ducked behind a tall, round headstone that read "Anatoli Kuznetsov." I thought about that as I lowered my face in the snow to hide. This man, this dead man who'd left this earth behind over fifty years ago, still got to keep his name. Yet, here I was, still alive and breathing but didn't merit anything more than a few stripes of ink on my skin.

I read in a book that it's disrespectful to stand on a grave, but I didn't give a skudge about respect at this point. Not for the dead, anyway. The dead didn't need anything today—not food, water, names, and least of all, respect.

CHAPTER 3
A POOR, LONELY MAN

THE CHECKPOINT WAS BUSIER than I would have expected. The city was at war, after all, and the wall had clearly been erected to keep the people inside safe from those outside. For all I knew, the war between Khizmit and Latvani waged two-hundred kilometers away.

The cemetery held five people. Well, five *living* people, at least. The two men digging the hole were accompanied by a long wooden coffin which I'm sure contained a body.

A man and two women wove past me, talking in low voices about the wind making it harder for them to find a certain headstone. I studied the women. They wore long dresses that extended past their boots, dragging through the icy snow. The colors, verdant green and light blue, darkened at the bottoms near their black boots where the snow and slosh had made them wet and muddy. Their gloves, thin and fashionable—likely ineffective at providing any real warmth —went clear up to their elbows where tufts of fur lined the edges. In that moment, I concluded women's fashion wasn't very practical. The fur would have been much more useful had it been on the inside of their gloves, like mine.

The coats went clear down their bodies, nearly to their knees. I reasoned this must have restricted the width of their steps as they shuffled along in the snow, making such a racket. I didn't worry about them hearing me as I nimbly moved between the headstones. Still, I slunk slowly as every step crunched and crackled the snow shifting under my feet.

The women captivated my attention.

Women. Not Warden Dulka but other women. *Everyday* women.

Their noses were so small, their eyes barely taking up any space on their faces at all. Their bodies were thin, even beneath the many layers of clothes.

I stared at the group, confused that the two men digging the hole practically ignored the two women who'd entered the cemetery. I might as well get all the staring out of my system now, since clearly it wouldn't be considered normal once I got inside Khizmit. *If* I got inside Khizmit.

The man with them wore a long black coat, but it didn't button all the way down the way the women's coats did. It fastened a few times in front with wide black buttons, and I realized this was the first man I'd seen outside of a military uniform. He wore a rounded top-hat rather than an ushanka on top of his head, with no indication of rank whatsoever, unless the maroon ribbon indicated something I didn't know about. I decided that was more likely. The color had to mean *something*.

"It's cold. Very, very cold," the woman in the blue dress said softly, but her voice carried over to me above the scrape of the men still chipping at the frozen ground. Her voice, void of venom and hate, filled me like a breath of fresh air. I smiled as she said 'very.' *She's right*, I thought. *It's skudging cold.*

"I'm sure he appreciates your efforts," the man said, extending his elbow to the woman as she nearly slipped.

"He didn't remember our anniversary in life," she muttered. "I don't know why he would in death." I wasn't sure, but her voice now had a bit of a bite to it.

The woman in green gripped the man and pulled him

closer. "Oh, don't give him more to regret. He didn't *try* to get shot, after all."

"He could have tried a little harder *not* to." The first woman looked down, frowning. Her lips were so thin, her voice delicate as a songbird. Although I could have kept listening, I redirected my attention to the men who'd now stopped shoveling and were sipping from their water canteens.

They weren't dressed anywhere near as nicely as the man escorting the women through the cemetery, but they looked better off than the men and boys I'd seen returning from the coal factory. Though, I'd never seen someone working with coal who didn't look like absolute slag by the end of the day.

One man stood almost a head taller than the other, sporting a thick, brown beard.

The other, younger by a few years, leaned against his shovel for support. "That's gotta be deep enough," he said before taking another sip of water.

The older man grunted. "Too shallow. Earth will spit him back out come spring."

"Fine." The younger one tossed his canteen back into the snow. It clanged as it hit a headstone.

The bearded one clucked his tongue, then returned to his digging. "Begging for a curse, are you?"

"An' who's to say we aren't already?" The younger man jumped on his shovel. "Cursed, that is."

"Cause we're not on the front lines is why."

"That's what the Lurper Legion is for! That's why it was made in the first place, wasn't it?"

"What do you mean by that?" The bearded man stopped his shoveling, fixing his gaze on the other man.

"They have the other inmates working in the mines, right? But do they really all need to be there? Why don't they send more of them to war?"

"Bah. I don't think they're even alive anymore," he said.

"In fact, even though the Chancellors say we have inmates up north in Predvoi or over in Vazenia, I don't believe it."

Vazenia?

Lockbox had mentioned it once. The prison for female inmates.

"Oh, they're there," the skinny man protested. "Word is he died up at one of those prisons!" He gestured to the coffin with his shovel.

"Another wolf attack in the woods? Or Latvani soldiers?"

"Neither. It was a lurper."

"I don't buy it."

"I've talked with soldiers who've guarded them. They're up there. They're the ones who should be on The Outskirts, keeping them Latvani soldiers out of our lands and away from our coal!" He stopped shoveling again for a moment.

The bearded man nudged him. "They keep them in prisons 'cause they can't be trusted with weapons," the older man said. "Just as likely to be our executioners as they are to be our saviors."

The last word resonated like a bell in my head.

Saviors.

The younger man unloaded another shovelful to the side of the grave. "But it's not out of the question."

"Maybe they're the curse."

"What?"

"Or maybe we're just cursed for what we did to them."

The skinny, young man swore. "Shut up about curses already and just finish the job so we can go back before another storm blasts us."

Was another storm coming? I looked up. I had no way of knowing what the skies usually looked like here, but a storm definitely wasn't out of the question, not with the weight in the air.

The woman in blue's voice rose again from the other side of the cemetery.

"No, that's quite enough. I'm done!" She started back toward me and the entrance to the city. "I said hello and happy anniversary. I feel that's more than adequate. But now I'm freezing out here, and we're going home!"

The man and woman, still linked arm in arm, walked up behind her.

They didn't talk as they followed her and then stopped at the guard shack. Four armed soldiers stepped out, wearing the all too familiar uniform and ushankas. Two had their backs to me. I realized they were both privates as I saw the gold circles on their right shoulders. Some privates had gold circles, some silver, and I didn't know the difference, if there was one.

"It's ridiculous. I just came out of this gate. I know you remember me," the woman in blue protested as she pulled off her gloves.

"Protocol is protocol, Ma'am," he said. He gave her wrist a cursory glance.

The man and the other woman also removed their left gloves for a quick inspection. The man stood, arms extended, while the soldiers patted down his sides and gestured for him to enter the gate.

I frowned. Of *course*, they checked their wrists.

Add that to my mounting list of obstacles. *It didn't matter*, I concluded. I'd gone through hell every day at Rhosivi. Just because I didn't know how the slag I was going to get into Khizmit didn't mean it couldn't be done. It just meant that when I *did* make it through, I'd have that much more self-satisfaction.

The men's heavy breathing caught my attention. I craned my neck around the headstone to get a better view. They gripped the edges of the coffin and slowly lowered it into the ground.

"Good enough?" the younger man asked, wiping his brow.

"Good enough."

The two of them made quick work of burying the coffin as more workers left out the back gate for the coal factory.

A small wooden shack sat inconspicuously toward the back-left corner of the cemetery. The grave diggers plodded their way toward it, grumbling the entire time about the cold. They deposited their shovels inside, locked it up, and returned to the relief of the gate.

They didn't wait to be asked to show their wrists. It was almost robotic. They held out their bare skin, unmarred by a designation, still talking about the bitter wind, then nodded and entered Khizmit.

I smiled, watching them disappear from my line of sight.

This could work, I thought to myself as a plan formulated. I just needed the cover of darkness, and I'd have both clothes *and* a way to conceal my tattoo from the gate guards.

I numbed some of the gnawing pain in my stomach just enough to get some sleep but make sure my senses were alert. I would hear any footfalls in the crisp snow if anyone approached and easily see them before they could see me.

The digging men had inspired an idea, but I had to wait for darkness before I could proceed with it. Nestling into the warm fur of the giant wolf, I took the opportunity to get some sleep but kept listening and forbade myself from drifting off too deeply.

The distinct sound of boots crunching through hard snow woke me. The sun had already set. I checked my darkened surroundings and identified the source of the sound. The two privates were doing a short patrol along the wall. They looked around and walked back to their shack before two new soldiers swapped out with them. The cemetery sat dark and empty, save me and the bones of the dead.

I enhanced my hearing. The wind whistled around the trees and stone, crying and loosening chunks of snow and ice that fell sporadically. With those sounds as my cover, I crept across the cemetery and approached the shack. If anyone saw the coat of the wolf in the cemetery, they'd shoot, thinking it was an animal. Luckily, there was still a great deal of snow, and I was able to blend in well enough in the shadows and drifts.

On the other hand, if anyone was to see a figure in striped prison clothes, they'd shoot to kill. Neither option thrilled me.

A heavy padlock held the door to the small shed in place, but when the next gust of wind arrived, loudly tearing sheets of ice from the branches of a nearby tree, I kicked the door in. It busted off the flimsy frame with ease. *Surely they didn't actually believe it would keep anyone out?*

I reached in and snagged one of the shovels and quietly pulled the door shut as the wind blew across my frosted grin.

By luck or fate, the fresh grave was far enough away from the guard shack that as long as I moved slowly, I could keep the sound down. Personally, if I were guarding a gate bordering a cemetery and I heard scraping near a new grave in the dead of night, I wouldn't dare venture out to see what it was.

Not that I believed in dead people rising or anything like that, but if someone was crazy enough to be milling around among the deceased in the dead of night, they'd be crazy enough to hurt me for interfering.

And I knew that's exactly what I'd have to do.

If the guards *did* hear me and came to investigate, guns leveled, I'd have no choice but to attack and disarm them.

Obviously, if that were my first choice, I'd be doing it now instead of slinking around in the cold, digging up coffins.

To the best of my knowledge, people weren't buried naked, so the dead man they'd placed in the ground had to be dressed. Still, I was making a lot of assumptions. I was assuming he hadn't died from some horrible, communicable disease that I'd contract by morning. I was also assuming, based on the lack of pomp, that he wasn't going to be some high-ranking military man dressed like Commander Markos.

Two men had buried him in a shallow grave. I held out hope he was wearing the clothes of a poor, lonely man.

The ground had frozen over again to some degree, but it wasn't as much work for me as it had been for the two men who'd dug the grave a few hours prior. And I was in far better shape. I'm not sure how much of that was due to my blood mutation and how much was due to the work I'd done at Rhosivi in the mine.

Wind blew through the trees, dropping huge mounds of snow from the boughs of the nearby pines, which muted the sounds of my shovel against the ice and rocks.

A hollow "thud" echoed up from the ground.

My shovel hit the coffin. I scraped and dug for a few more minutes until I'd moved enough dirt to see the top of the dead man's resting pall.

Without bothering to wipe the dirt off the top, I grabbed hold of the coffin's side tacked down with nails, waited for the next burst of wind to howl, and yanked hard.

The lid opened with a groan, the half-moon illuminating the corpse within. Thank the mines he wasn't naked!

It took only a single glance to know I was being haunted.

The man was pale and cleaned up, but I knew Goyle the moment I pried off the lid. Someone had cleaned the wound at his neck and changed him from his uniform into a thin brown overcoat with wide lapels covering a dark sweater. I didn't see any bloodstains on it.

Thanks to the darkness, I didn't have to see his face well, but I still tried not to mistreat his body as I unclasped the buttons around his neck. It was nearly impossible to do with gloves on, so I set them in the dirt and got to work. Though I was gentle with the brown overcoat, which I took off easily enough, I had to wrestle his stiff limbs while trying to remove the sweater and undershirt. As a branch in the distance cracked, I got an idea. I waited for another wind gust, then snapped the shoulder of Goyle's corpse, whispering an apology to the wind as I did so. *He's not a man anymore,* I told myself. *It's just a body.*

But the body had belonged to a man. The guard I'd named Goyle should have been at home with his family. Goyle's last ragged breath came to my memory. I'd killed him. The Chancellors had left me no choice. As a free man I hadn't hurt a soul. *Did my guilt indicate my humanity?*

I had to come to terms with the truth: I was a monster. I'd stolen this man's life, and now I stole his clothes to further facilitate my escape. He'd helped me once unwillingly. *Was I truly willing to rob him again?*

I dropped into the snow with my hand clamped over my mouth to prevent from sobbing aloud. Khizmit had done this to me. They were forcing me to become what I'd fought so hard to avoid. When compliant, they wanted me to kill. When rebelling, I had no choice *but* to kill. *How could I become the man I wanted to be when every turn led me to another impossible choice?*

Goyle is dead. He doesn't need these clothes and you do, I thought to myself. *His name wasn't even Goyle.*

Realizing that I didn't even know his proper name made me feel even worse. It was too late to turn back now. I ripped one of the sleeves and cursed but got it off. Then, hands shaky with the fear of being found, among other obvious things, I focused my attention on the waist of the pants.

I debated keeping on my prison rags for layering underneath the newly acquired clothes but decided it wasn't worth the risk. I had to get rid of them.

Once I'd stripped the body—and I had to keep thinking of it as just a body—I draped my prison clothes over it and started dressing in the dark garments. Every hair on my body stood up as the wind wound around my exposed skin, but the new clothes left me emboldened. Step one: complete. I had new clothes. Using one of the larger rocks I'd unearthed, I gingerly hammered the lid of the coffin back into place, climbed out of the pit, and finished burying the dead man for the second time that day.

If there had been a headstone, I would have read it. I would have apologized to him by name.

Now that my blood was pumping, the wind didn't bother me as much. "Rest in peace now," I said, packing down the dirt. I guess spirits don't hang around their bodies to see what happens after they die, or at least the guard I'd named Goyle now understood I needed his clothes more than he did tonight. Maybe he hovered above me, wishing he could exact revenge. Thankfully, no malicious spirit sprang from the dirt, choked me, or possessed my mind. In fact, I walked away from the grave and back to the small storage shed with newfound hope and confidence.

The wind had blown the door open, and the dark floor was now speckled with snow. I set the shovel back, pulled the door into place, and wedged it tightly, grinning as I returned to the icy path beaten into the snow.

For the first time in my life, I didn't have prison linens setting me apart from the rest of the world. That alone was reason to celebrate. I didn't even bother trying to conceal myself as I walked toward the coal factory in the darkness.

The hardest part was over.

Once I got rid of my tattoo, I'd be able to march into Khizmit without any issues at all.

But I had only one idea of how to do that, and it was quite possibly the worst idea I'd ever had.

CHAPTER 4
A GHASTLY BURN

NUMBERS WEREN'T MY STRENGTH, but Lockbox had figured about 50,000 people lived in Khizmit. With those numbers, I was willing to bet that not everyone who worked at this factory knew everyone else's face. Besides that, in my experience, cold makes people bitter and grouchy, so I didn't plan to get called out for coming to the factory at night.

The road I'd followed here led to the storage unit near the factory, a windowless metal building with four wide doors that slid up at least three meters to allow the trucks to back right in. At the moment, three of the doors were shut, but one held a truck not yet unloaded into the storage room.

Heavy bags of coal made the truck ride low. I'd loaded bags just like that. I'd mined, under the supervision of armed guards on weeks Markos was at Rhosivi, as well as cleaned, packed, and loaded endless amounts of coal when he wasn't there. And here it was, being used for the good of Khizmit. My whole life had been a string of hard work, trying to prove myself to a group of people who saw me as nothing more than slave labor. Still, I hoped my experience at Rhosivi would help me navigate the factory without giving any indication that I was an imposter. An invader. A runaway.

A long conveyer belt ran from the storage area up to the

bunkers in the plant. At Rhosivi, the bunkers only held enough coal to run the plant for four hours, but these ones looked large enough to run the plant for half a day, at least.

Beneath them had to be the mills where the coal would be pulverized to a fine powder. From there, the coal had to be heated in the boiler. That's where I'd find the maximum amount of heat possible, and where I needed to go.

Three gigantic smokestacks, the tallest I'd ever seen, stretched to the sky, belching out smoke and steam like an angry dragon from some fantasy story. Beneath them sat the factory, unassuming with its grey walls and small windows. Contained inside were workers, gears, vats, gases, steam, and coal that worked together to give the city electricity. The coal factory at Rhosivi, which had served the same function, only served the prison. This factory, on the other hand, made ours look like it was made for children.

In a very real sense, I suppose it was.

The path I walked from the storage unit led directly to two wide doors, above which hung several warnings on steel signs. As I drew nearer, I read them. *Caution: Boiler and turbine equipment operate at extremely high temperatures and pressures. Neither Khizmit authority nor any managerial staff is responsible for your safety.* Another said, '*You assume your own risk upon entry.*'

My heart hammered as I approached the doors, even though the gloves from Roman concealed my tattoo. All it would take was one person, one glance at the ink in my wrist, and I'd be as dead as the guard whose clothes I'd stolen.

Or they would.

I hadn't watched to see if they checked wrists at this door, but sometimes, you have to throw yourself into your plans face first and hope for a soft landing. I heightened my senses, turning them each up a little bit as I approached.

The clanging and pumping from the factory drowned out any sound the door hinges might have made as I pushed it open, which made me immediately turn down my enhanced hearing. Steam hissed through pipes, almost as if it carried the news of my entry like a secret, whispered only to those who were observant enough to listen for it.

Four men stood nearby, none of them bothering to look toward me. One glanced over and then tossed a white wrapper into a metal garbage can. With my sense of smell still heightened, I identified the food underneath the wrapper. Cheese.

Nearly animalistic with hunger, I felt myself lurch forward to grab the scraps. *Stop,* I told myself. *Wait.* But the food was so close.

I needed to satiate my hunger now. Though I had the ability to continue numbing the gnawing pain in my stomach, that would only intensify my headache, and I couldn't take much more of that.

I headed straight for the garbage can and picked it up.

"Wait," said the man who'd tossed the garbage into the bin, which fortunately, came close to spilling its contents over the top and onto the cement floor. An empty bin wouldn't need to be emptied. This, however, posed a perfect opportunity.

I spared a look up at the man who'd thrown out his cheese and didn't meet his dark eyes. His scraggly mustache was a few shades lighter than the hair that crept out of the sides of his hat. He wore a coat buttoned so high, it covered his chin, but his set eyes looked suspicious. Surely, they didn't wrist check garbage men. He stepped closer. His boots made soft sounds, barely audible over the pumping of machinery around us.

"Yes," I said, my fingers tightening on the metal handles of the can.

"My advice, get here on time or Brikenden will slaughter you."

How would a grown man behave? Submissive? Dismissive? I

had to assume he out-ranked the trash collector. "Okay," I said, shuffling my feet. *Where was I supposed to take this thing?*

"And don't forget to get the small bin by the back door on your way out."

Back door. There had to be more than one back door, but I needed to find the one that led to a larger bin. Not because I had to take the trash out like it was my job, but because if one of them saw me find a quiet corner and start digging for food, they might find me suspicious. I gripped the handles of the trash can and turned my back to the men.

"What a slaghead," he muttered, and I wove my way around the machinery, grateful for the heat, which was warming my too long chilled bones. I'd always preferred the hot to the cold, and too much of my life had already been spent numb from the frigid winters up in Rhosivi.

I glanced up, located the turbines, and used the pipes to guide me. The steam hissed, and one man yelped as he tightened a few pipes on a ladder above my head, no doubt getting a nasty steam burn in the process. The air around me grew hotter, and sweat now ran down my back as I skirted around the cylindrical vats. The ovens sat like lazy guards, not moving, but doing their work anyway.

The factory, though large, was easy to navigate since I knew the processes inside a coal factory. I called on the experiences I never imagined I'd be grateful for and found a small rear door just behind some turbines. The metal door opened easily, and I stepped outside, back into the cold.

I knew eating trash should bring me shame, but as I unwrinkled the papers and stuffed the bread crusts and tiny bits of cheese from the discarded sandwiches into my mouth, I felt nothing but joy. I sighed audibly as I swallowed.

Even if someone saw me, I wouldn't feel bad as I licked the sauce off the wrapper and then tossed it into the giant metal dumpster. No one was busy enough or picky enough to have thrown away a whole sandwich, but there was half an apple and enough remnants of the day shift's lunch to satisfy my appetite. Soggy crusts and bits of meat, could be rabbit, filled my stomach.

Whoever had been asked to empty the trash never showed up to complain that I'd done their job.

I stepped back into the warm factory, back to the heat, and grabbed the other bin. There wasn't anything worth eating from it, or else my standards had already risen above picked bones and coal-sprinkled bread.

After putting the bins back in place, I took note of where the other men stood. One still worked on the pipes above while another held his ladder. Nothing required their attention near the furnace, so I walked back to it, sweat beading my face. The tattoo was my last obstacle. The last task to complete before I could approach the guards at the gate.

I had to be fast. Silent. Inconspicuous.

You can't really erase a tattoo, but I figured you could cover it with something else. Something less grotesque to this world. Something the guards had seen before and wouldn't find suspicious.

I walked purposefully toward the round coal ovens that had no business being opened during operation. Only common sense stopped anyone from flipping down the latch and opening the thick metal door to the far side of the boiler. No locks. At Rhosivi, lurpers typically only opened these to clean up the ash out of the bottom.

Here goes nothing, I thought to myself. *Here goes everything.*

The gloves protected my fingers as I flipped a latch on the front of the furnace, and a wave of heat smashed across me as the door opened.

No time to spare or rethink this decision. *You can do this,* I said to myself. *You've been through worse.*

I slipped off my glove and rolled my sleeve up past my shoulder. The buttons would make it take too long to put back on, and besides, once I'd done what I needed to, I wouldn't be in any position to stuff my arm through the sleeve. Inside the furnace, the heat contorted the sight of the angry red coals.

Searing, suffocating heat.

I took a deep breath. "I'm not a Victor," I whispered. "It's not a name."

I threw up a block to pain and reached my left hand into the open door. The heat made my eyes water, but I couldn't look away.

Numb tingling crawled across my hand and arm, the hairs curling and withering off immediately. It would only take a moment, but I needed the hellish heat to scar me from the tips of my fingers clear up to my bicep.

Freedom would be mine, whatever the cost.

I hissed at the sight, making the same sounds as the pipes above me as the heat wrecked my arm. I had to pay close attention, as I couldn't feel anything, and I didn't want to burn myself clear to the bone, not knowing what tissue could regrow. My clothes could also catch fire at any moment, and that would cause a much bigger scene than I was willing to deal with.

I'd healed up fine after the wounds outside Predvoi, but I didn't want to test my limits. Could I even grow back flesh that no longer existed? Nervous fear flickered across my skin with the flames.

I pulled my arm out and sucked a breath of hot air into my lungs. Though I didn't feel any pain, my stomach roiled as I assessed the ghastly damage. No pain. *No pain?* It was entirely wrong to have such an injury and feel no pain.

My arm was thick with burned skin and livid black, red, and purple marks.

But it had to be done. If I'd only burned a small section of my wrist, I might as well have highlighted my status as a prisoner. The bigger the burn, the less likely anyone would be to give the concealed tattoo on my wrist a second thought. If it was too bad, then I'd draw too much attention to myself.

It'll be worth it, I told myself.

The burn was severe enough that instead of finding black letters in my skin, I found the skin itself had turned black along my hand and arm. The pain that I'd inevitably feel would bring me to my knees, the very edge of what I could endure; I just knew it. And I wouldn't be able to block the pain indefinitely.

With a flip of my hand, I checked my wrist once more to be sure. I'd effectively erased the tattoo. Burned out the ink. Blistering, blackened skin covered any sign of the previous etching.

I rushed around the front of the boiler where two men monitored the gauges, no doubt looking for the cause of the loss of pressure in the tank. My legs took me out the back door, and I put my hand into the snow. It melted a deep, black handprint as I kept it there for at least twenty minutes, ever so slowly turning down the block on my pain.

It worked like a dial, up to ten meant I felt nothing, and if I'd removed the block completely, well, I might not be able to stop myself from crying out or collapsing.

I turned the pain down to about a five. The pain made my body tremble. *What had I done?* I turned it to a four, and tears welled in my eyes. I gasped. The pain caused the edges of my vision to blur.

Down to a three. I was unable to bite back the tears that streamed down my cheeks. My arm—my whole skudging arm—felt like it was still in the furnace. I dropped the block completely and bit my bottom lip, drawing blood as I swallowed the scream that tried to escape. The wail roaring in my chest stayed put behind my throat, but I heard myself whimper.

I'd never felt pain like this. By comparison, the time Flak

had torn my face open felt like a blood blister, and Roman's stab wounds like a pinprick.

This skudging killed.

The shriek threatened to burst clean out of my chest, tearing a hole in its path to the sky, clear up to the clouds. I numbed it back up to a three. I don't know if it was less painful than death, but with my ability to heal, it was far less permanent.

It had to be done, I reminded myself. *You couldn't live like that.*

I dug my arm into the snow again until it had numbed my hand and arm, and then pulled it out, just long enough for it to thaw before placing it back in the snow.

When the sky to the east grew light, I knew I'd waited long enough. Morning was here. Today, I'd go to Khizmit.

Clenching my teeth, I struggled to get my glove back on.

My hand looked mangled, and the black skin blistered and peeled. The tops of my fingers bled, especially around my fingernails. The urge to heal part of it and take away the pain grew stronger as I noticed the red and black handprint I'd left in the snow. Using my right hand, I scooted a bunch of snow over the mark I'd made, in case any of the other workers came out, saw it, and wondered or worried. I gingerly rolled my sleeve back over my arm, gritting my teeth as I did so.

After a few moments of struggling with the glove, I took a deep breath and began the walk around the front of the building.

I tucked the staghorn dagger down the back of my pants. The guards hadn't checked anyone for weapons. Briefly, I considered tossing the knife into the woods, but what if I needed it?

It bumped against my back with every step I took as I walked from the back entrance to the cemetery and directly toward the guard shack. Fighting every instinct to duck my head, I made eye contact with the soldiers. They had no reason to expect an inmate from Predvoi. They had no reason to fear me.

As I got close, I had to speak to keep myself from panicking.

"I...uh...," I remarked. *Should I mention the weather while dealing with a wretched burn?*

"This wind is brutal," the shorter guard said as he drew closer to me. A glance at the gold circle gave him away as a private.

"I got...burned," I explained as I tried to remove the glove. I opted instead to roll my sleeve up. Wincing, my voice cracked a little. "That's why I'm heading back in now."

"Skudge," the private muttered as he saw the burn.

He took the lantern from the guard shack and brought it closer.

In the dim morning light, it had looked bad, and whether from the shadows or the direct light of the lantern, the burn looked even worse. I flipped my hands over, and I swear the tattoo burned the most. More than my fingers and the blisters which had torn open when I'd removed my glove. The letters, though invisible, had branded me deeper than the skin. In my very blood, I knew what I was.

"That's...concerning," he said. "Do you need an escort to the hospital?" He twisted his face away as a wave of nausea seemed to come over him.

The other soldier, a private with a silver circle, said, "I'm sure they'll see you right away. You know where it is?"

"Yes," I said, holding back a 'Sir.' I hoped that my haste came across in the form of pain rather than fear.

"Bet you regret signing up for the factory now," the private said.

"I'm an idiot," I said, swallowing hard. *Could they tell how scared I was? Could they hear my heart as it pounded in my chest?* I was sure they noticed the tears in my eyes even as I tried to hold them back. My hand was trembling. "I'm an absolute idiot."

The men stood aside, allowing me to step right into Khizmit.

I must not have looked too young for the job, or maybe they had seventeen-year-old boys working in the factories on the regular. I glanced back at the walls. It's not another prison, I told myself. It's a city, and Lockbox might be here.

I walked in.

Not as a Victor. Not as Victor-27. Not as a cunning, conniving inmate or a bloodthirsty convict.

Just a worker from the factory who'd been dumb enough to burn my arm.

I'd never been so happy to be misjudged.

———

The dirt path beneath my feet turned to cobblestone as I entered Khizmit. It was larger than I'd imagined. It would have taken at least a couple weeks to walk every street and read every sign. Only a few people wandered about and nodded to me as I passed, their faces mostly wrapped in layers and hats pulled low over their eyes. The wind didn't blow as bitterly here, maybe because the buildings blocked it.

As I ventured deeper into the town over the cobblestone paths under streetlights already blown out, the entire feel of the place changed.

Long green garlands woven with golden and crimson ribbons strung overhead reminded me that Koliada was later this week. Bold red flowers decorated balconies and store-fronts. Shop windows that had elaborate teal and gold snowflakes painted right onto the glass sparkled in the morning light. Green spruces had been brought in from the mountains, their verdant boughs liberated from the icy cages and decorated with metal ornaments. The gold, silver, and brass chimed in the wind as passersby skirted around the trees, rustling their branches.

Some held bright glass ornaments shaped like animals and foods, while other trees boasted paper ornaments folded like flowers and birds. The paper ones seemed to sag in the morning dew, but they contributed just as well as the others in creating a festive ambiance. Since standing around gawking at the decorations and whipping my head every time a bell chimed with the opening of a shop door didn't feel like a good cover, I tried to quell my fascination over all the sights and sounds.

Now that I'd safely entered the city, I walked deeper into it, past more shops, and wove a path away from the guards. I tugged the glove back on, not to keep out the cold, since my burn had seemed like a furnace itself at this point, but to keep any gawking to a minimum.

I took a seat on the wooden bench that overlooked a part of the path where the buildings almost seemed like they'd been scooted back for no other purpose than to make room for a gigantic pine tree.

I curled up on the bench and turned off any of my abilities that I'd kept on.

Pain took over me, centimeter by centimeter, from my legs which had been used more than legs should be, to a horrid drumming pain in my head. My hand felt like it was hot enough to set my glove on fire. With my eyes shut, I carefully healed the skin around my fingertips and at the tops of my knuckles where my flesh had split open and blood-stained the fur inside my gloves. I couldn't only keep the scarring over the tattoo, so I left most of the injury in place.

With my regeneration abilities, one might have thought I didn't need to sleep, but I did. *Slag, I needed vyco.* I pulled my legs onto the bench and slowed my breathing. My heart hadn't stopped racing since the moment I'd plunged my arm into the furnace, but now I steadied myself.

The buildings all around me shone in varied shades of white, beige, and tan, with an occasional pink. Down the hill, along a wider path that led to the heart of the city, I saw the bright red roofs. Beautiful arches decorated the doorways, and wrought iron railings twisted into spirals and floral designs did more than just protect anyone wandering along the second-story balconies. The beauty of the scene struck me as sharply as if I'd inhaled a gust of frozen air.

Rhosivi had been functional. Predvoi, too, with basic walls and floors, but this city was living and breathing art. Red flowers waved in the wind from the balconies and small tables near storefronts, as if inviting me to come inside and try the wares or taste the food. Somewhere in the distance, a group of people sang, their voices bringing emotions to my heart. A few flakes of snow blew down from the rooftops around me, and for the first time, I found it beautiful, too.

Embarrassed, I brushed my face quickly with the back of my glove. I had to be starving and exhausted to allow a simple scene to bring out such a reaction. As I shifted on the bench, turning to look beneath the bright blue awnings at my back, I knew I could never leave this place. Not when the very air here hummed with life and hope.

I'm safe, I reminded myself. *I'm free.*

I found myself tugging the gloves on tighter.

CHAPTER 5
LYING BEAUTY

"Where are you supposed to be?" someone growled at me.

I sat up and stared at the man who looked all the world like one of the guards from Predvoi or Rhosivi. But I wasn't in a cell. I wasn't a prisoner anymore. I had to keep reminding myself of that.

At his side hung a knife, but not with a staghorn handle. Wood and a golden metal, likely brass, made up this handle. The leather belt holding the dagger was buckled tightly around his waist, and just like the guards in Rhosivi and Predvoi, he had a gun slung around his shoulder.

Guards and soldiers were one and the same. Though I wasn't in the mines or cells, I'd never be free of the glares from guards it seemed. The same wool uniform with brass buttons was clasped from his waist clear up to his clean-shaven chin. Same ushanka with a rank patch. The silver birch leaf designated him as a first lieutenant.

In Rhosivi Mine and Predvoi Prison, I'd almost never seen an officer alone, but this man had no obvious comrades nearby. I glanced down the street, but no one else paid any attention to us. I turned back to the guard.

"Where are you supposed to be?" he repeated.

The guard had a certain look about him, one of strength

and compliance. The cut on his face showed how seriously he'd taken the task of shaving that morning, but what did it say about his work ethic? He seemed young, not as young as Roman, perhaps, but similar in age. With his brown eyes narrowed, he sized me up the same way I examined him, trying to learn what he could before I spoke.

At Rhosivi, I'd learned to identify the meaning of the patches on the guards' clothes. There, every soldier wore a patch of a pickaxe and a large piece of coal on their left shoulder. The patch of Khizmit's flag was worn proudly on their right. The flag was white with a large green triangle coming off the right side, pointing directly into the mouth of a black wolf with exaggeratedly large teeth and ears. A single star sat in the top left corner, and another sat in the bottom left corner. They wore their ranks on their ushankas and on the right shoulder of their uniforms.

At Predvoi, the patches varied but only slightly. The patch on the left shoulder bore an outline of a square with shackles inside—one open, one shut. I had little doubt they changed patches with assignments, and I had reason to believe that female victims of the Preemptive Initiative were responsible for hand-sewing all the patches based on a theory Lockbox had shared in passing.

This lieutenant's left shoulder patch bore a skyline, obviously Khizmit's, as it showcased the same tall building with a bulbous spire I'd seen just an hour or so prior.

"Excuse me?" I asked him as he cleared his throat again. His hair, where I could see it beneath his ushanka, was cut shorter than the lurpers at Rhosivi.

My gaze darted down to my wrist. *If I showed him the injury, would he make me go to the hospital? Would I have to explain myself to their doctors? And what if they had developed a way to heal it, and then the letters reappeared right before their eyes, telling them what I was?*

"Where are you supposed to be?" he asked for a third

time. I stared at the red scab forming along his chin where he'd recently been bleeding.

"I don't know what you mean," I said stupidly, knowing that everything I said put me at risk. One wrong word would reveal I had no idea what the rules were here, that I didn't belong in Khizmit. I'd never existed freely in society before. One misstep and I'd be back in front of the firing squad, and this time, Roman would be at my side for having helped me escape or at least for failing to kill me.

Maybe they'd make us fight each other to the death.

We wouldn't do it. At least, I wouldn't.

It wasn't just my life on the line anymore. No one could know I was alive, for my safety and Roman's.

"I take it you aren't a soldier, so you must work here in Khizmit. Why are you resting here instead of at home?"

"I was at work," I said quickly. I would have stood up, but he towered over me, and I was sure that standing up and pushing past him would have been seen as aggressive. For all I knew, there were rules against that too. Though it took a great deal of self-control, I stayed where I was on the bench.

"Why were you sleeping on the bench?" he asked.

I paused only for a moment, deciding to stick to the truth. "After my shift at the factory, I sat here to admire the tree there. Must have fallen asleep staring at it."

He didn't glance toward the tree, though I gestured toward it with the hope that he'd step back or give me a break from his suspicious glare.

"Then where do you live? What shift do you work? Do you have some identification?"

Identification. In all my daydreams of being in Khizmit, it never occurred to me that they had identification here too. Their identification was on paper instead of on their skin. *Right?*

Without the proper paperwork I'd die here. *I didn't want to believe it, but what choice did I have? Lie and say my identification had been lost or stolen? Claim I was experiencing amnesia to explain away my lack of understanding of Khizmit?* I reached for my pocket before thinking better of it. *Even if Goyle's clothes held his identification, I wouldn't be able to use it. I had no idea how known he was in Khizmit. This soldier might even have been friends with him.*

As usual, my brain had some idea of what to do. Not one helpful to my cause, effective as it may be. It involved choking the guard unconscious and running away. It guaranteed that I'd live, and he'd be unconscious long enough for me to run and hide, but then they'd have my description. And they'd be looking for me.

Were there any other options? I looked around as a few people strode along the cobblestone path behind me.

A young girl with long black hair, prominent cheekbones, and eyes curtained in gorgeous lashes stepped over and placed a hand on the guard's arm.

"Take a breath, Erik. He lives in Sector 4 near me." She threw me a wink and patted Erik's arm before taking a seat beside me.

"You know him?" Erik asked her as she scooted over.

My heart froze mid-beat. A girl. A real girl pressed her leg against mine. Fear and excitement hammered through me, and I could barely take my eyes off her, even with the imposing soldier standing over us. Though there was no way that her body heat reached me through her thick layers, my leg warmed nearly to the point of discomfort where it met hers. It became obvious to me at that moment, that going just a few days without the pills the guards had given me every morning in prison had some currently unwanted side effects as blood rushed away from my head.

"'Course I do," she laughed.

She turned to me, her face so close I could see the faint red makeup on her lips and the sparkling of the lights on the tree reflecting in her eyes.

"We missed you yesterday," she said. She leaned in, blocking my face from the soldier's, and I went completely rigid as I felt her lips graze the side of my cheek.

The greeting I'd observed at my hearing came back to mind, and I quickly made the softest sound with my lips. Surely it didn't sound like a kiss, but it sounded like I'd done something.

She moved her head to the other side of my face now, showing my profile to Erik once again. Under the weight of his supervision, I puckered quickly and brushed my lips on her cheek.

Her ears were as decorated as the holiday tree, with gold cuffs climbing from her lobe up the side like garlands. She pulled away and then leaned into my arm.

Her voice was not like Riah Dulka's. It came out cheerful, playful. "Sleeping on benches isn't a crime. Now go do something useful with that new patch of yours."

"Keep out of trouble, Lee," Erik said, ducking his head at her. He looked at me again as he took a few steps away. Still frozen solid in fear and concern, I watched him disappear around the corner.

Lee, the girl on my arm, laughed, and it sounded like birds sweetly twittering in the trees. I never heard birds in Rhosivi, but I had occasionally in the woods at Predvoi. Sometimes, when I'd stood out there slaughtering the rabbits, I'd heard them, as if they too had wanted to spread the word about the brutality I was capable of committing.

What was this girl up to? It wasn't as if she had me pegged as someone else. She didn't know me. I didn't live near her in Sector 4, and she knew it. This lying beauty had saved me, but *why?* Everything came at a cost. Lockbox had explained that all relationships are give-and-take. My throat felt dry as I avoided looking directly at her.

A girl. *Were they all this beautiful?*

"I'm Lee," she said as the few onlookers in the square returned to their business.

"Thanks," I replied, staring at her much closer than I should have.

"He means well."

My brain was mush. "Who?"

"Erik. He's trying to rise quickly. Promote early. You know." She waved her hand back in the direction the soldier had gone.

I didn't know.

"So, who are you?" she asked, squaring her shoulders toward me.

"I'm…" I didn't know what name to give. A bunch of names came to mind from books, but how could I know what names were considered normal here in Khizmit? No guards had ever told me their name, fraternization being severely punished and all.

"Pedrick," I said. At least, I knew it was a normal first name to have in Khizmit, unlike the names I'd read in books.

She raised an eyebrow. "You hesitated."

"I was trying to think of a fake name, but none came to mind."

"Why would you want to give me a fake name?"

"Because I don't know you."

"And you have a better chance of getting to know me with a fake name?" Her lips tightened.

"Well, when you put it like that…"

She laughed again. "Where do you really live?"

She wanted honesty, at least she thought she wanted honesty. Despite her smiling eyes and kindness when Erik had questioned me, I had no doubt she'd change her tune from songbird to warning cry if she had any idea where I was from and what I was.

"I'm…"

"Never mind," she said in my moment's hesitation.

"What?"

"Never mind. It doesn't matter."

While I wanted it not to matter, her sudden shift didn't exactly calm me down. "Why doesn't it matter?"

"You know why I came over here?" she asked.

The hope that she'd come because she was interested in me both shocked and horrified me. But that was only on account of the intense and immediate attraction I had for her.

"I hated the way you looked around when he asked for your ID. I knew you didn't have one, and I've been in your shoes before."

"You don't have ID?" I asked.

"Minors don't need ID. That's beside the point. I've been in situations like that when someone is intimidating me, and I didn't want you to have to go through that."

She saw me as intimidated. *Not intimidating?* She sympathized with me as a victim, not as a threat. While I couldn't give all the credit to my resurrected dimple, it couldn't have hurt the situation. The way she looked at me proved her motives to be true. She'd come to help me.

No one helped me.

But she did.

Just like I had with Lockbox, I considered how much it would hurt when that expression shifted, and she'd run away or scream once learning I was a Victor. *Was that reaction really guaranteed?* Lockbox had proven that it wasn't.

Lee patted my arm, and I thanked the mines she was sitting on my right, rather than my left. Still, her touch made my skin prickle even through the sleeve of my shirt.

"You look like slag," she laughed. *Slag?* Somehow, I hadn't expected to hear a word like that come from her. And to say I looked like...like slag? I felt myself blushing.

"That's probably why he asked for your ID. You look suspicious hanging out here without looking properly showered."

The heat from the furnace had singed more than the hair on my arms. For all I knew, it'd curled the small hairs on my face and eyebrows.

I blurted, "I'm not suspicious."

I was.

"It's okay if you got kicked out of the house. It's nothing to be ashamed of."

"I'm not ashamed, and I didn't get kicked out."

"So, you're not fighting with your wife."

The thought both amused and terrified me. My face must have shown the latter.

"No. I'm not married. No wife." I hated the way I nearly stammered out the last word.

"Just figured I'd ask. So, no ID because you're a minor?"

I nodded.

"Well, you should have just told him that." She heaved a sigh, her breath billowing in front of us like a cloud. "Let's go somewhere warmer." When she stood, she reached out her hand.

As I took Lee's hand, she tugged me away from the tree and the lights, down an alley opposite of the one I'd come down. Holding hands was completely unnecessary unless, of course, there were rules in Khizmit that I didn't know about requiring all underage couples to travel the streets like this. Though both of us wore gloves and my skin didn't touch hers, the gesture of holding her hand, feeling her fingers tighten around mine, felt intimate.

"I don't always look like slag," I said, wondering why I reverted to that right away. Besides, it wasn't really true. I did. My whole life I'd been caked in coal dust, my body bloody, bruised, broken, or frozen. Without a doubt, I always looked like slag. I probably smelled like slag too.

"You look like you could go for a strong drink."

"No alcohol," I insisted, unwilling to find out how it would fog my senses.

"No alcohol. But I know a place we can get something to help you feel better."

I almost said, "I feel fine." But that was an easy lie to spot. Instead, I said, "I feel—" I bit back, *"like slag,"* having the impression I shouldn't use those sorts of words around a girl.

Then she said it for me. Verbatim.

I laughed and agreed. "Yes. Like slag."

The headache in my temples demanded something to ease the pressure. Something like the drink Lockbox had given me. I reached down for my pocket. "I'd love something to drink, but…"

She squeezed my hand. "Peddy, let me buy you a drink. Maybe once you're warm, you'll warm up to the idea of having a real conversation with me." She winked, and it sent ripples of energy through me.

Peddy. I grinned at that, feeling my cheeks flush with heat as they dimpled deeply on both sides.

How strong had those pills been?

CHAPTER 6
PEKAREN

The shop Lee pulled me into had a small door with little glass windows iced with traces of fog and frost. The bold white letters on the door spelled out the name of this bakery: Pekaren. The red frame had a few spots where strips were peeled off, but it matched the bell which hung above the door, jangling as we stepped inside.

Cinnamon and peppermint, smells I'd rarely had the opportunity to experience before, hit me with such potency, I swear I could taste them with every inhalation.

Four tables, each with four chairs, sat together like friends on the far side of the café, and a spread of baked goods waited patiently underneath the curved glass of the display case to be purchased by eager patrons. A single strand of twinkling lights hung across the counter and along the wooden beams in the ceiling, which were painted to match the door.

The only exit to the room lay behind me, and if a group of soldiers came in, I'd be stuck, unless there was a door out back. I poked my head around the side of the display case to see if there was an opportunity for a retreat there.

There was a door, a stove, and an oven. Orange embers

inside the black stove pumped heat into the store. The sight of them caused my arm to hurt again.

"What are you doing?" Lee asked, peering around the corner with me. She leaned on my back for support, and I went rigid at her touch. I jerked my face toward hers and found her nearly nose to nose with me.

"What are you looking for?" she asked. "A bathroom?"

"Yeah," I lied.

A woman, wearing long sleeves and a frilly white apron wrapped around her large stomach, strode out from the kitchen.

"Washroom is for employees only," she said in an accent only slightly less raspy than Warden Velky's. "Oh, Lee!" The woman's round face broke into a smile. Lee sidestepped me and embraced the woman who lifted Lee up to her toes and then set her down again. "My license isn't expiring, is it?"

"No, I'm not here for work. Just came to show my friend around. This is Peddy." Lee grabbed my hand and pulled me forward. The woman stepped forward and smashed herself into me in a hug. *A hug.*

I twitched under the embrace. The only times I'd been held like this was right before a takedown. Right before getting lifted off my feet to have my face bashed into lumps of coal or shards of frozen snow.

I reached up and gently patted her back, overly aware of her enormous breasts that smashed into my chest as she hugged me.

"A friend of Lee's is a friend of mine," she said.

I couldn't breathe, and not because of the strength of the woman, but because I didn't know how to react to such...affection.

My muscles tightened up, ready to fight, because that's all I'd known physical touch to be, and yet, no one was here to attack me.

The woman, who smelled of cinnamon and yeast, released me and jerked a fat thumb to the back. "Washroom is back there," she bellowed before scooting her way behind the counter.

I took a few tentative steps toward the washroom but looked back to Lee. She shooed me away as she started up a conversation with the baker. "Oh, you're making szarlotka again! It smells wonderful as always in here, Leticia!"

The name halted me.

Leticia. I knew the name from a small piece of garbage.

Lockbox. They'd taken him. Warden Dulka had snatched him away somewhere to serve some purpose. I'd kept the words from the gum wrapper stored in my memory, *Leticia Varga,* still not convinced it was a lead at all, but I clung to it like Lockbox's life depended on it. For all I knew, it did. But it wasn't a random word, was it? It was the name of someone. Someone important to him.

It couldn't be this woman, could it? He didn't know her, did he?

I had to go use the washroom before asking anything else or Lee would know I'd been lying. She probably already knew. Everything I'd said so far had been a lie. And what? I now expected her to just tell me everything about Khizmit and help me find Leticia Varga?

Honesty had no purpose in the prison, but out here, I could see how it might prove useful. I'd have to win her trust before asking for her help. Otherwise, how could I trust what she told me?

Three steps into the kitchen took me to the entrance of the washroom. I could have spent all day standing there, the aromas of the bakery filling me as the heat from the stoves did. My gaze flitted around the kitchen, landing on a small mound of coal beside a thirty-kilo bag of it.

The front was stamped with a symbol. A pickaxe and a piece of coal. The same as the patch soldiers at Rhosivi wore.

Rhosivi—just thinking the word made my whole body hurt again.

The coal came from none other than Rhosivi, and, for all I knew, the coal cooking these pastries was coal I'd dug out. Granted, it'd been months since then, but I had no idea how long shipping took. Or how quickly they burned through the bags I'd busted my palms open packing up.

I stepped to the sink, expecting to find a pump like those at Rhosivi or Predvoi, but instead there was a knob. When I turned it on and rubbed my hand under the surprisingly warm water, I half-marveled, half-resented Khizmit for its use of electricity and indoor plumbing. Biting back a gasp of pain, I washed my hand under the water, which reopened some of the wounds. I cautiously healed them, just enough to stop the bleeding; I didn't dare heal them completely. Above the sink hung a mirror, and although the only light came in through the open door, it was enough to see that I didn't look like slag.

I looked far worse. The snow and ice that had fallen in my hair while I ran had melted from my body heat and then dried so strands of it whipped away from my face, making it appear more oblong. I leaned in and stared at my right dimple, running the tip of my unscathed finger over it as a headache drummed through my temples.

Gone. Healed. And all because my parents were criminals turned lab rats.

It was no wonder Khizmit feared me and wanted to kill me. I terrified myself at times, especially when I saw this face looking back at me. My lips were nearly blue, eyelashes and eyebrows coated in coal dust and melting ice, splotches of red smudging my cheeks. Gingerly filling my right hand with warm water, I splashed my face two times and then dried my hands on the damp white cloth hanging against the brick wall. The burst of heat from the furnace had curled the edges of my eyebrows. No wonder the lieutenant had questioned me.

I still looked like slag, but I couldn't do much about that without some more food. Hoping Lee wouldn't notice, I healed my eyebrows, eyelashes, and some of the reddish burn in my cheeks. No wonder my hair had seemed to defy the regular shavings.

A plan. I needed a plan now that I was here. I'd have to get some money if I wanted to eat and not be a criminal. And I didn't want to be a criminal. I'd have to find somewhere to live if I wanted to stay off the streets and park benches.

Why did Roman send me here?

Roman, for all his games, had followed a plan. The knife in the back of my pants reminded me of that. Maybe he sent me here to Khizmit because this is where Lockbox was. Somewhere in this city.

He knew that I wanted freedom and my friend. For the first time, I indulged in a daydream. One where I sat on the Judgment Board and voted for life every time. One where I earned respect and power, and then used my position to end the Preemptive Initiative.

I hurried out of the washroom, embarrassed at my daydream. I'd start by finding Leticia Varga, then getting Lockbox, whatever the cost.

The wooden floor creaked as I stepped back into the small dining area. Lee looked up as Leticia scooted her chair back and hurried away, indicating that the vacated seat was meant for me.

Two cups sitting on the table sent spirals of steam into the air. The one in front of Lee had decorative blue and purple flowers painted around the top and held a honey-colored drink. The large mug for me held a drink black as coal. Black as slag.

"What is it?" I asked, taking a seat.

"It's vyco," Lee said.

"How did you get vyco?" I raised it to my mouth and took a long drink. In moments, my headache would die down.

"Here in Khizmit, vyco is a controlled substance. If you have a doctor's note, it's easy to get, but Leticia doesn't require one, and she said after giving you the once-over, you needed it."

At her mention of a prescription, I wondered if they had other drugs here. Not that I wanted them, but my body had begun to react to Lee in a rather…distracting way.

"Don't worry, Peddy. Erik isn't going to come in here demanding to see your prescription for the vyco. You're not from here, are you?" As she asked it, my heart rate climbed.

What was it that made her think I wasn't from here? That I'd been surprised to see vyco? That wouldn't make sense. *Was it that I marveled at the decorations with barely bridled excitement? My accent?* At least I knew it wasn't my clothes.

She reached across the table and placed her hand on my wrist. Instinct told me to run and hide. But then I looked up to her face and saw her eyes filled with sympathy.

"What's her last name?" I asked, nodding toward the back room where Leticia had gone.

"Why do you ask?" She puffed on her tea. "Are you looking for someone in particular?"

I followed suit and blew into my drink, sending steam dancing through the air between us. A small smile played at the corners of my mouth, and feeling the dimple on my right cheek, I grinned deeper. "I'm looking for a friend."

"You already found a friend," she said with a soft laugh. She delicately lifted the cup to her lips and barely sipped at it before holding it in her hands.

Friends don't come that easily. Friendship comes with a cost, but I tried not to show any suspicion of her while I worked through figuring her out.

Her blue and gold gloves sat on the table. Evidently, that was the custom here, to take off your gloves to eat. But I didn't dare remove the one covering my left hand. No one could see the injury on my arm and wrist. Least of all, this girl with a thousand questions. Without adequate forethought, I removed my right glove, placed it on the table, and then regretted it. My left glove, still covering my other hand, drew attention. I should have kept them both on. But it was too late for that.

Lee looked at my hands and then up to me. "Her last name is Nowak." I guess the disappointment showed on my face because she reached over and placed her bare hand on my arm. "Can you tell me who you're looking for?"

"Someone named Leticia."

"There are lots of Leticias here. You'll have to be more specific."

"I will. Eventually," I attempted to tease, trying not to let on how scared I was of being found out. Fear in the prison was different. It was everywhere with such potency that there were days I swear I could taste it and see it like black clouds trailing on all our heels. But out here, now that I had a taste of the freshness of freedom, that fear of going back or getting killed bit sharper than it had before. Unlike a cloud hovering around me, it was a constant knife in my back, twisting itself through to my gut.

"What's your last name?" Lee asked, her hands back on her own cup.

"Let's stick to Peddy for now."

Her hair was straight and dark black and wove over her shoulder nearly down to her elbow. Though she kept her face down, her hair half falling in front of her, she lifted her gaze to me coyly before breaking the silence between us. "I've made up a story for you."

A story? "You what?"

"A backstory. I do it sometimes when I'm watching people. I give them names and stories."

"That's…interesting." Weird is what I meant. Unusual. And yet, my stomach warmed at the thought, as I'd been naming the prison guards and my former fellow inmates for as long as I could remember.

"You were a soldier on the front lines. That's why you're so strong." I blushed, and she didn't seem to notice as she continued, "But you weren't on the front lines fighting for Khizmit. You're completely unfamiliar with our culture here. You're a soldier, maybe even a young captain, from the Latvani Enclave. But you've killed too many people and seen too many of your own soldiers die, so you deserted. You ran away from the war, and since your face is well-known in Latvani, you had no choice but to come here, to Khizmit."

I smiled at her over my drink, which tasted like cloves and another spice I didn't know the name of. It had already taken a big bite out of my pain. The slightly bitter taste I couldn't quite place had to be vyco. This dose was stronger than anything I'd had yet.

"You look like a soldier. You've even got military-issued gloves." She blew on her drink again as she held it in her hands and then flipped her hand over, warming the other side of her fingers. "You keep the left one on because you have worse scars on that hand or perhaps a stumpy finger, deep scars from the battles you've fought, and you're self-conscious. A self-conscious captain from Latvani," she concluded.

"I'm not a soldier," I said before sipping the drink again, a little bit too fast. It nearly burned my tongue.

"Not anymore, but you were. You've fought. Just look at those scars on your hand. They must be from fights. Your knuckles have been split open more than once."

I looked at the white scars all over my right hand, wondering if I should have healed them. Probably better that I hadn't. Everyone has scars. Not having any would have been suspicious.

"I like your story," I said, grinning stupidly.

"Everyone deserves a new chance. Even traitors from

Latvani." She laughed at herself and, *skudge*, it sent my heart racing to see her smile clear up through her eyes. Not all girls or women could be like this. It was impossible. If every female were like her, every male would need to take the numbing pills in triple doses.

I didn't need to meet a million different females to know this girl was something special.

CHAPTER 7
ONE GOD WITH A THOUSAND FACES

I TALKED and laughed with Lee until the shop owner, Leticia, came out with some rye rolls and pats of butter. I thanked her quickly, worried that I'd be asked to pay a bill at the end. She disappeared into the back as Lee grabbed one of the rolls, smeared some butter on it, and took a large bite. She sighed and tossed her hair over her shoulder. I don't think she was trying to be attractive in that moment, but I'd never seen anything more beautiful in my whole life.

"Have one," Lee said, noting my hesitation.

"I still don't have any money." *Why did it embarrass me to say so?* I'd had a few koruna back in Rhosivi. I'd worked every day of my life and didn't have a single koruna to show for it when I needed it. I could have kicked myself for not having kept some of my coins with me at all times. As I'd been able to make money in prison, there had to be a way for me to make money here in Khizmit.

"I'll cover the bill. Don't worry." She pushed the plate of rolls toward me. It too had flowers painted in swirling designs of red, orange, and pink along the edge. I grabbed a roll and butter—we never had the luxury of butter in the prisons—and ate it, undoubtedly less attractively than Lee ate hers as I savored every bite.

"Are you going to tell me the truth about you?" she asked.

"Probably not," I said. "I like the story you made up anyway. Makes me sound heroic."

"Well, I hope you'll tell me your story someday."

"Hope," I muttered.

"What about hope? It's good to hope."

I debated biting my tongue, but I didn't. "Hope is the hand that leads you into the darkness of the unknown so it can torture and kill you there without any witnesses." Looking up, I saw her face and realized my mistake.

"You're really not from Khizmit at all." Her eyes shone with fascination. "Your face when you said that looked like you've been through hell. Like for a moment, you were back there. Back in hell. Back on the battlefield."

"Sorry, I just meant—"

"I know what you meant."

"I was kidding," I said.

"You were definitely not kidding."

"Fine, I wasn't kidding. Why would that mean I'm not from Khizmit?"

"It's obvious. I'm surprised Erik was too dense to see it right away. You know nothing about this place!"

I didn't dare correct her. *But would it really have been a correction? Wasn't prison its own battle? A battle to survive, whatever the cost?* She was right about one thing—I'd been through hell, and I was never, ever going back.

She nudged the plate toward me again as I finished the first roll. "You think differently. And I think...I think you've had more than a bad night."

I laughed uncomfortably and took another drink before reaching for a second roll. "It's not been all bad." I didn't like when people knew things about me.

The headache, which had been thudding like a metronome in my head since I'd healed myself, finally quieted to a whisper.

Another couple of girls entered the shop and glanced at me before lowering their voices to whispers, unaware that I could listen in without much effort.

"Nine," the one girl with a yellow shirt said.

Nine out of what? Nine out of fifty? Nine out of a hundred?

"Ten if he showered."

If who showered? If I showered?

It hadn't occurred to me to consider whether or not I looked attractive to girls. Probably because of the nummers, my daydreams of freedom hadn't included any relationships.

A nine? A ten? I laughed a little as the girls kept talking.

The girl with brown hair and purple gloves sighed. "I'd grab a fistful of that hair."

"Looks like someone already did," the girl in yellow said as she leaned back in her chair trying to see Lee's face. The chair creaked, and both Lee and I turned to see the girl sit back up quickly to keep from falling over.

"Who other than *Lee?*" The girl *humphed*, then spoke to us. "Is this one a captain, too?"

"Might be," Lee said. "Might not be."

"Has she skudged you yet?" The girl in the yellow shirt called loudly over to me. I didn't expect girls outside of prison to talk so crassly.

I turned to Lee, ready to defend her honor, only to see her grinning. "He's skudging me. I'm skudging him. Same thing really."

"Really?" The brown-haired girl looked at me forlornly, and her gaze went up to my hair.

My body went rigid as Lee leaned into me and pulled my arm over her shoulder.

"So you're just climbing your way up that ladder, huh? Sleeping your way to the top."

Lee placed her hand on my chest, and I'm surprised she couldn't feel my heart beating wildly under it. "Look at him, Aneta. This is the top."

"He is hot," the girl in yellow said quietly.

"Hotter than embers," Lee stated. The words sent a tremble through me.

The brown-haired girl named Aneta bit her bottom lip and eyed me somewhat morosely. The way she looked me down made me think she could visibly see in my face how aroused I was by Lee's compliment. *But she couldn't, right?*

The tension between the girls broke as Leticia stepped out from the back and stood at the counter. "Thanks for stopping in! Come back anytime."

"It was excellent," Lee said.

I still couldn't wrap my head around whatever game these girls were playing with each other.

Lee pulled her leather purse to the front and counted out six koruna before dropping them into Leticia's hand. Lee pulled her gloves on, but I kept my right one off, holding it in my left if for no other reason than to stop her from reaching for that hand.

"Thanks again!" I said to Leticia, trying not to look like a fool.

We turned for the door, Lee's body still pressed up against mine when she leaned over the girls table and said, "And for the record, there's not a lot of sleeping that happens." She winked, my face going hot as I turned back to the door, and she slipped her arm into mine, leaning into my shoulder affectionately as we stepped outside.

The wind in the air did little to cool my face. Only a few steps away from the shop, Lee moved away from my shoulder but kept her arm linked with mine.

"Sorry about that," she said quickly. "For the record, I don't."

"You don't what?"

"It's just a stupid rumor spread by stupid girls. Just ignore them. I try to."

"Sure," I said. "I'll ignore them."

She sighed and slid her hand into mine. Luckily, she was on my right side, so I was easily able to return the pressure to her fingers. "I realized that I can't control what other people think about me or how they see me, but I can have some fun with it." She laughed and kept guiding me down the streets.

While she was clearly still thinking about the conversation from the café, my concerns had nothing to do with her personal habits. *Where was she taking me? Could I trust her?*

"Where are we going?" I asked.

"You're lost, Peddy. And it's not safe for you to wander the streets like you were. So, I'm taking you home."

Home. Her home. It was certainly safer than wandering around out here. At the very least, taking me home meant I'd know where to find her again. *I had to see her again, didn't I? She'd want to see me again, right?* After all, she'd said I was the top. *Didn't that mean she liked me?* She'd said I was hotter than embers. I've been called many things. Slag for brains. Lurper. Dangerous. Lethal. A walking weapon. A threat. A mistake.

But never any synonym of handsome. My dimples were deeper than the mines in Rhosivi for how huge my smile was.

Were the compliments her way of making me feel safe? Or catching me off my guard so she could turn me in?

She thought I was a traitor from Latvani. She thought I was a captain.

I'd follow her for a while, learn what I could, and escape when I needed to. She was a girl, so I wouldn't hurt her, but I wouldn't need to in order to get away.

Arm in arm, Lee told me about all the traditions in Khizmit for Koliada, which was only a few days away now. Each sector had its own tree, and on Koliada morning at sunrise, everyone in the sector would come out and play music in celebration. Children exchanged gifts within their sectors, and everyone exchanged treats. Her mom apparently made caramels, some with nuts and some without, and Lee had to help wrap them up and tie them into little bundles for the neighbors.

"So Khizmit really is a utopia," I mused, looking at some artwork in the window of a business.

"It's not usually. But it's Koliada. You came at the best time!"

As she spoke, I realized that the Khizmit I'd hoped existed, did exist. Even if it was only at its peak once a year during Koliada. If a city could be that great during part of the year, then it could be that great year-round. Once TPI was overthrown.

Lee pointed out which shops along the way had the best hot drinks and which ones should be avoided since they used dirty water or didn't wash their hands or because the owners didn't understand boundaries.

"Don't go there. They don't like strangers, and they'll call the guards in if you show up without identification or an adult with you. They'd probably arrest you if you asked for vyco."

I nodded, making a mental map of the city I'd seen so far. Not every street had as grand of decorations as the one where she'd found me sleeping on the bench, but green garlands with handmade ornaments appeared to connect every house and building through all of Khizmit. Perhaps it was some great symbol of unity during the holiday.

"Do you celebrate Koliada in Latvani?" she asked as we slowed, turning a corner back near the center of town.

Latvani.

I suppose it couldn't be denied that I wasn't from Khizmit. It made sense that she'd assume I came from another enclave. After all, no one escaped from prison. Warden Dulka had to believe I was dead and eaten by wolves. But even if she'd known that I'd made it out alive, I couldn't see the government announcing that a dangerous prisoner had escaped and was roaming freely. I wasn't just any prisoner. Such an announcement would have brought mass panic.

"We don't celebrate Koliada where I'm from."

"In Latvani?"

I looked at her out of my peripheral.

"You don't have to confirm my suspicions, but can you at least tell me about it? It's not like I have anyone else to teach me about the world outside of mine."

"Where I'm from there are no holidays," I said. I wasn't afraid of lying. I was afraid that the lies I told would lead to the truth. But if she didn't know anything about Latvani, was it safe to assume she didn't know much about the Preemptive Initiative? *Was that possible? Was it possible that Khizmit didn't teach the younger generation about the past?*

Maybe she didn't know that Khizmit had needed stronger soldiers, and they'd tested their chemical creations on criminals. Or that those criminals had broken free, killed the scientists, destroyed the lab, and tried to go into hiding. Maybe she didn't know that her government had agreed to send out soldiers to hunt down the criminals from the experiments and then incarcerate their children. *I mean, what child wants to hear about other children who have worse lives?* I'd wished parents in Khizmit had taught their kids about us budding criminals and our lives in the mines to explain where the coal came from. Kids the same ages as them, living completely opposite lives. If it could be called living.

"What do you celebrate? What do you worship?" she asked.

"We worship coal," I said quickly. I didn't intend on inventing a whole religion, but if I'd said we didn't have a god, that our faith was in a Freedom Tunnel, well, then she'd know exactly where I came from. "We have lots of mines, and we all work in them, and we gather up our coal and pray."

"To a coal god?"

"It's a bit more…vague than that." I had to keep it vague for myself.

"Monotheistic or polytheistic?" Lee's eyes widened in curiosity, and I decided she wasn't trying to trap me or trick me. If that was her intent, she was a professional.

"One god with a thousand faces and a thousand appetites."

"A god with an appetite? What for?"

"The god battles within himself. Whichever face he shows is the one we worship and the appetite we feed. Lately, it's been coal, but it can be other things too. Rye. Water."

"Is that how you explain things in Latvani? Through gods?"

"It's not a matter of explaining things. No one explains things." That last part was true.

She tugged at my arm until I looked at her, and we stopped walking for a moment.

"Too bad we can't open up trade between our enclaves. We have plenty of coal. You have something to trade, don't you? Maybe that's what this war is all about. You don't think you could convince some of your leaders to offer some as a peace offering, do you?"

Plenty of coal? That wasn't exactly what I'd been told at Rhosivi. I worked my jaw and tried to respond to her politely. "My leaders wouldn't give a slag what—" I paused and rephrased it. "They wouldn't listen to me. Your version of my story paints me as someone high ranking, but that's not the case."

"I have alternate versions if you want to hear them." She fiddled with a few of her gold ear cuffs.

"I think I'd like to keep the version you've already shared. Me. An officer." I chuckled.

"So that's what these are from?" She traced her hand along a scar on the top of my wrist, drawing back my sleeve as she followed it to its end. "Mining? Are there lots of mines in Latvani?"

I tried to swallow, but it felt like there was a piece of ore stuck in my throat. She stepped back.

Her cheeks looked red, either from the cold air or maybe from embarrassment. She tucked some of her hair over her ear.

"My people aren't...very affectionate." I said, trying to explain. "We don't embrace or touch each other."

"Just men don't, or just women don't?"

"What?"

"You don't hug women, or you don't hug men?"

"I don't hug anyone."

"Just you or everyone in Latvani?"

"No one hugs anyone, and the women mostly stay away from the men."

"Are the men dangerous?"

My heart started racing. *That word.* "What?"

"Are you dangerous?"

"Me? I guess that depends on who you ask."

Lee stared at me, narrowing her eyes. "I'm asking you."

I don't know what prompted me to reply honestly. Maybe to see if she'd leave me in the road. Maybe I felt like I owed her a warning. "Yes," I said. "I am. I would say I'm rather dangerous." I didn't want to sound like I was making a threat. "But that's not why the women stay away from the men."

"Oh, is it a cultural thing? Are there arranged marriages? Is that why you ran away? Did you show up for your wedding and get assigned a mean bride? Or was she an old bride?"

"There are things far worse than an old bride. How young do you think they're getting married over in Latvani anyway?"

"How am I supposed to know how old you are?"

"I'm seventeen."

She smiled. Something about that made her eyes light up. "Too young to be a captain. Too young to be a husband."

I should have lied and said twenty-one. I liked when she thought I was an officer.

We continued down the path; the buildings were taller here, and some were painted white. Her black hair stood out as she leaned against the side of one.

She caught her breath. There was no one else around. No guards. No pedestrians. Lee had foolishly brought me somewhere we could be alone.

I trusted myself, but the novelty of the moment rattled me. Left me feeling exposed, but she was the one who should feel exposed. I'd just told her I was dangerous. *Did she think I was joking?*

"Why did you leave Latvani?" she asked.

"I never said I did. I never said I didn't."

"Are you from Latvani? You can't be from Dovaberg. It's too far. It's too…they're all…"

"I'm not from Dovaberg."

"In my culture, lying is frowned upon." The wind blew some snow off the roofs, and it tumbled around us, settling on the top of her hair.

"In my culture, the best liars are the most successful. So, in that way, lying is rewarded."

"Well, that's definitely true here, too." She laughed. "When we get inside, I just want you to know that my dad can smell a lie from a kilometer away. Trust me, I've had seventeen years to try and trick him, and it never works. That's why the rumors people spread about me and his soldiers don't bother him. He can always tell what's true and what isn't."

Her mentioning the rumors again seemed to hint that even though she'd fueled them and laughed them off, they bothered her.

I started speaking audaciously. "I know what it's like for people to make assumptions about you and then spread those rumors far and wide. So, I'm just saying, you don't have to worry about me believing everything I hear. About you or anyone else." Look at me, giving advice. Trying to share a heartfelt moment. And yet, it felt like the truest moment I'd had with her. It was the most genuine thing I'd said, and somehow, she knew it. I could see that in her face.

"Same for you. I've heard Latvanians are quite brutal, but you seem nice enough."

I chuckled and found myself reaching forward to brush some snowflakes out of her hair when I dropped my hand again and instead ruffled my own hair.

"I appreciate the offer to come inside, to meet your dad, and all that. And I can't thank you enough for the vyco and bread, but I can't come in."

"Where will you go?"

"I don't know yet."

"You'll get arrested."

"Why?"

"Because you don't know what you're doing."

Would I be…?

But she said her father could smell a lie a kilometer away. For all I knew, that was possible. I could block pain, amplify my senses, predict movements in a fight, and heal myself. A human who could smell dishonesty didn't seem that far-fetched of an idea. *And what had she said? His soldiers? Meaning they reported to him?* He had to be an officer of some sort for her to call the soldiers "his."

I couldn't go with her. The risks were too high. I'd come so far. I wasn't about to deliver myself into the hands of some high captain.

My misgivings must have been obvious.

"Come in. Meet him. Then you can leave if you'd like."

Leave? Just like how I'd left Predvoi. Leaving somewhere

wasn't that simple. A house could be a prison. Trapped in on all sides, nowhere to run if I needed to make an escape.

But besides that, what if someone found out she'd been kind to me. That she'd housed a lurper. *What danger was I putting her in?*

"Have you considered that maybe I'm not the sort of person you want to bring home?"

Lee ignored my question as she stuck the tips of her fingers into her mouth, bit onto the mitten, and used her teeth to hold it while she dug around in the small satchel at her waist with her bare hand. With a small key in her hand, she turned toward the building and stuck it into the keyhole. That probably meant the door would lock behind me, and I'd spent enough time locked behind doors.

"Thank you, again, but I can't come in."

"And what's your plan, Peddy? To sleep on the bench? Hang out with the homeless while you find a way to blend in? Because that's going to take a long time. I won't say impossible because I suspect you're capable of a lot, but you don't blend in. Most men your size and build are in uniforms. So, unless you're going to somehow attack one and steal their clothes, you're going to stand out. Thank your god or whichever face of your god is hungry today that I found you first."

I chuckled. I'd have to remember that lie about a many-faced god with appetites. My plan had always just been to get here to Khizmit, but I'd never considered that I'd stand out so much.

"My dad will help you. He can get you a job; he can help you blend in." *Did all young girls think their dad was some hero? What if he wasn't?*

"Is he a high captain?" I asked.

"No."

He had to be a captain then. I'd dealt with captains before. The cold steel of the dagger against my skin reminded me that I was armed.

If he tried to take me to another prison, I could slice his throat. I could—

I disgusted myself. *How dare I imagine killing her dad!*

"Can you just trust me?" she asked.

The answer was "no," but I wasn't about to say that. She could read the fear on my face. I hadn't masked it well enough. She reached out and placed her hand on my arm, my burned arm. I winced.

"I'm not going to hurt you."

If she knew what I was, if she knew what I could do, she would have screamed.

And yet she stood there, reassuring me that she wasn't going to hurt me.

"I don't want you to get arrested," she said. It was her sincerity that finally convinced me.

Maybe going with the story that I was from Latvani wasn't such a bad idea. *Or could I make up some other city further south?* Latvani was south. North would only make her think of Rhosivi and Predvoi. I didn't believe there was anything more northern than Rhosivi. *What if I said I was a slave who'd been sold to work in the mines in Latvani and then escaped and came here?* That had to be a good enough story.

As Lee opened the door, I committed myself to that story. Peddy, the slave from some city named…Or maybe I'd just stick with Latvani. I could invent an accent and feign a language barrier. That way I wouldn't have to say much until I understood more. Except that Lee already knew I didn't have a language barrier. *What were my options?* If I hadn't been so distracted by her beauty and kindness, I might have thought of something better than following her blindly to her home.

She stepped inside, and I followed.

Just inside the door sat a wide staircase with twisted iron railings leading up to the interior of the house. Heat crept around my face as I cautiously stepped in.

"I'm home!" Lee called, shutting the door behind her. It clicked, the lock sounding as loud as a gunshot in my head.

Please let her father be a good man, I thought to no god in particular.

Lee dashed up the stairs and practically jumped into the arms of a man standing just out of sight. He stepped forward.

"Emberly!" He buried his face in her shoulder and all I could see of him were his arms and the top of his head. I didn't have to have Lockbox's memory to know the name Emberly. Lee. Emberly.

Skudge. I was skudged.

The hair on my arms stood on end, and my whole body tensed because even in that one word, I knew who this man was.

Commander Markos held his daughter close, and I had a single second to decide what to do.

CHAPTER 8
THE WOLF'S FACE

Pedrick Markos who had pulled Romeo-22 off me when I was twelve years old. Markos, as I'd called him affectionally, who'd driven me to Predvoi and then, just two days before, had raised his hand and voted for my death.

Commander Markos stepped aside from his daughter to face me. He didn't have his ushanka or his overcoat on, just his uniform pants and a tan undershirt with small white buttons. I'd have recognized him no matter what he wore.

Hope was all I had to hold on to. Hope that he wouldn't recognize me without the scar and the prison garb. He hadn't been able to remember my name in the back of the truck. He'd had to have received the news that I'd been killed. He'd seen me run.

Markos took one look at me, and his face turned to stone. I instinctively reached for the dagger in my pants as he launched himself over the railing, cleared all the stairs, and grabbed my hands.

He pinned me to the thick door, twisting my arms up so the blade hovered at my own neck.

"Sir," I whispered.

"Give it to me," he growled.

I struggled for half a second before reality slammed into

me. There were many ways he could kill me and not a single situation where I came out on top. My fingers released their hold on the handle. "Sir, I—"

"Not in my house," Commander Markos said. "Not here."

The door opened behind me as Commander Pedrick Markos turned the handle and herded me out of his house. *No key.* It hadn't been locked after all.

The growl out of his throat sounded almost like it came from a wolf rather than a human. I almost tripped over my boots as I stumbled backwards.

Crossing the threshold, he turned back to Emberly and said only two words, "Stay here." His tone wasn't gentle, but the command clearly came from a place of concern.

If I ran, Markos would catch me. If I fought, I'd lose. I could hardly breathe. Her father wasn't a high captain. What a skudging stupid question! Commander. She could have mentioned that her father was a commander!

I couldn't process any of it. *Had she known I was a lurper? Had he known I'd survived? Was he looking for me? Was Lee a member of the Task Force?*

As I walked backward toward a narrow, dark alley, I looked at Markos's face, trying to read his expression. Bricks blocked one way. Stone walls blocked the other. This would be my tomb.

Once both of us stood in the tight space away from the eyes and ears of everyone, or so it seemed, Markos moved for me. I prepared myself for the wretched pain of a blade in my side, but instead, Markos's arms moved around me in an unmistakable embrace.

I was too stunned to even move.

Markos's voice came out as a whisper, "I thought you were dead. The report said that…"

The hug from the shop owner had been startling enough, but the act of Warden Markos actually embracing me shocked me more than the moment Roman had stabbed me.

Markos stepped back and wiped at his eyes. *Tears? For me? I had to be misinterpreting everything right now.* "Are you alone?" he whispered.

"Yes, Sir," I said, my voice weak.

"How did you find me?" he asked.

"By accident. Coincidence."

At this reassurance, he tucked Roman's blade into his pants and put out his hand. I knew he wanted to see my wrist.

"Please," I pleaded as I handed him my arm. I almost asked him to be gentle with me.

He moved slowly as he pulled the glove away from my charred skin and shuddered. "What the skudge did you do?"

"I burned it in the factory outside the city. I guess you won't be able to check—"

"I don't need to check your wrist to know it said Victor-27." His voice was stern, but the smallest smile played at the edges of his mouth.

"Right," I said.

"Do you have any other weapons?"

"No, Sir. Just…myself."

He smiled now, actually smiled at that, and it helped me to relax a little.

"I'm going to bring you back inside where we won't be interrupted. Don't say anything to Emberly."

He wanted to take me back inside his house? Back past Emberly?

"Are you going to kill me, Sir?"

"No."

Was he going to call a company of soldiers here to finish the execution that I'd escaped?

"If you are, I'd rather you make it quick. Private."

I couldn't stomach the idea of my murder being made into a public spectacle.

Markos turned to me and moved close. He placed his

hand on my right shoulder. I tried not to flinch. "You're okay." He put his arm around me. "You're safe now."

Safe? Would I ever be safe?

I wanted to run, but I didn't stand a chance. Markos knew these streets, these buildings, these people. *Would he follow me at all, or just open fire?* He had no firearms on him that I could tell, and he had few places to hide one without his overcoat on.

But he'd had tears on his face.

The tears were the reason I followed him back to his house.

We crossed the pathway, and Pedrick Markos unlocked the door for me, just as he had back in Rhosivi. *Was I entering another prison? Or finally leaving one?*

When we stepped back through the door, Emberly was waiting for us. I didn't look up at her. I stared at her feet instead, wrapped in leather boots with decorative rabbit fur on the tips of the laces.

"What was that about?" Emberly asked, her voice angry.

"What did he tell you?" Markos asked gently, guiding me up the stairs to the living room.

"What did he tell *you*?" she replied. "I told him he'd be safe here! That you'd help him."

"He is safe here." Markos turned to me. "Do you feel safe here?"

"Yes, Sir," I said, not because it was true but because I knew it was the right answer.

"See, he's perfectly safe and happy here."

"You attacked him the second he entered the house! Did you cut him?" Emberly peered at my neck, but I kept my head down. "Are you okay?"

"I'm fine," I said.

"Like he said, he's fine," Markos echoed me.

I followed him into their living room at the top of the stairs.

The room had a small black stove, beside which sat a bin of the all-too-familiar coal from the mines. The heat from just that small fireplace warmed the home, and I would have removed my gloves if I wasn't so concerned about the attention it would draw from Emberley.

The couch, with a thick green cushion on top, was on one side of the room. Two large wingback chairs sat across from it. Though it was by far the nicest furniture I'd ever seen, it still seemed like a man of Pedrick Markos's prestige should have been living in even more luxurious conditions.

"What did he tell you?" Markos asked again, his voice a bit gentler this time.

Emberly sat down on the couch and picked up a pillow that she clutched to her chest. "Do you know each other?" she replied instead.

Markos took a seat on the couch near to her, and I sat in one of the chairs furthest from the fire. Sweat began to trickle down my back.

"Yes, we know each other. No, I didn't cut his neck. We just had a brief misunderstanding," Markos said. He reached out to console his daughter. She batted his hand away.

No one batted Markos away.

"Why'd you pull a knife on him then?"

"He pulled the knife on me, actually," Markos said with a grin. It shocked me that I had done that, and now he sat there, declaring it proudly to his daughter.

"You had a dagger with you this whole time?" Emberly turned to me. "So, you *are* a captain. That's a captain's weapon. Why'd you pull a knife on my dad?"

"I…I was…"

"He was just being careful," Markos said. "He's not a captain."

"What the—" she stopped herself from what most certainly would have been a curse. "What's going on?"

Markos took a breath. "He was being careful. I had to

make sure he was alone. I trust him, but I wasn't sure if he was…himself."

The answer didn't satisfy Emberly, but I finally understood. He didn't know if I'd come to hurt him. After all, he'd just voted for my execution. Maybe he feared I'd escaped and hunted him down to hurt him or his family. It wasn't something I'd ever considered, but it wasn't outside of my range of abilities either. He'd used my blade against me to keep me on the defense until he knew for sure that I wasn't here to harm him. I didn't blame him for it. Emberly, however, looked like she might never forgive him.

"You two know one another?"

"Yes," Markos said. "He's a soldier from my unit. He went dark, doing some clandestine work, and he and I need to debrief immediately. I'm very grateful you brought him here. No one can know what he does while he's here, do you understand?"

I finally looked up at Emberly. I wished I'd looked up sooner when she was mad. Now her expression showed hurt and confusion.

She made eye contact with me. "You mean, you knew who I was? And who my father was? And you were just trying to get me to take you here?"

"I…" I had no idea what to say. Several great lies came to mind, all of which I could sell. But to lie to her would only deepen those sad lines in her face.

"Is your name really Pedrick?"

I shook my head.

"So you just told me that name…you gave me my own father's name."

Markos reached out again to comfort her, and this time, she didn't bat his hand away.

"He was supposed to find me at my station near Latvani, but things didn't go according to plan. I'd been called to Predvoi, and he forgot it was the first Saturday of the month. I had to participate in some…responsibilities there." *She didn't know he was on The Judgement Board?* Markos continued, "He didn't know how to find me, but tracking you down was clever. He's good like that. You did the right thing bringing him here."

I've seen boys die, and while it's never made me happy, it usually didn't hurt in a deep, personal way. But as pain clawed across Emberly's face, it simultaneously clawed into my chest.

Her voice wasn't playful anymore. "You used me?"

"I…" I turned to Markos. "I'm not sure what to say."

Markos sighed. "The less we say, the safer you are." He rubbed her arm, and she glared at him. Her lips tightened.

"Well, I'm glad I could help." The words, though nice, were delivered with such anger it might as well have been an insult.

"What's your real name?" She stood, ready to leave, asking me for one single truth.

"I…" I turned to Markos who was no help at all. I looked back at her, hoping she could see the sincerity in my eyes. "I don't think I can tell you that."

Emberly huffed. "Of course not."

She stomped down the stairs and flung the door wide open, letting in a flurry of snowflakes and chilly wind.

"Where are you going?" Markos asked.

"Out. Be back later," she said through gritted teeth, and then she shut the door behind her with such force that I'm sure snow fell off the edges of the red roof outside.

If anyone else was home, they kept to the back rooms even as Emberly slammed the door. In the awkward silence that followed her exit, I looked around the house. I had no memory of being in a home.

The wall in front of me held a large mirror with a decorative silver border. In the corner away from the fire stood a narrow shelf crammed with books—far more books than I'd had in my trunk. On top of them in a display case was Khizmit's flag—the wolf's face in the center of the flag only half-way exposed through the glass.

The iron tools for the fireplace would have made great weapons. I hated that I thought of them that way. I turned around to the small table in the kitchen where six chairs were tucked neatly beneath the dark, worn wood.

Markos cleared his throat, and I turned back to him. "Tell me everything. From leaving Predvoi to meeting my daughter."

I didn't say a word. *What would happen if I did? What if I didn't?* "Why?" I asked. The word echoed and had to have landed like a blow, but what reason did I have to confide in him? He'd voted for my execution.

"Because I brought you back inside my house as a guest, and I'm going to continue giving you the protection you've enjoyed so far in life because, with my help, you have a chance of survival. So, it's about time you started to trust me."

"Trust you? Trust *you*? You sent me to Predvoi! You broke my nose. You voted for my execution!"

His voice grew rougher. "I kept you alive. I sent you to Predvoi when they gave me a new station. I had no choice but to accept the commission to become a commander, and you wouldn't have survived a day under Head Warden Velky. He's been advocating for your termination from the day you arrived at Rhosivi ten years ago."

"You mean, you knew you were leaving…and you didn't want me to…" Hearing it was one thing, but processing it required a little bit of time.

"Doctor Bolest had been asking for an opportunity to study you for almost as long as Velky had been arguing for you to be sent to the front lines or requesting permission to kill you himself. Doctor Bolest has been fascinated by Victors, and Head Chancellor Dulka finally granted him permission to study one at Predvoi. She took him out of the Lurper Legion and sent him as a gift for Bolest, a mistake I recognized immediately."

"You're talking about Victor-14?" I asked.

Markos grimaced. "You heard then, what happened. What Riah Dulka did."

I'd believed it when Lockbox had told me, but the pain on Markos's face almost made it look like he'd been there, too, and was, at that moment, reliving the grisly horror.

"I kept you safe at Rhosivi, even when others advocated that you be sent to the front lines."

"So, you kept me…to study?" I asked.

"I used that as my excuse, but I kept you because little boys have no business being used as fodder in a war any more than they should be used as slaves in the mine. Your survival was more likely under conditions I could control."

I mulled over his words. "Did you know…" I took a breath. "Did you know that my father was an X-ray and my mother was a Victor?"

"Yes."

"But you weren't…scared of me?"

"Scared of you? No," Markos scoffed. "I'm proud of you. Of what you've resisted and overcome. Of the young man you've grown into."

Proud. I didn't mean to smile, but how could I help it?

"But when you left me at Predvoi, you…broke my nose."

Markos scratched the back of his neck. "Yes, and I'm sorry about that. It was too soon for you to know that I was helping you. I was worried you knew the truth already. That I sympathized with you, and if you were aware of it, I worried someone else might be aware of it as well. If I sent you inside, bleeding and broken like that, Riah Dulka would have no reason to suspect that I cared about you, despite Andrei Velky's insistence that I was giving you special treatment."

I had no recollection of special treatment, but I certainly had no intention of arguing with him.

"I would have taken you with me when I took command, but it would have been too suspicious, especially considering Velky's accusations. The safest place to send you was Predvoi. I knew that Doctor Bolest, as twisted as he is, wouldn't kill you because that would be killing his last chance to amount to something. You were the last identified Victor in Khizmit, and the Victors on the front lines are too volatile to bring back. Victor-14 proved that." Markos heaved a sigh, relaxing deeper into the seat.

I opened my mouth to ask more about the others, but Markos went on.

"I knew that sending you to Predvoi would keep you alive."

My voice became a bit sharp. "For only six more months. What difference did it make?"

"What diff—" He clenched his jaw and leaned over his lap, closer to me, keeping his voice low, though no one else was home, and the neighbors definitely couldn't hear us. "I have stuck my neck out for you time and time again. I had to make it look like I was doing it as a favor for Dulka since she'd recommended me as Commander. But I have two daughters who need my protection more than you do. I have a wife who spends more sleepless nights worrying for my safety than she does resting."

I didn't want to relive the painful memory, but I had to bring it up. I spoke a little louder than he did. "But you voted for my termination. At The Judgement Board. I saw you—"

"Of course, I did! I had to. If I'd voted that you live when no one else did, it would have revealed that I care."

He kept talking, but the words hit my ears as a buzz while that word echoed in my head. *Care.* He did care. He did know me. The relief at knowing that I wasn't crazy for thinking he did was like a shot of straight vyco.

"Listen," Markos said. "While you pulled that stunt in the courtyard, I was pulling strings getting you assigned to my unit. I wasn't going to let them shoot you."

"Captain Kral stabbed me," I said.

"I heard. And I hoped that…I hoped that Captain Kral had enough time to tell you what to do."

Captain Kral. Roman. "Where is he?"

"Still at Predvoi."

"Who is he? Did you send him?"

"How else would he have ended up watching after you? To tell you what you could do?"

"Took him long enough."

"The captain took a lot of risks with you. Some gratitude wouldn't kill you, you know. I reassigned him as a disciplinary measure at Predvoi."

"What did he do? To deserve that punishment?"

"Nothing. I just needed eyes on you. Someone I could trust to keep you from getting killed and report back to me. Didn't Lockbox figure any of that out and tell you?"

He called him Lockbox. He knew his name. He'd coordinated the transfer with both of us in mind. I knew my transfers were orchestrated by Head Warden Markos, but to realize the way he'd been so integral in the details of my life took more than a few moments to process. Roman's position at Predvoi. The vote at The Judgement Board. My trunk. My friends. He'd been behind all of it. I looked up into his eyes, pushing aside my habit of avoiding doing just that.

Markos's face appeared more gentle, and I recognized the look of concern and relief. He'd worried about me.

I didn't know what made me happier—that I'd been right, and Commander Markos did give a slag about my life, or that I was finally out of prison. Freedom, as precious as it was, didn't outweigh validation. Concern. Care.

I could have laughed or cried; I didn't know which would have been more appropriate.

"Lockbox had figured some things out. The war. The legion with lurpers."

"Good. And you and he got close? He trusted you?"

I nodded, worry taking the place of words.

"I'd reviewed his file and Foxtrot-10's."

"Who is Foxtrot-10?"

"I believe he went by 'Spikes' at Predvoi. I wanted you to be roommates with Lockbox. After all, I'd been slipping him information for years. Information about Test Criminals and other enclaves."

"That was you, too?" I asked, incredulous.

"Believe me, it wasn't easy. He's been one of their high-interest inmates since he arrived. They've taken note of how the other inmates, even Juliets, Kilos, Mikes, Romeos, and Sierras fear him. When you gain some power in Khizmit, it's easier to have influence in a lot of places. I told the Chancellor Supreme that I would send you to Predvoi for Bolest to study if she gave me Foxtrot-10 for the Penal Legion. She couldn't understand why I wanted him, but she agreed. I assumed that they wouldn't want to disrupt politics among inmates, so they'd put you in with Lockbox who could then share what he knew with you."

"He did," I said, still processing. "Until they took him away."

Markos dropped his eyes. "I heard about that. I mean, I'd heard that you'd killed him, but I also knew it wasn't true."

What would he say when he found out that I had killed someone?

"Where is he?" I asked.

"Somewhere hard to get to. He's alive, I can assure you of that."

I said what I feared, "I thought for a while that Roman had killed him."

"Roman? You say it just like that. Lucky he didn't get flagged for fraternization."

"Is he okay?"

"Looks like you've been fraternizing" he said.

"Why's that?"

"Most people aren't that happy to hear they'll meet their assassins again." He had a point. Roman had stabbed me twice and threatened to kill me almost daily. His actions had saved my life. Contrary to Lockbox's warnings, I *had* become friends with Roman.

"Yes," I consented. "I suppose I did fraternize with Roman."

Markos finally bent to untie his boots. "First name basis would suggest so."

"Maybe I'm not supposed to ask, but what is his real name?"

He stared at me. "What do you mean? Didn't he tell you to call him Roman?"

"Actually, he told me repeatedly *not* to call him Roman."

"Then why do you call him that?"

A bit embarrassed, I told him how I named a lot of the guards based on their traits, physical or otherwise. I even mentioned Captain Bitter. Markos laughed, and I joined with him nervously.

"Oh, the Roman numerals earned him a name, huh?" he pondered. "I can tell you why he didn't want you calling him Roman."

"Because of fraternization?" I guessed. He'd warned me of it repeatedly.

Markos chuckled. "Sure looks like it. His real name is Romulus Kral. You probably scared the slag out of him by calling him something so close to his real name."

"He probably thought Lockbox had figured it out, since he had the Kral piece right."

"It must not have done too much damage, since the other guards didn't know his first name anyway," Markos said, still chuckling.

"I worried that Roman had killed Lockbox."

"Why would you think he'd kill a teenage boy?" Markos was vehement over this.

"He shot Smoke. He was a teenage boy."

"That's a bit of a different circumstance."

"He drugged us, both me and Lockbox."

"I drugged you, too. Every day! Some things can't be avoided. But Lockbox was too important of an inmate to kill. No one is going to kill him."

"So, he's safe?"

"What does it mean to be safe? Are any of us?" Markos sighed. "He's safe for now."

"Is he here in Khizmit?"

"I suspect so."

Hope fluttered in my chest. "Where?"

"I don't know, and honestly, that's not the priority right now. I promise we'll get to addressing Lockbox's situation. Right now, I really need you to tell me everything about your escape. From Predvoi all the way until you got here. Please," Markos said.

Please? Now that was a word I'd never heard him say. A word he didn't need to say, least of all to me. I'd have licked the snow off his boots if he told me to.

I took a breath and shared my story.

I didn't elaborate on any of the dialogue with Emberly, and I neglected to mention how I felt around her. But my face must have grown red when I talked about her.

"Oh, the nummers," Markos said, suddenly remembering my daily pills in the prison. "I'll try to snag some for you when I can, but in the meantime, keep a safe distance from… girls. Okay?"

Obviously, he meant for me to keep away from his daughter. I didn't want to agree. I wasn't some Charlie, genetically altered to comply. But after all that Markos had done for me, why shouldn't I agree? Based on the way Emberly had stormed out, she wasn't in any rush to spend any more time with me anyway.

"Sure," I said. "I wasn't going to—"

"It should go without being said."

"Of course."

"Of course." Markos insisted that I take a shower before dinner. He'd throw away Goyle's clothes and find some new ones for me.

He walked me down the wide hallway to the first door on the left. He said he'd be in the living room and his wife would be home soon. We had to keep up appearances for her, too.

"What about my hand and wrist, Sir?" I asked, standing in the doorway to the bathroom.

"Heal anything that's bleeding, but keep most of the burn intact. Victor-27 is supposed to be dead. If Dulka finds out you're alive, well, I'm sure you can think of at least one person she won't be happy with."

Roman.

"I have a vyco for when you're done taking care of what needs to be taken care of. No nummers, but I'll look for something that might make your time here a little more…comfortable." Markos reached in past the doorway and flipped a switch which turned on the lights in the ceiling.

"Uh, thanks," I said and shut the wooden door into place.

I turned around. Two white towels hung from a towel rack on the far wall above a toilet. Not a hole in the ground. Not a pot to slag in. A toilet with plumbing in his home, like the one I'd seen at the bakery, but cleaner. Nicer. A porcelain sink with two silver handles stood beside it, upon which rested a small clear vase holding some dried green plants.

The shower head came from the wall but was enclosed with glass doors that slid open as I pulled on them.

Peeling my clothes off felt nice as they'd been stuck to my skin with a cool sweat. The gloves were another story entirely. I could have numbed the pain, but it would have resulted in more work for me to do later with healing. I kept my senses intact and slowly peeled back the gloves, wincing and audibly crying twice. The room echoed, but I don't think anyone heard me. From the bathroom, I heard the front door open and shut and muffled voices, a female's and Markos's, but I couldn't understand any of it.

I adjusted my hearing in time to hear Emberly say, "I don't care. I'm not mad."

But she definitely was mad. I'd have been able to tell that from a single word.

Two knobs controlled hot and cold water, and it burst from the head of the shower with impressive force. Though I could have made the water warm or even hot, I kept it cool for the sake of my burn and because I'd never showered in anything other than tepid water. While standing under the shower head with streams of water running along my back and face, I focused on my hand, carefully sealing up the skin where it had peeled away inside the glove. I kept the scars and the blackened flesh. The healing felt a lot like the cool water on my skin.

I was almost finished showering when Markos cracked open the door to set some clothes on the floor. I dried off and dressed, only ruffling my short hair in the mirror before leaving.

Markos knocked as I finished dressing. I knew it was him by the way he walked down the hall. "Come in," I said.

The brown pants he'd given me were tight around my thighs as I pulled them on but roomier below my knees. They only made it halfway down my ankles. The shirt, a white linen V-cut tunic had black embroidery along the collar and shoulders as well as along the bottom which fell several millimeters below my waist. It was clearly a more traditional outfit for the occasion. Because it came so low, it covered the thin leather belt which held up my pants. I think they would have stayed on well enough without it.

"Where'd you get these?" I asked.

"The tailor next door."

"You just asked her for some clothes? She didn't wonder why you needed them?"

"No, her son died a few weeks ago, and she'd mentioned that she wanted to donate them. I just hadn't picked them up yet."

I suppose this meant I was destined to wear the clothes of dead men until I joined them in the ground.

"Head Warden, I mean, Commander Markos. Uhh, what do I call you?" I asked, feeling very young.

"Markos is fine while you're here."

"And Markos, Sir, what will you call me?" I'm sure he had the same realization that I did. He couldn't call me Victor, and as much as I wanted the black letter V on my wrist to be a name, it wasn't. It never would be. I hadn't minded when Lee called my Peddy, but going by Pedrick Markos's name was theft. Markos didn't say anything, but I know he heard me.

"Markos," I said again, and he looked back at me. "What will you call me? What should I go by out here?"

"Well," Markos paused and swallowed hard. "I always thought of you as...Luka."

"Luka?" It sounded foreign in my mouth. The name wasn't a new title or a letter or a number, but an actual name. *Always?* "Why Luka?"

"Because..." He scratched the side of his face and then said in a low voice, "because that's what your mother named you."

CHAPTER 9
LUKA

Luka. My mother named me Luka.

I had a name. "But how do you know that's what my mother named me?"

"She told me," Markos replied. "Right before she asked me to take care of you."

"And my father…" I felt stupid for even thinking it. "Do you know anything about him?"

"Your father was named Stefan Krajnak. I was there when they killed him, too. Someday, when we have time, I'll tell you more about them."

Stefan Krajnak. I committed the name to memory and poked my head out the door. "But my mother, they said she would have killed me."

"Well, add it to the list of lies they told you. Your mother was named Ilona, and she was enchanted by you. Her death…was one of the most tragic I've ever witnessed." He choked out the last line, and I knew he was telling me the truth. "I'm the one who took you in my arms when the soldiers marched her away. I'm the one who heard her last words."

"What did she say?" I whispered. Ilona. Ilona.

"She said, 'Take care of Luka for me.'" A creak from the

front door told us someone else was home. "Get dressed, Luka. Dinner's here." Markos pulled the bathroom door shut.

I heard him walk back to the front door where someone entered. I picked up on a more mature woman's voice greeting him and assumed it was Zuzana, Markos's wife, who was walking quickly up the stairs, carrying something that rustled.

In hushed tones I could hear without issue, Markos simply explained that I was one of his soldiers here in town on assignment and that I'd be staying for a couple of days before he would take me back to The Outskirts with him.

My parents *hadn't* skudged up?

And my mother had been enchanted by me?

I could hardly breathe.

I checked my face in the mirror before leaving. *Luka.* I stared at myself, tracing the place on my cheek where the scar used to mar my face. Thick hair sprouted just as dense there as it did on the other cheek, despite not having grown for years on account of the injury.

New face. New life. New world. It seemed only fitting that I needed a new name. One that didn't designate me as inmate. My mother named me Luka. And Luka I would be.

I stepped out into the hallway, expecting the tile floor to be cold underfoot, but it wasn't.

"Welcome," Zuzana said from the kitchen where Markos helped her unload some large brown paper bags onto the dark countertops. "Boots go in the entryway," Zuzana said, catching sight of them in my hand.

I carried my boots down to the entryway where I dropped them beside the door just as it opened again.

Emberly nearly ran right into me. I put my arms out to catch her and then yanked them back, Markos's gaze heavy on my back. Fortunately, Emberly caught herself on the wooden doorframe and then grabbed her younger sister's arm who'd followed her inside. Unlike Emberly, Milena had only one pair of earrings, and they matched. Gold foxes smaller than my fingernail hung from her ears.

"Excuse me," I said, scooting backward.

"This is one of dad's soldiers," Emberly said to Milena who regarded me with wide eyes. Emberly removed her tall boots and dropped them beside mine. Emberly's expression didn't seem malicious, but she didn't look at me long. And it was a far cry from the look she'd given me at the tea shop. She scooted beside me, careful not to make any physical contact, and hurried up the stairs.

"Hi," Milena said to me as she passed, trailing her sister.

"Hi," I said.

She didn't flinch. She didn't glare. And I found myself smiling.

"Dinner's about ready," Zuzana called. Her voice, though accented, didn't sound much like anyone I'd ever heard. Her accent was more like mine, striking me as subtle.

I stood in the entryway, not entirely sure where to go or what to do. I adjusted the shirt which fit snugly across my shoulders. Dinner plates clanged as the girls set the table, and I hurried into the kitchen.

Tall, dark wooden cabinets covered the far wall. The cabinets below wrapped around the corner of the room which led to a stove. Dark countertops were now covered with groceries as Markos finished emptying the last bag, and Zuzana hurried around sticking the items into the cabinets and refrigerator. The refrigerator, slender and almost as tall as I was, illustrated Markos's social status. I knew we had some freezers at the prison, but I never imagined individual families could afford a refrigerator for their home. Shelves covered in living plants were stacked above the window, and below that was the large rectangular sink currently sitting empty.

Zuzana wore a brightly embroidered dress that nearly swept the floor as she hurried around.

"What should I do?" I asked Markos, not sure if he wanted me to talk to his girls or his wife.

But it was Zuzana who answered. She hurried over to me and leaned in kissing my cheeks so quickly I didn't even have time to pretend to kiss her back. "I'm Zuzana," she said, giving me a quick hug.

"I'm…" I hesitated. *Was I really supposed to own this new name?*

"Luka, right?" Zuzana smiled, her eyes wrinkling slightly at the edges.

"Yes, Ma'am," I said, glancing briefly at Markos.

"Oh, no need for 'Ma'am' here," Zuzana said.

I'd try.

Markos caught my eye and waved me over. On the far side of the kitchen, Emberly and Milena took their seats at a table. The table was round with six matching wooden chairs around it. Milena took the seat which faced the corner, Emberly took the one beside it. On her other side, no plate was set. I took the seat beside the empty one, and Markos sat to my right.

In the center, dinner waited for us: potatoes, a jar of butter, a carton of cream, spinach, and boiled meat simmering in a thick gravy.

"This is Luka," Markos said mostly to Milena at this point. "He'll be staying with us for a few days, so you'll be moving your bed in with Emberly."

I'd be staying here? In his home? I suppose it was for the best, since this way he could keep a closer eye on me.

For the first time ever, I dished up my own food and took such small rations that Markos ended up scooping up some more meat and gravy over my potato.

Throughout dinner, I said nothing as I mulled over my name and my parents' names. Luka. Ilona. Stefan.

I kept looking at Markos, memories from Rhosivi coming back to me.

He'd sent me away to protect me. He'd assigned Roman to Predvoi to help me. What else had he done? He had to have sent my trunk of items from Rhosivi. He had to have altered my paperwork to say I was just a Victor.

He knew my parents? He *knew* my parents.

Emberly and Milena sat opposite me, Milena eyeing me curiously and Emberly doing everything possible not to look my way at all. Milena had small eyes and a quick way about her. She talked about her day at school, some of the boys who'd been teasing her, and that she didn't push any of them.

Zuzana said, "That's what I'd expect, Milena."

Personally, I thought she should have pushed them back harder and then beat the slag out of them. Milena was a small girl with small arms and a wide smile even while telling about the bullies at school. If I'd been there and saw a boy push her, well, I'm not sure he'd leave with any of his teeth.

Those thoughts left me wondering if there was a place for me in Khizmit or if I'd interfere with normal events, provided that normal events included 14-year-old boys pushing around girls at school. I wanted to ask if there were guards at school. I imagined guards everywhere, but perhaps kids here were allowed to play and interact without armed supervision. *How did that work out?* Evidenced by the one-sided fight, it didn't seem to be going well. But that's just because Milena wasn't an inmate. Any inmate would have thrown hands if someone touched him. I assumed it was true for female inmates in Vazenia, but maybe they didn't. I wondered if girls were less violent than boys, but then I looked back at Lee.

She looked ready to murder me.

We cleaned up dinner all together. I helped dry dishes and then swept before Markos asked me to follow him down the hallway. There were four doors. He pointed to the one at the far end and told me that room belonged to him and his wife. Emberly's room was beside the bathroom, and Milena's was across from it.

"We'll move her bed over and make one up for you," Markos said, pushing open the door. Milena's room was decorated with teal and yellow. Three books rested on her nightstand beside a little black lamp. A painting of the mountains in springtime with flowers in full bloom was signed by both Milena and Emberly.

"Sir, did they paint this? Your daughters?" I asked, peering closer to see the detail of the mountains.

"Yes, earlier this year. And you don't need to call me 'Sir' while we're here."

Markos grabbed the top of the mattress near the white pillow, and I moved to the foot of the bed.

"We don't need to upheave your family. I can sleep outside," I offered. "Just find an alley and give me a blanket. I'm sure I'll—"

"You'll risk getting swept up by a patrol or getting sick, and I'm not taking you to a clinic. It's too dangerous."

"But if I got sick, couldn't I just heal and—"

"You're not sleeping outside like a stray animal." The finality in his voice was non-negotiable.

We carried the mattress into Emberly's room, which had ornate wood around the doorframe. We set the mattress on the floor between the bed and the window, which looked over many of the rooftops.

Emberly's room had one tall bookshelf in the corner, but the books, as loved as they might have been, were disorganized. Some sat on their sides, others were piled haphazardly, stacked in such a way that they would surely tumble down at any moment. Scraps of paper littered the upper shelves and the floor around her nightstand. A matching black lamp sat on her dresser.

Back in Milena's room a huge pile of blankets lay where the bed used to be. Zuzana was just sweeping up a pile of dirt, dust, and small wrappers when Markos and I walked in.

I figured there were some barracks of sorts that guards could usually use when they came to town. At least, I assumed there were some Charlies and Alphas who'd graduated who didn't have a home yet. There would never be a place for a Victor or an X-ray.

I was both.

I was a dangerous mutt of a lurper, and Markos of all people knew that. He'd known it longer than anyone. It was he who had them brand me with "V-27" when I first arrived at Rhosivi almost ten years ago. *But he was fine letting me sleep unshackled in his home? With his daughters across the hall?* There was no way. He had to be planning to sleep in the hallway, rifle or revolver at the ready, just in case I tried anything.

"You can lock me in, Sir. Just like the good old days." I gestured to the door. "Just take the knob off and turn it around."

"I'm not going to lock it," Markos said, his voice insistent.

"I don't mind. I'm used to it."

"Well, that's part of the problem, isn't it?" His accent always got stronger when he was upset.

"I'm just saying, I know you can't trust me to—"

The indignation in his voice warmed me. "And why can't I trust you? Give me one good reason."

I lowered my voice. "Remember what I said. I killed a man. Back at Predvoi."

Markos moved forward and placed his hand on my shoulder. "I've killed too. But you've never given me a reason not to trust you. And you won't, will you?" He pulled his dark eyebrows low over his eyes.

I shook my head. I wanted to say, "You can trust me." *But was it true?* I scarcely trusted myself. "I'll stay in the room." I'd pretend it was locked. I had no reason to leave. Nowhere to go. No one to go to.

Markos stepped back. "If you want to lock your own door,

go ahead. You'll stay in here until morning unless you need to use the bathroom. You won't leave the house."

"Yes, Sir," I said.

"Tomorrow morning, I have an appointment at the Parliament House. I'll be back by early afternoon. The next day is Koliada Eve, and I have no work. We'll have time to talk then, but Emberly, Milena, and Zuzana will be home too, so we'll have to be discreet. We'll celebrate Koliada here with my family, and then the morning of the thirtieth, we'll ship out to The Outskirts."

Koliada. For the first time, I'd be celebrating the holiday. I'd heard guards discuss their traditions with one another, from gift exchanges to bread pudding and feasts so lavish they left everyone in a lethargic stupor for hours.

From there, Markos and I would go to The Outskirts. The Lurper Legion had been the only future I'd been able to see myself having. *Would I feel safe there? Would it be just another prison?*

But if Lockbox really was here in Khizmit, I couldn't just leave him. I couldn't move on with my plans and my future not knowing where he was being kept. If he was being fed. Was he okay, or was he injured?

I told him I had his back. But in three days, I was supposed to leave Khizmit for The Outskirts. Once I got there, would I be overwhelmed with a sense of belonging? In three days, I'd meet other Victors and X-Rays. Maybe they wouldn't treat me like slag, but like a brother. That's what they called it right, 'brothers-in-arms'? With other Victors there, would they call me Luka? And if they did, would it feel like my name? Without letting hope carry me away too far, I climbed over to the pile of blankets and curled into them. They were comfortable, but I wasn't sure I'd get any sleep at all.

Markos had been working in my best interest for my whole life.

Lockbox was somewhere in Khizmit.

My mother had been enchanted by me.

I had a name.

Luka. My mother had named me Luka.

But why was Markos at my birth? Why did she ask him to keep me safe? I was born six years after the Preemptive Initiative had been passed, so she had to have known what my life was going to look like. *Why did she have any hope for my safety at all?* After all, a Victor alone had no need for a name since we had little to no chance of living past graduation. The world would never get to know us as individuals.

If I remembered correctly, the initial paperwork which Markos had destroyed also proved that my father Stefan Krajnak was an X-ray. That meant whoever else was there at my birth to hear my mother name me Luka was also aware that both of my parents were Test Criminals.

I'm surprised they didn't kill me right then as a baby, aware of what I could do. *Who would care enough to write my name down, those four letters, at all?* Even the wish of a dying woman couldn't have persuaded them to do much since they still killed her.

A curious little question climbed into my head. *Did Markos know my parents before my birth? Was he the only one there?*

I wiggled deeper into the blankets as the house all around me grew quiet. A time would come for me to ask him more about that day, my birthday, and my name. Markos and I would be going to The Outskirts soon, a trip that would afford us plenty of time together, and somehow, I'd work that question in.

But I wouldn't go to The Outskirts without Lockbox. I was left with little choice. I had to find Lockbox tomorrow morning while Commander Markos was at the Parliament House. There was no other time.

Though the name on the gum wrapper hardly constituted

a lead, it was all I had. I decided I'd look for Leticia Varga, and if I didn't find her, I'd ask Markos to help me.

He'd been helping me. He'd help me again.

One way or another, I had to find my friend.

CHAPTER 10

BLATANT FRATERNIZATION

"Stay here," Markos directed me.

Morning light streamed in through the wide windows of the Markos's home. I stood in the living room beside the fireplace, watching Emberly and Milena shrink away in the distance through the window as they walked down the sidewalk. Zuzana had already been gone for over ten minutes. Commander Markos looked more like his imposing self today since he wore his full uniform sporting his ribbons and rank. The wolf on his ushanka matched the one on the Khizmit Flag on display in their living room.

"Where are they going?" I asked.

"Ember is going to work. Milena is going to school. And you're going to stay here until I get back."

"When did she finish school?" I was curious since I knew she was still a minor.

"Some finish school at sixteen. Some start trades earlier. Young men can be drafted as soon as they're seventeen."

"But how...if she's working like an adult, is she considered one?"

"She's not an adult until she's 18. Many start work at fifteen, while still in school."

It wasn't unusual then, for me to be in the coal factory

outside of Khizmit. I was, apparently, exactly the right age to be working or fighting after all.

"But if you're working, you need special paperwork, which you don't have."

I almost asked Markos if he could find some for me. Or forge them for me and thought better of it, asking instead, "Does she go by 'Ember' or 'Lee'?"

Markos finished fastening his top button. "Depends. I've always called her 'Ember.' I think with some friends she goes by 'Lee.' I'd prefer you call her 'Emberly' to avoid any familiarity." He glanced sideways at me.

"Fraternization," I clarified.

"However you want to think about it is fine." He turned around to face the large, gold framed mirror beside the front door. "If anyone knocks, ignore it. They might be dropping off Koliada treats. Don't open the door."

"I won't open the door," I promised, but even as I said it, I felt like a traitor. I had every intention of going outside again, appreciating the beauty of Khizmit, and trying to find someone named Leticia with the hopes of leading me to Lockbox. My official plan consisted of me acting like I was on a mission from Commander Markos and seeing if anyone could direct me to Leticia Varga. Someone was bound to recognize the name "Leticia Varga," and once I put a face to the name, I'd ask her about Lockbox.

It wasn't a great plan. It wasn't even a good plan. But if I told Markos my intention to explore, he'd tell me to stay at his house. If I told him I wanted to find Lockbox, he'd tell me to leave it to him. I knew above all else that if I sat in this house while my friend was still missing, it would make me more of a monster than I already was.

A warning bit at me, telling me that Lockbox wasn't okay. I had low expectations for success, but even if I found no lead to Leticia Varga, looking would assuage my guilt.

Markos turned back to me before opening the door. "Luka."

At first, I didn't turn toward him.

"Luka."

My face grew warm as I stood and moved closer. "Sorry, Sir. It doesn't feel like me yet."

"It will." He smiled. "What are you going to do today?"

"What should I do?"

"Read. You like reading."

He remembered my book collection.

"Did you arrange for my things to be brought to me at Predvoi?" I asked suddenly.

"Yes."

It was humbling, realizing how much he'd done for me without any recognition or gratitude on my part.

"Thanks for letting books circulate at Rhosivi," I said. Books I'd never see again now.

"I didn't *let* them circulate," Markos laughed. "I brought most of them myself. We have to get you boys educated somehow." And with that, he opened the door and left me alone. In his house. With his stuff. Unguarded and unchained.

Freedom really was amazing. So was this oddly unbridled trust in me.

I sat alone, waiting for the right amount of time to pass before going to look for Lockbox. The more I considered leaving this house, the more nervous I became. This wasn't a prison, but leaving would put me at risk again. Maybe I should have feared Markos or worried that he was not going to a meeting at all but instead had gone to Predvoi to hunt Roman down and bring him back for a public execution alongside me.

But I knew Markos wasn't about to do anything like that. I'd always known.

I'd have felt a lot better leaving the house if Markos had returned my dagger, but he hadn't. It was undoubtedly in the house somewhere. I decided I'd rather go outside unarmed than violate Markos's privacy by rooting around his bedroom for the blade, even though it was mine. Gifted in a most unconventional way.

If I stayed here, I'd betray Lockbox; if I left the house, I'd betray Markos. Staying here all day wouldn't be so bad. I would have plenty of time to ruminate on my parents' names and Markos's involvement in my past, my name, but Lockbox's voice echoed in my head over and over again.

"C'mon roomie, you've got my back, don't you?"

"I've got your back," I'd said.

That sounded like a promise to me.

My attention suddenly jarred, the front door creaking as Emberly stepped in, a flurry of snow blowing in around her long dark hair.

She shut the door and pulled off her gloves. Her hair hung around her face and shoulders speckled with snow. I stood and walked over to the few stairs leading down to the entryway.

"Forget something?" I asked, watching to see if she'd grab a hat or scarf from the entryway closet where Markos had stored his.

"Yes, I forgot to tell you that I'm positively livid! You tricked me. You refused to tell me your name. You made me feel like—ugh—like an idiot!" She marched up the stairs toward me. Why was her anger endearing? She wouldn't have appreciated knowing that was my reaction.

"You're mad at me."

"Hell yes, I'm mad at you! You tricked me! Deceiving me! You toyed with me and made me look like an idiot in front of my father. You could have just told me you were Luka. *THE* Luka. My father has talked about you enough that I'd have known who you were. I'd have helped you."

She hurried up the stairs toward me. No one rushed toward me like that without a weapon in their hands. I backed up quickly to avoid reacting to her approach, not because I was threatened, but she would be much more than angry with me if she knew I was a lurper. I had to keep my distance.

My retreat didn't slow her. It absolutely took my breath away that she dared to approach me upset rather than running for her life.

I couldn't tell her that I didn't even know I was Luka when I met her. "I didn't dare to disobey your father. He's intimidating," I said.

"Well, I didn't think someone like you would find him intimidating. You work with him. You shouldn't need to find him intimidating."

"Have you seen him in his element? In his role as a warden?" I raised an eyebrow.

"He's only like that with lurpers, young boys who need discipline. And men who step out of line."

I was all of those, wasn't I?

I couldn't admit to her that when he wanted to be, Pedrick Markos was the most terrifying man I'd ever seen. Not as big of a risk to me as Warden Velky but considerably more powerful.

"Well, I didn't lie about my age. I am seventeen," I said. "I'm sorry for the deception. I didn't intend to upset or embarrass you."

"Then set the record straight," she said, dropping into the couch beside me. "Because I don't like looking like a fool."

"I don't think you look like a fool."

She brushed some snow off her shoulders and scowled at me. Not knowing exactly what she wanted me to do, I just stared at her.

"You look great," I said. *Why did I say that?*

She tucked some of her hair behind her ear, and again, the jewelry going up the edge of her ear caught my attention. Three gold bands went around the upper shell of her ear, two studs—one turquoise and one with a diamond—were below that. Then, dangling from the bottom hung a small feather earring with a black bead.

"Well," she said expectantly, having not heard me or choosing to ignore me completely.

"Well, what?" I asked, looking back into her face. Her cheeks were red.

"Tell me the truth. From the beginning."

Initially, a story began to weave itself in my mind. Lying after all came easily. *But did I want to risk her wrath?* Even though the story was partly mine, it wasn't one I could tell. Wouldn't tell. And I'm quite certain Markos wouldn't be pleased at all if I did tell her, especially the bit about his involvement in helping me.

"I can't tell you the whole truth. But I'll tell you part."

She sighed. "Fine, tell me part."

"Why do you care about the truth, anyway?"

She looked away from me, her mouth set. "Like I said, I don't like feeling like a fool."

Her father told me not to become familiar with her. He probably preferred I said nothing and grabbed a book to read instead of talking to her. But talking to her was worth the risk. Talking to her had brought me more joy than just about anything else had in my entire life.

"Do you want to ask me something specific?" I finally offered. *Would it ever be like it was those first few hours alone together?*

"Yes, but I have no reason to believe you'd tell me the truth anyway."

I shifted on the couch and turned to her. "Just because I'm an incredible liar doesn't mean I'm incapable of telling the truth."

"Prove it."

"Sure," I said. *Why was I so desperate to feel that connection with her again?* Was I destined to break every promise I made to Markos? When he asked me to stay away from his daughter, was it asking too much?

I hadn't asked her to come here. I hadn't sought her out. She'd come back here. She's the one who hadn't stayed away from me. Was I really violating Markos's trust by sitting alone with her in the house within an arm's reach?

"What are you?" she asked. "Who are you?"

"Who am I? Or what am I? I suppose it's all the same to you." I stopped short, not meaning for my words to come out as sharp as they had.

Lee moved to stand up. To leave.

"I'm a lurper from Rhosivi," I blurted out the truth, monitoring her expression for fear or disgust. She gasped and said nothing for a moment. Her eyes didn't move from my face. I'd expected to see malice enter her expression. I watched for fear to compel her to scoot away from me. Instead, she stared. *Did she think I was still lying?*

"That's how I met your dad. He was my High Warden. But I'm not an inmate anymore," I added, hoping she wouldn't ask for clarification as to why I wasn't an inmate anymore. For all I knew, she'd assume I'd graduated early.

"I understand now," she finally said.

"Understand what?"

"When I approached you in the square, you gave me a look."

I remembered seeing her for the first time. I hadn't considered what my face had done. "What sort of look?"

She shifted her eyes to the side and pursed her lips. "You looked at me like I was the first girl you'd ever seen." She sounded breathless. "And now I know, it's because I was."

"You weren't the first girl I'd seen. I've seen girls." I thought of the drawings in books and the women in the cemetery.

"Up close? Like this?" She scooted closer, and my heartrate rose.

"No," I confessed, looking down at my hands. My gaze lingered on the burn. "You were the first."

"That's why you said you stayed away from girls where you're from. Why you said you worship coal and rye. That's why you reacted the way you did when I leaned in to greet you."

She leaned in again, as if to kiss my cheeks once more.

I scooted away. Kissing Emberly was absolutely a violation of my promise to Markos, cultural or not.

She paused, scanning my face for any indication that I was lying. "Can I see your wrist?" She reached for my hand. My burned deformed hand. She must not have known she was supposed to be terrified of me as she moved closer.

"I have a burn. You can't see the tattoo under the burn." I gave her my hand. Her touch, gentle and concerned, didn't cause any pain.

"Can you even feel this?" she asked, dragging her fingertips along my palm.

"No," I said flatly. "But I feel you there." I pointed to where her left hand rested higher up on my arm. She blushed and leaned in closer to my wrist. After examining it for a few seconds, she moved away. The worst part of the burn was black and numb to her touch, but further up my arm where some of the blisters still oozed, the pain thrummed like each one had its own heartbeat.

"You can't see it, can you?" I verified.

Lee sighed and relaxed on the couch. She knew I had been an inmate, and yet, she continued to sit with me, alone in the house, completely unarmed. "What happened there?" she asked.

"I got burned…"

"I know you got burned; I mean, how did you get burned? It looks recent."

I flipped my hand around, palm down. Even though she knew I'd been at Rhosivi, the idea of her seeing the mark on my wrist brought shame into my throat. She knew the burn on my hand covered a tattoo designating me as dangerous in some form or another, and even though she didn't know if I had a V or an X or an H, she shouldn't have been so calm alone with me.

"In a furnace. In a coal factory."

"Did you do it on purpose?" She met my gaze.

I stammered. "W-why would I do it on purpose?"

"Because if you worked at Rhosivi for the last decade, you know how to behave in a coal factory. You know the risks. And that burn is severe. Why didn't you pull your hand away sooner? These marks, they go pretty high." She walked her fingers up my wrist to my arm a little way, to where the burn ended.

"I..." *What should I confess to her?*

"You wanted to hide your mark, didn't you? You burned your whole arm to conceal a few little symbols."

I gritted my teeth and said nothing. I couldn't tell from her tone if she was impressed with my actions or amused by the desperation that led to the horrible scarring. She took her hands back into her own lap, and I found myself trying to hide mine beneath the brown pillow at my side.

I thought Lee might ask me a few questions about the prison since she'd been so interested in me when we first met, and she thought I was from Latvani.

"What did the tattoo say?" she asked.

I shook my head. I couldn't. Not only because it posed too big of a risk for her to know, but because if she knew that my wrist said V, she'd know I was dangerous. Her father had to have warned her about lurpers like me. He had to have given her rules from a young age of how to avoid inmates of all sorts, especially the more dangerous ones.

"Sorry." I offered an apologetic expression. "I don't..."

She grinned and placed her hand on my shoulder. "It doesn't matter anyway. I was just curious."

Doesn't matter? I mused. *How could it not matter?* It had been the only thing that had ever mattered about me. The ink on my wrist had been, up until then, my most interesting and defining feature.

"Why are you still looking at me like that?" she asked, and I wished she would touch my other hand. The one with feeling. She didn't reach out. *What if I did? Would she run away? Would she tell her father?*

"Like what?" I asked.

"Like, with your eyes like that. With your face all...you know!"

What would I say? I'd read a lot of books, but none of them gave guidance on how to talk to a girl. I'd daydreamed about leaving Rhosivi and Predvoi, but I'd never imagined, even in my wildest daydreams, that being around a beautiful girl would make me feel like this.

I looked down at her lips for far too long.

"Oh, I get it." She laughed softly. "You've never been around a girl before at all, have you?"

"No, I—"

"And you want to kiss a girl?" She didn't move away when she said it.

"No—"

"You don't want to kiss me?" She reached up and touched her own lips.

My hand shot out on its own and grabbed hers in an act of blatant fraternization. "No, Emberly, I don't want to kiss a girl. Not to kiss a girl, just to kiss a girl. Yes, I suppose I do want to kiss you. But I have no idea what I'm doing. I don't know how to talk to you or look at you. And yes, you're the first girl I met, but I saw lots of girls yesterday in Khizmit, and none of them make me feel so..." I trailed off, dropping her hand.

She reached across and took it back, resting her soft

fingers across mine. "I imagine it's a bit of a shock, all of this. Being here. Adjusting to a lot of things."

I nodded.

"Is your name really Luka?" she asked, graciously changing the subject.

"According to your dad, yes."

She studied me for a moment, as if she hadn't already studied me enough. I had to wonder if she'd spend so much time looking at my face if it was still marred by the scar from Romeo-22.

"You don't seem like a dangerous criminal. But Luka is a name for a nice, sweet boy. I'm not sure it fits you either."

She wasn't wrong. I wasn't a dangerous criminal or a nice, sweet boy. "What do you think I am?" I asked.

"I think you're a boy who hasn't taken his pills," she said. I must not have been able to hide my surprise that she knew about the nummers. *Did all boys take them, even those who weren't incarcerated?* "I'm not trying to tease you. I'm sure you have to adjust to a lot of things now that you're out."

My face grew warm. I'd hoped she didn't know that much about inmates.

She scooted away. "I'll try to do better at keeping my hands to myself."

Not even a cup full of pills would be strong enough to dull what I'm feeling, I thought. But I stood up to leave the room instead.

I turned around as I reached the hallway. Emberly still sat on the couch, looking at me, no doubt keying into my frustration. "You said before that I was hotter than embers."

"I did," she said slowly.

"Did you mean it?"

She hesitated. "Yes. I can appreciate a good-looking boy when I see one."

"It wasn't true," I said, not having thought through my next words. "I'm not hotter than you. Cause, you know, you're Ember. And you're more…attractive…"

She laughed. "You're terrible at this." She finally met my gaze. "I'll help you find your friend. The Leticia you were looking for. Assuming that wasn't a lie."

She remembered? And she knew I was going to keep looking? "I wasn't—I didn't say that so you'd help—I just—" I tripped over my words so clumsily, I think I would have rather fallen down the stairs.

"You don't need to manipulate me to get my help. Just be a little more transparent."

"I'll try," was all I could offer.

"I'm an intern at City Hall. I have access to the census. If we go to my office, we can find the paperwork and get the address for the friend you're looking for."

The offer left me confused. If she wasn't Markos's daughter, I'd have thought she was setting me up.

"Why are you helping me?"

"Because I think you need it. I'd hate for you to stick your other hand into a furnace." Emberly walked down to the entryway and turned the knob. "Come on. You need to be back before my dad is. And I'm already late for work." She grinned and pulled the door open. I was glad she did, because this way, I could keep my promise to Markos.

I didn't open the door.

Emberly did.

CHAPTER 11
LETICIA VARGA

In a few moments, Emberly and I were walking along the slick cobblestone path, side by side but not hand in hand. She must not have touched me this time out of respect.

Respect for me, a lurper.

She walked purposefully with wide steps, and I kept up, trying not to let too much space come between us. These roads, much like the ones I'd first seen, were elaborately decorated for Koliada. Candles burned in the windows, some of which bore paintings of bears and goats with tall, twisty horns. The decor distracted me from making a mental map of the city.

The streets bustled with people, most of whom carried steaming cups as they hurried their way through the crowd. *Was it sveetin? Rakia? Tea?* The faint smell of cinnamon and licorice wafted toward me. I found myself wishing that Emberly would take my hand again. Though I didn't dare take hers.

We passed another colossal spruce lit up and decorated with painted pinecones and golden, glass ornaments.

Then we passed a group of kids that had to be around our age. Some were dressed in all black, others in all white. A few people wore masks made from animal skin, and others sported tall horns.

"What are they doing?" I asked as soon as they were far enough behind us.

"Getting ready for the celebration." She must have known that her answer didn't actually tell me anything helpful. She turned back to me, slowing just for a moment. "I hope you'll be here in Khizmit long enough to make some good memories."

"I have some good memories already." She'd come close to me, very close, and hadn't shied away even after learning I was a lurper. And she continued to offer me help without a trace of fear.

As if she knew what I was thinking, she grinned and then faced forward once more. We passed only a handful of guards on our way, two of whom recognized Emberly with a wave and a short nod of their heads. I wasn't sure if this was because of her astonishing personality and beauty, or because they knew her father's high-ranking status.

Emberly slowed to talk to me as we continued walking. "We have some rituals as we celebrate Koliada. All the youth ages ten to eighteen participate in the Koliada Bonfire. Everyone brings a log to add to the fire, and then around that great fire, we drink wine and rakia and chase away the bad spirits in preparation for the new year."

I'd heard of hot rakia. The guards seemed to prefer that tradition to the bonfire or the ceremonial dance.

"There is a pretend battle where half the people wear white, and the other half wear black. Those dressed like the spirits of the gods don masks and dance in the outer circle while good battles evil."

In prison, fighting didn't happen as an approved ritual. It was an eventuality, but not a custom. The fact that they fought here as a way to celebrate made no sense at all.

We passed a group of three soldiers—two privates and one sergeant. They didn't look at me. Didn't notice me at all.

"It's not a real fight," Emberly said as we passed another group of teenagers dressed in black.

"Okay."

"Just staged. And white always wins. Symbolic of good prevailing over evil. I'll be there, all in white, participating in the fight against evil."

"That suits you," I said, grinning. "Will I be attending this ceremony?" I suppose part of me was curious what a staged fight would consist of, and the other part of me was interested in connecting with my heritage, despite having been ostracized and sequestered.

"I'm sure my dad will bring you. Our whole family always goes together. Besides, I imagine he'll want to keep a close eye on you once he finds out that you've left today."

My stomach dropped. "Why will he find out?"

"Oh," she said casually, "he always finds out. He'll know what we've both done today, and there will be consequences, but it'll be worth it. Right?"

I nodded. I'd rather hoped he wouldn't find out about today. It wasn't necessarily a guarantee. If we found the information about Leticia Varga quickly and I hurried back home before he got there, I doubted he'd know I'd left. And he wouldn't know Emberly had come home. "I'll bet we can keep a secret from him," I said. I'd prefer Markos learned that I'd left the house before he'd learned that I'd let his daughter run her fingers all along my hands and arm.

"We can try," she said. She stopped in front of a tall, yellow building and winked at me. "This is it. City Hall."

City Hall stood four stories tall with a peaked roof that jutted out from the rest of the building. The front had been decorated for the upcoming holiday with a few garnished trees and some garland wrapped around the two columns out front.

"Am I allowed in?" I asked.

"Only vaznov officers check wrists within the city, and only on those vaznov they're assigned to monitor." She paused, and my entire body froze at the word. "I can call them graduates if that's better."

Vaznov. In the prisons we didn't say the word. Didn't think the word. While I'd dreamed of becoming a vaznov my whole life, I'd avoided the word as if it would condemn me.

Vaznov. They were the ones who'd made it out. Who'd won. For us, it was a word reserved only for those who actually graduated. It was only after you got your mark of freedom that you could even think the nearly-sacred title.

Their wrists were marked with the date of their graduation and a random symbol selected by the Judgement Board. That way, no one would be able to tattoo a date and the correct symbol since it was assigned randomly at graduation and kept on record. Lockbox said he knew a Charlie who'd graduated and come back to Predvoi as a vaznov guard. His mark of graduation was a single dot.

"I'm just saying, you don't need to be worried about him checking for your designation or whatever," Emberly said, jerking her head toward the soldier standing outside the double doors. He was only one of a few soldiers I'd seen on our entire walk. We had to climb long white steps to get up to the doors, but I recognized the man with pale skin and short hair from the square awaiting us at the entrance.

"Hello, Erik." Emberly waved as we approached him.

He glared at me and stepped forward to open the door for her. But then he moved in front of it, blocking our entry. I felt my shoulders go taut.

"I thought you said he lived near you, not *with* you," Erik said, his voice low and annoyed. "After what happened with the captain—"

"Who said he lived with me?"

"Aneta said she saw you with him yesterday. She said she followed you and that you took him home."

"And?" Emberly stuck her hand on her hip.

"And that he didn't leave." Erik threw another glance my way.

Emberly sighed. "Lieutenant, aren't you a little old to be involving yourself in drama and gossip?"

"It's not about me," Erik said coolly. "But there's someone who wasn't too pleased to hear about the sleeping arrangements."

"People should mind their own business."

Erik reached out and placed his hand on Emberly's arm. The tension in my shoulders spread down to my fingers which curled into fists. *Erik's voice was gentle—not threatening*, I thought, willing myself to calm down.

"He's upset, Lee," Erik said. "You need to be careful."

"He needs to be careful," I growled a low warning from behind my clenched teeth. Whoever 'he' was.

"He's always upset," Emberly said as she turned to me. "I'm not sure you two were ever properly introduced. Erik, this is Luka. Luka, this is Erik."

Erik extended a hand to me, and I shook it, gripping it tightly even under Emberly's gaze. Erik had at least managed to shave without cutting himself today. His clean-shaven face made me more aware of the beard growing on mine.

"Luka is working with my father. You can pass that along if you'd like. You know how my father likes his privacy. Anyone who puts their nose into my business, or Luka's business, is putting their nose in my father's business."

"I don't need veiled threats," Erik said. "I'm just passing along what I heard. Alex is the one you should watch out for."

Emberly leaned in close to Erik, though she had to push up on her tip toes to get close to his face. "I'm not afraid of anyone, and if Alex is mad, that's his problem."

Erik sighed, as if accepting that his warning fell on deaf ears. He opened the door and gave me a look as I passed, albeit not an angry one. "Luka," he said quietly as Emberly continued ahead. He grabbed my arm, and I had to subdue the images that came into my mind of how I could throw him down the steps. I turned to face the Lieutenant, ever aware of his weapons. "If you're going to get her into trouble, you better stay close to make sure you can get her out of it."

Not sure what to say, I just nodded.

Erik continued, "If you're really working with Commander Markos, you should know he's very protective of his daughters."

I drew a breath. "Well, that makes two of us."

Aneta had, no doubt, passed along the little rumor Emberly had begun about us. My throat grew tight in embarrassment.

Erik let go of my arm, and I hurried after Emberly. The entry area of City Hall had a tall ceiling. The tallest I'd ever seen. The peach and beige floor sparkled from the light coming in the dozens of windows in the front of the building. A wide, wooden desk sat before us, and a woman with dark curls sat behind it.

She looked at Emberly and then to the large clock on the far wall. "You're late, Ember," the woman chided in a friendly voice.

"Sorry," Emberly said. "And he's with me."

"Fine," the woman said lazily. She looked at me briefly, evidently not trying to conceal the fact that she found me attractive. I felt out of place in this outfit. I didn't miss my prison garb, but these clothes were tight on my arms and chest. They drew unwanted attention.

Or else I drew the attention.

Emberly and I walked through two more doors and into a back room which had square drawers from floor to ceiling.

Khizmit had a filing system that couldn't have been that different from the ones in Markos's office at Rhosivi.

"Do they keep records on everyone here?" I asked as Emberly went to work unlocking one of the bottom right drawers.

"More or less. Some have just their name and address."

"What do you do here?"

"I approve business licenses, and I'm supposed to report expired ones to the right authorities," she said.

"What do you mean, 'supposed to'?"

She flipped through papers so fast I wondered how she didn't get a paper cut. Lockbox had a few from his more intense workdays at Predvoi.

"I mean I usually go to their physical address and remind them to renew their licenses. They usually pay for them there, I sign the paperwork, bring back the copies here, and update their files. That's what I was doing when I met you the first time, so you might as well be grateful that I didn't follow the instructions to the letter."

I grinned. Apparently, Khizmit didn't mind if their youth were non-compliant. Just their lurpers. "Is this where they keep business license files?"

"No. This isn't the room I work in." She worked hurriedly, flipping through yellowed tabs before she pulled out a sheet of paper. "Leticia Varga lives in Block 13. House 3F. That's close by."

She put the paper back carefully, shut the drawer, and hurried out of the room to the next one. Inside were more metal filing cabinets and a single desk completely littered with papers. She leaned over the desk, shuffling a few sheets around before snatching up a small blue one and a thick-lined pad. She grabbed a pen and stabbed it through the back end of her ponytail.

Her speed impressed me.

"Are you taking me to Leticia Varga's house?" I asked.

"Do you know where Block 13 House 3F is?"

"Of course not," I stated.

"Then, of course, I'm taking you."

We hurried out of the room, back through the entry, past the woman who looked nearly asleep, and out through the front doors.

Erik seemed as surprised to see us as I was that we'd found Leticia's address so easily. But I suppose if you knew where to look, it didn't have to be complicated.

"See you soon," Emberly called to Erik as she dashed down the stairs. I don't know how she managed not to slip on the ice.

Erik gave me another look, and I followed Emberly as she veered left at the base of the stairs, taking an uphill road. We passed a shop selling embroidered bags and another one with earrings and bracelets on display. Many of the shops showed wrapped packages with deals for the upcoming holiday, but Emberly didn't even stop to glance in the windows. I don't know who was more concerned about her dad catching us—me or her. Then it occurred to me that perhaps she wasn't scared of her dad finding out, but she knew I was.

We turned another corner, and she pointed to a small white sign on the corner of a large red, brick building. "This is Block 13." She smiled at me. "Meaning, we're close."

Erik's warning to be careful sounded in my head, though Emberly seemed to have completely forgotten it.

"I'm going to the house alone," I said, trying to keep my voice kind but immovable.

"Fine," Emberly shrugged. I'd expected more of a fight. "It's just over there."

She pointed to a row of houses tucked in the far corner, side by side. Most of the doors boasted festive wreaths or golden bells. "The third cluster of houses is 3, and you should see a small 'F' on the front door of Leticia Varga's house."

Though I couldn't see it from where I stood, I now knew where to go.

"I'm going to let Mr. Topanky know that his business license will expire in three days. I'll meet you over by the small fountain." Emberly pointed to a small fountain nearly hidden behind a huge tree.

"Okay," I agreed. Even though she wouldn't be near me as I approached the house, I worried that I could still get her into trouble. *What if it went badly? What if I got caught and she got caught helping me?*

I was dangerous. I'd never hurt Emberly, but association with me had led to Lockbox's disappearance. What if I was scouring the streets of Khizmit, looking for Emberly next?

Emberly disappeared around a corner, and I took a deep breath. I hated that I'd left Markos's house. I hated that I'd allowed Emberly to help me. But Lockbox was my only friend, and I owed it to him to follow this lead, even if it took me to a small house in Khizmit when I'd have preferred to stay at the Markos's reading a new book.

As I approached the houses, I found that they turned with the street, each door identical except for the decorations and small painted numbers and letters.

The door labeled with 'F' had drawings all over it, taped haphazardly at various angles. The drawings, though difficult to decipher, had trees, bells, and a scribble of black overlapping with a scribble of silver.

I stood there frozen, my body suddenly made of lead. I'd done much more nerve-racking things than knock on a door. I'd run forty kilometers at once. I'd spent hours from dawn to dusk dismembering furry rabbits. I'd killed a wolf with my bare hands. *Why was this so hard to do?*

Grow a pair, I thought as I steadied myself and prepared to talk to a stranger.

My knuckles hit the door hard, and I swear the sound echoed down the street despite the chiming of bells and the muffled talk of a few women sitting outside a shop, haggling over prices.

Through the door I heard someone approach, unlock a bolt, and open the door just a few fingers wide.

"Leticia Varga?" I spoke to the slit between the door and the frame.

Sunlight only showed a sliver of her face, narrowed eyes, and set lips. In the dim light, she appeared grey. Her watery eyes searched my face and the top of my head, no doubt looking for an ushanka and rank patch. She glanced up and down at my clothes. I know she would have responded differently if I'd been a soldier.

"What do you want?" Her voice was about as friendly as a wolf's growl.

"I'm trying to find someone. Some information about someone."

"I don't know anything," she said coarsely and began to shut the door.

I stepped forward, and the door hit my boot with a thud. My voice grew a little softer. I attempted a nicer approach to try and undo the fear I'd planted in her eyes by blocking the door. "I'm sorry, but I've come a long way, and I haven't even told you who I'm looking for yet."

She stared at my boot which held the door fast and then looked up at me again. "Are you a worker or a soldier?"

"Neither."

She looked me over once more, as if this third time she'd see something different than she had the first couple times.

"Show me your wrist," she finally stated, her gaze lingering at my left hand.

"Excuse me?" I asked.

"If you aren't a guard and you aren't a worker, I have to assume you're a vaznov."

Was that my best play here? Without wanting to delay, I

slowly removed my gloves and showed her the burn on my wrist.

"How am I supposed to tell by that whether you're a vazzie or not? Where's your officer? Graduating doesn't mean you're allowed to wander the streets at will, knocking on doors," she growled.

"Please, just hear me out," I said, trying to look as nonthreatening as possible. "I'm here concerning Lockbox. I don't have any intention of causing trouble."

"Lockbox?" she asked with absolutely no familiarity at all.

"Oscar-17," I whispered, though the nearest passersby couldn't have been listening anyway.

She stepped away from the door, and for a second, I thought she'd slam it in my face, but instead, she unlocked the chain and opened the door a little wider. She wore a yellowed apron with embroidery that seemed to be coming undone at the edges. When she poked her head out the door, she looked left, then right, then left again. "Are you with Commander Markos?"

I nodded since it seemed to ensure the highest chance of success. She looked to the right again. "Come in. Just for a moment," she said quickly.

I stepped over the threshold and into the house. Wiping my boots on the grey rug, I looked around.

Her home opened to a small front room with a fireplace, three chairs, a padded bench, and a table upon which sat a vase with mostly dead trimmings. The house smelled of dirt and coal. The basket beside the door held more shoes, some too large for me and some that were too small for her.

She didn't ask me to take a seat, so I remained standing on the rug. Emberly had made a good point—I knew nothing of the culture here.

Leticia began pacing, smoothing her loose blonde hairs over her sweaty forehead as she sighed. My eyes adjusted to the light. A single long braid came down her back. Wrinkles decorated the edges of her eyes and the center of her forehead. Her stockings slid silently across the floor as she paced in the front room.

"Do you know him?" I asked impatiently.

"Yes, I know him," she whispered.

"Do you know where he is?"

"They took him away as soon as I found out who the father was. I did my part. They said he'd take care of the problem and that I wouldn't hear from them again. But then Commander Markos sent a letter informing me that Oscar-17 was on track for graduation from Predvoi, and he asked if I was interested in reunification services. I said no." She stopped pacing. "Did he get the letter or not?" Her raw voice came out in a sharp whisper.

"You're his mother?" I searched her face for any familiar features.

"People don't know that," she snapped. "I like to keep it that way. I don't like it to be common knowledge that I birthed one of those lurpers. I'm not a skrag! Now give me whatever forms I need to sign, and be off."

On the table was a small drawing of a stick figure family done in crayon. "Do you have other children?" I asked. "Did you have more after Lockbox?"

"Lockbox is what they're calling it now? Instead of Oscar-17. I swear I can't keep track of these things."

"Yes, some people call him Lockbox, and others call him Oscar-17. I'm just asking if you've seen him."

She began pacing again. "I haven't seen him, and I wouldn't like to. When I found out what its father was, I reported it right away. I can't be convicted of anything. I'm innocent. I can't and won't be involved. Just leave me out of this." She wagged a finger at me, then tucked it back into her shaking hands.

"I'm not here to accuse or convict or anything like that," I assured her. *She'd sent her baby boy to Predvoi.* It made my stomach churn.

"What are you here to do?"

A lie formed quickly based on what she'd said. "I'm here at Commander Markos's request to make sure you're still not interested in reunification services. The note you sent was difficult to read."

"Ah, yes, well, I'd written it in haste. My husband, he doesn't know, Veles bless him. And my other kids need to be protected. Oscar-17, did you set it free?"

It. I bit back the words I wanted to say and consciously released the tension in my shoulders. "You're safe," I reassured her. "Oscar-17 is not a threat to anyone. But if you're not interested in seeing him again, I'll make sure that he is not able to contact you or anyone in your family."

Leticia's gaze went back to my burn. "Did you know him?"

"Yes," I stated.

"How?"

"I worked with Commander Markos at Rhosivi."

She bit her lip and picked at the loose strings on her apron. "But I was told that Oscar-17 was kept at Predvoi."

A spark of panic started inside my chest, but I kept it off my face. "I was later transferred to work with Warden Dulka at Predvoi, where I met him." I turned for the door.

"Wait," she said, growing frantic. "I might—" She hurried to the window and moved aside some of the dark curtains. "Wait here." She pointed to the chair nearest me. "Take a seat." Her voice still wavered.

I stepped into the room, finally leaving the rug, and sat in the hard chair.

"I'll be right back." She opened the door and rushed outside, leaving it open a crack. I sat for a moment, unsure if I should get up and shut the door or wait for her. *Was she getting some information that would lead me to Lockbox? Or did she have something for me to give him when I finally met up with him again?*

With coal in the fireplace, it didn't seem like she'd want her house to get cold, so I got up and walked over to the rug again. But as I placed my hand on the door to shut it, I looked down and saw her shoes. She hadn't bothered to put them on. When I looked up, I saw that her bare feet had melted footprints on the path outside.

I gripped the door and opened it wide just in time to see Leticia running back toward her house, apron strings flying behind her, and she wasn't alone.

Four soldiers sprinted toward me, their boots hammering along the path.

Stay calm, I told myself. But the other voice in my head told me I was skudged.

CHAPTER 12
CREASES AND GARLIC

ONE PRIVATE, two junior sergeants, and a captain stopped in front of me. The women down the street who had previously ignored my presence, now turned to stare at the scene. Leticia hunched behind the captain, but I gave her an incredulous look before walking calmly toward the captain.

"Who are you?" the captain asked me.

"I'm Luka," I stated.

"What are you doing inside a private residence?"

"I knocked on the door. I asked if I could come inside and ask some questions. She opened the door and let me in."

The captain turned to Leticia.

"Check his wrist," she said, her voice trembling. She pointed a shaky finger at my left wrist, as if they wouldn't know which one to check without her direction.

Since I didn't want to find myself on the wrong end of a knife or gun, I held out my hands, wrists up.

He moved the sleeve up, only becoming slightly gentler once he saw the burn.

"That's convenient," the captain said, surveying my injury. His eyes were small and shiny, like little glistening beetles. Three deep creases spread across his forehead. Captain Crease it would have to be.

"I got burned," I explained, pulling up my sleeve further for him to see.

"Did you come to this residence asking her about an Oscar?" Captain Crease turned up his authority. There's a voice that men use when they want to intimidate, and it always pissed me off.

I tried not to glare at Leticia. "Yes, Mr. Chief —" His expression shifted. I'd skudged up. "Sir," I finished.

Captain Crease's eyes narrowed. He knew. He knew I was about to say, 'Mr. Chief Preemptive Officer.' "Grab him," the captain commanded.

The two junior sergeants grabbed my arms. I could have fought them all. In seconds, I could have killed the lot of them and then faced a terrified Leticia who'd probably die of fright having witnessed what I was capable of. She deserved to die of fear for everything I now knew. She'd turned in her own son, abandoning him for the rest of his life.

But fighting these soldiers off wouldn't result in my freedom, or Lockbox's, for that matter. I had to be compliant.

"I'm happy to come in for questioning," I said, successfully keeping my voice pleasant. One of the guards pulled out handcuffs, and memories from Rhosivi surfaced. "Those aren't necessary." My tone grew angry now. "I'll come, but I'm not letting you put those on me."

Captain Crease's hand went to his pistol. No way his aim was as good as Roman's, but I wasn't willing to risk another life-threatening injury. "Who gave you the information that you should go to the Varga's home to ask about an Oscar?"

"What?" I asked, moving my arms enough that the guards hadn't been able to grab hold of them yet to strap on the handcuffs.

"Hold still. What did you say your name is?" Captain Crease asked.

"Luka," I said again. "And I'm here under Commander

Markos. If you have questions about my actions, you should ask him."

The guard who'd been chasing my arms with the hand-cuffs stopped moving. "Commander Markos?"

"Yes," I said, turning to him, glaring. "I'm here under his orders. If you have an issue with what happened here with Ms. Varga, take it up with him."

Their hesitation only lasted a moment. "The problem is this—I don't believe you." Captain Crease waved his hand. The junior lieutenant pulled out his knife and pointed it directly at my ribs. Though I'd healed, the pain of having been run through with one was fresh in my mind. "Your wrist is burned, so we can't confirm whether or not you're a lurper or a vaznov."

"Are there any missing?" I asked.

Captain Crease replied through clenched teeth, "If there were any vaznov acting out of order, we'd have heard about it. However, there are several lurpers from The Outskirts that haven't been accounted for. Though they're assumed dead, I could see one making their way back here."

"That wouldn't be very clever of them," I said.

I didn't fight out of fear that if I did, they'd suspect I was a Victor or a Juliet or something. I had every intention of dragging out this back-and-forth and maybe eventually slipping away from them, but a crowd had begun to gather behind the soldiers. In a single glance, I saw a face that made me comply immediately, my arms going slack.

Emberly stared at us from the group of women who covered their mouths, as if it would do anything to keep me from hearing their whispers. Fear that Emberly would approach and try to talk us out of this had me reaching for the handcuffs.

I strapped one of them on myself. Her gaze met mine for a brief moment, and I shook my head, praying that she'd keep herself safe. "This scene is unnecessary, and it puts a real damper on the festive mood, so let's move it along," I said, stepping toward Captain Crease.

The click of the second half of the handcuffs reached my ears even over the conspiratorial whispers. Hands cuffed in front of my body, I marched in the middle of the four soldiers. Captain Crease led the way, one soldier stood on each side of me, and the last one trailed behind as I followed Captain Crease.

Though I strained my ears, I didn't hear Emberly say anything. She didn't protest like she had with Erik. *Where would she go now? Back to work at City Hall? Would Erik be pleased to see that she was alone?*

I shouldn't have been worrying about Emberly as I marched in cuffs through the back streets of Khizmit. *At least, I mused, I broke my record for time out of custody.* But my mood grew more somber with each passing moment.

I'd failed Lockbox.

I'd betrayed Markos.

Captain Crease would eventually discover that I was a lurper. He'd ask around. They'd eventually bring in Warden Dulka and Warden Velky to see if either of them recognized me. Both of them would, and either would kill me on sight. Or they'd wait, and they'd bring Roman into it. They'd bring Lockbox into it. They might even bring Emberly to the execution.

My stomach threatened to empty itself.

Captain Crease took us to a small, non-descript building made of grey stone. Inside, a soldier with an impressive number of chins sat at a desk. The air in here was warmer, and since I didn't see a stove, I had to assume it was because this large man had successfully heated this entire space with his body. It smelled strongly of garlic and foul body odor.

I made the decision to be friendly to him anyway.

"Hello," I said, waving a cuffed hand.

The man offered me a bemused smile before directing his

attention to Captain Crease. "Who's this?" His voice was higher than I'd expected.

"Don't know. He said his name's Luka, but check out his hand."

Captain Crease and the garlic-smelling human heater looked at me expectantly.

"It wouldn't kill you to just ask me about my arm," I said. "But I confess, I'm a bit embarrassed by what happened." I lifted my hands up and set them on the desk. The two men stared at my burn.

Captain Crease wiggled the metal on my wrist around, looking for a tattoo. The motion caused a large piece of my dead skin to flake off, and I started bleeding onto the wood.

"That hurt," I said.

Garlic Man grimaced. "What did you bring him in for?"

"He entered a private residence and was asking questions about a specific inmate. As if he was looking for someone. Then he told me he was working for Commander Markos."

Garlic Man raised an eyebrow at this. "If he is, and you detained him, you'll be skudged."

"And if he's lying, which he has to be, then I'll be rewarded. We have no idea who this man is."

"I'm not a man," I said, scooting back to sit on the wooden bench. "I'm a minor, so don't expect to find any identification on me."

It was a gamble, but I hadn't seen Emberly with any identification. Markos had said she worked as a minor. When Erik had first seen me in the square, he'd asked for identification, but no one had asked her. Granted, most people seemed to know who she was.

"Tell us who you are, and you can get on your way," Garlic Man said.

"I told you, my name is Luka, and I work with Commander Markos."

My response didn't alter their expressions. If anything, it increased their suspicions.

Captain Crease leaned over the narrow desk. "I'm not crazy, right? This guy says he's a minor, but look at how he's built. Working for Captain Markos. And that burn, it can't be coincidental."

Garlic Man leaned around Captain Crease to get a better view of me. I tried my best to appear innocent, widening my eyes and keeping my lips in a straight line, even though it's never worked for me before.

"He does have the look of what you'd expect to see from one of *them*," Garlic Man concluded.

"Let's put him in the back room. We'll see if he talks in a few hours once he gets bored." Captain Crease stood back up to his full height and approached me.

"I just answered you!" I protested. "You said if I told you who I was, I could be on my way."

"The problem is, I don't believe you. And I'm the ranking officer," Crease said.

Half a dozen ways to escape flashed in front of my eyes. On his own, Captain Crease would go down easily, and I could choose to choke him with his own collar, knock him unconscious, or deliver a fatal blow with one of his own weapons. If he wasn't expecting an attack, I could run for him, lower my shoulder into his stomach, and grab both his legs. He'd go down hard, and if I lifted him high enough, his head and neck would land first. Garlic Man would be even easier to evade, and from the looks of him, I could probably shout loudly enough in his direction to get him to lock himself in the back room.

The grisly image of Captain Crease's busted neck at my feet knotted my stomach. *I wanted to attend Koliada with the Markos Family. I wanted to see Emberly again.* The memory of her hand in mine is what I held onto as Garlic Man and

Captain Crease herded me back to a room in the far corner of the building.

There couldn't be more than four rooms total in this building, and though I wasn't able to see into the two small rooms with closed wooden doors, I knew they had to be barely larger than closets for how small the building had been on the outside.

Despite the panicked alarm in my head that urged me to fight these soldiers and escape, I resisted. If someone came to test my blood, I'd escape. But until then, I made the very deliberate decision to hold onto hope.

Just like Lockbox had told me to.

Garlic Man grunted as he heaved open a heavy door, and Captain Crease told me to get inside and make myself comfortable.

Comfortable, I thought incredulously. The concrete was certainly suited for comfort, just like the cells back in Rhosivi and Predvoi.

Don't panic. But it was its own kind of prison cell. Here was a captain pushing me inside. *Breathe. You're not caught yet,* I told myself.

Three deadbolts, each as thick as the barrel of a rifle, were welded to the metal doorframe. Once they shut them, that door wasn't going to move.

"This will be an embarrassing mistake for you very soon," I said. I couldn't tell if my voice was full of anger or fright.

Would there be time for me to escape later if they sent someone in to take my blood? And what if that person they sent ended up being Bolest? The image of his grey teeth and yellowed lab coat slapped across my memory.

"We'll see," Captain Crease said as he shut the door.

The three bolts ground into place, and I took a seat on the tile floor. This, too, could have been a closet. Clearly, it wasn't intended as a long-term cell, since there wasn't even a cot or a trunk. The space wouldn't have held a cot anyway, but the excessive number of bolts for this room told me that I wasn't the first person they'd confined here.

It's not a prison, I reminded myself. *It's just a closet.*

Captain Crease left, and I heard the door shut behind him as Garlic Man muttered something about not getting paid enough. Exhausted, I rested my head on my knees and tried not to imagine the look Markos would have when he found out I'd disobeyed his direct orders.

Besides that, Leticia Varga hadn't gotten me any closer to finding Lockbox. What I had learned was something darker. She'd turned him in herself. Given him up and then given up on him. Maybe, in some ways, having a dead mother who had named me was preferable to a living one who called you 'it'.

Time is always weird in a cell without light to tell you how much of it has passed, but I'd learned a few tricks to help me count, though they usually required my heartrate to be at resting. I could count the beats and use it like a timer. Not only that, it gave me something else to do besides worry if Warden Velky or Bolest was about to march in.

The floors, cold and dirty, reminded me a bit of Rhosivi but with less mold. The walls, smudged with dirty finger-prints and minor chips, were made of concrete.

Time felt slow.

I grew hungry.

The desire to escape left me restless.

It had been almost two hours, by my estimation, when the front door of the building opened again. Enhancing my senses, I tuned in, anticipating that I'd know if a man or woman entered, how large they were, and if they dragged anything behind them, like say, a trunk, a suitcase, or a cart with medical supplies.

Despite being three rooms away from the entrance, I

recognized the footsteps immediately. One set was deliberate and heavy, the other set was heavy and sure. I breathed a sigh of relief.

Commander Markos had come for me.

And he hadn't come alone.

CHAPTER 13
CHARLIE-10

MARKOS'S ANGER laced his every syllable so emphatically, I was surprised it didn't make the roof shudder. I didn't need amplified hearing to understand his words as he spat them out. "Where the skudge is my soldier?"

His soldier? With my senses amplified, his voice resounded throughout my skull.

"Sorry, Commander Markos, Sir," Garlic Man said. It sounded like he was scrambling to stand up. "Captain Ivankovic found his burn to be suspicious. He directed me to keep him here until he returns."

"And where is Captain Ivankovic now?"

Garlic Man stuttered. "H-he went looking for a medic wh-who could test his blood." I could smell the garlic on his breath from back here. I tried to dial down my senses a touch, while still being able to hear every word of the conversation outside.

"So, now Captains think they have the authority to detain people without any evidence of wrongdoing and then subject them to blood draws?" Markos's anger had never brought me so much joy. Except, perhaps, the one time I'd heard him scolding Warden Velky. "I'll ask you again: where is my soldier?"

Garlic Man's voice quavered again. "I didn't think he was a soldier. I didn't know he was. He-he said he was a minor. Minors can't be soldiers. He-he had no rank or uniform. No assigned unit—"

"I told him to say that!" A few more heavy footfalls told me Markos had stepped closer to Garlic Man. "I told him to say he was a minor in the event of an incident or interference. He followed my directive, something that's proving to be too difficult for you."

"I'm sorry," Garlic Man said. His feet shuffled as he walked across the floor. "He's right back here. Again, so sorry. I'm just trying to follow orders. My own chain of command. You understand, don't you, Sir?"

The bolts scraped as Garlic Man moved them away. I stood up, adjusting my hair and clothes before the door opened. Light flooded in, and I raised a hand to shield my face. Lowering my hand slowly, my gaze met Commander Markos's.

Beside him, his gold pinecone shining like a star, stood Roman.

I had to hold back a smile.

I remained stock still while Garlic Man fumbled with the door. Roman briefly flashed me a grin. I'm surprised I didn't have tears in my eyes for the relief I felt.

"Luka," Markos said. The irritation in his voice was definitely genuine.

"Commander Markos, Sir," I said, "I tried to return but was detained. Thank you for coming for me, Sir." My voice nearly squeaked with emotion. *Had being a free man for a few days already made me soft? Or had those pills I'd taken in prison also limited my emotional range?*

"You left your comrade," Markos said.

"I'm sorry, Sir," I repeated to Markos. I turned to Roman. "I'm sorry, Captain Kral, Sir." I raised my hand to salute, feeling like that was the best course of action. *Did I do it right?*

"Come on, we're already late." Markos's voice was stiff.

He nodded to Garlic Man, who saluted him uncomfortably. Roman followed Markos, and I trailed behind as we walked down the hallway to the front door. Markos had his hand on the handle, but he wasn't the one who opened it as it pulled from his grasp.

Captain Crease held open the door, letting in a stout woman in a blue lab coat who carried a white case in her gloved hands.

I knew what it contained. Needles, vials, test kits. Everything they needed to prove that I had abnormalities in my blood, revealing me to be a lurper—both a Victor and an X-ray.

"Captain Kral, Commander Markos," Captain Crease said, his jaw dropping slightly at the sight of the three of us together. "I didn't expect…"

"You must have connections," Markos said, nodding to the box of needles and long test strips speckled with lightly colored boxes. "Tests?"

"Yes, Sir."

"Well, it won't be necessary. Luka is one of my soldiers."

The woman, doctor, nurse, whoever she was, fidgeted uncomfortably. Captain Crease must have noticed too because he directed her to take a seat on the bench while they sorted things out.

Captain Crease cleared his throat. "You understand if I want to get him tested. Just to be sure—"

"Those test kits don't come cheap," Commander Markos said. "And we already know what they'd tell us."

"Sir, his hand is suspiciously burned."

"Yes, it was strategically placed to cover his designation. We didn't want to run into any problems while we ran our op. Vaznov tend to stand out, and we needed to make sure he didn't."

"You admit that he is…that there is a…" Captain Crease looked at my blackened hand again.

"Didn't you hear me the first time? Yes, Luka here was a lurper. I determined it was in our best interests to conceal his vaznov tattoo so that he could more easily move around Khizmit under my direction."

"But not your supervision," Captain Crease said more as a statement than a question. The lack of respect in his tone left me gritting my teeth. "He lied to us. He said he was a minor. Did you graduate a minor early and enlist him?"

"What I do or don't do is none of your skudging business. He is not a minor, or he could not be a soldier. He was a lurper who has passed the Judgement Board and became a vaznov, got the name Luka, and is working with me on a covert operation here in Khizmit. An operation you compromised when you caused a scene arresting him!"

Maybe I should have said less when they'd taken me in. Garlic Man, the nurse, and I all remained still, watching Markos's face turn red.

Roman stood tall and motionless, his expression stoic.

I couldn't get over it. *Roman was here. Roman had come for me again.*

"But even graduated lurpers aren't supposed to lie to figures of authority. If he's a soldier, then he should have respected my rank!"

A few drops of spit flew from Markos's mouth as he shouted, "What the skudge do you think he's going to say and do? He's a Charlie. He's required to comply with *my* orders."

"A Charlie? The Charlies we've encountered have all complied with our orders. I wouldn't call him compliant!"

"Did he come willingly and without a fight?"

"Yes."

"And he allowed you to lock him in the holding cell without resistence?"

Captain Crease hesitated and then answered, "Well, yes."

"That sounds like compliance to me."

I could have laughed if the situation wasn't so serious. In what I hoped was a gesture of passivity, I moved my hands behind my back and inclined my head slightly so that I was looking at the floor, just as Roman did. I ducked my head to hide the small smile that betrayed my emotions.

"But, Sir, we could test him just to be sure—"

"Watch your tone with me, soldier." Markos slammed a fist into the tabletop. "I'm the Commander of the Lurper Legion. It's no surprise that I am capitalizing on their abilities to better serve Khizmit. I picked a Charlie unlike all the others. I needed one I could trust. One loyal to me who wouldn't follow the orders of every officer in sight."

Crease pointed to my hand. "But, Sir, he wasn't behaving like a Charlie. He lied. He defied direct orders I gave him to be honest."

"He's not your soldier! He's mine."

"We can't read his designation beneath his injury. We can't prove—"

"Then you'll just have to take my word for it."

"Yes, Sir, I believe you, Sir, but…" Captain Crease lowered his voice but still seemed suspicious. "What was he doing asking after Oscar-17?"

"It's classified," Markos growled.

"Respectfully, Sir, I'm the company commander of Khizmit's security force. If there is any reason to believe that an unregistered lurper is in our Enclave, that information wouldn't be classified from me."

Markos sighed, making no effort to mask his impatience. "I was informed by Captain Kral regarding Oscar-17's location here in Khizmit. But Oscars are tricky, and this one has a history of being a bit subversive. I asked this solder"—Markos gestured to me—"to approach Oscar's mother under the guise of being a friend to make sure that she didn't know where he was. To make sure that he hasn't found a way to communicate with her. We have no reason to believe she'd be forthcoming with me, but if she's sympathetic to her son, she'd be sympathetic to one of her son's friends. To another lurper."

"And?"

"And obviously, because we're having this conversation and you've detained my assistant, we've no reason to believe that Oscar-17 has had any communication with his mother since his incarceration."

Captain Crease furrowed his brow. "But why is that classified?"

"You've heard the whispers. You've read reports. There are parents who are upset. Residents of our great Enclave who think The Preemptive Initiative was a mistake. Part of my job is to find those who pity the inmates. Root out those who sympathize with the threats to our safety and our way of life. I'm using this Charlie to help me find them."

"Even if you're using a lurper to help Khizmit, he's supposed to be under constant supervision."

Roman spoke up. "I was supervising him. He's my comrade. The only moment he left my line of sight is when he approached Leticia Varga. I decided not to intervene during your public arrest, lest I compromise the op. I went to Commander Markos instead."

"You're not supposed to leave a vazzie alone for any amount of time while they're in public, Captain," Crease said.

"I will discipline him accordingly," Markos said as he bristled visibly at the use of the crude name given to graduates by those less than kind to any one of us given freedom after eighteen years behind bars.

"From what I've heard, this isn't the first time you've had to give Captain Kral disciplinary—"

"What the skudge does that have to do with this?" Markos cut in.

"It causes me to question your ability to select trustworthy members for your cadre."

"I don't give a slag stack about your opinion," Markos said. He turned to Roman. "You should have accompanied your vaznov into the private residence. You'll lose pay for this week and have extra duty all next month."

Roman nodded. "Yes, Sir."

Crease looked so happy you'd have thought he got Roman's pay for the week instead.

"We have other matters to attend to, Captain Ivankovic," Markos said. "We'll be on our way."

He turned to leave, but Captain Crease had the balls to stop us. "Before you go, I'll need this vazzie's designation and accompanying mark."

"So, you can verify my claims?"

"We have no choice, Sir. I apologize for the inconvenience."

Markos growled. "Charlie-10. His mark is an incomplete triangle."

"Charlie-10?"

He looked at me.

"I'm Luka. I'm Charlie-10," I said.

Crease looked from me to Roman to Markos. "I'll send this down for verification. It'll be just a few minutes." The captain pulled Garlic Man out the front door and gave him some directions that I would have eavesdropped on, but Markos turned to me and gave me a look that made me feel utterly humiliated.

The nurse cleared her throat gently. "Sorry, but are we doing a test or not?" She readjusted the plastic container on her lap.

"No need to waste a test," Markos said.

The woman stood. "They're getting advanced rapid tests soon. They've isolated the variable for Victors, thanks to Doctor Bolest. You know of him, don't you?"

"Yes," Markos said.

At Bolest's name, I recoiled. *Did what she said mean Bolest had finally found what he'd been looking for in my blood?*

"Well, it's good news. Chancellor Dulka commissioned them, and they're in the final stages of development. I'd think you'll find it to be quite helpful, especially given your previous position at Rhosivi, Commander."

"Rapid tests for all seven serums?" Markos asked. "And they can isolate the variation of each one?"

"Yes." The woman looked around to make sure no one else was listening. "First, they'll use them on our military men, just to make sure no unregistered lurpers are serving as soldiers. Then, they'll use them on all the guards at all the prisons—Rhosivi, Predvoi, Vazenia—and eventually, we'll test the whole population."

"What would be the purpose of mass testing?" Markos asked.

"The Task Force never found all the Test Criminals. Maybe some went to Latvani, but if there are any more hiding out here in Khizmit, don't we deserve to know?"

Commander Markos nodded. "That will be very revealing."

The woman's voice became excited. "It's very in-depth. The tests will be able to tell us which serum they carry. Which mutation they have."

"The rapid tests are that reliable?" Markos asked.

"Extremely. We won't need to rely solely on tattoos anymore. We can prick everyone's finger, and their blood will tell us how much of the serum is in their blood, so we'll know if they're an original Test Criminal or lurper."

Commander Markos nodded and thanked her for sharing these advancements. "You better hurry back to work before someone tries to keep you here all day." He was no doubt referring to Captain Crease.

"Thank you, Commander," the nurse said. "I'm sure I can

trust you not to share what I said widely. The general public is better not knowing. We wouldn't want to alert anyone in hiding to go running."

"I wouldn't dream of making such a mistake," Markos said. He seemed barely able to force a smile in her direction before she pushed the door open and left. When I looked up at Markos, he was working his jaw, something he only did when very upset.

"What—"

"Not now, vazzie!" Markos barked.

I shut my mouth immediately.

We stood in silence for a few minutes, and based on the tension in the room, Markos's concern was only mounting. *Would his lie about me being a Charlie-10 be found out? If he knew they were about to catch him in a lie, would we still be standing here?*

Roman barely moved and didn't glance my way.

Captain Crease reentered the room. He didn't bother looking at me. "Commander Markos, our records indicate that Charlie-10 was executed at Rhosivi Mine on December 6th of this last year."

"Correct." Markos's voice was steady. Unfazed.

"But you claim that this is Charlie-10?" Now, he looked at me, his eyes narrow.

"Before leaving Rhosivi Mine as the Head Warden and taking command of the Lurper Legion, I was asked to pick two assistants and a Legion Aid. After reviewing files, I selected Captain Kral as my Aid and picked two assistants who I'd personally interacted with during my time as Head Warden. Two prisoners who I'd recommended for graduation who had abilities I could exploit for our enclave."

"But—"

"But," Markos cut in, his voice louder and sterner, "for my objectives with them to remain clandestine as we hunted down those who sympathize with lurpers, I had to keep their identities a secret. On all official paperwork, you will find that I left those lines blank. It appears that I didn't take any assistants, when in fact, the assistants I selected were only executed on paper. As you can see from Charlie-10 standing in front of your eyes, I only wanted the paperwork to reflect his execution. If you read back, you'll see that I consistently recommended Charlie-10 for graduation. Why would I suddenly vote for his execution?"

"You lied on official paperwork?" Crease asked.

Markos lowered his voice, "I have reason to believe, as I'm sure you do, that there are Test Criminals and lurpers vying for positions of power. If we are going to find them out, we have to catch them off guard."

This explanation left Captain Crease speechless. Then he asked, "Will you allow me to check your paperwork?"

"You've held us up much longer than necessary, and I'd say I've been extremely patient. Check whatever paperwork you want to. You know where to find me."

Roman rushed forward, opening the door for Markos. Roman and I followed him out into the cold.

My heart raced.

I was free again.

No one followed us as we walked along the streets, around shops, and through narrow alleyways. Markos had told me not to speak. I could at least obey this request. I couldn't ask Roman how they'd found me or how long he'd been back in Khizmit. *Was Emberly safe?* The guilt I felt at having disobeyed him was overpowered by the relief at being safe again. At having my freedom restored.

We walked on in silence, and my stomach growled as we passed a few places where they sold sandwiches and warm drinks.

"I'm going back to the Parliament House," Markos said as he came to an abrupt stop.

"I'm sorry," I said quickly. "I was looking—"

"For Lockbox. I know. I told you I'd help you find him. Why didn't you wait?"

I said nothing.

Markos nodded slowly as if he understood. And maybe he did. The truth was that even after everything he'd done for me, I didn't trust him. I didn't believe that he really would make getting Lockbox a priority. Not in the way that I could.

"We will help Lockbox as soon as we can. *We*." Markos drew a circle in the air, connecting me, Roman, and himself. "Will you two stick together?"

"Yes, Sir," I said.

Markos offered a tight smile. "Try not to get arrested again, Luka. We need you out here."

"Yes, Sir."

"I'll be back tonight," Markos said. He and Roman locked eyes. "Get him home safely." Markos handed over Roman's staghorn dagger.

"I will," Roman said as he sheathed it.

Markos turned to leave.

"Sir," I began. He turned back. I asked my question in a quiet voice, "What really happened to Charlie-10?"

Markos didn't blink as he answered, "He was executed."

CHAPTER 14
MAKE PEACE

MARKOS HAD JUST LEFT my line of sight when Roman grabbed my shoulders and turned me to face him.

"Look at you," he said, admiring my cheek. "I told you you'd look better when both sides matched."

The memory of him holding his dagger up to my face flashed in my mind. I'd considered it a threat at the time.

"Thank the gods," he whispered. "You had me worried there." He looked over his shoulder as a group of soldiers approached. "Predvoi isn't far. While I don't think anyone would recognize you, they'll recognize me."

I hadn't thought about guards on holiday here. For all I knew, I'd run into Dent or Captain Caterpillar. Maybe Stork.

But not Goyle—definitely, not him.

I followed Roman as he skirted around a large tree in the path and ducked beneath some low-hanging garlands. He wove his way through the streets with such ease and familiarity. It shouldn't have surprised me. He grew up here. He knew this city the way I knew the tunnels at Rhosivi. Our childhood playgrounds.

Not wanting to stay too close to Roman, I lingered behind. We were too recognizable side-by-side.

Roman approached a large tree pressed into the corner of

a low brick wall and fished around beneath the branches before pulling out a large black bag.

Did it contain weapons? He looped the strap over his shoulder and continued through the streets. I tried to imitate the balance he had for moving quickly without drawing attention.

We passed through a few more blocks, and I became completely lost in Khizmit.

Roman stopped outside of what was, unmistakably, a wooden church. It had three steeples proudly extending toward heaven and rose three times higher than the buildings around it. Even the impressive height of the church was diminished by the enormous building in the distance with the golden dome topped by a tall green spire, the inspiration for the patches of the soldiers serving here in Khizmit.

I followed Roman through the double doors into an entryway lit by thousands of small white candles placed haphazardly around the room, either on the floor or in candelabrums.

Our footsteps echoed uncomfortably in the small area.

Roman waited for me inside the next set of doors and closed the door behind us slowly.

We stood alone in the chapel. A few dozen pews stretched out around us, facing an altar and paintings that went from the floor nearly to the ceiling of what I assumed to be the religious figurehead of this particular denomination. Floor candelabrums lit this room too, but inadequately.

Roman turned the lock on the door.

Weeks previous, I would have slagged my pants in fear that he'd lock me in a room to kill me, and now I found myself staring into his face, considering giving him an embrace.

"I shouldn't have twisted the blade when I pulled it out," he said. "Sorry about that. The other guards were so close. I could hardly breathe with the other captain breathing over my shoulder."

"Captain Bitter," I said.

"If you say so." Roman chuckled and led me down the aisle to an empty pew four rows from the front.

I sat beside him on the wooden bench. The air, musty and dry, made this church feel not entirely different from parts of the mines. The most notable distinction was that I could see in here.

"Did you give all the guards names?" Roman asked.

"Yes. I guess I still do—we just got away from Captain Crease and Garlic Man."

Roman laughed at this, shaking his head. "Oh," he said, as if realizing something for the first time. "Oh, you called me Roman because of..." He held up his hand, showcasing the tattoos that were all too familiar to me. I'd seen his inked fingers grab for his Luger often enough that they looked almost empty without the weapon in his hand.

"I didn't know Romulus was your name. Lockbox hadn't told me."

"And here I'd resented the little lurp for being unable to keep a secret." He clapped me on the back so hard I almost fell over.

The 'little lurp,' as he'd called him, needed me, and here I was, sitting in a church. I ran my thumb along a deep groove in the bench. "Lockbox is, hands down, the best at keeping secrets of anyone I've ever met," I said.

Roman unzipped the bag and pulled out a change of clothes. He made quick work of the buttons on his uniform and put the top back into his bag.

I'd seen the looks people gave him in the streets. A captain was, evidently, almost as rare here as it was in the prisons. He folded the uniform top and placed it into the bag.

"Don't want the attention?" I asked.

"I only needed it for the clout." He didn't have to remind me how stupid I'd been for getting caught.

Roman changed his pants and finally tucked all his uniform pieces, including his ushanka, into his bag.

While I'd have recognized him anywhere, it would have taken me a moment to know for sure that it was, in fact, Captain Kral in front of me. The uniform aged him a few years, for starters, and without it, he relaxed. His entire posture and demeanor changed into something more casual, more approachable.

Roman dropped the bag to the side and looked over at me again. "It's good to see you, Lu— wait. Did Markos tell you? He wanted to be the one to tell you."

"Tell me what?"

"Your name."

The memory of Roman beginning to say my name back in Predvoi returned to me from the time after I'd fallen from the Mills. I'd thought he was about to call me "Lurper."

"You knew my name, my real name?" I asked.

"You know mine," he replied. "I can keep calling you 'Victor' if you prefer."

"Why, so I can keep calling you 'Sir'?"

Roman scoffed. "No, please, I get enough of that from the crusters."

The crusters…but Roman was a cruster. All guards were.

"All healed up then? Can I see your side?"

I pulled up my shirt, showing Roman the smooth skin where he'd stabbed me.

"That's skudging incredible." He looked back at my face. "You look good."

"Yes, no thanks to you."

"I think you mean *all* thanks to me."

I did mean that. Swallowing my pride I said, "Thank you."

"I would have warned you to block pain, but I was afraid that if you did, we wouldn't have been able to sell the story."

I understood. I understood a lot of the reasons for the things he'd done. "Thank you," I repeated. "For making me run and not shooting me and leaving me with your knife and gloves and—"

"Were you going to kill me?" Roman asked. His eyes made him look vulnerable. "In the woods right before I told you about healing, were you going to kill me?"

I could have said 'no' convincingly. I could have told him I suspected he was trying to help me. "I don't know," I said. "I hadn't decided."

"Good."

"Why is that good?"

"You didn't know what to think of me. You didn't know if I was going to kill you for real or help you. It means I did my job."

"Not your job of killing me."

"You were right. I'd have missed you."

"I hated you," I said. "I have thought of killing you so many times. In so many ways."

"I know."

"I'm sorry."

"I'm not," Roman said. "We did what we had to do. We did it successfully. You didn't kill me, and I didn't kill you. I'd call that a win." He stretched his arms across the back of the pew as if making himself at home here in the empty chapel.

"What happened after I left?" I asked, my voice low.

"Dulka sent a few guards out to look for any remnants of your body. They found a lot of blood and wolf tracks. Then she sent me away. My job was done."

That was days ago. He'd been released from his position. Without me, I suppose he had no reason to be there.

"Where were you?" I asked.

"I went to see someone first."

"Who?"

Roman looked at me as a boyish grin crossed his face. "A lady. My lady."

"You have…you're married?"

"Engaged to be. You sound shocked."

I was.

"With a face like yours and no tag on your wrist, you'll get a lady, too, if that's what you want. I should warn you, some of the girls here are pretty…forthcoming…and assertive."

"I noticed that already," I said.

"I bet that's an adjustment for you. Sorry I couldn't get the dose dialed down before you left."

He'd considered doing that? "I'll adapt. Markos said he'd look for some pills for me. Maybe wean me off them."

"You met Markos's daughters. Did you meet Emberly?"

"Yes," I said. "I met her all right."

"Oh." Roman playfully batted my arm. "You've got it bad!"

"Why do you say that?"

"Look at you! Your face is all red. And you hid your hands."

"Well, you can't blame me, can you? I mean, you've met her!" She truly was skudging gorgeous. But it was more than that. She was daring and considerate. Selfless and courageous.

Roman nodded. "She's something. I won't risk saying anything else except good luck."

"Why won't you say anything else?"

"We have…something of a…history, I guess I should say."

"A history?" *Why did that suddenly make me so angry?*

"Not a romantic history, not like that. Don't worry. Skudge, you get scary when you're mad!"

He was scared of me?

"I can see it in your eyes. Not the bloodlust I'd mentioned, that's all slag, but you do get a look. And you have it now!"

"I barely know her," I said. It was true, and yet, my face was warm. The idea of Roman having a history with Emberly left me with the not-so-simple emotion of jealousy. Roman knew Khizmit. Roman was a cruster, not an inmate. Roman knew the Markos family and got to drink rakia.

I turned away from him to look at the paintings on the walls.

"Is this an old haunt of yours?"

"Yes," he replied. "I come here when I need to make peace."

"With what? God?"

"No. Well, maybe. I come here to make peace with myself." Roman cleared his throat. "I saw how you looked at me after what happened with Smoke. I didn't mean what I said about you being useless. Personally, I never expected that you'd comply with the order."

"Should I have?"

"You made your own choice. I admire you for that. I had to make my own choice too."

"You shot him in the head. He was just a kid."

Roman just nodded and pressed his thumbs into his forehead. "I know. And he didn't deserve it. And I didn't deserve to have to do it." He sighed and ran his hand through his hair before looking back up to the front of the chapel. "I come to this place to make peace with myself over my choices." He turned to me, a pained expression on his face. "I brought you here just in case you needed to find some peace in your choices."

Goyle. He meant Goyle. I hated that he knew how that haunted me, because it meant he did know me. But I loved that he knew I didn't have any joy in the action.

The image of the knife flying from my hands and sinking into Goyle's throat came back to me. The thud of his body on the floor. The spewing red—

"How do you do it?" I asked. I had to get the memory out of my head.

"I say a prayer. I ask for forgiveness from whatever higher powers may be. I remind myself what I am," Roman said. "Then the hardest part."

"Which is?"

"I forgive myself."

The sputter of the candles took up the place of our conversation, and I shut my eyes. With my head bowed, I thought a prayer. *I had no choice but to kill Goyle. I did the best I could in the situation with what I had. I took no pleasure in it. I didn't know it was his grave I'd dug up until it was too late. Does it matter that, in some small way, I've only wronged one man instead of two or more? Forgive me.*

I tried for a few minutes to forgive myself, but the guilt gnawed at me. "How long does it take…to forgive yourself?"

"I'll let you know when I get there," Roman replied.

I tried not to think about what Roman had said. I tried not to wonder what it meant, but it bothered me. It was the only conversation that kept my mind off the image of Goyle's last gasping breaths, off the snap of his shoulder when I'd taken his clothes to get into Khizmit.

"What's your history with Emberly?" I asked.

"Well," Roman said. He scratched at the back of his neck. "I figured you'd ask."

"Are you going to tell me to skudge off? To mind my own business? To kiss ass a little more and then maybe you'll tell me?"

"This is a church." Roman chuckled. "Have a little respect."

"Sorry."

"No, I'm not gonna tell you to skudge off. We're not fraternizing. We're friends." Even in the flickering light, I could see him smiling so big he had a few wrinkles around the edges of his eyes. I should have realized what they meant when I first saw them. It meant he smiled often.

Roman leaned over the seat, cracking his back a few times. "I sort of ruined her reputation," he said abruptly.

My mind considered the worst for a moment, and the anger flared like a fuel induced flame.

"Not like that," Roman said. "In short, I needed to get a message to Markos. He'd been promoted to Commander just before Velky was to be promoted to Head Warden. If we didn't get a certain Victor out of Rhosivi in a timely manner, well…Velky has a thing against Victors."

Me. It all came back to me.

"While looking for Markos, I ran into Emberly in the square here in Khizmit. It would have been fraternization to the highest degree if anyone saw me, a captain, go to Commander Markos's home. I had no reason to be there. At the time, no one knew we even knew each other. It would have jeopardized your safety and mine. I couldn't trust Emberly to take the message to Markos because he's wanted his family to stay out of it."

"So, you…what?"

"It was her idea. We'd already been seen together by a group of her friends. She took me by the hand, and we pretended to try and sneak away. I pretended that I was going to her home for…other reasons."

"You went home with her and gave the public impression that you two were up to…something else…"

"We weren't. Nothing happened. She did kiss me on the cheek a bit longer than necessary, and sort of, well, cuddled into me by a public fountain right when her ex-boyfriend, Alex, was looking. She said it was a win-win. She got to have a bit a revenge on him since he wasn't about to start a fight with me, and I got a cover story for why I was at Commander Markos's house."

I imagined her kissing him longer than necessary. She was

clever to do it in front of Alex. He sounded like nothing less than a skudgeface. I wished it could have been me that she'd used to make him jealous. That it could have been me she'd kissed and cuddled into in front of her friends.

But I hadn't been here. I'd likely been robbing Fox's trunk at the time or arms deep in filling bags of coal.

"Don't be angry with me, Luka. You two are a good match. I'm not a threat. I have my Alba."

If I hadn't met Emberly, I might not have believed it had all been her idea, but I'd been around her enough to know that she wanted to help her dad. She wanted to keep Roman safe. Her action of sacrificing her public appearance might have played a role in my escape.

"Alba," I repeated. I should have asked about her. Asked how the two of them met and when they planned to get married; instead, I asked the questions that sat at the forefront of my mind. "Is that why you got punished? Is that the reason you were sent away to Predvoi?"

Roman nodded. "It all worked out, didn't it?" He refrained from mentioning how it had ruined his own reputation as well.

"That's why the other guards at Predvoi didn't like you," I said.

"They didn't call me 'ink hands' on account of these." He gestured to the Roman numerals on his fingers. "They said it because they believed I liked to get my hands dirty."

They thought he'd skudged the Commander's daughter, so he'd been sent to Predvoi as a disciplinary measure.

And they did it all for what? It couldn't have all been for me. I wasn't worth all that.

"Luka," Roman said, his voice sounding happier. "I know where Lockbox is."

My heart started racing.

"I asked you so many times! The one time I don't ask you, you know?"

"I always knew. I couldn't always tell you," Roman said. "Warden Dulka really did think you were going to kill him based on the reports Bolest had written. Since Lockbox was a high-interest inmate, they didn't want to risk it. She asked me to drug Lockbox so they could transfer him and drug you so you wouldn't remember that night. That way they could skudge with your head. Warden Dulka and Doctor Bolest decided to see how you responded to being told you'd murdered him because, historically, Victor's become much more blood-thirsty after their first kill. Bolest knew you hadn't killed Lockbox but pretended to believe you had to see how you'd react. To see if it brought out a more violent side to you."

"They were trying to break me," I said.

"Yes."

"And you went and skudged up their plan."

"That was always my intention." Roman shoved me playfully again before wrapping his arm around my shoulder. "Crusters, they're all a bunch of slagheads, am I right?"

I leaned back, looking at his uniform, the patch, the weapon, and the flag on the shoulder as it poked out the side of his bag. "Roman, you may not be in uniform right now, but you're still the biggest cruster there is."

Roman looked offended and almost taken aback. As a captain, he surely knew what that made him. He cocked his head to the side. "Lockbox didn't figure it out, huh? You didn't either…"

"Don't insult me, Roman. It's been a long day."

Roman laughed and punched me lightly in the shoulder before leaning in near my ear. "I'm like you, Luka," he whispered. "I'm a skudging lurper, just like you."

CHAPTER 15
THE KILO

"WHAT DID YOU SAY?" I asked.

Captain Kral, a lurper? It wasn't possible. *How could he be?* Roman was just a gifted soldier. He wasn't tainted like me. He didn't come from criminal parents like I had. *How could he be one of us?*

"I think you heard me. You have carefully calibrated hearing and can hear many more things than even the average lurp." Roman gave me a knowing look.

"But..."

My gaze went down to Roman's wrist. It was, ironically, the only part of his hand and arm left unmarred by traces of black ink. He held it up for me to see in the dim light of the empty chapel.

"You were never found," I said softly.

"And I'd like to keep it that way."

"What are you?"

"What do you think?" Roman asked. His tone was playful.

"Charlie?"

"Oh, come on! I can do a lot more than just follow orders."

The image of him shooting the can off the rabbit hutches and then the impossible shot he'd made dropping Smoke resurfaced.

"Juliet?" I asked. "Lima?

"Close," Roman said. "I'm an unmarked Kilo."

I couldn't speak. He had to be at least twenty-five years old, and according to the timeline Lockbox had told me, that was too old to be a lurper and too young to be an original Test Criminal.

"My mother was an inmate in Zalar Correctional Facility when they decided to toy with everyone there and shoot them up with serums." He answered my questions as if he could read my thoughts as easily as he could spot a target in the fog. "She was pregnant at the time. That's why I'm older than most of the rest of us."

"A Kilo?" I asked.

"That's how I heard you when Velky came to Predvoi. When he and Bolest tried to bleed you out. I think my better eyesight is on account of the slight variation in the Kilo serum. Juliet only helps with hearing, Kilo with both. At least, that's the best I can figure."

"You're really a Kilo." I hated how dumbfounded I sounded. If Lockbox had any suspicions, he's sure done a good job keeping them to himself. "Your mom...was she caught? How did you evade the Task Force?"

"My mom had me almost a year before they found her. I grew up with my aunt, who knew what I was but claimed me as her own son, even after they found my birth mother and offered rewards for any leads to, well, kids like us."

"But didn't people realize your aunt suddenly had a son?"

"No, because my aunt did have a son. He was a few months older than me, but he passed away in his sleep as a baby. No one knew why. My mom saw it as an opportunity to get me to safety, and she gave me to my aunt before anyone found out my cousin had died. Sadly, she was the one who had to take care of his body, so he was never buried properly for my aunt to visit his gravesite."

"And your uncle?"

"He'd been away at the war. He never met his real son. Didn't protest when she started calling me Romulus instead of my cousin's name, Jozef."

I couldn't decide if it was more incredible that Roman was a lurper, that he'd evaded capture his whole life and had an aunt who watched over him, raising him as her own, or if the most incredible part of it all was that he'd chosen to confide everything in me.

"You're a lurper," I said aloud. "And you're a captain, and you have tattoos." I paused. "You are violating so many laws."

Roman laughed, and the sound rang out around us.

"That's true," he said. "And it won't be the last of the laws I break, either."

"I hope that means you're going to help me get Lockbox. Where is he?"

"Lockbox is an information slave in the Grand Palace."

"Where's that?"

"You know that building with the gold dome and green spire? It was probably the first one you saw when you came over the hill."

I knew it by sight. I'd admired it with awe. Here I'd thought I was an expert on prisons, but there'd been one gleaming in the sunlight, right under my nose.

"When Lockbox's mom declined reunification services, it put Lockbox up for auction. He'd been recommended for early graduation, but since he was a high-interest inmate, they auctioned him off instead."

"Auctioned?"

"They do that with high-interest inmates. Markos bid the most for him, but Supreme Chancellor Dulka forbade the sending of an Oscar to the Lurper Legion. She doesn't exactly support the Legion as is and vetoed the Commander's bid."

"So, someone else got him?"

"Chancellor Eldrat wanted him as an information slave. Sometimes they call them analysts. I've heard it's not all bad."

"Why'd they take him? He'd been failing some of the tests. He'd hoped it would make them think he didn't have that great of a memory," I said.

"Yes, but they don't make decisions based only on the tests. Predvoi is full of inmates who feared Lockbox when he was there. That sort of respect and fear among inmates doesn't go unnoticed, and the only way it could have been explained in Lockbox's case is that he had information that others didn't."

"Who's in charge of the Grand Palace?" I asked.

"The Chancellors all hold equal power over Khizmit," Roman said. "Commander Markos is now the face of the military. Chancellor Eldrat sits in the Grand Palace. He presides over education and information. Now that Lockbox has been exposed to the intelligence we have on Latvani and Dovaberg, our plans with the war, and our history with the Test Criminals, they will never let him leave there alive."

"Never?" I couldn't help the crestfallen feeling spreading through my chest.

"I said *let* him. We won't be asking permission."

We had to get him out. Lockbox knew there was a risk of him going there, and he'd fought it. He must have known something about it that made him aim for graduation rather than being privy to Khizmit's secrets. "What's the plan?" I asked.

"I could get in okay, but I wouldn't be able to get out with Lockbox alone. I'd need someone who could take a bullet for me and then walk away unscathed."

"Easy," I said.

"It's not that easy though, because if we go in and you get shot up and leave so much as a drop of blood on the floor, they'll know it was you. Their rapid tests will pop red on X-ray and Victor. You're the only one with blood like that.

They'd know you were the one to get in. They'd know I didn't kill you."

"And we'd both be dead."

"No, we'd *all* be dead. Commander Markos, me, you, and Lockbox."

"Then how do we get out?"

"You're not listening. I still haven't figured out how to get you in, let alone how to get all three of us out."

"Is he safe there? I mean, do they feed him well?" It couldn't be that cold. It wasn't backbreaking manual labor. As much as I wanted to liberate Lockbox, maybe life as an information slave was better than an early death.

"I don't know," Roman said. "Commander Markos has been gathering intel on the situation."

"He's going to help?"

Roman raised an eyebrow at me. "All he does is help. He made time before his promotion to Commander, which for the record was supposed to be a surprise, to personally escort you from Rhosivi to Predvoi. You still don't trust him?"

Did I? Could I? I should, that was clear, but as much as I'd imagined Markos as something of a father to me, it was different to decide that I should trust him. First, I had to stop breaking the promises I made to him. "Trust is a complicated thing," I said.

"Things change. Things will have to change. We're a team now."

"I had a teammate. Lockbox was my teammate."

"He still is. We're on his team, too."

A door to the right of an enormous painting swung open with a groan, and three men in brown robes shuffled inside the chapel. They began to intonate harmoniously with one another as they walked across the front of the chapel, swapping the candles that had burned out. They cupped their wrinkled hands around the flames of lit candles as they used their light to bring the new candles to life.

"Who are they?" I asked. "Priests? Bishops? Pastors?"

"Monks," Roman replied.

"Are they eunuchs?"

"What?"

"Are they eunuchs?"

"That's not how you pronounce it," Roman said. "It's you-nick, not ew-newk."

That's the risk when you learn everything solely from books for the latter half of your formative years, I thought to myself.

"And I have no idea. I've never asked."

One of the monks wandered down the aisle closer to us, but he didn't look at us or give any indication that he saw us at all.

"You want to ask?"

"No," I replied. "I just read about that once. Wondered if it's common."

The monk nearest us wandered farther down and exited through a back door.

"What do they do to the analysts?" I asked. I preferred that title to, 'information slave,' but slave labor is what it was. It's what lurpers were good for.

"I don't know much, only rumor. It might just be rumor."

"What have you heard?"

"Sometimes the analysts get too clever. One almost escaped once. I've heard that sometimes—just sometimes —they…"

"Roman."

"Sometimes they cripple them. Khizmit doesn't need the analysts to be able to walk. They're capable of working without the use of their legs."

Crippled? My stomach sunk. The edges of my mind flashed with crimson. Khizmit claimed that they didn't want me to be a weapon of mass destruction, but if I'd been given a chance right then, I'd have entered the palace with deadly force and liberated every Oscar in the building.

If they so much as harmed Lockbox, I'd kill them, and I'd do it with far less mercy than I had assassinating Goyle.

Roman looked at my hands. "You really do get scary when you're mad." He laughed, though it was uneasy. "We're going to get Lockbox, Luka. As soon as we can do it safely, I swear."

"On what?"

"On the mines. On my mother."

Above us, loud and resonant, the bell chimed. The wooden walls around us vibrated with its reverberations. It chimed again and again and again. It was time for me to get back to Commander Markos's home.

The bell chimed for a fifth time. I had to face Markos after what I'd done.

I had to trust him.

Roman stood, shouldering his bag. We made our way toward the door. One of the men in a large brown robe opened the door for us, bowing as we exited.

It was brighter outside than I'd expected; only a few of the shops and homes had lit their candles. Both of us scanned the crowd for any familiar faces. It unnerved me to realize that guards from Predvoi or Rhosivi could be traveling these streets, and they would most likely not be in their uniforms.

"When will I see you again?" I asked.

"Maybe tomorrow. I usually come to the chapel in the evenings."

"Every night? I thought you just came here to make peace?"

Roman didn't smile. "I have a lot to make peace with."

CHAPTER 16
MARKOS'S PLAN

ROMAN LED me close to the Markos's home but not all the way. He hung back as a hooded silhouette while I walked the final few blocks. Roman had to head back to Alba's house. I didn't know how much she knew about Roman, his abilities, or his relationship with me. He'd tell me what he wanted me to know, but I got the distinct impression that he didn't want to share too much about her with me, or anyone else, for that matter.

Markos met me outside his front door as if he'd been waiting for me based on the small pile of snowflakes that sat atop his black ushanka. His nose and cheeks were rosy from the cold.

I'd considered how much more comfortable I'd have been if I could have stayed at Roman's rather than Commander Markos's home, but Roman didn't have a home. He stayed with Alba. And Alba didn't know either of us were lurpers.

As soon as Commander Markos and I entered his home, Emberly hurried over to look at us over the railing. Her long hair flowed over her shoulders as she moved. The way she chewed her bottom lip told me I wasn't the only one who'd noticed the telltale signs of Markos's anger.

He didn't even remove his boots as he marched in,

tracking muddy snow all across the rug and entryway. Markos shut the door forcibly, making the wreath outside smack into the wood before he looked up at Emberly.

"Dad, I—"

"Not now," Markos said in what was clearly an effort to keep his voice down.

Her almond eyes met mine. "I wanted to make sure Luka—"

"Luka is not your concern." He flashed me a livid glance as he picked up a patterned burgundy scarf and held it out for Emberly.

Markos wasn't even my father, but knowing that I'd let him down left me feeling hollow and despondent.

As Emberly hurried down the stairs past me, I wanted to say something. To thank her. To apologize for putting her in a position where her father was disappointed in her. We looked at one another for only a moment, and I hoped my face expressed gratitude for her help. She'd saved me, whether she knew it or not.

"And Ember—" Markos said as she reached for the doorknob with her gloved hands, "Thank you."

Without another glance at either of us, she hurried outside.

The silence that followed was punctuated by the hum of my pulse in my ears and the familiar warnings in my head that I was in danger here alone with Markos.

I'm not in danger, I told myself. Markos climbed the stairs, and I followed, after removing my boots. Keeping to the far side of the steps, I avoided the small lines of dirty snow left by him.

When we both stood in the living room, Markos turned to me. The fear of him that had always lived inside me grew larger. Even as a Victor, I'd been impressed by his strength and size. His arms dwarfed mine. It was no wonder they'd selected him as the

Commander of the Legion. If any man could keep a bunch of lurpers from killing each other, themselves, or their superiors, it was Pedrick Markos. I'd known it before, but as I stood there, looking at his well-fitted uniform, the arced sabre at his side, and his face tight with anger, I feared him. I respected him.

"What the skudge were you thinking?" Markos asked. "You risked more lives than your own by going out there today and asking after Lockbox."

For most of my life, I felt brave, strong, and capable, but standing there, I felt like a useless piece of slag.

I dropped my chin, submitting to whatever punishment Markos had for me. "I'm sorry; I wanted to find Lockbox. After what Warden Dulka said, I thought that he might be in danger."

Markos stepped a few paces to the side and then walked back to me. Placing a hand on my shoulder, he said my name. "Luka." It was nearly a whisper. The anger wasn't completely gone from his face, but now he looked more concerned, more sympathetic. He spoke softly as he continued, "I understand that you're used to doing it alone. To not being able to rely on anyone to help you. You're used to being used and manipulated and lied to, but Luka, I'm not going to do that. I need you, and you need me. You can't go running off by yourself like that. I thought…"

But he didn't have to finish. I knew what he'd thought.

"I'm sorry. I shouldn't have left. And I shouldn't have let your daughter help me. Risking my own safety is stupid enough, but risking yours…risking hers…" This time I was the one who couldn't finish.

He removed his ushanka and ran his hand through his damp hair, and even though it was short, it stayed back against his scalp. "I asked you to leave her alone. To keep your distance from her."

"Yes, Sir," I said. I intentionally didn't agree to anything this time, only acknowledged that he had clearly asked me not to get close to her.

"I wasn't able to get any pills for you," Markos said, placing his ushanka on the chair. "Not without drawing suspicion. But you're strong, and you'll adjust."

It wasn't a loss in my book. I wasn't sure I ever wanted them anyway. "Yes, Sir," I said.

"She shouldn't have come back here at all. I sent her to work, and I'd assumed she'd be there, but the mystery of you, of having you here, I should have known it would be too much for her to resist. She told me that she came back here and freely offered her help to you."

I sighed in relief. She must not have told him that we'd been sitting on the couch together. *Was it not a big deal to her? For her to run her delicate hands along mine the way she had?* I couldn't imagine those sorts of interactions were normal or acceptable or even commonplace. Something told me that Markos definitely wouldn't have allowed it to happen if he'd been in the room with us.

Markos began unbuttoning the brass clips on the front of his uniform, and I fidgeted awkwardly for a moment as I considered how to ask about Lockbox.

"Sir," I said, trying to keep my hope in check. "Do you have a plan for getting Lockbox back?"

Markos walked across the room to the kitchen, leaving a trail of snow from his boots, and pulled out two drinks from the cooler and a sandwich wrapped in brown paper. "Not yet," he finally said as he returned to the couch and handed me the sandwich and one of the drinks.

"Thank you," I said, hastily unwrapping the sandwich. I dropped onto the couch.

"If you eat in here, don't let Zuzana catch you or leave any evidence you were sitting there."

I nodded, my mouth full of the rye bread and cheese as I made sure to be careful of the bites I took.

"I was in communication with Warden Dulka this morning. She has no reason to believe you're alive, and we need to keep it that way. Captain Kral will keep his distance until we return to The Outskirts."

Markos took a long drink as I opened mine and sipped at it. The carbonation made my nose feel funny. I didn't know how Markos was able to guzzle it so easily.

"The good news is that Lockbox is safe, and even if Warden Dulka wanted him back, she wouldn't be able to reach him at this point." Markos stared at me, leaning forward. "I swear to you, as soon as it becomes possible for me to help your friend, I will."

There was no way I could distrust him. I nodded, and this time, I meant it. As much as it pained me, I wouldn't go looking for Lockbox.

"What's happening right now in Khizmit, it's so much bigger than just you." And yet Roman had sacrificed his reputation for me. Markos allowed his daughter's own reputation to suffer for me. I'd run off and put everyone at risk, and he'd still come for me.

"You didn't leave me today. You didn't tell them what I was, what I could do."

Markos sighed. "If I have to cut you off and let you die, I will, but I swear, it'll kill me. If they find out I've been helping you, they'll investigate every guard and inmate I've worked with. You heard what that nurse said. With rapid tests right around the corner, they'll find a lot of unmarked carriers."

"What does it mean?" I asked.

"They track markers in the blood. That's why your blood was so difficult for Bolest to crack, but once he figured out you were an X-ray and a Victor, he was able to isolate the variables. Yours was the last genetic code to be cracked. They can identify everyone by their blood now."

"And that's bad because..." I asked.

"If anyone tests your blood, it'll tell them you're a Romeo, Hotel, Uniform, and Juliet."

"Roman explained that. But why would anyone test my blood randomly? As long as I keep my blood inside my body and avoid any injuries, I should be good to go."

Markos shook his head.

"Why do they need rapid tests when we've all been tattooed already? Isn't checking wrists enough?"

Markos leaned in close. "Don't think for a moment that all the Test Criminals were caught, because they weren't. The reason there are so few Victors is because many of the people who'd been given that serum haven't been caught."

Lockbox had been right, and he'd probably been right because Markos had slipped that intel to him.

"There were a thousand inmates injected at Zalar. In the breakout, they killed the scientists who'd altered them and destroyed the records kept of them. The Task Force has found some of the criminals but not all of them. Once they mass produce the rapid tests, people will die. People we care about. People we've been trying to protect."

He'd been protecting me, but something told me that I wasn't the only person he'd been keeping safe. "So, you don't believe that we're dangerous?" I asked.

"I believe that anyone can be dangerous if they want to be and that your abilities don't define you any more than your parents' crimes should. Their crimes shouldn't have defined them either, and they wouldn't have, but then Khizmit got reckless with their serums."

"But you've told me my whole life that I'm dangerous."

"You are. You can be. If you want to be, and under the right conditions, you can be one of the most dangerous weapons we have. You're more than that though. You're a boy robbed of his childhood because of mistakes certain adults made. I'm not trying to reduce you to something you don't want to be, but right now and in the coming months, I *need* you to be dangerous. I need you to be everything Khizmit has feared that you are."

The passion in his voice lit a fire in my chest. *What did he need me to do?* I didn't dare ask, but I knew that I would do it. Not because I was forced to, but because Commander Markos believed in me and needed me. He'd been fighting for me, for my life, for my freedom for seventeen years. I'd fight with him now.

A moment of silence swirled around us and then Markos readjusted his position on the couch.

"What are you planning?"

He smiled, and I knew he wasn't about to tell me everything. "I'll tell you what we're going to do now. We're going to celebrate Koliada here. You're going to lay low until we reunite with Captain Kral on The Outskirts. In the meantime, I'm going to figure out a way to get Lockbox out of the Grand Palace."

CHAPTER 17

KOLIADA CARAMELS

WE ATE dinner mostly in silence that night, probably because Markos had told Zuzana how Emberly had disobeyed. The only one who seemed immune to the tension was Milena, who chattered through the meal. We'd had variations of cabbage stew in the prison but never like this. For one, this stew was seasoned and had small pieces of meat mixed in. In the prison, what we called cabbage stew usually just meant slightly steamed cabbage in hot water.

Again, I wanted to compliment Zuzana on the meal but didn't want to repeatedly remind her that I'd been in prison.

I went to bed right after dinner, without even a moment to talk to Emberly, which I assumed had been intentional. I didn't have to be a Charlie to be compliant. My respect for Markos could compel me to be strictly obedient. Besides, I'd gotten Emberly into trouble, and I didn't want to do it again.

I struggled to keep Lockbox from my every thought, but with the excitement of Koliada Eve in the air and Markos's promise to help him as soon as we could, I managed.

I'd been sleeping and dreaming of something to do with rabbits in a coal mine when Zuzana's voice woke me. I don't know what she and Markos had been discussing before, but my name is what jolted me awake.

"I thought you'd want to take Luka with you tomorrow," she said. "You've never complained about not having a son, but you might like to have him with you. I know how you see him. Besides, it's not like he has a dad to take him. The girls won't be offended."

"I would take him with me," Markos said. "But I don't think he should be leaving the city right now."

"What aren't you telling me about Luka?"

"There's a lot I can't tell you."

A moment passed.

"They didn't graduate him, did they?" she said finally.

"Zuz—"

"You can just tell me! You should have told me before. I thought they'd graduated him. You said you were going up for his Judgement Board at Predvoi. I assumed they'd followed your suggestions."

"Well, they didn't. Riah found some reason to hate him and urged the rest of the board to vote for termination."

"Makes me sick," Zuzana spat. "And we all know how Andrei Velky voted. He'd shoot all those inmates himself if you hadn't set up those new rules."

Markos sighed. "Zuz, you can't—"

"How many times are you going to say that in our marriage? I know. It's not like I go into the council meetings and share any of this."

"I know. I just can't risk him getting caught. Not after everything he's been through."

Zuzana's footsteps stopped. "I can't believe they voted for his termination after everything you put in his file. You told them about him saving that inmate from the cave in? And sharing with the younger inmates?" Her voice became incredulous.

"I wrote it all in there. But they were too scared to take the chance with him."

He knew about all that?

"Why?" she asked. "Why've they had it out for Luka since day one? What is he anyway?"

"It doesn't matter," Markos said stiffly.

"You'll never tell me, will you?"

I took a deep breath in. She didn't know who I was. She didn't know I was a Victor and an X-ray. Markos, who'd known since my birth, hadn't even told his own wife.

"If Luka didn't graduate, how did he get here?" Zuzana whispered quickly. "Did you help him?"

"I had to—" Markos began.

"Of course, you had to. You couldn't let him go. You've never been able to. You've loved that boy since the day he was born. But how did you get him out?"

"He got out," Markos whispered, and his voice was so quiet that I struggled to hear it over the crackling flames and settling logs in the front room. "He burned his hand to cover the tattoo, but I can't take him outside of Khizmit and expect that I'll be able to convince the guards not to worry about it simply because I say they shouldn't."

"They respect you, Rick."

Markos laughed. "Not the captain I met today. He barely let us leave without a full interrogation."

"My heart aches for the boy. I feel like I've known him for as long as you have. I hate that I have to say goodbye to him so soon."

"Don't worry about it right now. Just enjoy Koliada, and we'll take what comes next."

I thought they might have gone to sleep, but then Zuzana spoke again. "You're not upset with him, are you?"

"He scared me today. Emberly, too," Markos said. "But I'm not upset. I just want to keep him safe."

"He's almost a man. You can't keep him safe."

"Yes, he is almost a man. That's what kills me. He didn't even get a chance to be a kid yet."

———

I woke up to lively music coming from the street. Only one small window sat in the wall of this room, but through it, I could see down the street a short distance. Enough to see kids running with ribbons streaming behind them. A few older kids carried their instruments, and one plucked happily on the balalaika. It took me a moment to remember the tune. Khizmit's national anthem.

Once a year, on April 2nd, I'd heard the anthem. Though, I confess, I'd never been very interested in celebrating Khizmit's Founding Day. *What had Khizmit done for me?* The day, a holiday for most of the Enclave, had held nothing for me other than a delayed start to my work. A single guard had come in with an old balalaika and played our anthem while all us inmates had listened impatiently.

The tune that came through Milena's window was the same and yet, different. Now that I stood in Khizmit, had tasted the food, and met the people, I had to admit that I felt more for this place than loathing. More than tolerance. The Preemptive Initiative was total slag, but there were things about this place worth fighting for, worth staying for.

The song stirred my emotions.

When I heard the rest of the house get up, I knew I hadn't been the only one who'd heard the music. I waited until I knew Zuzana was in the kitchen before I left the bedroom.

"Happy Koliada Eve," she said, tying an apron around her waist. "How'd you sleep?"

"Well," I said politely. "You?"

"Okay." She pulled a large black saucepan from a lower cabinet. "It'll be a busy day today! I don't imagine you've celebrated Koliada in Khizmit before, have you?"

"No."

"Can you bring me the milk?" She pointed to the fridge.

I walked over, pulled it open, and took out the tall glass

bottle. Meanwhile, she'd dumped something from a box into the saucepan and was uncapping a small jar of raisins.

"I'm making porridge now, and we'll have rabbit stew later for dinner before the parade. And we still have some baking to do for the neighbors. Then Rick will get the yule log. He usually brings a few." She talked about as fast as she added ingredients to the pot.

"Do you want me to help with anything?" I asked.

"No, go ahead and take a seat. I'll have you grab some bowls in a minute, but the porridge is not going to be ready right away."

I pulled out a chair, and she sighed before turning back to me.

"Actually, can you get a fire started?" She smiled and looked all the world like Emberly. "Oh, sorry." Her expression became apologetic. Her gaze went to my blackened hand. "I forgot about your burn. I'll have Rick do it when he gets up."

I stood. "I can do it."

I walked into the front room. Beside the fireplace was a tall, steel rack, which had previously been teeming with wood. Now it contained only half a dozen logs.

"If you're sure," Zuzana said from the kitchen. "You can use some of these bags to get it going."

I stepped back into the kitchen and found the paper bags from before folded neatly in the cabinet beside the refrigerator. In the same cabinet was a box of matches.

Zuzana hummed the anthem under her breath as I went back to the front room. Crumpling them up and tossing them in, the wrinkled brown paper caught fire quickly as I adjusted the logs above it, using only my right hand. The heat, even in small doses, caused my left hand to twitch in pain. I had to keep it away from the flames as they grew, licking and then engulfing the dry wood in the grate.

"It's tradition to cook over a fire today and tomorrow," Zuzana explained, bringing out a pot with a long handle. She transferred the contents of the small pot over to the larger one with the handle and then hung the porridge over the open flames on a trammel hook.

The door to Emberly's room swung open, and I walked toward the two girls as they emerged. Milena hurried ahead to the front room where Zuzana stirred the pot.

"Are you making caramels?" Milena asked, getting closer to the fireplace.

"Not until after breakfast," Zuzana replied. "Happy Koliada Eve." She kissed Milena on the top of her head.

I cleared my throat as I turned to Emberly. She wore her hair pulled up in a bun surrounded by a large braid. She shook her head at me when I opened my mouth to talk to her.

I shut it briefly, not sure why she'd silenced me. "I just wanted to say thank you," I said quickly. "For letting Markos know where I was. Otherwise, I…"

She spoke very quietly. "It was my fault. I talked you into leaving the house when my father had asked you not to. I gave you directions to Leticia's house. I let you go there alone. I never should have—"

"No," I reached for her, but then remembering that Zuzana or Markos could see us, I dropped my hands. "You helped me. I asked for your help. It wasn't—"

"It was my fault, and I'm very sorry." I can't say that I preferred this submissive, apologetic version of Emberly.

"I might have gone looking without you, and then I'd still be there," I said. "What you did was—"

"Stupid," she said loudly enough that Milena might have heard it over the clatter of dishes as they dished up some food.

"You're the furthest thing from stupid," I insisted, stepping toward her. She put out her hand, as if to ask me to stay away. I stepped backward.

"What I did was stupid, and I apologize." There was something in her tone that seemed almost demonstrative, even though we stood alone in the hallway. It wasn't the care-free attitude I'd seen every other time I'd been with her. There was a new formality, similar to how I spoke to Roman when he'd asked me to call him 'Sir.'

I realized what she was doing. She was building a wall between us. She was trying to obey the rules on fraterniza-tion. Though bizarre, I could almost hear her tacking a 'Sir' to the end of her statements to me.

"Well, thanks," I said, trying to end the conversation.

Markos opened his bedroom door. Behind him, I caught sight of a huge bed covered in a bold, blue blanket. He pulled the wooden door shut behind him just as Emberly slipped toward her bedroom. "Luka. You're up."

"Yes, Sir," I said, before remembering he didn't want me to be too formal with him in his house.

"Happy Koliada Eve," he said, glancing from me to Emberly. She stood in her open doorway staring at us.

"Happy Koliada Eve," she replied. She stepped out of her room and moved to hug her dad. I'd been right, back at Rhosivi, when I'd assumed he was a good husband and father. Watching them, I understood why he didn't want to involve his family in his work at the prisons.

"Breakfast is ready," Zuzana called from the front room.

Markos, Emberly, and I joined Milena and Zuzana in the kitchen.

"I'll get the pot," Markos said, grabbing a cloth and moving to the front room.

While he brought it in, Zuzana walked over to Emberly. "Happy Koliada Eve," she said, kissing her eldest daughter on the forehead.

Emberly returned the greeting and kissed her mother on the cheek. Markos set the pot on the table and smiled warmly before we all began to eat.

Distracted by everything I wanted to say to Emberly, I could hardly appreciate the porridge but still managed to finish two large bowls while I listened to Milena tell Markos all about the Koliada party they'd had at school.

Everyone cleaned up from breakfast, and then Zuzana and Emberly began reading a recipe from a small book. Milena, who'd been hanging on her dad's arm, went to join them when it became obvious that they were starting to make the caramels.

"I'm heading out for the yule log," Markos said as he pulled on his boots. "I have to go out to the woods, since you can see we're low on fuel anyway."

"Why don't you just use coal?" I asked, mostly sincerely, but there was a hint of unavoidable sardonicism in my voice.

"Khizmit spends so much time trying to find coal when we have all this lumber around us, and it's a perfectly good source of fuel. I think they just like making things complicated. Coal does have its advantages." Markos looked at me knowingly. "And it's disadvantages." He laced up his boot and pulled on the other one. "I won't be gone long. Just stick around here. Zuzana wanted to show you around the neighborhood."

"I'll be here," I said. He'd leave me alone with his wife and daughters. *How could he put so much trust in me?* To facilitate keeping my promise to him to stay away from Emberly, I thought maybe I should stay in my room until he returned.

"I'd take you with me, but I don't want to risk the guards asking about your burn at reentry."

"I understand," I said.

He walked down to the entryway and pulled open the door. After placing his revolver in its usual spot on his hip, he pulled out a long axe and heaved it over his shoulder.

Markos left me with a weighty feeling of responsibility that bore upon my shoulders. I was alone in the house with his wife and daughters. I had to, above all else, keep them safe. *But why did I feel this way?* It wasn't as though any of them were in danger. In fact, quite obviously, the most dangerous thing in the vicinity was me. I sat in the front room, on the couch, as I watched Markos disappear down the busy streets, passing groups of kids already half-dressed for the parade the next day.

I might have stayed sitting there until Markos returned if Zuzana hadn't invited me to join them in the kitchen.

"You don't have to," Zuzana insisted as she tied the back of Milena's apron. "But it might be fun."

"I'll help," I said, but it didn't appear that they needed my help at all. The three of them worked together as if they could communicate by thought alone. One of them stirred the milk constantly while the others measured out sugars and syrups and dumped them into the heating liquid.

"Can you bring us a bowl of clean snow?" Zuzana asked, passing me a large metal bowl.

I took it and went to the entryway where I slipped on my boots and unlocked the door. My gloves hung on a small hook, but since the chafing of the fabric made my burn hurt more, I decided to go without them.

Outside, snow covered everything, from the tips of the small fences and upper balconies to the branches of the trees and garlands strung between the buildings. Even the pathways, which had been muddied with dirt, currently were as white as the rooftops.

Down the street several paces, someone had parked a small food cart on the side of the road, and the snow on its roof looked to be the cleanest within reach. With my burned hand, I held the bottom of the metal bowl. Careful not to dig to the bottom, I scraped the snow into the bowl with my right hand until it was full. The bowl, now freezing cold from the snow, soothed my hand, even though I'd done a fair amount of healing on it.

With a creak, the door of the house nearest me opened, and a man in a dark overcoat stepped out, carrying a large axe.

"Happy Koliada Eve," he said. He looked at the bowl in my hands with a question in his expression.

"Happy Koliada Eve," I replied.

"You're staying with the Markos family." He looked back toward their front door.

It wasn't exactly a question, but I answered anyway. "Yes," I said.

"You a family friend?"

"Yes." I wanted to hurry back inside without giving any indication of my haste. Not family. But a friend. *Should I mention working with the Commander?* I didn't imagine it was normal to house your soldiers, so I kept my answers short. "Well, I'm one of his soldiers," I added quickly, just in case the neighbors began talking.

I decided to tell him a truth, since it seemed the least likely to get me into trouble without fueling any rumors about Emberly. I had to keep our stories consistent.

As the man continued to fasten the buttons on his coat, his expression was one that seemed ready to ask a question. "Wow, I didn't expect the Commander would be taking on interns."

"Yes, well, he doesn't usually. Made an exception for me. Not sure why." I took another few steps toward the door.

The man spoke again, and I had no choice but to turn and face him again. "I thought I'd seen you leave this morning with him. To get the yule log."

"Oh," I said, moving slowly back toward the Markos's door. "No, actually, I've injured my hand, so I wouldn't be much help with that."

The man looked at my hand which held the bowl, as if he'd be able to assess the problem. "What sort of injury?" he asked.

"A burn."

"Must be bad," he said, and this time, he didn't try to conceal his disbelief.

Perhaps, I thought, *if I show him the burn and he can see that this part of the story is true, he'll be more inclined to believe the rest of what I've told him.*

"Do you want to see it?" I asked. "It's not pretty."

I moved the bowl to my right hand. Here in the white world, my hand looked displaced and sinister. Scabs covered large cracks along my knuckles and fingernails.

"That's something," he said, getting up close.

With my palm and wrist down, keeping his attention on my hand, I agreed with him. "I better hurry inside," I said. "Zuzana asked me to bring this in for the caramels."

The man finally smiled. It seemed that my burn had inspired him to trust me. "Be sure to bring some by. My wife loves those."

"We will," I replied and hurried back to the Markos's house.

Zuzana was counting out loud over the boiling pot of caramels. Milena dumped some water into the bowl with the snow, which melted it just before Emberly took a spoonful of the caramel and dunked it into the ice water. After keeping it in for a second, she pulled it up, and the caramel slipped off the spoon like thick honey.

"A little longer," Emberly said.

Milena reached a spoon into the pot of caramel and followed suit, dropping it into the bowl I'd filled. Once it had cooled, she popped it into her mouth. "Mmm," she said. "But probably still not ready."

"Grab a spoon," Zuzana said to me, pointing with her free hand to a pile of them beside the fireplace. Somehow, despite how quickly they worked, there wasn't a sense of urgency as much as excitement.

I scooped a small portion of caramel out and put it in the water.

"You can try it now," Emberly said.

When I popped the spoonful of watery caramel into my

mouth, I wished I'd scooped twice as much. It was smooth and warm and rich.

"How is it?" Zuzana asked.

"Delicious," I replied.

"And the texture?"

"I don't know what it's supposed to be," I confessed.

Emberly took another sample and tested it in the water. "It's ready," she announced.

Her mother grabbed a cloth and grasped the handle of the pot. As she rushed into the kitchen, we followed. While I'd been outside someone had chopped nuts and placed them in the bottom of a rectangular pan. Zuzana poured the caramels on top of them, slowly enough that they didn't scatter as the caramel flowed and filled the pan.

The pot sizzled as she placed it into the wet sink, and then, using the same cloth, she wiped her forehead which had beaded with sweat.

While the caramels cooled, I told Zuzana about my exchange with her neighbor. Though she said it was fine, lines of concern crossed her face.

"Ember, will you take these outside while they cool?" Zuzana asked as Emberly bit back any comments about the neighbor I'd spoken to. She had thoughts—I could see them flickering behind her eyes. She just smiled at me and then took a cloth, covered the caramels, and went through the front door to set the pan on their snowy steps.

Zuzana went to the back room, and Milena snacked on the few nuts scattered across the tabletop that hadn't made it into the pan. Zuzana came back with three pairs of scissors and colorful paper which she explained was for us to cut and then wrap around the caramels.

"How long will you be here?" Milena asked me as we cut paper.

"Just a couple more days."

"And then are you going with my dad to The Outskirts?" Her words were weighted and heavy.

"Yes."

"When he comes back, will you come back with him?" She moved her blue papers to the center of the table and began cutting a piece of paper with yellow birds.

"I don't think so," I replied.

"Well, you should." I smiled at this to her, and she blushed. "I like having you here. Ember is too shy to say it, but she likes you."

"Milena," Zuzana chided, but her tone wasn't serious.

"She does," Milena said, and the squares she'd been cutting began to have crooked edges as she used the scissors more aggressively. "She told me you're the most handsome boy she'd ever met and that you're brave and—"

"Would Ember appreciate you telling all of this to him?" Zuzana took some of the squares Milena had cut and fixed the edges.

"She's too shy to admit it, but it's true. She can't stop thinking about you." Milena smiled at me, as if the information should have been embarrassing to either me or Emberly, but instead, it made me want to go outside and check on the caramels. At least, it meant that she wasn't upset with me.

"Milena," Zuzana said, her voice sterner this time. "When someone tells us a secret, they're trusting us. You don't want to compromise the trust your sister has in you."

"Fine," she muttered, looking up at me through her eyelashes. "But when Ember gets all weak in the knees and falls on her face, you don't have to worry. It's just because she's obsessed." The grin on her face told me how pleased she was to have gotten a last word in.

"Milena." Zuzana sighed.

"Well, I'm not too shy to say it. I think you're very handsome and I like you and I hope you also come back from war with my dad."

"I'm sorry," Zuzana said to me before turning back to her youngest daughter. "That's not really a way to make our guest feel welcome. You're going to make him uncomfortable."

Milena scowled. "Everyone in this whole family talks about Luka. Dad and you and Ember, and the one time I do, I get into trouble."

"It's fine," I said. *Obsessed?* I couldn't help but smile. *Ember was 'obsessed'?*

"Why don't you go switch places with your sister now," Zuzana suggested, but we all knew it wasn't optional.

Milena got up, sighed dramatically, and then hurried down the steps to the front door.

"Probably best we don't mention any of that to Ember," Zuzana said suddenly. "She'd be so embarrassed."

"I won't bring it up," I agreed.

But I wasn't going to forget it either.

CHAPTER 18
THE NEPHEW

FOR SOMEONE WHO WAS OBSESSED, Ember sure did a good job of not talking to me much once she came inside. Walls, that's what it had to be. Walls to keep me out.

Commander Markos must have asked her to stay away from me. Or maybe she'd only pretended not to be scared when she found out I was a lurper. Maybe now that she'd had some time to think about it, she'd have some good sense to keep me at arm's length.

But she didn't keep me at an arm's length. Not exactly. Once, her hand brushed mine, but she didn't notice or didn't care. I tried, unsuccessfully, to brush my fingers across her hand again, but by then, she'd scooted away and had begun cutting the red ribbon into smaller pieces.

Milena brought in the cooled caramels about fifteen minutes later. She tried to take the seat beside me, but her mother insisted she sit across from me instead. It took a bit of effort to suppress the chuckle that rose when I saw her scowl before obeying.

We cut the caramel into small pieces and began wrapping them in the paper before putting them into the little bags that Milena tied with a ribbon. I wasn't a great help with my hand stiff and sore, but I could hand Ember single pieces of the paper for her to use.

We snacked on the caramels with such frequency, it was a wonder we still had as many to deliver as we did. When Zuzana announced that we'd be making our rounds to the neighbors, I offered to stay home.

"I don't want to raise any suspicion," I said.

"They already know you're here, and I'm sure they've all discussed what you're doing at our home anyway. If we go see them, they can ask their questions, and maybe that will give some relief to their insatiable need to gossip."

Zuzana handed me four bags of caramels to carry. She knew, just like Ember and Markos, that beneath my glove and burned hand was a tattoo. She didn't know what I could do, and somehow, she showed me kindness anyway.

By the time we left to deliver the caramels, small rivulets trailed down sides of the buildings and railings as the snow melted in the bright sun. The path, which had been pristine before, now bore deep brown tracks where wheels had packed down the snow and mud.

To avoid needless looks, I'd tugged on my gloves, wincing soundlessly as I tightened the strap around my wrist. Just as I'd winced, the pain disappeared, without any prompting from me. Curiously, I poked at my burned hand, feeling nothing more than the subtle sensation of pins and needles. *Were my abilities becoming unconscious? Would it get to the point where my body would stop pain before I ever felt it?*

Lest I draw any attention to my concern, I hurried behind Emberly, Milena, and Zuzana. Milena, in a floral yellow coat, had brown boots that turned dark as they became wet. Zuzana, wearing a light blue coat that fell past her knees, looked like a dancing snowflake as she walked along the path. A word came to mind from earlier as I looked at Emberly in her bold, navy-blue coat. *Obsessed.*

I smiled just as she turned and caught me looking at her. I

don't know who blushed more between us, but I didn't look away.

The first door we stopped at had a bushy green wreath adorned with a small candle in the center, which, for obvious reasons, hadn't been lit.

A girl, somewhere around Milena's age, opened the door. "Lena!" she said, wrapping her arms around Milena. "Happy Koliada Eve!"

Milena handed her a bag with the caramels.

The girl's wide brown eyes paused as she looked at me, but she didn't ask any questions. Her gaze flitted over my ill-fitting pants and my military gloves, which were quite obviously the nicest thing I owned.

"Mama," the girl said. "The Markoses are here."

As a woman approached the door, Emberly, Milena, and Zuzana began to sing:

"We come to your door,
With caramel,
Sharing the news,
All will be well."

The music grew livelier, and Milena drummed on her legs, the soft thump adding rhythm to their carol.

"Spring is on its way.
Night will turn to day,
Brighter and brighter
Brighter and brighter."

Here, their voices separated, Emberly's voice rising higher than either of the others as she held a single note. Then they sang together again, and the pleasant song slowed.

"Life will be kind,
Life will be long,
This is our gift.
This is our song."

As the song ended, the audience, which had grown to five

by now, broke into applause. If not for my hand, I would have joined in.

"Absolutely lovely," the woman at the door said. As she clapped, small plumes of flour fell from her hands. "Thank you, Zuzana. Happy Koliada Eve!" She turned back inside the door and reached for a small bag from one of her own children. She handed the bag to Zuzana. Then she turned to me. "I packed enough for everyone. I heard you had a guest this year."

Zuzana turned to the side to allow a full view of me to the family inside the door. "This is Luka. He works with Pedrick."

"Nice to meet you," the woman said, dipping her head to me. The man, who I'd only seen briefly through the doorframe, stood and approached us. As he came to the door, the three children hurried back inside, their giggles only interrupted by the wrinkling of paper as they dove into the caramels.

"Happy Koliada Eve," the man said, extending his hand to me.

I reached out and shook his, repeating the customary greeting.

"You're a soldier then?" he asked.

I nodded.

"It's a noble profession," the man said. "Even if this war has gone on too long."

"Far too long," I said, since it felt like a safe reply.

Zuzana, bless her, must have felt my apprehension at continuing the conversation anymore, because she leaned in and kissed her friend on the cheek before quickly saying, "Well, we have lots to deliver before it gets late."

They finally shut their door, and we began walking down the path again.

"Mom, can I have one of these?" Milena asked as she peered into the bag the neighbor had given them.

"Just one," Zuzana said, noticing that I hung back with Emberly. "Bring me one too." She smiled at me as Milena hurried forward, giving me and Emberly a little distance.

"What's the war about?" I whispered to Emberly. "If someone asks me, I want to be able to answer. Why is Latvani attacking Khizmit?"

She stopped walking as she answered, "We're an Enclave. It means we're the minority here. I don't think war ever has a simple explanation. It's not about resources, since Latvani has plenty. And I don't think it's about territory either. The simplest explanation I've heard is that they feel threatened by us. They want to take over Khizmit and put their own leaders in power here. I heard my father once say they were motivated by revenge, but he didn't elaborate. You know how he can be secretive at times."

I nodded. "So, they don't want to kill us all?"

"I don't know," she said. "They just want to take over."

"And what? Incarcerate everyone?"

She didn't even look to see if her mother was watching as she placed her hand gently on mine. "Don't worry, Luka. You're not going back to prison." Her eyes, wide and reassuring, glistened with sincerity. "You're free now."

Zuzana knocked on the next door, and Emberly dropped her hand. She hurried forward to join her sister and mother as they began their song again.

The next four houses also gave us goodies, and I only knew what the bags contained because of how Milena dug through each one immediately, announcing the contents with glee.

"Fried cookies!" she said after one.

"Spiced honey cakes!" she announced as she ripped open another bag.

At one house, they gave us a decorative tin, which Milena had barely touched before pulling off the lid. "Zserbo!" she said, pulling out a triangular layered cookie.

"Try one," she offered, holding the treat out for me.

The cake was frosted with dark chocolate and filled with apricot jelly and toasted nuts. I swallowed, wishing I'd taken smaller bites. It was in moments like this that I decided Khizmit really was a utopia. In some small way, I didn't entirely blame Chancellor Dulka for wanting to keep these people and their traditions safe.

I thought about all the inmates in Rhosivi, Predvoi, and Vazenia. The taste of walnuts and cocoa turned bitter in my mouth. I thought of Lockbox, used only for his mind and memory, certain he wasn't currently enjoying spiced honey cakes or zserbo.

"Want another?" Milena asked, scooting closer to me with another piece in her gloved hand.

"No, thank you."

We stood in front of a yellow door decorated with a mask rather than a wreath. The mask had horns and looked as if it had been made, at least in part, from a real animal skull. Tiny designs had been painted into the sides, and feathers were tied around the base of the horns with fine twine, only visible if I adjusted my eyesight to focus on it. Of all my senses, hearing was the one that responded best to my amplification. Sometimes I wondered though, if other Juliets, Kilos, or Limas could smell, taste, or see in an amplified way with their mutations. Maybe Roman's assessment was right about Kilos and eyesight.

The door swung open, revealing a man with a black cane. His eyes were alert compared to the rest of his face, which looked somewhat mournful. His knobbed fingers gripped the handle of the cane, and as we sang, a slight smile crossed his face.

"Come over, Brita," he called over his shoulder.

A woman, who didn't appear to be quite as elderly, shuffled down the steps and listened to the song. While most of their neighbors had looked at Emberly and Milena as they sang, or hungrily at the bag of goodies, Brita stared unflinchingly at me.

She didn't even clap as the song ended and instead broke through the last note with, "Who's he?"

"This is Luka," Zuzana said, holding out one of our last bags of caramels.

Brita took them and continued to look at me. "Is he a relative?"

"No," Zuzana replied. "He's a friend."

Brita smiled and turned to Emberly. "A friend of yours?"

"A friend of the family," Zuzana answered before Emberly could.

"Worth asking. I've heard you're quite popular with the young men."

At her remark, Emberly clenched her jaw so hard I could see her cheeks and neck tense.

Brita leaned into Zuzana. "Not that I blame her one bit. Or them. You have lovely daughters."

"Thank you," Zuzana said with little more sincerity than I'd ever given Warden Velky.

"Please excuse my wife," the man said, placing his free hand on her back. "Won't you come in for a minute? I hate to complain, but we did just get the house warm."

"We'll be off," Zuzana said.

"Please stay," the man urged. "Just for a moment."

"My fingers are getting cold," Milena said, blowing warm air into her cupped hands.

"Just for a minute or two," Zuzana agreed.

Hesitantly, I followed Zuzana as she stepped inside the home, which had an identical layout as the Markos's house. We walked into a small entryway where a basket of boots rested in a mound on the brown tile.

The scents of peppermint and pine slammed into me. Though I tried to dial back my senses, I'm not sure it worked, for in those few moments, the thud of boots hitting the floor as both Emberly and Milena removed theirs and tossed them into the basket nearly forced my hands up to my ears.

Their living room, warmed by a fire which roared in the grate, had three small couches. Two almost matched, but the last one, with thick wooden legs and discolored patterned cushions, looked out of place. As out of place as me with the Markos women.

I took a seat as Brita shuffled into the kitchen. "Emberly, can you give me a hand?" she called.

From here I couldn't see into the kitchen, but the clatter of cups and whistling tea kettle told me what was coming. Emberly followed her, and then the two of them returned with hands full of small teacups.

"Luka, was it?" the man asked as he settled himself onto the brown couch nearest the fire.

"Yes," I said.

"I take it you don't have family to spend the holidays with?"

I paused before answering as Emberly returned with the kettle and began filling the small mauve and beige cups. "No, unfortunately not," I said, reaching for a cup.

"Well, it's nice they let some of the soldiers come home for the holidays. At least Latvani is civil enough not to fight this week."

Brita bustled back in with some napkins which she placed on the table before taking her own teacup. "I'd hardly call agreeing not to kill anyone on the week of Koliada kindness." She sighed and took a sip, but even as she drank, it was clear she had more to say. "It's a shame the guards at Rhosivi, Vazenia, and Predvoi don't get to come home for the holidays."

"Mmm," Zuzana murmured before blowing into her cup.

Milena had removed her gloves and was using the teacup to warm her fingers. "I think working in the prison is the most important job someone can do," she said, no doubt thinking of her own father and how many nights he'd spent there instead of home.

"Where is Pedrick?" Brita asked, looking back at me suspiciously.

"The forest. Getting a yule log."

"Of course," Brita said, sipping her tea, which seemed to have almost burned her for how quickly she drew back. "And why aren't you with him?"

"I'm not his son," I said, deciding that explanation was better than bringing up my burned hand.

"True." Brita looked to Zuzana. "He might have liked having a son, don't you think?"

Zuzana inhaled sharply through her nose and lifted her head up. "He likes having daughters."

"Well, in any event, I was hoping to see Pedrick. I wanted to ask him about Rhosivi and Predvoi. He must know about Predvoi even though he didn't work there, right? He was the Head Warden at Rhosivi all those years."

Zuzana gulped her tea, which must have been quite warm, but maybe she was trying to rush out the door. "He was, but he isn't anymore. He's serving at the war front now, so I'm afraid he wouldn't be able to tell you much about our efforts in the prisons. Most of it's classified anyway."

"Oh, no, you misunderstood," Brita said, setting her teacup down. She leaned forward and took the bag of caramels from the table. "I wanted to ask him about Rhosivi. Maybe *you* could answer some questions for me."

"I doubt it," Zuzana said as Brita opened her first caramel.

An uncomfortable silence followed until Milena adjusted in her seat so obviously about to speak that no one else did. "You could ask Luka your question," she said innocently. "Luka worked with my dad at Rhosivi."

All eyes were on me in that second. Milena must have heard Markos talk about me to his wife and undoubtedly concluded that I was a guard rather than an inmate.

"Did you spend time at Rhosivi?" Brita asked, leaning forward curiously as she chewed the caramel with a partially open mouth.

"Yes," I said. "More time than I would have liked."

"I'm sure. Terrible place. They said Predvoi is safer than working at Rhosivi, but I haven't heard of a casualty from there in at least a year."

I knew at once that by casualty, she meant guards. Inmate deaths didn't count. I grit my teeth.

She reached her finger into her mouth to dislodge a nut from one of her molars before she sucked on that fingernail. With a pop, she took her finger out of her mouth and turned her attention to me. "How about Predvoi? Have you been there?"

"Yes," I said, keeping my answer clipped.

"Better than Rhosivi, wasn't it?"

I shifted on the couch, only glancing over to Emberly once. In order to keep Markos's family safe, I had to lie convincingly. That didn't have to be difficult. I sat up straighter, deciding to act like Roman as I answered her questions. "Predvoi has a very different setup than Rhosivi. Fewer guards at Predvoi, but lower risk inmates."

"Did they send you into the mine sometimes at Rhosivi? I heard that's one of the more dangerous aspects of that station. Sometimes, they send guards down into the tunnels to find inmates or make sure they're working. I can't imagine going down there." Though the woman had kept talking after her question, she stared at me, waiting for an answer.

"I've been into the mines at Rhosivi. They sent me in there often."

"With a weapon."

"Not usually. It would have been too easy for some of the inmates to disarm me and use the weapon on guards or other inmates."

"Terrifying." She shuttered, the teacup clattering against

the plate as she moved to set them both down. "That they would send our young men down there with those skrags—"

"Brita!" her husband cut in. He jerked his head toward Milena. "There are children present."

"I'm not sorry," she said bitterly to her husband before facing me again.

"Our nephew was stationed at Predvoi," she said, unwrapping a second caramel. "We'd hoped he'd be safer there than on the front lines. After all, we hear the stories of that Lurper Legion getting out of hand and so many cases of..." Her gaze went to Milena. "...friendly fire." Brita reached out and grabbed Zuzana's hand. "Not since Pedrick took command, mind you. But even he can't expect to control everything that happens out there."

"No, he can't," Zuzana said, obviously trying to keep a smile on her face.

I tried to make my face a stone as I'd often seen Roman and Markos do. Friendly fire. Lurpers killing lurpers. *Mind your breathing,* I told myself.

"You know what happened to our nephew just last week at Predvoi?"

"Brita," the man said, prodding the fire. "Let's not bring down the celebration with our news."

She didn't respond to his request in the slightest. "He was killed at Predvoi Prison. Just four days ago, a skrag killed him."

My blood went cold. *Four days ago.*

"One of his friends said it was a Victor who did it. Another said it was an X-ray."

All at once the memory suffocated me.

I'd thrown the knife right into his throat. The sticky gasp echoed through my head. His body falling, his red blood melting the snow around him.

"But, Brita," her husband said, giving Zuzana an apologetic look "they don't even keep those at Predvoi. You've seen

Dulka's graduation rates. She doesn't accept those prisoners anyway. She sends them to the front."

I couldn't swallow. The room seemed to be shrinking and spinning around me.

"He died a hero. He was the only thing standing between that monster and Khizmit, and he stood his ground."

Monster. That monster.

Milena gasped. "What happened?"

Brita, evidently happy to have an audience no matter the age, stared Milena right in the face. "One of those inmates tried to escape, and our nephew, may he rest in peace, stopped him. He held him off long enough for the rest of the guards to get him."

"So, he didn't escape?" Emberly asked, offering her first comment of the visit.

"No," the husband said. "Don't worry. No one can escape from Predvoi. They killed the inmate."

"They killed him for trying to escape?" Emberly asked.

"They don't really need a reason to kill them. Do they?" the woman asked me.

I looked to Zuzana, whose expression didn't give me much direction. "They need a reason, but certainly attempted escape would do it," I answered. Successful escape. I succeeded. They didn't suspect me. I glanced over at Emberly. *Did she suspect me?*

Her attention stayed fixed on Brita. Her expression of irritation gave me hope. She sympathized with lurpers. Obviously, I'd known that from how she'd reacted to my confession, but here she sat, almost defending us to her neighbor.

Markos wouldn't have approved.

Brita spoke loudly. "I've heard Velky's proposition. He thinks they should bury all the skrags—"

"Brita!" the man said again.

She scowled. "Fine. He thinks we should bury the lurpers

in those mines and shut the prison down permanently. Redirect all our efforts to the front lines rather than waste good men at Rhosivi. It's not like they're worth the money and time. Don't you think so? You were there. What was your impression?" Brita bulged her eyes at me.

I had to be careful. *What did I think? It didn't matter what I thought. I could have woven a lie and sold it without a problem, but I wondered what I thought should be done with people like me.* I thought Velky should be buried in slag or thrown into the furnace with the coal he'd valued above the lives of boys.

But having been there, I also didn't think they should throw the prison gates open and let everyone re-enter Khizmit freely. The image of Romeo-22, Flak, or Ice walking down the street where Milena played with her friends ignited fear in me.

I took a breath and answered the best I could. "I think Chancellor Dulka has a better idea. Reform who we can. Test them for threat levels. Track them if they graduate."

"But she graduates so many of them!" Brita complained before stuffing another caramel into her mouth. "She kept an inmate there who murdered our nephew. Can you imagine how devastated my sister is? Days before Koliada, a captain comes to her home to deliver her boy's body. He'd already been dead for two days before they were allowed to bring the body back here. They tried to clean him up, but his throat…" She reached her wrinkled hand up to her own throat. "I think they should kill them all."

A shiver went down my spine, and I must not have kept my expression as controlled as I should.

"Look at you," Brita said, wagging the paper in her hand at me. "You're sick just remembering your time there." She picked at a nut in her teeth again, and I looked down at my gloved hands. The hands that had killed her nephew.

"I'm so sorry for your loss," Zuzana said, taking advantage of the silence. "We have to get going."

"Yes, just a moment." Brita dabbed at her eyes with the corner of her apron. She went back to the kitchen, so we all stood, except for her husband, and moved toward the stairs. Brita met us at the top with a loaf of braided bread.

"Thank you," Zuzana said, taking the loaf and walking down the steps. She began putting her boots on, and I moved to join them.

Brita caught my arm as I walked past. Her watery eyes met mine. "Thank you for your service," she said sweetly. "I wish my nephew hadn't been killed, that he could join us this holiday, but thank Veles you made it home." A tear trickled down her face as she said it.

"I'm sorry," I said, my hands shaking in my gloves. "I wish he could have made it home, too." I paused momentarily before patting her gently on the shoulder as I asked a question I didn't really want the answer to.

"Your nephew, what was his name?"

CHAPTER 19
PRIVATE PETROV

A WHIRLWIND of emotions spun inside me as we left the neighbors, and Zuzana, either cognizant of my emotional state or tired herself from the interactions, led us back to her house rather than on to another neighbor's house.

I hurried to my room and locked the door before dropping to the blankets.

"Yatsenko. Dimitar Yatsenko." I repeated the name in my head, muttering it as I committed it to memory. Goyle's real name was Dimitar, and he'd had a family that cared for him. A future. A life. And I'd stolen it from him.

I covered my face with my hands, still gloved, and sobbed silently. For what I'd done. For what I was.

But then Brita's other words came back to me. She'd called people like me 'skrags.' She wanted every single one of us to die. It had come down to me or Dimitar. I only did what I had to do to survive. To get a chance at a life. *Was that fair, or was I trying to justify a horrific crime?*

I tried not to think too hard on Dimitar, even though the memory of the moment I'd killed him resurfaced time and time again.

To keep the guilt at bay, I indulged in daydreams of marching through Khizmit with an army and taking over under Markos's leadership. I smiled, imagining locking Dulka and Velky in the cells I'd grown up in. I must have fallen asleep at some point because the next thing I heard was Markos's voice. I sat up, wiping a small trail of spit off my cheek.

"Where's Luka?" his voice carried to me. I sat up, then listened as Zuzana relayed what Brita had said. I had no doubt Markos would know that I'd been the one to kill their neighbor's nephew.

Sounds from the kitchen told me that dinner was in progress. Despite my hunger, I couldn't eat, not with the roiling in my gut.

Milena and Emberly were both helping their mom make rabbit stew, and soon the sound of chopping vegetables and the scraping of dishes replaced the conversation about what gift Milena hoped she'd be getting at the end of the festival.

I almost left the room to go talk to Markos, but I heard him already coming down the hallway. He knocked on the door and whispered my name.

When I pulled the door open, Markos gave me a quick look. His face was red from the cold, especially around his eyes. Small icicles covered his eyebrows and eyelashes. He still wore his thick pants, and his socks were dark where the snow had melted through his boots. Though he presently didn't have any hat on, it was clear he'd only recently removed one by how disheveled his hair was.

"Can I come in?" he asked. I stepped aside and he entered. "It's a bit warm for those, don't you think?" He gestured to my gloves.

I removed them slowly, ashamed of the burned black skin as if it were an extension of the black ink on my wrist.

"I heard about what happened."

I just nodded.

"Dimitar deserves to be mourned, just as much as Smoke or any other boy or man. But no one mourned Smoke. No one missed him this Koliada. That's something we're fighting to change. This is a war no different from the one on the border, and while Dimitar's death was tragic, it wasn't preventable. As a guard at Predvoi, he picked a side." Markos took a seat beside me, dropping a few chunks of snow onto the pile of blankets as he did so. "You had to escape. You deserve a life just as much as anyone. Dimitar wouldn't have allowed you to leave. You had no choice."

"I could have chosen to stay. You said you were trying to get me assigned to your unit. I should have waited rather than escape."

Markos shook his head and clapped me on the shoulder. "There were no guarantees with Dulka. You did what you had to. You've always fought against hope. But it's resilient, like you. There were days I didn't see it in your face, and other days, it shined so brilliantly, I was sure you'd grow wings and fly out of Rhosivi. But you've learned that hope isn't just sitting around, waiting for someone else to do something, waiting for things to change all on their own. Hope is actionable. You had hope that you could change your future. You acted on that. You escaped."

He was right.

He turned to me. "You've changed," he said. "You've changed a lot since Rhosivi. Not just the scar." My hand went to my cheek. "But that makes a difference too."

I absentmindedly scratched my face. I'd never gone so long without a haircut or a shave.

"I'm sorry that you have someone's death on your hands. It doesn't get easier. If we dwell on the past, we can't live in the present. We can't plan for the future." Markos stood back up. Noticing the small drops of water now falling from his coat, he moved away from the blankets. "Luka," he said, and I stood. "I'm proud of you."

The four words shouldn't have felt as good as they did,

but their effect was like a healing balm for my guilt and grief. "Thank you, Sir," I said.

"There's a certain Oscar I'm planning to visit tomorrow."

Hope flickered inside my chest. *Lockbox.* "Tomorrow?"

"You thought I spent all day finding a log?"

"I...I don't know."

"If we don't do it tomorrow, it won't happen."

"What's the plan, Sir?"

"I'm heading back out to get a few supplies. You going to join us for dinner?"

I shook my head. "I'm going to stay in here for the rest of the night, if that's okay."

He nodded, not asking why. "Get some rest. I'll tell you everything tomorrow morning. At the church."

I understood what he didn't have to say. Roman, Lockbox, and I were about to have one helluva reunion.

———

Markos walked alongside me part of the way to the church.

The sun had barely graced the sky with its light when Markos had woken me up. Not with "On your feet, lurper," like so many times before. He'd tapped the door lightly and called my name. 'Luka' sounded more like me now. It no longer took me a few seconds to respond anymore.

Though the sun was up, the wind still carried a frosty bite, which reminded me of Rhosivi. Here I was, trailing Commander Markos through Khizmit. It was far beyond anything I'd imagined.

Despite not wearing his uniform, many of the people we passed recognized him. Some greeted him with a wave, others hurried past in the other direction, and some looked at him with reverence in their eyes.

When we were only a few blocks from the church, Markos

whispered directions for the rest of the way, and I hurried on without him.

A row of candles illuminated glowing halos on the sides of the dark wood of the church. I approached reverently, Dimitar's name in my head. *Forgive me,* I thought as I pulled the cold handle of the door.

I recognized the sole silhouette as Roman, even from across the chapel.

He turned and stood. "You alone?" he asked as I got close.

"Yes, Markos should be coming soon."

"Good," he said.

I debated telling him Dimitar's name. Maybe confessing his name and admitting the final act of desecrating his grave would give me closure. Perhaps telling Roman what I'd done would seal the act into my memory, and his, forever.

"We can't walk into the Grand Palace, grab Lockbox, and leave," Roman said as he pulled a black bag from beneath a pew, his voice drawing me back to the present and our current objective. "We can't stash him in a sack, fake his death, or fight our way out."

That was a long list of things that we couldn't do. Roman unzipped the bag. It was filled with pieces of a uniform but seemed to take up much more space than it had yesterday.

"We can't give anyone a reason to test your blood."

"Can we get him out or not?" I asked impatiently.

Roman pulled out a uniform top and held it out to me. "Markos believes we can. And if he says we can, then we can."

I took the uniform into my hand, and Roman pulled out a matching top.

"Do I..." The uniform disgusted me.

"We're going as soldiers under Markos on official business. You're Private Petrov."

"Who was Private Petrov?"

"Could be anyone. There are almost a hundred soldiers with that last name in the Enclave."

Wearing this uniform would make others see me as a cruster. Private Petrov.

Roman changed his pants. I followed suit.

Had it been any other lurper who needed my help, I'd have said forget it. But this was Lockbox. *For Lockbox,* I thought. *Only for Lockbox.*

The uniform fit perfectly, and with it on, I could have passed as Roman's brother. He pulled out a silver circle patch and slapped it onto my shoulder. I fastened the buttons of the shirt and flattened the fabric. Skudge it all, it fit better than anything I'd ever worn.

"Looking good, Private," Roman said. He checked his own patches and adjusted a couple of mine.

"Was this yours?"

"All except that patch." He motioned to the patch that told the world I was a private. "Wasn't too hard to get a hold of."

"Is there a difference between the gold circle and the silver?" I asked.

"You get silver when you've been in longer but aren't promotable to korporal. They're all called privates, so you don't need to stress it."

The door to the chapel creaked open, and Markos stepped in. He turned and slid a giant beam into place to seal the door before he strode toward us.

Markos carried a large bag out of which several long poles protruded. He had to have stuffed it full of supplies the previous day and stashed it nearby.

"This is your gear. If anyone asks, tell them you just got it from the Central Issue Facility."

"What are the poles for?"

"Constructing a tent."

"What do I need a tent for?"

"You don't. But if anyone asks, that's what it is."

I grabbed the bag and slung it over my shoulder.

Roman tossed a small brown ushanka over, and I pulled it on. It didn't have a place for a rank patch, but perhaps that was common for lower ranking soldiers.

"Strap this on," Roman said. He handed me his staghorn dagger and the leather sheath.

"Privates don't usually…" I trailed off. *What did I know about what privates did or didn't do?*

"Yes, they don't usually have anything more than a palka, but trust me, you'll need this."

I strapped it on my right side without any further questions.

Markos quickly talked us through the plan, which relied heavily on Lockbox being able to ascertain our motives and work through what we expected from him.

"Did he read all the books I sent?" Markos asked.

"The books you sent?"

"The books in your trunk that I gave Roman to give you. Did Lockbox read them all?"

And to think, I'd assumed the trunk had been from Dulka.

"I think he read them all, yes."

"That's fine," Markos said. "If he read them, he'll know what to do."

I dug deep in my memory to see if the supplies in my bag reminded me of anything from my books, but all it did was make me certain that I was not an Oscar.

Our job was not to free Lockbox. Our job was to give him the tools he needed to escape on his own.

"We have one shot at this," Markos said. "Let's try not to skudge it up."

———

The doors to the Grand Palace were plated in gold just like the giant dome at the top that sat beneath the weathered green spire. Armed sentries stood at the doors and saluted Markos as we walked up the steps. I followed behind Roman, carrying my bag of gear.

The sentry nearest the door pushed it open for Markos and saluted. Markos stiffly saluted back. Roman saluted back. I hurried and raised my own hand in a salute to the sentry. The two silver bars of his rank patch told me he was a korporal.

I'd have assumed that door duty would be given to lower ranking soldiers. The job was more serious than I'd thought it to be.

We walked past a desk, and no one stopped Markos. He was in his element now. He marched across the lobby, his familiar, assertive gait guiding me.

No one asked him any questions or for any identification until we'd climbed two flights of stairs and passed at least two dozen guards. Three of them had been Captains.

A korporal stood, rifle in hand, blocking the door in front of Markos.

"Good afternoon, Sir," he said.

"I'm here to discuss a security threat with Chancellor Eldrat or High Captain Voboda."

"We can have a messenger patch it through."

"We cannot," Markos replied. "Open the door and let High Captain Voboda know I'm here concerning Oscar-17."

"Yes, Sir," the korporal replied.

He stepped to the side, and we hurried down another hallway through three more steel doors that required keyed entry and climbed eleven flights of stairs.

The bag over my shoulder grew heavy. My fingers became sweaty with every step that took me closer to my friend. Not from exertion, but from anxiety of what would come next.

We reached a small landing at the base of the dome and paused briefly while Markos discussed his reasons for being here with another korporal. To my right, a small window afforded a minimal view of Khizmit, so there wasn't much to see from this vantage point.

Markos had explained that security was light today as many of the guards were away on account of it being Koliada. Our options for helping Lockbox were limited to today or tomorrow. And tomorrow was never guaranteed.

If this was the Grand Palace with light security, Lockbox really didn't have a shot at escape. I'd have thought they'd spare more of these men for detail up at Rhosivi or Predvoi.

But those were prisons. They held lurpers.

This place held secrets.

"Who is with you?" The korporal in conversation with Markos stepped to the side to look at us.

"Captain Kral and Private Petrov."

"He will need to place his bag in the briefing room before advancing past this point," the korporal said.

He opened the door closest to us. It was as Markos had described back at the church. They occasionally used this room for meetings since the wide window looked out over the east of Khizmit. It was stunning in the brightening morning as all the city lights and candles began to wink out below, day dawning around the city.

I dropped my gear into the far corner so it wasn't immediately visible when someone opened the door. The rest of the room was completely empty.

When I exited, I immediately identified the High Captain. It wasn't just the silver pinecone that gave him away. It was the pungent air of authority he exuded even in Commander Markos's presence.

High Captain Voboda was thin. He had a pointed nose and chin. His dark hair was slick and shiny as if it hadn't been washed in weeks. He stepped out from behind the heavy steel door and shook hands with Markos.

"I know you're disappointed with the auction, but this is a

bit extreme," High Captain Voboda said. "Chancellor Eldrat has made it clear—"

"There's a security threat." Markos didn't wait for High Captain Voboda to respond. "Oscar-17. We need to see him immediately."

"Oscar-17 is contained."

"The security threat regards intel he may have."

"And you think you'll be able to get him to crack? You think he'll share something with you?"

Markos stepped to the side, making me completely visible to the High Captain.

"This is Private Petrov and Captain Kral. They both know the Oscar from Predvoi."

"So?"

"They know where to apply pressure on the Oscar. I believe they can get the Oscar to give us the information we need. As soon as we have it, you'll be privy as well."

"What is the nature of the security threat?"

Markos cleared his throat. "I was at Predvoi, voting for the execution of a high-interest inmate there. Did you hear about him?"

"Only rumors."

"What did you hear?"

"An X-Ray, Victor mix? Is it true?"

"It's true," Markos said. "As you may know, Oscar-17 was cellmates with the inmate known as Victor-27 before his auction. Victor-27 made an attempt to escape Predvoi. He got skudging close, too, before Captain Kral caught up to him and subdued the threat."

"Subdued?" High Captain Voboda asked.

"Respectfully," Captain Kral said, "I buried a dagger in his chest."

I felt my breath catch at the memory.

"Good," High Captain Voboda replied. "How close did he get to escaping?"

Markos replied. "Technically, he did escape. He nearly made it to the outer fence. We need to know if Victor-27 had confided any of his plans to Oscar-17 or if Oscar-17 gave him any information regarding how to escape. We aren't sure the Victor would have been smart enough to get as far as he did on his own. We think he may have intimidated or beat information from Oscar-17 prior to his auction."

"I see," High Captain Voboda said. "In order to prevent future escapes, you want to know how involved the Oscar was?"

"Yes." Markos tapped the handle of his revolver impatiently. *Or maybe*, I thought, *maybe he tapped it when he was nervous*. Maybe I'd read him wrong this whole time.

"Oscar-17 is in Room 5." High Captain Voboda turned to the korporal and gestured for him to let us in.

This all felt too easy. Too fast. But Commander Markos did carry a lot of clout. His rank patch had the power to sway and persuade.

The heavy door clicked open, and I followed Roman and Markos into the bright, sterile hallway. My heart hammered. Lockbox was close. I found myself reaching out with my thoughts as if I could somehow communicate with him like that now that we were so close.

We passed doors one and two; my pulse roared in my ears.

We passed doors three and four. Sweat began to bead on my forehead.

We stopped outside the door with a large black '5' on the front.

The korporal stood at attention. "Sir, would you like me to provide backup in the event the Oscar remains uncooperative or combative?" He placed a hand on the knife at his waist.

High Captain Voboda scoffed. "Combative? Both his legs are broken. How combative do you possibly think he'll be?"

CHAPTER 20
BE A CRUSTER

THE EDGES of my vision flashed crimson at the High Captain's words. *Both his legs are broken.*

I couldn't use my rage against High Captain Voboda. I had to redirect it. The image of reaching out and choking the High Captain with his collar brought me some satisfaction, as did the image of me taking the dagger at my hip and driving it though his shoulder before I broke both of *his* legs.

Roman placed a hand on my shoulder. "Private," he whispered. "Are you ready?"

He didn't say what he meant. What he meant was, "Don't do what you're thinking about doing. Don't skudge up the plan."

I made eye contact with Markos. He'd gone so far as to break my nose to maintain our cover. He knew, to some degree, what I was thinking. Roman had said I was scary when I was mad, and he knew that I was well beyond mad at this point. *Did High Captain Voboda have any inkling of how close he was to experiencing nauseating pain at my hands?*

"I wish you better luck than we've had," High Captain Voboda said. He slid a key into the lock and turned it.

"Oscar-17," Roman shouted as soon as the door swung open. "Don't move, and hands where I can see them!"

I took my rage with me into that room. I'd use it to be convincing in my role. I'd use it to get Lockbox out.

Lockbox sat in a metal chair, wearing the same clothes he'd had on at Predvoi. The stripes were faded now. He sat facing us, his chin tucked down, his hands raised high above his head. They were covered in black ink.

His legs were both wrapped in thick, hard casts which smelled like they'd been dipped in wax and resin.

Had he lost weight? I tried to meet his gaze, but he didn't look up.

"I know that voice," Lockbox said. His voice lacked its usual energy. He sounded tired. Just as he had the last time I'd heard him, but he'd been drugged then.

He wasn't drugged now.

He was broken.

"I know a secret about you, Captain Kral," Lockbox said. His voice was slow but still carried an edge of power.

"Oscar-17," Markos said. "We have reason to believe you may have assisted your cellmate Victor-27 in escaping Predvoi Prison."

"Did he escape?" Lockbox asked. I'd have thought he'd react more to seeing Commander Markos himself in the room. He'd been shocked to learn that he'd been the one to personally escort me to Predvoi. A familiar grin crossed his face. He lowered his hands and raised his face.

Not even a glimmer of recognition showed when he faced me.

"No," Roman said. "Victor-27 was unsuccessful."

Lockbox's expression dropped. *Couldn't he see me? I know I was in a cruster's clothes, but didn't he know me?*

"Tell me what happened, and I won't tell Commander Markos your secret," Lockbox said.

Roman stepped closer to Lockbox, but Lockbox's gaze didn't follow him. His blue eyes looked cloudy.

"I stabbed him twice and left him for dead in the snow for the wolves," Roman said.

I stepped closer, and Lockbox's gaze fell on me. His expression stayed fixed; my stomach dropped.

He couldn't see me.

"Did you really?" Lockbox asked.

"Yes," Roman said.

Ever aware of High Captain Voboda's presence in the doorway, I was careful not to speak, but I knew the hell of thinking my friend was dead.

Lockbox had already been through too much. I had to hope he wouldn't react and give me away.

"I was there," I said loudly, stepping closer to Lockbox. "The blood melted the snow around his body."

Lockbox's entire body snapped to attention.

"What else?" he asked.

He knew. He knew my voice. I stepped closer.

"We aren't here to discuss the death of Victor-27," I said, letting all my hatred for Voboda come into my words. "He was inconsequential. We're here to figure out how the skudge you helped him get as far as he did!"

I rushed toward Lockbox, biting back tears. *Would he even be able to escape in his condition?*

With a trembling hand, I pulled out the dagger and placed the tip against Lockbox's chest. "The Captain is telling the truth. Lurpers like you go down much more easily than you'd think," I growled. Then, in a whisper, I said, "I can heal."

As I whispered, Markos began to speak, covering any low rumble coming from me as I made it look like I was threatening Lockbox's life.

"What did you tell him? Did you help him willingly?" Markos began shouting questions so loudly and quickly, I couldn't listen to them.

"Attack me," I whispered frantically. "They'll take you out of this room. There are instructions and supplies."

"How did Victor-27 know where to escape towards?" Markos roared.

"Can you see?" I asked through clenched teeth.

"A little," Lockbox said. "Enough."

"Use the tools. Remember the books," I said. "Attack me and get away."

"If you tell us, maybe we won't leave you in the same condition we left your cellmate!" Markos finished.

The room became silent except for my ragged breathing. My instincts told me to kill High Captain Voboda, scoop Lockbox up, and rush for the door. He'd die. I might not die, but he'd die for sure.

I wished I could reach out and lend my ability to heal to Lockbox. I wished I could block *his* pain.

"Victor-27 nearly killed me," Lockbox said. His voice grew more angry and violent with every word. "Everyone there saw him choke me in the yard. I wouldn't have helped him! And I won't help you!" I pushed the handle of the dagger into Lockbox's hands.

He snatched it and whipped it forward, catching the side of my neck with the tip.

I screamed and dropped to my knees, ignoring all the ways to prevent the next swipe from the dagger. My neck seared from the pain and my hot blood. My blood. I heard myself scream again out of anger and agony. My hands turned bright red as I reached up to stop the bleeding. I had to keep as much of it off the floor as possible.

Lockbox swung his arm forward again. This time I scooted back. Instinct forbade me from letting the blade get me a second time.

Roman moved forward. He grabbed Lockbox's wrist. Lockbox cursed as Roman wrenched the dagger away from him. He held it to Lockbox's throat. In their haste, Roman nicked Lockbox's hand with the knife.

My pain rose briefly, and as I blinked, it disappeared.

Skudge! I didn't want to block it. I had to feel it! I willed it back, and it returned like a fresh injury. I gasped.

Lockbox's milky eyes flitted back and forth as if desperate to see what he'd done to me.

I began cursing loudly so he'd know I was alive.

"Check him!" Roman shouted to the korporal. The korporal rushed toward me.

"Get the Oscar out of here!" Commander Markos directed Roman. "Get him in isolation!"

High Captain Voboda opened his mouth to protest, but Markos shouted over him, "Down the hall!"

Two more soldiers hurried down the hallway to join Roman as he dragged a flailing Lockbox away and out the heavy metal door.

"All the rooms are occupied. We can't put two Oscars in the same room! If they combine intel, they'll be too resource-ful. They'd know too much!" High Captain Voboda shouted.

"Then open another room!" Roman replied.

The heavy door down the hallway clanged, and I imag-ined Roman had thrown it open forcibly.

I had to pray they'd put Lockbox in the right briefing room. With Commander Markos here and High Captain Voboda staring at my bleeding neck, that left Roman as the ranking officer in the hallway. He'd tell them to put Lockbox in the right room.

Lockbox would find the supplies. He'd see the note, and then he'd swallow it, just as it directed. Anxiety left me writhing on the floor as much as the pain in my neck. It was a very small note with very small writing.

"Private Petrov," the korporal said. "A medic is en route."

I waged a battle within myself as half of me tried to numb the pain, and the other part fought to keep it. If my pain was authentic, they couldn't suspect us. If they had even a milliliter of doubt in our motives, we might all die. We might all fail.

I leaned into the pain. I couldn't give them any reason to test my blood.

"Get a medic in here!" High Captain Voboda shouted.

Moments later, Roman and a korporal medic hurried into the room. The medic began pressing bandages against my throat, assessing the damage with the other korporal. I strained to listen to Markos and Roman.

"Oscar-17 is contained," Roman said. "We will continue our interrogation by less friendly means after Private Petrov's injury is addressed."

The medic held pressure to my neck and pulled out a first aid kit.

"Get him on some vyco right away," Markos said.

The medic dipped the needle of a syringe into the top of a small glass vial and tipped it upside down before filling the syringe with the medicine.

He injected the shot into my shoulder. His hands moved quickly as he brought out a needle and thread. He pulled the yellow lid off a tube of ointment and smeared it across my wound with a brief apology and some explanation about how it would help the blood coagulate and numb the area before he sutured it up.

Disoriented by pain, I found myself lying backward on the floor while soldiers worked away at my neck.

Be a cruster, I thought. *Don't let the pain end yet.*

High Captain Voboda stood over me, assessing the damage Lockbox had done. "He shouldn't have let the lurp get his weapon," High Captain Voboda said. "Good thing the injury isn't fatal, or we'd have to put the Oscar down."

"I'm willing to bet Private Petrov here learned a valuable lesson," Roman said.

"There's a reason they don't send many privates up to Rhosivi or Predvoi. Underestimated him."

"I'll break his legs," I said through gritted teeth. High

Captain Voboda, Markos, Roman, and the medic all looked at me. "I'll break his arms."

I locked eyes with High Captain Voboda. Maybe bloodlust was a bunch of slag Doctor Bolest made up when writing his report on Victors. But I felt it now.

I'd put High Captain Voboda down before he so much as touched Lockbox again.

"His legs are already fractured," High Captain Voboda said to me. "But if you're feeling up for it after this, you're welcome to break one of his arms. Either one." He turned to Markos. "The lurp's ambidextrous. Warden Dulka didn't have that in his file."

"I'll break you," I hissed through my teeth. High Captain Voboda had no idea I was talking to him. I was dying to break *him*.

"He's in the other room where he'll remain until you're ready," said the High Captain. "Clearly, you can't approach him with a weapon, but we can talk you through how to break his arm. It's not all that complicated."

My rage swelled until it outweighed the pain in my neck. Everything in the room had a faint red glow to it. I could breathe and contain my anger. But every word from Voboda's lips threatened to break the dam.

I didn't have to pretend to be dizzy as they stitched my neck. The medic counted aloud every time he put a new one in. I stopped listening after he got to twenty.

Voboda went on, oblivious to everything I felt. "I'd have thought he'd be a bit more compliant after I broke his first leg."

"*You* broke it?" I asked.

"I broke both. It's one of the privileges I enjoy at this assignment. But after seeing what he did to your neck, I'm willing to let you have a taste of revenge."

"What did you do to his eyes?" I sat up.

"His eyesight was already bad enough without his

glasses. Sometimes, we need him to read reports, but he'd been disrespectful, so we gave him drops to blur his vision. It wears off after a few days."

The medic cleaned up all the blood from the floor and stuffed all the soiled bandages into a garbage bag.

We'd previously discussed that Roman couldn't volunteer to take the garbage out, since it was far beneath him as a Captain. I needed to bring out all the blood that I'd brought in.

"Thank you, korporal," I said to the medic. I grimaced. "I'll take that down with me. Might need to throw this top out too." The blood would dry and make the shirt crisp.

I wasn't sure we'd given Lockbox enough time alone. It had only been a little more than twenty minutes since Roman had shut him in the side room. We couldn't stay too long, and we couldn't rush Lockbox. We'd planned to give Lockbox about half an hour. I was supposed to let him injure me in a way that would not require a trip to the hospital, but one that would take about half an hour to treat.

The medic was fast. I prayed Lockbox was too.

The medic helped me to my feet and made sure I wasn't too dizzy. "Drink plenty of water," he said. "Eat some red meat to get your iron levels up."

"Thank you."

High Captain Voboda looked impressed at the stitches on my neck. "Still think you can get the lurp to talk?"

I grit my teeth together. I couldn't speak. I could scarcely contain my bloodlust for him.

"Come on, Private," Roman said. I don't know how he kept his tone so casual. "I'll show you how it's done."

I nodded, shuffling to the door. It hadn't been half an hour.

I prayed Lockbox was ready.

CHAPTER 21
THE CONTRAPTION

ROMAN'S VOICE was harsh and convincing. "When we open the door, you go in there and put the skudging lurp in his place, got it? He's got broken legs. Give them a kick. Remind him that you're in charge."

"Yes, Sir," I said.

"Do you know how to break an arm?"

"I think I can manage." I tried not to look at High Captain Voboda, but I couldn't help but catch his smirk. He had no idea what I was. He doubted I could so much as break Lockbox's finger, let alone his arm.

"High Captain Voboda, permission to shoot if the Oscar becomes hostile again?" Roman asked.

"Try to avoid center of mass. Chancellor Eldrat has briefed this particular Oscar on some key strategy points regarding Latvani. I know he'd like to use him, but if we can't get him to comply, then it doesn't really matter what's going on in his brain, does it?"

"Roger that," Roman said.

I couldn't tell if I was numbing the pain or if the shot of vyco was, but I nearly forgot about the injury on my neck or the twenty-something stitches holding it together.

Lockbox's legs were broken.

If Lockbox wasn't ready when the High Captain opened the door, the plan was skudged anyway. I'd already decided to fracture every single bone in Voboda's body before leaving with Lockbox.

I'd go rogue. Roman might have to shoot me in the head for real to maintain Markos's reputation. I was having a hard time containing myself as it was. If we opened the door and I had to go in with the expectation that I'd harm Lockbox, Voboda was coming in with me. I'd force the door shut behind us. I'd break the lock. I'd use his head to bash open the glass window, and then Lockbox would be free.

We stopped outside the unmarked door where I'd left my gear.

This was my cue.

"He's in here?" I asked, facing High Captain Voboda and hoping I sounded incredulous enough.

"The other rooms are full."

"That may be a problem, Sir." My voice didn't sound scared. I sounded, as Roman had put it, scary. I tried to fix it. *Sound submissive.* "High Captain Voboda, Sir. That korporal directed me to leave my gear in there before we entered."

High Captain Voboda whipped around to face the korporal. The korporal became pale on sight. "Is that true?"

"Yes, Sir."

"What was in your gear bag?" he asked as he unholstered his Luger.

"A lot of things. I just came from the Central Issue Facility. A tent. Poles. Eye protection. The list is in the bag."

"Code Black!" High Captain Voboda shouted.

Markos imitated his alarm. "Code Black!" he bellowed even louder than High Captain Voboda. Markos turned on me and took several steps in my direction. "How many ways are you going to skudge up a single assignment? You've armed a lurper!"

I tried to stammer. "S—sir, I…There are no weapons in the bag, S—sir."

"He's an Oscar, you slaghead! Everything is a weapon for something as clever as him!"

"I didn't—" I had to take the blame. "I'm sorry, Sir. I didn't know."

"Get in there and see what damage he's done! We're not risking our lives for your mistake." Markos shoved me toward the door.

High Captain Voboda stood waiting. I had one job in that room: I had to repeatedly position myself between Voboda and Lockbox. Voboda turned to Markos. "You want to send him in first? Unarmed?"

"He's the only private here. The most dispensable. And he's the slaghead who brought a bag of gear onto this level."

"Yes, Sir," High Captain Voboda said. He turned the lock, and I twisted the knob.

"Oscar-17!" I yelled. "Hands where we can see them!"

The gear bag had already been pilfered. Pieces of cloth and gear were strewn across the floor. Lockbox stood in the center on his bandaged legs. Wings constructed from the tent poles and canvas extended from the backpack on Lockbox's shoulders clear to the edges of the small room. Each wing was nearly twice the length of my body.

This was Markos's plan?

An image from a book flashed into my memory. A flying machine. A glider. The book wasn't fiction. In twenty minutes, Lockbox had turned the bag of gear into a complicated contraption.

High Captain Voboda shouted, "What the—"

"Shoot him!" I shouted.

It was the signal. I looked away from Lockbox, trying to appear confused and terrified as I strategically remained close to High Captain Voboda. He aimed to take a shot, and I moved to the side to block it. He shoved me, attempting to get a clear view, and I pushed him back.

Roman's gun barked. The thick glass stopped the bullet, but deep cracks spiderwebbed their way out from the black bullet.

The window hadn't broken. My heart raced.

"Don't hit the window!" High Captain Voboda yelled. "He can't go anywhere!"

Lockbox moved next, and I anticipated the action with relief. He bent, grabbed a small brick from my bag, and chucked it at the big window.

The glass crunched, and in the same moment, he was sprinting after the falling brick. Roman fired again. And again. In the mayhem, I bumped into Voboda, sending him tumbling sideways as I rushed after Lockbox.

The brick and large shards of glass fell out of sight; Lockbox diving through the window after them. His hands worked quickly with the handles of the glider, and the wings extended even further.

I held my breath. *Fly. Fly!*

The metal creaked. I thought I heard a piece of canvas tear. Unblinking, I stared at Lockbox's hands as they adjusted their position. He leaned to the side as I leaned forward to get a better view, and his nosedive turned into an upward glide.

High Captain Voboda fired off a few more shots, but the sun glared directly into our eyes, making getting a clear line of sight impossible. Only Roman could have hit him from here.

I could breathe again. I realized I'd grabbed some shards of glass in the window ledge and kept them in my fingers. There couldn't be any evidence of Victor-27 here.

Not smiling was nearly as difficult as not shoving High Captain Voboda out the window proved to be. He leaned forward, mouth agape, as Lockbox flew away. I could have pushed him out.

It would have been so skudging easy, too.

Lockbox's legs were broken, but he'd made wings. He flew over the rooftops of Khizmit, and I only looked away when the sun threatened to blind me.

Markos picked me up and threw me against the wall. We hadn't planned this far.

The terror across my face was genuine as he shouted at me. "You're demoted. No pay. Extra duty. You will spend the rest of your life looking for Oscar-17, and you will never find him!"

"I'm sorry. I'm sorry—"

"Your gear bag facilitated his escape!"

"I didn't know not to bring it here. The korporal told me to—"

"We'll never find him now!"

Roman stepped closer to us. "Sir, if it's any consolation, I got him at least twice as he…well…as he flew away. I don't think he'll last long."

High Captain Voboda looked the slightest bit less concerned.

"Are you sure, Captain?" Markos asked Roman.

Roman nodded.

"Center of mass. If the mechanism he built doesn't break and drop him from the skies, he'll die from blood loss or infection. If anyone tries to treat him, they'll know what he is."

"You don't think he could make it to Latvani?" High Captain Voboda asked.

"Not a chance," Markos said. He rounded on me again. "But I think we'll send this one there to keep an eye out and ask around some Latvani soldiers himself!"

It was meant as a threat. "Sir, you don't mean to send me to the front lines—"

"I'll deal with you later," Markos snapped.

The finality in his tone shut me up. He wheeled around. I

dropped to my knees to begin gathering pieces of my gear that remained.

"Leave it!" Markos said. "You'll have to pay to replace it all anyway!" I jumped back to my feet. I scanned the floor again. The note Markos had put inside the bag was nowhere to be seen. I held onto the garbage with all my blood on it.

We'd done it.

Lockbox, wherever he was, was free.

"Get moving!" Markos barked. "We have an Oscar to find."

CHAPTER 22
HIDEOUT

Commander Markos, Roman, and I rushed out the doors and sprinted down flight after flight. The entire building was on high alert. All lurpers were locked away.

But Lockbox was free.

I didn't know where he was, but I had enough faith in his makeshift glider to believe that he hadn't crashed, at least, not because of a malfunction.

Maybe because his legs were too heavy in their casts. Maybe because he couldn't actually see. Did the goggles Markos had thrown in the bag help much, if at all?

I ran down another flight of stairs.

Lockbox was free, but what about the other Oscars here? What about the other lurpers with broken legs who I'd left under High Captain Voboda?

Maybe I should have shoved him out the window after all. It would have haunted me, but maybe I should have taken that load onto my shoulders. Was it going to be easier to live with the guilt of knowing that I was so close to other prisoners and hadn't saved any of them?

We reached the ground floor and hurried outside with a few other groups of soldiers.

Markos shouted some directions, assigning off different blocks to different parties. Someone mentioned the Task Force and where they'd go looking.

The glider would have drawn attention. It was still early but not so early that everyone was in bed. Someone would have seen a boy with a backpack with canvas wings flying through the morning sky.

And since his legs were broken, wherever he landed, he'd stay.

A few of the soldiers looked my way, because even with the chaos of a missing lurper, the vivid red blood on my uniform top claimed attention.

Roman moved in front of me, shielding me from the eyes of the soldiers as officers shouted orders.

"Come on," Markos said to me and Roman when most of the groups had finally moved on. If Lockbox was able to maneuver the glider, he'd land where Markos told him to. But there were too many variables for me to feel confident in the execution of our plan.

We were four streets away from the Grand Palace when Markos stopped abruptly.

"Get those out of his neck," Markos said to Roman. "Luka, heal up."

I didn't insult him by asking if that would be suspicious. He clearly didn't think anyone would recognize me as Private Petrov, the idiot who'd been sliced open by an Oscar.

I healed the cut with careful precision not to make any alterations to my burned hand. Just my neck.

It must have looked strange to have thick black thread in my neck and no injury.

Roman pulled out his dagger and used the sharp point to cut at the threads. His hands were steady and precise.

"Go faster," I said.

"I was trying to be careful."

"We don't have time for that."

"Fine." Roman cut a single slice across all the rest of the stitches at once, and I numbed the pain as a fresh stream of blood flowed from the shallow cut. He picked out the stitches and nodded, signaling that I could heal completely now.

"See that?" Markos asked. He gestured to the flickering flames ahead of us through a small crowd.

An outdoor café had a large fire in the center of their dining area.

"Take off your shirt and throw it into the fire along with the bandages," Markos said.

"That will draw a lot of attention."

"Pretend you're drunk," Roman suggested. "And I'll come apprehend you."

"You seem to like it when I act like I've got slag for brains," I muttered, pulling off the shirt. I'd have to be an absolute fool taking off clothes in this weather.

"You've been acting stupid for a full decade. I'm sure you can manage being dumb one more day," Markos said. "Out of necessity. You were stupid because Velky expected you to be. It kept you alive. Being stupid now will keep you alive too."

I hadn't had a lot of exposure to drunkenness. Guards seldom had enough rakia to make them tipsy, let alone completely drunk. Roman took my bloody shirt into his hand and using it and some snow, cleaned any remaining blood off my neck and shoulders.

Assuming Markos or Roman had access to another shirt, I moved forward with the plan. A plan that made me look like a drunken slaghead.

I prayed Emberly wasn't watching and staggered forward with the bag of bloody bandages and my shirt.

"Happy Koliada!" I sang, slurring my words. "Time to celebrate!" *What was I supposed to say?*

I stumbled over a chair, and it crashed to the ground,

immediately bringing all eyes to me. My burned hand ached beneath the glove. What idiot wears gloves and no shirt? The burn on my arm and shoulder should have drawn attention, but it was, evidently, not the most unusual thing about me.

"I took a trip," I said, scrambling to get up.

A few women at the table nearest me stood and hurried out of my path. A man rose, looking combative. I ran for the fire and threw the garbage in. The flames leapt and consumed the evidence of my involvement at the Grand Palace. The crowd of over a dozen people stared at me. Some amused, some concerned, and one downright angry.

"Happy Koliada!" I sang again and tripped.

Roman stepped forward. "You're disturbing the peace," he said. He apologized to the crowd for the commotion and led me away down another alley.

I stumbled and let him half-drag me until we were well out of sight. "That was humiliating," I said. "Where's Commander Markos?" I worried that he'd gone off to find Lockbox without us.

"He'll be right back."

A bell chimed above a door, and Roman and I turned to see Commander Markos exit, his arms full of black fabric.

"Put this on," he said, shoving the material into my hands.

I held it up to find it was a lightly worn overcoat, adorned with brass buttons, and lined with rabbit fur along the neck.

"Thank you, Sir." I slipped into it. While I struggled with the buttons, Markos walked back to make sure all the evidence had burned. "I'll return it in good condition."

"It's yours," Markos said. "Happy Koliada."

This was mine? Not a dead man's. Not stolen. Not loaned to me. Mine.

"Thank you," I said. I could have embraced him.

"We need to move," Markos said. Roman and I followed him as he took purposeful steps down a narrow road. "If Lockbox was able to follow my directions, he's six blocks away, hiding in the garbage plot. I told him to land there and dismantle the glider."

The gear, dismantled, would blend in with the garbage. Lockbox, on the other hand, wouldn't.

He didn't have a burn on his wrist to conceal what he was. He didn't have a coat to keep him warm. My steps quickened, quietly urging Markos to move faster.

My heart beat faster as we hurried along. We were so close to finding Lockbox, I just knew it. We had to find him first.

"It's just past this wall," Markos said. We hurried alongside a tall brick wall and turned to come face-to-face with a twisted iron gate.

Beyond the gate were piles of metal and stones and discarded pieces of furniture. If Lockbox had landed here, the dismantled glider would fit right in.

Movement caught my attention as someone stood up from behind a pile garbage.

It wasn't Lockbox. It wasn't a boy at all.

Emberly Markos took a few wide steps over piles of garage and walked straight toward us.

"What are you doing here?" Markos asked.

"Picking through the trash. Looking for some materials to build—"

"Ember."

Emberly smiled. "I think you know why I'm here."

Markos looked around her, scanning the piles of garbage and discarded materials just as I did. I wouldn't know if there was a sign of Lockbox.

"Did you see anything?" Markos asked.

Emberly smiled coyly. "You'll get a more specific answer if you ask a more specific question."

"We don't have time for this."

"Then be direct."

"It's official business."

"Somehow, I doubt that." Ember stuck her hand on her hip. "You think I don't know you're up to something?"

"I don't know what you mean."

"If you hated lurpers like you're supposed to, you wouldn't tell Mom how bad you feel for them. I've heard you crying late at night after holding Judgement Boards."

"Don't question my loyalty." Markos sounded nervous.

"You hate lurpers, then? You liked being Head Warden? You liked being able to kill them at will?"

"I have always tried to use any authority entrusted to me for the good of Khizmit."

"But not always for the good of the Chancellors. Not always for the Chancellor Supreme."

"I have obeyed the orders given to me. I value life, yes, even the lives of vaznovs and lurpers. But they aren't the same as you and I." Markos scanned the surroundings again and then lowered his voice. "Did you see a flying machine or a boy with casts on his legs?"

"Is he a lurper?"

"Yes. A lurper escapee from the Grand Palace on a glider, and the last we saw of him, he looked like he would land around here."

"Is that where you all were this morning?" Ember looked us over. "At the Grand Palace? How'd you help him out?"

"Ember!" Markos hissed. He stepped closer to her. "This is serious! We have reason to believe that there's a lurper loose here in Khizmit."

"Oh, I'm sure there's more than one." Emberly looked at me obviously. "But you already know that."

Markos stared at me momentarily and narrowed his eyes. "Luka graduated," he said through gritted teeth.

"No, he didn't," Emberly said. "If you're not honest with me, you can't expect me to be honest with you."

"I tell you what I am able to tell you."

"Why are you looking for the missing lurper?"

"To bring him to justice."

"Dad, admit that you have a soft spot for the boys you watched grow up in Rhosivi. Just tell me what you want the Oscar for."

Markos didn't say a word. *Oscar. She'd said Oscar, not lurper. Markos didn't miss that detail or the tone of disrespect in her reply.* If anyone else spoke to him like this, he'd have gutted them with his words. The time I'd insisted he admit that he knew me as more than just the mark on my wrist, he'd broken my nose.

Ember stepped toward me instead of her father. She spoke to him though. "If you hated lurpers and feared them the way you pretend to, you wouldn't have brought one home."

Markos flashed me a look that guaranteed we'd discuss my mistake later.

"Ember, please—"

"You think I don't know that you volunteered to be the Commander of the Lurper Legion? I heard you talking to Mom. Even after everything that happened to the previous ones, you volunteered! You've spent half my life with them and half my life with me and I'm not complaining, but you sure as hell owe me the truth! I'm not a child anymore!"

Markos sighed and reached his arms out for Ember. She crossed her arms and looked from me to her father.

"I don't want to endanger you by involving you. I can't risk it. I can't risk losing you."

"But you're willing to risk me losing you? I've already proven that I don't care what people think." Emberly gestured to Roman. "I can help you a lot better if you tell me what you're doing. I can help all of you!"

"Where's the Oscar?" Markos asked.

"He's under the protection of the Vaznov Adjustment Association."

Markos became instantly irritated. "The Vaznov Adjust —" He scoffed. "The Vaznov Adjustment Association...

Emberly, you can't be serious. He's not a vazzie, and you can't just —"

"It may not bother you adults, but there are a lot of us here in Khizmit who sympathize with the lurpers. It could have been us sent to those prisons! It could have been me in the tower. It could have—"

"You think I don't know?" Markos shouted. "But you are in danger when you affiliate yourself with them. Just tell me where to find the Oscar, and forget this Lurper Liberation idea."

"Why?" she asked.

"Because it's not safe."

"Are you safe?" she asked her dad. She turned to me. "Are *you*? Why then should I prioritize my own safety above the safety of others? I won't do it. My *dad* taught me better than that."

I finally dared to speak. Markos was getting nowhere with his daughter. Other soldiers would be here soon. I knew speaking would risk his wrath, but I was already going to get in trouble for what I'd revealed to his daughter. "Lockbox was my roommate at Predvoi," I said. "Please, Ember. Do you know where he is?"

"Lockbox is all you had to say," she said. "I'll take Luka with me."

"Why just Luka?" Markos asked.

"Because he isn't really a soldier anyway. The two of you can keep up the farce of looking for Lockbox. You're the Commander, and you draw too much attention. And I'm sorry Romulus, but—"

"I don't exactly want to be seen alone with you again anyway," Roman said. "I've had to explain a lot to Alba already. I'd rather not go through that a second time."

Markos sighed, his breath billowing out in a momentary cloud. "Fine. Take Luka." He grabbed my shoulder, and he didn't have to say a word. I had to leave his daughter alone.

Even when we were by ourselves. "Meet you back at the house tonight?" Markos asked.

Emberly nodded. "Come on," she said as she started walking down a side street, and I followed, but not before turning back with an apologetic expression.

As soon as we were out of sight of Markos and Roman, I reached forward and took her hand in mine.

CHAPTER 23
LURPER ON THE LOOSE

"What's this for?" Emberly asked, giving my hand a gentle squeeze.

"I thought this was the normal way to walk around the city," I said. For the most part, I wasn't lying.

"It's normal enough for me." She took a quick turn down a narrow alley. "Lockbox is in a vacant building. I keep the keys to places like this handy to help vazzies in trouble. Never imagined I'd be able to help lurpers like you."

Lurpers like me. She'd said it so casually.

"But you didn't take me someplace like that," I said. "You took me to the Commander. To your dad."

"Wasn't that your intention all along? Didn't you two need to meet up?"

"Actually..." I began.

I wanted to tell her the truth. She hadn't so much as bat an eye when I revealed to her I was a lurper. *How would she react if I told her I'd escaped?* I wanted to see. I wanted to tell her about my time at Rhosivi. Her dad breaking my nose. Meeting Roman. Watching Smoke drop dead. Learning what I could do.

There wasn't time for it all. Maybe there wouldn't ever be time.

"Actually what?" Emberly asked.

I opted for a different story. "When I was twelve, another inmate attacked me. Head Warden—your dad, he broke up the fight. Otherwise, that kid would have messed me up pretty bad."

Ember stopped and turned to face me. "I remember that day." She scanned my cheeks. "My dad came home shouting about how someone had cut up your face. I heard him telling my mom about it. He's always had a soft spot for lurpers, free or not. I think that's why he wanted to work at Rhosivi in the first place!"

He'd told Zuzana about that?

"I feel like I've known you for a long time," Ember said. She started walking again. "And somehow, I feel like I still don't know you at all."

She scooted down another narrow street and stopped. What might have once been a blue door now stood nearly naked, curled pieces of paint sitting around its base. She dropped my hand and lowered her voice. "He's here." She turned to me. "Was he really your cellmate?"

"Yes." I tried not to sound too anxious.

She dug around in her pocket and pulled out a small key which she inserted into the small keyhole. *Was Lockbox jailed here?* I preferred to think she'd done it to keep him safe.

I hated myself for not trusting her more.

"Is the Vaznov Adjusment Association a real thing?" I asked.

"Yes," she said.

"What do you do?"

"Besides helping vazzies adjust to the cultural climate here and use their freedom in a way that won't land them behind bars or put them at risk of execution, we do some... less legal things as well."

"Such as?"

"Protest TPI. Vandalize political messages. Sabotage the

Task Force. And keep our eyes open for vaznovs in Khizmit who need our help. I intervene when I think a vazzie is in trouble with a guard. Khizmit doesn't do much to take care of you guys. And former lurpers are surprisingly easy to spot, including you."

I didn't bother defending the remark. I'd done my best to blend in when I'd arrived, but even the way I'd fallen asleep on the bench had drawn attention.

"Are there many vazzies here?"

"Not a lot," she said. "Some vazzies get in trouble within their first week, and even though they graduated, no one told them how to adjust, leaving them with no choice but crime. Many go directly to the Lurper Legion to help, despite being graduates. I assume it's more comfortable for them there than here. I wouldn't want to be here if I were a vazzie. But maybe we can get more vazzies to stay. Build a community for them and lurpers. Find a way to encourage more lurpers to break out and make their way here."

Her optimism left me smiling. There was no breaking out. No freedom tunnel. No way to leave without getting a dagger buried in your guts.

"Thanks for helping him," I said as the door opened a crack. I was almost ready to go inside when I predicted what the first word out of Lockbox's mouth would be.

If Emberly heard Lockbox call me Victor, she'd know what I was. It wasn't that I loathed the idea of her knowing, but I wanted to be the one to tell her.

"Mind if I go in alone?" I asked.

Her expression gave me the impression that she absolutely did mind, but she didn't say so.

"Promise he's safe with you?" she asked. "You were his cellmate, but were you on good terms?"

I couldn't decide if I should laugh because of the absurdity or if I was touched that she wanted to ensure his safety.

"He's my best friend," I reassured her. "The one I was looking for. He's the reason Leticia Varga sent that Captain after me."

That must have been reassuring enough because she pushed the door open for me.

With my heart beating wildly, I stepped into the dark room and pulled the door shut.

"Lockbox?" I called out. Light dimly filtered through the slats in the wood over the windows, illuminating swirling dust in the nearly empty room.

"Victor," Lockbox whispered. He poked his head up from behind a short desk. "Is your neck okay?"

"Are your legs okay? Can you see?" I rushed across the room and caught him in an embrace. "Lockbox, I…I missed you."

He patted me on the back. "I made the molds myself to stabilize my bones while they healed. I can see much better with these goggles. Still not great. But I won't complain."

I stepped back and stared at him. "We don't have much time alone. She'll come in soon."

"Who is she?"

"Get this—she's Commander Markos's daughter!"

Lockbox chuckled. "*That's* Emberly Markos."

"She knows I'm a lurper. She doesn't know I'm a Victor. She can't know."

"Does that mean you finally picked a nickname you like?"

"Luka," I said. I didn't want to mention that my mother had given me the name, while his mother had given him over to the Task Force.

"Luka. I like it." Lockbox adjusted his goggles and attempted to look at my neck. "You can heal rapidly. That's the Uniform. The final serum. I should have guessed!"

"They made it their life's work to keep it a secret from you," I reminded him.

"Emberly, she's sympathetic to lurpers…That must mean that…" Lockbox trailed off. I knew he'd get more satisfaction if he could solve everything himself, but I didn't think time would afford us that luxury.

"Markos has been giving you information for years. Helping me for years. Helping lurpers like us his whole life under the pretense of hating us."

"He took you to Predvoi himself because the move wasn't approved by Velky. It was his last act as Head Warden. He wanted to make sure you were…safe?"

I nodded, then said, "Yes," since I wasn't sure he could see me very well. "He sent Roman to—"

"Keep you safe," Lockbox finished. "So, you know then? What he is?"

"Yes."

"A Kilo, right?"

"Yes," I said. "He had to tell me though. I didn't figure it out. Is that why Roman drugged you? Is that what you'd figured out?"

"I had figured it out, but no one knows he's a lurper, do they? Except Markos, which is why he actually assigned him to watch you."

"Now, you can keep on knowing stuff." I laughed. I told him about my burned wrist to cover my tattoo.

Emberly shifted outside the door. I expected her to come in at any moment.

Lockbox adjusted his position on the floor. "Your name is Luka, Commander Markos is on our side, Captain Kral is a lurper, and you've escaped Predvoi. Anything else I need to know?"

There was so much more. My abilities. My escape.

"I met your mother," I said. I didn't even mean to. "I thought maybe the name in the bottom of your trunk was a clue to finding you, but when I found her, she—"

"She doesn't want me."

"No," I said.

"I know. I always knew. I'd hoped to meet her someday though."

"Save yourself the trouble," I muttered.

A man's voice came from just outside the door. Lockbox and I both froze in place. I had a scar on my wrist to conceal what I was. Lockbox had nothing. Even in the dim room the O on his wrist was prominent.

"Can't you just mind your own business?" Ember shouted. I calibrated my hearing.

Erik, the lieutenant who'd found me in the square and guarded the building where Emberly worked, sounded upset. "What are you doing over here? Are you alone?"

"I'm not alone."

"Is there another captain in there waiting for you?"

"That's just a rumor, and you know it!" Her voice became barbed.

"Then why don't you have lunch with me? If you and Alex are—"

"I have plenty of reasons, Erik, but I don't have to give you an explanation."

"Who's in there?"

"Luka." Her feet shuffled against the path as if she'd moved in front of the door.

"Why sneak out here if you're already in the same house?"

Emberly huffed, and her hand hit the wood. "It's none of your business!"

Someone turned the knob and pushed against the door.

"You know someone could arrest you for trespassing," Erik said. *Would he really attempt to arrest the Commander's daughter?* I'd like to see him try. Really, I found myself enjoying the idea of throwing him onto the ground and running off with Ember. But that left Lockbox here alone.

"Arrest me? Honestly?"

"I could. You're interfering with official business. I'm looking for someone."

"I have a key. I don't think that qualifies as trespassing. Besides, you haven't seen me go into the building."

"You told me Luka is in there."

Emberly huffed. "You were a lot nicer before you became an officer, you know that?"

"You weren't interested in me then, either."

"Wasn't friendship good enough for you?"

"You gave every indication that it would evolve into something else."

"And you gave every indication that you weren't going to turn into an absolute slaghead!"

Erik chuckled. It was a low taunt. "You know, before long I might have a gold pinecone patch. Everyone knows how you like—"

"Shut up already! Are you really so skudging jealous of a rumor that you're going to treat me like this?"

"How do you like to be treated?"

Thud! Initially, I thought it was Erik's fist pounding at the locked door in frustration, but then Emberly gasped. and I realized it was her head and back hitting the door.

If he put his hands on her, Markos would tear him apart.

I'd tear him apart.

"Stop—" she said. "You can't have the key. You can't go in there."

"It's not Luka in there, is it?" Erik's voice grew incredulous. "I swear to the gods, if it's the lurper—"

"A lurper?" Emberly asked. "In Khizmit? You sound like you've been drinking rakia on duty."

"I'm serious, Lee. There's a lurper on the loose, and he's probably around here. If you're helping him, you could get locked up and branded yourself!"

Emberly scoffed. "Stop pushing me!"

The edges of my vision began turning red. If I went out there, I risked Erik spotting Lockbox. But I wasn't sure how long I could stay here while Erik pushed her around.

Another thud sent me barreling toward the door.

"Let go!" Emberly hissed.

"Get out of the way!" It sounded like he pushed her aside.

With little effort, I threw my shoulder into the door, and the wood splintered at the hinges.

It must have hit Erik hard enough as it came down to send him to the ground because when I stepped out of the doorway he was scrambling to his feet, looking slightly disoriented.

"Leave her alone," I growled. My voice sounded foreign for how predatory it came out.

Emberly's expression went from surprise to pride. She scooted closer to me and placed a hand on my arm. It was trembling. Her fear was mild, but I'd make *him* feel true terror.

Erik would be trembling before I was done with him.

"Luka," Ember said. "We should go."

She was right. If I fought Erik, he'd have reason to suspect me. *And what had he said? The punishment for aiding a lurper was jail time and branding?*

Erik walked over the doorway and peered inside. "Step aside," he said. He wasn't quite as tall as I was even as he took a deep breath and rolled his shoulder back.

"Is this your shop?" I asked.

"I'm looking for someone."

"Look somewhere else."

Erik faced Emberly. "I recommend you ask your newest guard dog to step aside." He fingered the handle of his dagger.

Emberly's face flashed with concern. *For me?*

"You really think I'd help a lurper?" She tried to make her voice sound light, but I picked up the fear in it. "Get a grip,

Erik! My dad was a Head Warden. I grew up hearing horror stories from Rhosivi. I know how dangerous they are."

I fought the urge to glance behind me and see if Lockbox was completely hidden behind the few pieces of furniture in the shop. Now that the door was missing, light blazed inside, making it much more difficult for him to conceal himself.

"Then let me investigate this shop."

"No," Emberly said, coming to stand beside me in the doorframe. "Now it's a matter of principle." Her gloved fingers found mine. My burned hand. As she squeezed my hand out of fear, the pain turned into anger toward Erik.

"She asked you to shove off," I said. "You're insulting her reputation and her integrity at this point."

"Who are you?" Erik asked.

"Who are you?" I echoed. "Who are you to come here, pushing her around, accusing her of criminal activity, and demanding that we follow your directives? We're not prisoners. You're not some Preemptive Officer for us. So, I recommend you mind your own business and shove off."

Erik's mouth twitched. His hand was slow as it drew the dagger. Clumsy. Uncertainty in his movements. He pointed it in Emberly's direction, and my hand flew out. I grabbed his wrist and twisted it to the side, forcing him to drop the weapon.

It clattered to the ground as he cried out in pain. I released him and snatched the blade up.

Erik's eyes narrowed to livid slits, and he straightened himself. I tucked the dagger into my belt.

"How dare—"

"Never," I said. "Never point a weapon at her again."

Don't kill him, I told myself. *Don't break him.* After fighting other lurpers, I could easily see myself accidently killing Erik. *Would it be such a tragedy?*

Yes, I reminded myself. *Yes, it would be.* Emberly tightened her grip. The pain in my hand wasn't entirely uncomfortable.

It grounded me to the dangers of showing what I could do. What I was.

Erik took a few steps away from us. "I'll be back," he said.

What choice did we have? Standing in the doorframe made us look guilty as slag, but if we'd moved, he'd have seen Lockbox. His striped clothes. His legs in casts. The 'O' on his wrist.

Erik slipped twice on the path as he sprinted away.

Once he was out of sight and the door shut again, I whipped around to the dark shop.

"Lockbox," I called. "What do we do?"

"You expect me to have a foolproof exit strategy?" he asked, pulling himself from beneath a small blanket in the corner.

"You're an Oscar, aren't you?"

"Oh, I see, you're allowed to tell her what I am, but I can't share your secrets," he jibed. "Get these off me. They're too noticeable." He gestured to the casts on his legs.

I hurried over and got to work with the dagger. Erik had kept it sharp. I cut the casts off quickly.

"Anyone who glances your way will know you're an Oscar," I said. We all looked at his wrist.

"Hide those under the blankets," Lockbox instructed. "Get me a strip from them."

"A strip?" Emberly asked. She dropped to her knees and began ripping a few thick strips of the worn cloth. "Like this?"

"Yes," Lockbox said. "Prefect. Bring them here please."

"I could carry you somewhere," I offered. Lockbox began wrapping the cloth around his wrist and hand. We couldn't go to the Markos's home. Taking him out of the shop only exposed him to more danger. More likely to be seen.

"Got any other keys to abandoned shops you could stash me in?" Lockbox asked Emberly.

"Not nearby," she said. She threw the pieces of his cast

over to the corner and covered them with a few loose boards and other pieces of worn cloths.

Lockbox and I shared a look. I made an offer with it. He shook his head.

"What?" Emberly asked.

"Luka here wants to know if he should have killed him. Knocked him out. Tied him up. Something like that."

Emberly reached out for my hand again. "It would have made things worse."

Lockbox shivered in the wind. I pulled off my new coat and wrapped it around him. I might have been wrong, but it seemed to me like Emberly's gaze rested on my bare chest for a moment longer than necessary. And it seemed like a small smile tugged the edges of her lips up.

Hotter than embers.

The memory of her compliment warmed me enough that I didn't think I needed the coat anymore. The coat was long enough that it nearly covered all of Lockbox's prison clothes, but we had to cuff his pants a few times to get them beneath the layers. *Would it be better if he took off the clothes and I stashed them somewhere?*

In the distance, we heard Erik's voice. He was already on his way back to us.

"Sir, they're over here!"

Heavy footfalls came toward us on the path. If I needed to, I'd fight a whole platoon to keep Emberly and Lockbox safe. Erik rounded the corner first, and even from far away, the malicious glint in his eyes was obvious.

Erik bent over, hands on his knees while he caught his breath as Captain Kral and Commander Markos rounded the corner.

I exhaled.

"I know she's your daughter, Sir, but I think she's found the Oscar we're looking for." Erik pointed a finger in our direction, as if me standing in the doorframe wasn't indication enough of our location.

Commander Markos stopped in front of the door, eyes darting from me to Ember to Lockbox, who was entirely too visible for my comfort.

"I'm sorry," Markos whispered to us, his expression soft. "I'll do what I have to."

CHAPTER 24
THE BODYGUARD

"WHAT THE SKUDGE is going on here?" Markos yelled.

It was immediately clear from Emberly's reaction that she hadn't seen this side of her father before. Her whole body became tense as she stood half a meter away from me, almost protective of Lockbox.

Erik and Roman stood on the street outside the door, both staring over at me, Lockbox, and Ember in the small shop.

"Who's this?" Markos said, glaring at Lockbox from where he sat in the shadows. Lockbox scrambled to try and get to his feet. Prison rule number five rang through my head —*All prisoners in a cell will stand when a Warden, officer, or other figure of authority stands at the door of, or enters, the room they occupy.*

Lockbox heaved himself up on his right arm and worked his legs beneath him, grunting. I scooted beside him. With my arm around him, I hoisted him onto his feet, still bearing most of his weight.

He shouldn't act like a lurper, though I knew the habit was nearly impossible to break.

"What the skudge is wrong with your legs?" Markos shouted.

Emberly grimaced again. However, I could have smiled,

even with Erik's sneer creeping in the side of the doorframe. This was the Markos I knew best.

Markos stepped out of the shadows of the nearby buildings, past Erik and Ember, right into the shop and turned on me. "Where is your shirt?"

There were a thousand ways I could have taken the story. *Which way did he want me to? Was I still Private Petrov?*

"Sorry, Sir," I said. It was the safest thing to say.

"Emberly Markos, what are you doing here?" Markos's voice became only slightly softer. The wind blew her dark hair across her face as she stepped closer to the doorway. "Lieutenant Ivanov claims you refused him entry to this shop. Are you aware there is a hunt underway?"

"I was protecting a friend," Emberly said, her tone confused but determined. "Erik said he was looking for a lurper. My friend isn't a lurper."

"You seem to have a lot of male friends these days," Markos growled.

Emberly's bottom lip quivered, just slightly and only for a moment, but I noticed it. Erik took a step forward, and Markos raised his hand.

"Wait outside with Captain Kral," he directed.

Erik stopped his advance, but he didn't back up to where Roman waited. Markos marched up close to the pair of us. He glanced at my bare torso.

"Is it asking too much for you to keep your clothes on around my daughter, Luka?"

"I lost my shirt, Sir," I said. "And her friend was naked, so I gave him my coat."

"We're supposed to believe you're half-naked because of altruism?" Erik asked from the doorway. He looked at me with disgust. "What happened to your arm, anyway?"

The burn had healed a lot more than I'd expected. Pink and purple scars only covered from the base of my palm up to my elbow. *When had that happened?*

"Did you get burned?" Erik asked.

"None of your skudging business—"

"Luka!" Markos thundered. "I will not permit you to speak to Lieutenant Ivanov in that manner."

"Sorry, Sir," I said.

"Who the hell is he?" Erik asked, ignoring Markos's directive to wait outside. He stomped into the building, leaving Emberly and Roman out in the drifting snow.

Markos walked up to Lockbox and bent down, not even looking at Erik as he responded, "One thing at a time, Lieutenant. Remember your priorities." Then to himself he muttered, "Lieutenants get a little bit of power and still can't keep their slag straight."

Erik straightened and briefly checked all his patches to make sure they were on straight.

Markos reached for Lockbox's wrist. "Who are you?"

"Peter," Lockbox said.

"What are you doing hiding in an abandoned shop? Why is your hand wrapped?"

"Commander Markos, Sir," Lockbox began.

"Hold still. I'm just checking." Markos peeled back some of the cloth to check his wrist. Erik leaned to the side, trying to see beyond Markos so he could check the wrist himself, but Markos was situated in a manner that it was impossible for Erik to see anything. "What are you wearing beneath Luka's coat?"

"Nothing, Sir," Lockbox said.

"Am I to understand that you were naked in the presence of my daughter?"

"Yes, Sir."

"And I take it that you were naked because you ditched your uniform?"

"Yes, Sir."

Markos readjusted the wrapping on Lockbox's wrist to

make sure his lurper tattoo was completely concealed and gently released it. "You are Peter Petrov?" Markos asked.

"Yes," Lockbox said.

Markos stood up and sighed. "This isn't the Oscar. His wrist is clean. He's a fresh private who escaped from the clinic earlier this morning." Markos directed his words to Erik. "Private Petrov injured himself on purpose to dodge getting sent to The Outskirts. He's assigned to the Bear Legion. He's not a lurper—just a coward." He spat the last word with such convincing hatred, I found myself feeling protective of Lockbox all over again.

Erik stepped to the side, trying to get around me, but I wasn't about to let him get within striking distance of Lockbox. I scooted alongside him. Irritation spiked in Erik's voice as he addressed Markos. "Can I check his wrist too? Not to insult you, Commander Markos, Sir, but protocol recommends two witnesses." He put his hand on my shoulder to move me to the side, but I planted myself, waiting for him to look me in the eye. He didn't. "Sir, I'm sure you—"

"Captain," Markos barked.

Roman took the invitation to enter the shop, and as he got closer to us, he effectively shoved Erik out of his path.

"Wait outside, Lieutenant," Markos barked for the second time. "You're making me claustrophobic!" As Erik backed out to the doorway, Roman moved forward and adjusted the wrapping on Lockbox's wrist. I didn't catch sight of the tattoo. Roman had successfully kept it covered.

"Slag," Roman muttered. "You've got some nerve running away from the clinic with your wrist this swollen and bruised." He straightened and turned to Erik. "No tattoo, Lieutenant."

Erik grew restless in the doorway. He knew. Somehow, he knew we were all lying to him. His face twisted in frustration, but he didn't speak. Didn't dare insult the Commander and a Captain.

"He probably injured his legs jumping out of his window to escape the clinic," Markos muttered in Roman's direction. "Can you walk, Private?"

Lockbox nodded, then attempted to take a step forward.

"Captain Kral," Markos said. "Take Private Petrov back to the clinic where they will treat him." He shook his head disapprovingly at Lockbox. "You will face a trial for desertion, and know that I personally will press charges for indecent exposure to a minor."

Lockbox bowed his head.

Captain Kral scooped Lockbox up in a fluid motion, making him look like he weighed less than forty kilos. He was careful not to expose any of his prison clothes as he walked away.

Erik blocked the doorway.

"Excuse me, Lieutenant," Roman said. "You heard the Commander. I'm sure you'd love to be the one to find the missing lurper, but this isn't him."

Erik didn't move out of Roman's way. "Sir, you must see how suspicious the situation is." Erik locked his gaze on Roman's. "They routinely break the Oscars' legs in the Grand Palace. His left wrist is wrapped, and that's where they mark the lurpers. He could be naked because he removed his prison clothes. If we search the area, we might find them."

Markos whipped around and stomped between Erik and Roman. He towered over the lieutenant. "It would take a great fool not to notice the correlations between Private Petrov's injuries and those we would expect from the escaped Oscar. But it would also take a greater fool to assume that those coincidences alone would indicate they are the same person." Markos took a deep breath, and his tone became menacing. "I have worked with lurpers longer than you have been alive, boy. Are you suggesting that I wouldn't be able to recognize one? You think after my time at Rhosivi that I could be duped by a lurper, even one as clever as an Oscar from the Grand Palace?"

"No, Sir. Of course not, Sir," Erik sputtered.

"He has no tattoo. His legs aren't broken anyway—just sprained."

Erik stumbled backwards as he made room for Roman and Lockbox to slip out the door.

I watched them hurry away until I couldn't see them anymore, though I ached to follow. Roman wasn't taking him to a clinic. I had no idea where he was going to hide him, but I had to trust Markos had some semblance of a plan.

Markos turned back to Emberly who had been uncharacteristically quiet and meek as she'd waited in the corner. "Emberly Markos, what made you believe that deserter was your friend?" His voice was necessarily harsh, though my hands still curled into fists as he shouted at his daughter. "And he was naked? Shouldn't that have been some indication that you should have stayed far away or called for help?"

"I'm sorry."

"And the way you treated Lieutenant Ivanov? Haven't I taught you better than that?"

Emberly's face was red. "He said he was a minor and that his father was drunk on rakia and had beat him and then turned him out. He looked like a minor to me, and I just wanted to help."

Markos dragged his hand across his face. He exited the shop, leaving a fresh trail of boot prints in the dust before Emberly, and I followed. I took in a shallow breath as the wind tore across my bare skin.

"Go home," Markos said to the two of us. "Luka, while I appreciate you protecting my daughter from the…view…I can't honestly say I prefer the present situation."

While I wasn't an expert at knowing the difference between Markos acting angry and when he was genuinely angry. I knew one thing for sure—he didn't want me to be this exposed around his daughter.

"It won't happen again, Sir." I shivered. I turned to walk home, assuming Emberly knew the way.

"Commander," Erik said. I halted even though he hadn't said my name. I turned to face him. Shoulders back. Pretending that I didn't feel the cold.

Slag. Just like that, I didn't. I glanced down at my skin flecked with snowflakes. Nothing. No cold. I'd blocked it.

"My weapon..." Erik kept his mouth partially open then fiddled with his belt.

"Luka," Markos said.

I pulled the weapon out, flipped it dramatically in my hand, and then caught it by the blade before I held it out for Erik to grab.

"Why did he disarm you?" Markos didn't ask me why I'd taken it. His voice, sharp as the dagger, was directed at Erik.

Erik winced as if cut by the words. At the very least, he sensed danger in Markos now more than he had before.

"I...there was reasonable suspicion that..." Erik fumbled over his words.

Markos was out of patience for Erik, and anyone within three kilometers could have seen it. A few people down the street, milling around now that it was lunchtime, glanced our way. Markos turned to me. "Luka, why did you take Lieutenant Ivanov's weapon?"

"He drew it on your daughter, Sir," I said.

"I...I asked her to step aside so I could investigate," Erik said.

"You threatened my daughter?"

"Sir...I...even you agreed that the situation was suspicious. I had to do something to get them to move so I could check the shop."

Markos's jaw went tight. His eyes became narrow. "You asked me earlier who Luka is. Or, as you so eloquently phrased the question 'Who the hell is he?'" His hand moved slowly to his sabre. "Luka is interning with me. He is, for lack of a better term, Emberly's bodyguard for the time being."

Erik glanced from me to Emberly. "Her bodyguard?"

Markos followed his gaze and paused on me. "Lieutenant, give Luka your overcoat."

"Sir?"

"It's not standard issue, and he's freezing. Don't make me ask again."

"But, Sir, this coat was a gift—"

"And my warning is a gift. You drew your weapon on my daughter and threatened her. You're out here without a comrade and out of regulation with your coat anyway."

Erik reached up and began to unclasp the metal clips on his coat. As he removed his coat and handed it over, I caught the threat in his eye. "Her bodyguard?" he asked again, still not seeming to believe the Commander.

"There have been a few attacks on her character, as you've heard, and some threats against her safety. Someone might want to get to me by getting to my daughters. It shouldn't come as a surprise that I assigned a personal detail to follow my daughter."

"Did you also ask him or assign him to hold her hand?"

"As a matter of fact, yes." Markos nodded to me as I hesitated to put on the coat. "Unlike you, he is not an officer, and he is not supposed to be in uniform or accompanied by a comrade. It's not common knowledge that he is her bodyguard. It's in the best interest of her safety that people assume they are a couple rather than guess at the true nature of the situation. I don't want anyone getting any ideas that could endanger my family."

"But what about her reputation?" Erik's mouth nearly curled into a smile.

Emberly stepped forward. "You're an absolute slagsack, Erik—"

"I'll have you know, Lieutenant,"—Markos placed his hand on Emberly's back. She continued to breathe heavily, shoulders rising and falling as Markos spoke to Erik—"at the time of the incident you're referencing, I'd asked Captain Kral to be her personal detail. The rumors which you yourself have made sure to circulate around Khizmit are based on a lie."

Erik glowered.

Emberly looked ready to punch him, and I wished she would. I imagined her catching him in the face before I stepped in between the two of them to finish the job. *Her bodyguard.* I could have been glowing for how much I loved the title. The role.

The lie. *Was it a lie though?*

Erik folded his arms across himself to keep warm. "I would have been happy to be her bodyguard, Sir. It would have garnered less suspicion from the local community for them to see us together than for her to be seen in personally compromising situations with an older captain and a previously unknown...boy." Erik looked at me.

"You are not under my command, Ivanov."

"You could have requested me."

"I know too much of your character to make a mistake like that."

Emberly laughed. Markos knew how to hit hard.

Erik's mouth twisted as if he'd been slapped across the teeth by a palka.

"You drew a weapon on her yourself," Markos said, clarifying his insult. "All for the promise of getting praise. Promotion. I know where your priorities are, Erik."

The use of his first name didn't escape me, or him.

Erik's face paled. "You look like you need some lunch," Markos said.

"No, Sir. I can wait, Sir." Erik's words were as stiff as his arms now. "I have another question about this bodyguard you've selected."

Markos brushed some snow off his sleeve, drawing attention to the rank patch there. "Lieutenant, there's still a lurper on the loose in Khizmit, and we waste precious time discussing matters that are, frankly, none of your skudging business."

Erik dipped his chin. "Yes, Sir. Sorry, Sir."

"Go find yourself a comrade and get looking for the Oscar."

Erik gave me a last glance and hurried away through the snow.

"We'll talk tonight," Markos whispered. "I'm sorry, Ember." He reached out, and she stepped forward to embrace him. "I'm proud of you. You're so brave. Forgive me?"

She nodded, and I thought maybe she had tears in her eyes.

"Luka," Markos said softly and scanned the area. We were alone. "I was right."

"Sir?"

"I can trust you."

CHAPTER 25
TRUST

I can trust you.

Markos's words were probably meant to instill confidence in me. Instead, they made me feel twice the pressure to be trustworthy. Emberly and I didn't speak as we hurried through the streets. We did, however, hold hands. *It was my assignment, wasn't it?*

We were supposed to look like a couple. Commander Markos himself had said so—*I can trust you.* Was the rest of that sentence supposed to be, "I can trust you not to actually develop feelings for her? I can trust you not to let her look at you like she did when you took your shirt off? I can trust you not to follow her down a side street and stare at her face, count the freckles on her cheeks, and memorize the earrings that climbed up her ear?"

I wanted to do all of that.

I wanted to take off my glove and feel her bare hand in mine. I wanted to tell her who I was and what I was and how being around her made my heartbeat rage in my ears.

She was brave, but she was more than that. She was beautiful, but it was far deeper than her face and her hair even as the wind blew it over her shoulder. Perhaps it was her compassion that attracted me to her the most. Her compassion for me and for Lockbox. When Markos said he trusted me, was it because he knew what I felt and trusted me not to do a thing about it?

Emberly led the way and could have been winding us deeper into Khizmit and farther from home, but I doubted she was.

She finally stopped and caught her breath.

"You aren't winded," she stated.

"No."

She seemed to glance briefly at my wrist, as if to see if my tattoo had appeared to announce what I was to her.

"Thank you," I said. "For helping Lockbox. For not letting your friend—"

"He is clearly not my friend," she spat. She adjusted her gloves and pulled the sleeves of her coat over them again. "He's an absolute—"

"Slaghead." I grinned. "I completely agree with you."

She jumped at me, throwing her arms around my neck. She made a quiet choking sound. I could tell from the way her chest heaved as she sucked in a breath that she was crying. She buried her face in my neck, her nose cold against my skin.

For the first time in my life, I was completely full of self-doubt. *Was she crying because her father had yelled at her or because of Erik?*

"How can I help?" I whispered. Her ear was so close to my face, I could have put my lips to her skin. *Would the earrings be cold?*

Emberly shook her head.

"What do you need?"

She held me tighter, and I pulled her close, breathing in the fragrant scent of her hair.

"I wanted to kill him," she finally breathed. "I wanted to hit Erik right in the face and send him sliding across the ice. I wanted to knock the wind out of him and—" She stopped abruptly. She shook her head again.

"It's okay," I said.

"When he pulled that knife on me, I froze. I wanted to take it from him. Shove it into his face, not literally, but close. Close enough to make him step back. Make him rethink treating me like that."

"It's okay."

"We were friends for so long, and now I feel like I don't know him at all." She dropped her head onto my chest. Her hair smelled faintly of the cinnamon from the shop. I took a deep breath and held her closer as she said quietly, "He would have turned Lockbox in. He'd turn you in if he knew."

"He's not here," I said. "You're safe with me."

I heard my words before I'd thought them through. But she was safe with me. She was safer with me than alone.

All my life I'd been told I was a threat. I was dangerous. I had to be contained because of the peril I posed to others, girls especially.

They knew so little about me. Because as I stood in the lightly falling snow in the early afternoon, I had only one desire. One goal. My talents and abilities served a singular purpose.

To protect.

Far sooner than I wanted her to, Ember released her hold on me and dropped her arms back to her side. I reached up and wiped a tear off her face.

"Don't think me weak, I can't handle—"

"You're not weak," I said. She was too beautiful. I wanted to pull her back to me. Wrap my arms around her again. I wanted to kiss her. If she made the offer to me again like she had at the house, I'd give in.

Had she offered at the house? Or had my desire been so easily read on my face?

I couldn't be physically closer to her, but I could share something. I could expose myself emotionally.

"Roman was my guard at Predvoi. I thought he'd been assigned there to kill me if I became too big of a threat, but your dad assigned him to help me. To teach me what I could do. To protect me from the Head Warden."

"My dad cares about you."

"I didn't know. He had to play the role of hating me." I wiped another stray tear off the side of her cheek. "Did he ever tell you about breaking my nose?"

"My dad broke your nose?"

"Yeah," I laughed. "It's fine now. He did it because I was asking questions. Sort of like you were back there. Trying to get him to confess that he gave a slag what happened to me. Hit too close to home, I guess."

"He actually broke your nose?" Disbelief was written all over her face.

"Yeah," I said. "I didn't know what he felt for me. I'd assumed, at times, he saw me as a son and other times that he saw me as a problem. A burden. A risk. He's done a lot for me though." I swallowed hard.

"Why'd you let him hit you?"

"I didn't let him. I didn't see it coming."

She raised an eyebrow. "You're not the sort to accidently get burned or *let* someone have the drop on you."

"No, not usually. I think your dad has some sides you haven't seen. Like today. That was normal for me."

"It was…scary," she confessed. Her gaze locked onto mine. I wanted to warm my cheek on hers. If I got closer, I could smell her hair again.

I could lean in and see if she'd kiss me on her own without a formal invitation. I could ask her outright if she wanted to. I could lie and tell her we should do it to seal the rumors that we were a couple.

But Markos trusted me.

"I don't want to disappoint him," I said, dropping my eyes from her face. Looking at her only made this harder. If she didn't close her eyes, or if I didn't turn away, we'd be here forever. Frozen in the moment when I had to decide what I wanted more.

"Roman won't take Lockbox to the clinic, will he?" Ember asked. The way she cared about him, knowing nothing but that he'd faced some injustices, was beyond my comprehension.

"No, he'll keep him safe."

"Good," she breathed.

"We need to go home," I said, because if I stood alone beside her a moment longer, I wasn't sure I could resist the temptation to put my arms back around her and plant my lips on hers.

———

I waited until dinner was ready before emerging from my room. I'd found, to my surprise, more clothes in my size sitting on the bed. Zuzana had to have brought them in. I made a note to thank her later as I pulled on a pair of warm brown pants, a white shirt that slipped over my head, and a soft green sweater that was only slightly too small for me.

As much as I liked the warm coat, I didn't want to keep it. I figured I could find a way to get it returned to Erik somehow. I was no thief. Not anymore.

As the stew cooked, the girls went back into the room across the hall.

The herbs in the leftover rabbit stew filled the house with a woodsy aroma as Zuzana reheated it over a fire. I only came out of my room because I heard Markos walk in through the front door.

"We didn't find him," he announced for my benefit and for Ember's.

She and I nearly collided as we hurried to the top of the stairs.

"Dinner's ready to eat," Zuzana announced.

"I'll just need a moment with Ember and Luka." Markos removed his boots and came up the stairs.

The three of us went to my room, Milena's technically, and Markos shut the door.

"Ember," he said softly. "What you're doing is admirable. What you desire is good, but I can't let you be involved with anything that supports the vaznovs and now, the lurpers. The risks are too high."

"But—"

"I've thought about it all day while I pretended to look for the Oscar. I can't tell you more. I will make you a promise, and I'm going to ask you to make me a promise."

She nodded.

"I promise not to lie to you. I promise to use every bit of power and authority that I've worked for to help the lurpers. I am and have been working to exact justice for them, to liberate who we can, and to give the vaznovs more assistance and better rights …" He glanced at me. "And to change what can be changed. I have big plans in the works, and I know you would never want to interfere or sabotage them, so I need you to be what Khizmit expects of you. You need to pretend not to care about the lurpers and the vaznovs. I'm sorry; I know that's hard for someone with as big of a heart as you have."

Emberly sat on the bed and pulled a blanket over her lap. She rested her head against the wall. "What are you planning?" she asked.

"I can't tell you."

"You said—"

"I said I wouldn't lie. But I can't tell you everything."

"Does your plan involve Luka?"

"Yes."

"And Captain Kral?"

"Yes."

"Can it involve me?" she asked.

Markos sighed. "No. It's too dangerous for you."

"Dangerous! Dangerous like the lurpers? Dangerous like Luka?" She moved as if to get to her feet.

"Shh," Markos urged. "Yes, dangerous."

Ember dropped back to her spot on the mattress. I took a few steps closer to her and sat down. "I'm starting to doubt that you know what dangerous means," she said to him while looking at me. She didn't think I was a threat. She never had.

I grinned.

"For your information—and this is a secret— Luka is the most dangerous individual you've ever met," Markos said without hesitation.

"Are you?" she asked me.

"I don't know everyone you've ever met."

She laughed. "Are you really dangerous? Have you killed people?"

"Not people. One person…so far." *Why had I added 'so far'?* I knew why. I added it because the future wasn't going to be clean and easy.

"Are you the most dangerous person I've ever met?"

"Probably," I admitted. I glanced at Markos. "Yes. Honestly, yes, most definitely."

"More dangerous than Lockbox? Even though he's an Oscar?"

"Yes," I said. "Much more dangerous than Lockbox. Though I don't necessarily see Lockbox as—"

"Listen," Markos interrupted. "We have traditions to upkeep. A parade to attend. Then presents to unwrap. We still have a few days before Luka and I go to The Outskirts. I can tell you more tomorrow, but I need a promise from you, Ember. I need you to promise me that you'll stay away from the vaznovs. Stay away from the politics of it all. I need you to stay safe."

Emberly looked to me as if to gauge what I wanted her to do. I admired her bravery and love for lurpers like me. It was only because of her curiosity and desire to help that I'd made it here safely.

She'd saved me and Lockbox.

"Please," I said. "Trust him." I didn't think I could call him 'the Commander' to Emberly, and I wasn't sure I wanted to call him her dad in front of Markos. "Please stay safe."

"I can make the promise on one condition," Ember said. "You find a way to involve me, or I'll find a way to involve myself."

CHAPTER 26
THE PARADE

I walked into the kitchen, and Markos handed me some bowls to set around the wooden table. I couldn't believe that he'd agreed.

A few minutes later, Emberly entered, wearing her usual tunic but half-dressed in costume for her part in the Koliada festival.

"Is that for the parade?" I asked her, gesturing to the long white skirt.

"Yes," she said, and I noticed she maintained a formal tone with me. I redirected the rest of my questions to Markos as we finished setting the table. I wanted to say it looked nice. That she looked beautiful. But I didn't want an elbow in my face, so I pretended not to notice that her cheeks were rosier now and her lips pinker.

Zuzana set a fat round roll on each of the plates and then took a seat.

"Where's the yule log?" Milena asked as her mother filled our bowls.

"On the front step," Markos answered.

"Oh, you brought back plenty," Milena said as she caught sight of the tower of split wood beside the fireplace.

"Come and eat," Zuzana called.

Milena hurried over, and we all began to eat. Milena seemed to be the only one in the home oblivious to how silent it had become. Conversation felt fragile after the promises exchanged.

To avoid saying anything, I bent over and ate my stew. From what I understood, Zuzana worked in the government doing something with counselors, so I wasn't sure how she also cooked well enough to have opened a restaurant. The salty broth combined with the carrots made even the caramels seem mediocre.

Emberly ate quickly, glancing at me often enough that I noticed, but not often enough for me to catch her gaze. It was only once she'd finished eating that she spoke. "Is Luka coming to the parade?" she asked.

"I'm not sure," Markos said, beginning on his second bowl of stew. He blew on it, sending a thin tendril of steam through the air.

"You're not going to make him stay here alone and miss the festivities, are you?" Emberly's voice became impatient.

"I considered it," Markos said. "I don't want to draw attention to him."

She huffed. "Well, the neighbors have already seen him. It would draw more attention if he wasn't at the celebration."

I took a large bite of the roll, hopeful that if my mouth was full, no one would ask me to state my opinion. There was a comfort in staying here, but a parade... *Would I be able to resist the urge to leave the house and get a glimpse of the festival?*

Zuzana shrugged. "I don't see any harm in him coming at this point. Rick?" She refilled his water and then offered to take mine.

"Thank you," I said. I didn't dislike being served by her, but it left me a bit uncomfortable. While I hadn't done anything to deserve incarceration, I'd also done nothing to deserve their kindness either.

"He should stay with me," Markos said as he held a spoonful of stew above the bowl to cool.

A tug at my arm startled me so much, I nearly dropped my piece of bread.

"Sorry," Milena said. My reaction had drawn everyone's attention. "I'm in the parade. I play—"

"The balalaika, right?" I said.

My eyes darted over to Markos to see if it upset him that I knew. He lifted his eyebrows, and I turned back to Milena. It was the most common instrument, so it would have made sense as a guess.

Milena blushed as I stared at her. "Well, yes, I do play, but not for the parade. I'll be on the spoons. Do you want me to show you?"

I began, "Sure—"

"He'll see you in the parade," Zuzana said, taking note of my nearly empty bowl. "And we heard you practicing. It sounds great, but we don't have a lot of time right now." She buried the ladle into the bottom of the steel pot and pulled out another scoop of the stew, brimming with carrots and rabbit meat. "More?" she asked, but she didn't wait for an answer. With a smile, she emptied the scoop into my bowl.

"Thank you," I said.

"So, you don't want me to play right now?" Milena asked irritably.

"Not right now. Not while we're eating," Zuzana said.

"Well, all the rest of the youth are in the parade," Emberly began, and I can't have been the only one who noticed how deliberately she was choosing her words. "It might be strange if Luka is just watching with a bunch of adults."

"He looks like an adult," Markos said.

"But the rest of the men will be in uniform. Except for the workers."

Markos seemed to consider this as he broke a potato into two with the side of his spoon.

"He doesn't have a uniform yet, does he?" Emberly asked, glancing from me back to her father. "So, he doesn't look like a soldier."

I had the pants. I'd had the uniform until I'd bled all over it.

"What do you want?" Markos asked, wiping his face with the brown cloth napkin.

"I just think he should be in the parade."

"With you?"

"With the rest of the kids our age."

Markos shook his head. "No." He scooted his bowl forward and rested his hands on the table. "Luka will stay with me, and we will watch the parade together."

I dipped my bread into the stew and took a bite. One would think that having butchered so many rabbits, I'd have lost my appetite for them, but I think it had the opposite effect. Instead, I savored every bite, knowing what it cost to get it. The soup warmed me clear down to my feet.

"Do you want to be in the parade?" Zuzana asked. She buttered another roll and held it out for me.

"I'm full, thank you." I held up a hand. She waited for my other answer. Though it was clear that Commander Markos didn't want me to be in the parade, it was also clear that Emberly wanted me to join her. *Was it possible to please both?* "I don't know anything about the parade. I can't say I know what would be better. But I trust Commander Markos," I added respectfully. "Just being able to watch it would be a privilege."

Zuzana leaned in and placed her hand over her husband's. "Don't you think he'd have more fun if he had the chance to be in the parade? Besides, I don't like the idea of Emberly being alone out in the streets after dark, especially when so many parents hand out rakia like its water to any hungry hands, no matter how reckless. They act like Koliada gives anyone the right to get drunk all in the name of celebration."

Markos narrowed his eyes as he looked between Emberly and me. Then he turned back to Zuzana. "She won't be alone. Aren't you meeting up with some friends?"

"I was..." Emberly began. "Most of them are too old to be in the parade anymore."

"What about Aneta?"

Zuzana coughed, not so subtly.

Markos turned quickly to her. "What happened with Aneta?"

In a quiet voice that we could all still obviously hear, she said, "She's spreading all those rumors...you know."

He worked his jaw for a second. "I suppose it wouldn't hurt to keep your bodyguard around for tonight."

"It's fine either way," Emberly said reservedly.

"I'll have a word with Luka. Then we can decide if he'll be in the parade with Ember or not." He picked up his bowl and went to stand.

The girls cleared the table and washed the dishes in what had to be record time with the anticipation of the parade right on our heels. As soon as the table was wiped down, Zuzana followed them both back into the bedroom to help them get ready for the parade.

Markos called me into the front room where he tossed another log into the fireplace before taking his usual seat in the large recliner. I sat on the couch.

"Last time I left you alone with Emberly, you ended up half-naked, and she had a dagger pointed at her," Markos said.

"Yes, Sir. I know." I stared at his knees.

"You can look at me when we're talking. This isn't Rhosivi."

"Yes, Mr. Chief Preemptive Officer," I said, a lilt in my voice.

The corners of his mouth slightly turned upward before he dragged a hand across his face. "You deserve to have some fun, but I worry about her. Can you keep a close eye on her?"

"Sir, I'd protect her with my life."

"I believe you."

Perhaps I shouldn't have gone so far. A 'yes' would have been adequate. I hadn't said everything I wanted to though.

Markos went on, "It's Ember's last year in the parade, and I know she wants to participate. But with all her friends gone, I just…I don't want her out there alone."

I nodded, afraid that if I said the wrong thing, the conversation would take a sharp turn in another direction.

"You'll stay close to her."

I nodded.

"But not too close?" he added, his voice quieter.

"I'll keep her in my sight, and I promise to keep all my clothes on."

He didn't laugh, digging his fingers into his hair with a sigh. "Luka, it's one night here. And I know you might be tempted to try and experience it all at once before we leave for The Outskirts, but just…don't. Okay?"

"Yes, Sir."

"No rakia," he said.

I nodded. Though the answer scared me, I had to ask him. "Are you afraid that I might give in to my dangerous tendencies? That I might give in to my predisposition for—"

"We're all human, Luka. We all have predispositions of one kind or another. And while I confess, I have some concern for what could happen, you're not the one I'm worried about tonight."

"I understand." Back in Rhosivi I'd always assumed Markos was a good dad, but even that estimation had come up short. He adored his daughters, and outside of the prison, I was able to see it now more than ever. Deciding to lighten the mood, I said, "Let me guess, if I threaten anyone or start any fights, you'll kill me—"

"I will not kill you," he interjected, his tone serious again.

"If I threaten anyone or start any fights, I'll be subject to disciplinary action. If I drink rakia, conduct myself in a disrespectful manner, or otherwise pose a threat to the community, I'll be subject to disciplinary action."

Markos finally smiled, although it was brief. "Have fun, Luka. And keep both of you out of trouble."

———

Emberly emerged from the bedroom, looking like white moonlight. Her skirt had been hiked up and tied so she could use her legs more freely, and the long tunic went a little past her wrists. Her joy was almost palpable when her father told her I could go with her to the parade. In the meantime, Zuzana went to her closet to find some white clothes for me to wear.

Milena, on the other hand, was wearing bold reds, blues, and yellows, and holding her wooden spoons with pride. Though she'd applied makeup in the same way Emberly had, she still didn't look a day past fifteen, which I'm sure wouldn't have pleased her. Her green skirt came down to her knees, showing white tights on the small section of her legs that wasn't covered by her tall, decorated boots.

"Where's your mask?" Milena asked Emberly.

Ember hurried back to her room and returned with a mask that looked more like a crown because of the tall bones that stuck up from the top. Wide holes were left for her eyes, and the rest of the fox's pelt covered her head like a reddish orange hat. She carried a small scrap of the pelt in her hand.

"It's not great, but it will work," she said, looking to her mother for approval. Zuzana took the small piece and cut two eyeholes into it, and then strung a black ribbon through the sides.

Zuzana put the soft mask across my face and tied it around the back of my head. The orange fur poked into the edges of my vision and tickled my nose, but judging by the way Emberly was blushing, I couldn't have looked that bad.

"Looks good to me," Zuzana said, placing the scissors back on the table.

After putting my boots on, I followed Markos to the front porch, where a huge log, partially split, sat like a wide seat. Snatches of music filled the air as if musicians from all over town were taking a few final moments to practice before the parade. Once Emberly, Milena, and Zuzana joined us outside, Markos hoisted the giant stump onto his shoulder and began walking down the street.

Markos led us through town, catching up to a few more families who made a bit of a parade themselves en route to the festival. A few streets down, he stopped and turned back to me.

"Be careful," he said, then with a nudge from Zuzana, he added, "Have a good time."

CHAPTER 27
THE KOLIADA FIGHT

EMBERLY GUIDED me down the cobblestone street, where we snaked around a few families carrying logs of their own toward the square. She explained as we ran that the parade would end at the bonfire, but we had to get to the start where the rest of the performers were waiting for the music to cue our start.

As I tried to get my bearings, I decided that the parade must take place in a circle, rather than a straight line through the block. Ahead, in what had been an open square, at least a hundred youth congregated, dressed in black and white and masks as varied as snowflakes.

"Wait here," Emberly said. "I'll be right back."

"Where are you going?"

"I just need to talk to someone really quickly." She grinned and then slipped through the crowd of laughing performers before I could follow her.

Markos told me to stay close to her but not too close. Maybe keeping her in my line of sight was what he had in mind. While I stayed in place, I continued to look out for her. Several performers were sharing a cup that they passed back and forth, laughing. They sat on a short wall, kicking their feet. Some had already removed their masks and were swaying as if to a beat I couldn't hear.

But I could hear everything else.

I wiggled between a few of them and stood on the short wall, watching the top of Emberly's red fox crown as she made her way to a guard standing beside a nearby alley. Though I wasn't sure, I had every reason to believe it was Erik. I tried to listen to her from this distance, but instead, my head echoed and pounded as I heard all the conversations, belches, shouts, and cries from the performers.

My ears ringing, I jumped down from the wall as some of the boys sitting there scooted over, nearly knocking me down. I'd barely straightened myself back up when someone approached me.

"Hey, there handsome," a voice said, just as a slender arm slid into mine.

I jumped back, and the girl smiled at me coyly from behind a black mask, if what she wore could be called that. It didn't cover her face at all, except for a small strip of black fur that hung down above her nose. The top looked like a nest of her hair with sticks, and feathers.

"You don't need to be scared. I don't bite."

The girl wore all black and had drawn heavy black makeup all around her eyes. Though I'm sure it was meant to be attractive, or maybe somewhat menacing, it came across like she'd been digging in coal all day and had rubbed her eyes without washing her hands first.

"Hello," I said slowly. She stepped closer to me and reached for my arm again.

"I was hoping I'd see more of you." Her gaze traveled down my body slowly before climbing back up to my eyes.

"Do I know you?" I asked, but there was no way that I did. *Was it common practice for girls in Khizmit to pretend to know random boys they found in the street?* There was something vaguely familiar about her, but I couldn't place it.

"I want you to know me. I want you to know everything

about me." Her sultry voice made her sound threatening. More threatening than most of the inmates I'd met. She might not bite, but I had a feeling she was capable of much worse.

I looked around, hoping to catch sight of Emberly again. In the pressing crowd of restless teens all preparing for a fake fight, the air hummed. I should have gone with her, at least to the building.

"Don't tell me you're looking for *her*." The girl at my side sighed.

"For who?" I barely glanced back at her, just to make sure she wasn't advancing on me again. Her dark hair, pulled tightly back into a bun, made her high cheekbones look nearly sharp in the dimming light.

"For Emberly. I take it you two are a thing now?"

"We're friends."

"Friends with benefits. Okay," she said, creeping closer again. "You can have more than one friend, you know." In that moment, she'd sidled between my arms, placing her hand on my bicep.

"Please stop touching me," I said as she moved a hand across my chest. Instinctively I wanted to push her away, but if I pushed too hard, I could see her slipping backwards, smacking her head on the hard pavement, and never waking up again.

She completely ignored my words. I stepped backwards, but the thick crowd made it impossible to move away without pushing someone over, and the pretend fight hadn't even begun yet. "What is it? You don't think I'm pretty?" she asked, pouting.

"You are pretty," I said, holding my hands out to try and keep some distance between us.

"Then what is it?"

"I..." I struggled to come up with a reason before I realized that I didn't need one. I owed her nothing.

"You do look better now that you've showered," she said. Then it clicked.

"You're the girl from that shop."

"Pekaren's. Yes." Her eyes widened along with her smile. "You remember me. My name is Aneta. You're Luka?" She evidently had an impossible time keeping her hands to herself.

"Don't touch me," I said again, this time with more of an edge to my voice. For the first time, I missed the physical distance usually granted to me given my status as a Victor and an X-ray mutt. But she ignored me again. I gently grabbed her wrists and pulled her arms down.

"Ouch," she complained.

"I won't ask nicely again," I said before letting go of her.

Aneta rubbed her wrist, but I didn't think I'd grabbed her very hard. "So, what? Only she's good enough for you?"

"We're just friends," I said again, jumping once to get a view over the crowd of black and white clad teenagers.

"Then why don't you want to get to know me?"

I finally looked at her.

She was, undeniably, very beautiful, despite the weird black marks around her eyes. Her skin beneath my hand had been smooth. But the look behind her eyes was a look I'd seen before a thousand times. She saw me as a thing, not as a person. It was, more or less, the same look Bolest had given me. She liked what she saw; she'd made that much obvious. But I was the same thing to her as I had been to the doctor. A very interesting specimen.

"Because I'm busy," I finally said.

I jumped again, finally catching sight of Emberly, who was making her way back but was blocked by a crowd of performers dressed in black. I didn't need to amplify my hearing to make out their voices, though it wasn't easy.

"And you brought him here tonight?" the boy beside Emberly said. His voice rang with unpleasantness.

"Let me through, Tibor. I don't have time for your games."

"Oh, but isn't that what tonight is all about?" The boy named Tibor had scraggly hair that hung down past his eyes and arms that might have been threatening to a Bravo or a Delta, but they didn't seem to have any effect on Emberly. She tried to push past him, and he held out his arm to stop her.

She didn't need my help. In just a short time, I'd learned she was capable of a lot more than even she gave herself credit for, but what kind of a friend would let a man push a woman around like that?

And we were friends. We were at least that.

I only stopped listening to Tibor and Emberly when Aneta prodded me in the shoulder.

"If you knew the truth about her, you might not be so loyal," Aneta said once she knew I was listening to her again. "She's just passing the time with you."

Without even bothering with goodbye, I pushed past her, gently enough that she wouldn't get hurt, but with enough aggression that there was no way for her to misinterpret my dismissal.

I shoved past a few more groups until I came upon Emberly and, not so accidentally, knocked Tibor over.

"Oh, excuse me," I said a bit less than sincerely as I stepped into the space Tibor had occupied moments before. Then I turned to Emberly. "You ready?"

The look of relief that flickered across her face was subtle, but I noticed it.

"Yes," she said and grabbed my arm. I led the way, cutting a path through some more groups of kids, opposite of where I'd left Aneta. I considered telling Emberly I'd met her but thought better of it.

"You okay?" I asked as we found a small space beside a tall fountain, where a cluster of other performers in white stood.

"I'm fine," she said. "Don't worry about them."

"I'm not worried about them."

"Don't worry about me either," she said, her voice a bit more playful. But she looked over her shoulder briefly. With her hand still on my arm, I felt her body go tense.

"I'm not worried about you. But I'm not about to sit on my ass while some skudger pushes you around."

She turned back to face me, her hand relaxing again. "Thanks," she said.

We both took a seat on the cold, icy concrete of the fountain. Water trickled out of the mouth of the stone bird, leaving a thin trail of ice down its belly and along the outer sides of the pool. In its base sat a few discarded wishes in the form of loose change.

Some of the masks carried the pungent smell of leather, while others already stunk with sweat. The press of so many people in one place gave me the smallest hint of panic. My senses wouldn't dial down.

What if a real fight broke out? There were no soldiers here. No palkas. No lieutenants with rifles in a guard tower to take down a threat.

I didn't want there to be. There wasn't a need, and yet, there was too much that could happen. Too many unpredictable variables in a group like this for me to relax.

"Who were you talking to?" I asked, noticing that Emberly still glanced over the crowd, no doubt looking for someone. I had little doubt it was Tibor.

"I was just getting something sorted out. For this parade, we're supposed to bring the fight here and parade down this street, onto Ulica street, past Pekaren, and finish in the town center."

"And the performers in black, are they just supposed to lie down in the street and stay there?" I imagined it to be some sort of punishment to get cast in such a role.

"No, they can get back up. They're just supposed to stay there until we move on, then jump up and fight again."

I laughed a little.

"What's funny?"

"It's just not how a real fight goes."

"Mr. Most-Dangerous-Man-I've-Ever-Met, I take it you've been in many?" she asked curiously. I wondered if she'd care, but knowing her, she wanted the truth, even if it wasn't pretty.

"Yes," I said, and instinctively my hand went up to my face. The scar was gone, but the memories would last forever.

"I figured." She took my hand. "Based on those scars I've seen on your knuckles."

She touched me so casually, and I could barely return the pressure in my fingers without feeling like I'd had the wind knocked out of me.

Music, carried on the wind, began down the street. I stood up, looking for the source.

"It's beginning! You want to see them?" Emberly asked excitedly. She stood up and tugged my hand. "Let's go look. We have time."

The music, lively and bold, filled the air. Emberly guided me through back alleys, and we jumped over a low wall before skirting around the back side of a few shops. As we reached the side of the street where a crowd of people watched, we stopped. A few of them eyed us critically. Our attire made it obvious we were meant to be in the parade, not spectators of it. But I didn't look at them. I couldn't, not when the musicians came into view around the corner.

Men and women danced around the corner, expertly playing the strings on their balalaika's while they moved in time with them. I'd seen pictures of these instruments in books, but I'd never heard them played. The notes, like lyrics, told a story as they sang through the hollow wooden bodies. The women, in bold red dresses, turned back and forth, sending their skirts rippling around their feet as they played. The dresses boasted beautiful floral patterns that matched the vests worn by the few men in their company. Their fingers strummed the strings of their triangular instruments so quickly, they blurred. The wooden bodies of their balalaikas were as ornately decorated as their dresses. Others used their domras so expertly, it was as if they were extensions of their own selves.

Behind them, dancing in a row, came women with braided hair, each carrying a ceramic bird. Then, all at once, they raised them to their mouths and blew. The whistles sounded like a chorus of birds all singing in synchronization. The women's fingers slid over the tiny holes on their whistles, creating music so beautiful, I wondered how it didn't thaw the world around us. The cadence of the song grew faster until suddenly, they all stopped. Everyone froze in place for a moment, then another group of musicians began to play.

The instruments they carried were small round wooden frames, with leather stretched over the top, and dozens of small bells secured to the sides. Using only their fingers, they began to drum, the bells chiming with every deliberate twitch of their hands.

I was awed; I don't know how long Emberly had been staring at me before I noticed her.

She moved close to my ear. "That's called a buben," she said, barely loud enough for me to hear over the music.

"I've read about them." I leaned in closer to her, still staring at the musicians. I forced myself to focus on the joy in the moment, but the crowd put me in fight mode. The crowd had grown, making it harder for me to pick individual voices among them. The few conversations that I tried to listen in to had grown rowdy as the rakia flowed. My mind was hyper-aware of those around us and anything that could be a weapon.

The last group was the younger children, Milena among them, who carried and clapped wooden spoons together. They clapped them against their own hands, their legs, and even one another's arms in an orchestrated performance. Worried that Milena might see us since we were supposed to be in the back of the parade rather than watching, we ducked away from the crowd.

Besides, we could already see our part of the parade beginning to advance. Our pretend battle was meant to take place in earshot of the music, to heighten the drama of the small fights. I supposed it was really more of a dance than anything else.

"Come on," Emberly said as we moved through the crowd again to the empty roads. We hurried back to the rest of the "fighters."

But when we got back, a group of black fighters were waiting for us. Tibor and Aneta glared at us as we approached, keeping up with the fighters who were listening for the musical cue to begin. Another boy, with a wide nose and a tragic attempt at a mustache, had his arms crossed across his chest. His mask made him look like an overgrown raven with a long beak made of bone and painted black that extended past his chin.

"Is that him?" the boy asked, shooting me with a frown.

"Yeah, that's him," Aneta said.

Then the music stopped, a cymbal crashed, and all around us, the performance fighters began. Some carried sticks, and they swung them slowly, giving their opponents time to feign injury or dodge. Others threw ridiculous punches at each other from several meters away, which had to be about as amusing as it was convincing.

The raven boy in front of us didn't react to the cymbal crash at all.

"Not now, Alex," Emberly said to him, pretending to throw a punch at a girl in black. The girl in black slowly moved around her, dramatically cried, and lowered herself to the cold cobblestone ground.

"Is it true then?" Alex asked, rounding on Emberly. He

threw a high kick to the side of Emberly, and although I knew the fight was strictly for show, I couldn't keep concern from creeping into my chest.

"Is what true?" Emberly replied, exasperated.

"You said no to me," Alex said, his voice terse. "But you said yes to him?" He picked up a discarded stick and swung it toward me. It came at me so fast, it whistled through the air, and I'm not sure I would have dodged it if I hadn't already been in a defensive position.

"It's really none"—Emberly ducked beneath the stick as Alex whipped it through the air toward her—"of your business."

"Aneta said he's been staying at your house. I know you don't have an extra bedroom." Alex rushed me, and I side-stepped. At our side the crowd clapped.

"I don't have to explain anything to you," Emberly said.

Alex's stick clattered against the icy road. "He won't love you like I do. No one else will ever care for you like I do." His words, lies, set me off.

But Emberly responded before I could. "Shut up," she said, not backing down. "I'm not dealing with your manipulation or slag anymore. Ever again." Though she spoke directly to Alex, she kept her eyes on Aneta as they continued in a choreographed fight, though executed with more intensity than those around us.

"I've been patient with you," Alex said, coming up behind Emberly. "I always hoped you'd become something more than a cheap whore."

My vision became tinged with crimson. If blood could boil, mine began to at that moment, and it was a good thing it did, too.

Alex pulled back the thick stick again, winding up to strike Emberly while she was blocked in by Aneta and two of Alex's friends. The stick flew forward, and I jumped in front, catching the end of it in my gloved hand. My burned skin cracked beneath the force, and warm blood began filling my glove, but I didn't care.

"It's time for you to go," I said, ripping the stick from Alex's hands. With a quick motion, I broke the long staff in half and then in half again before dropping the pieces onto the ground beside the few teens so committed to their roles that they didn't move. However, they stared at us, mouths open. They must have sensed I didn't know how to fake a fight. I only knew one level of intensity, and my self-control had no more patience for this slaghead.

Alex didn't know to fear me, or he would have pissed himself and rolled onto the ground. But his ignorance would make this more fun for me anyway.

"You know what I think would make this a little more of a performance?" Alex tilted his head to the side. "A little more commitment."

Three of the guys around us, Tibor among them, adjusted their positions. They leered, and I caught myself smiling. As much as I hated to admit it, I lived for this. This adrenaline spike that brought my senses to high alert.

I laughed. "You wanna start a fight? I'll let you throw the first punch. Make it a good one."

"Don't," Emberly said, but she might as well have shouted "go," because as soon as she spoke, Alex stepped forward and threw one of the most pathetic punches I'd ever seen.

It came toward me, almost in slow motion, and I moved my head to the side. I stood back up now that he was close, grabbed his collar, and scooped up his leg that was closest to me. I let him jump around on the other one for a second as he tried to stop the inevitable, before I kicked his one free leg out from under him. As soon as he hit the ground, his mask fell off, and four other guys in black rushed me.

After fighting inmates, these boys were little more than toys to me. I practically danced around them to the beat of the music, dodging their punches. The crowd beside us clapped louder, and some spectators from further down the line scooted to get a better look at us. They wanted a show, and I was about to deliver the best one they'd ever seen.

Alex began cussing as I circled away from him, forcing him to follow me. He picked up a new staff and began swinging it in wide circles. The grin stayed plastered to my face until he moved toward Emberly again. She pulled up her own staff, and even the other performers stopped to watch as Emberly blocked his first strike.

A new sort of rage overtook me, and I was behind Alex, gripping his clothes in tight fists before he'd even had a moment to draw back his new staff. I swept his leg, sending him falling to the ground again. At that same moment, his three friends came up to me from behind. One jumped shamelessly onto my back and went for a chokehold. With a quick movement, I launched him over my shoulder, where he landed on top of Alex. Alex groaned and then shoved his friend off him.

I didn't notice the blood until my fist made contact with Alex's ribs. Dark red blood, bright and fresh, demanded attention as it stained my white clothes. At first, I couldn't be sure where it was coming from, but then I removed my glove and found thick cracks all around my knuckles and wrist.

If they tested it, they'd know what I was. They'd know everything. I quickly healed the cuts beneath the glove and allowed the healing to creep down to the base of my wrist.

Although the blood seemed to give the audience pause, their cheers quieting a measure, it didn't deter Alex and his friends in the slightest. Instead, Alex aimed a kick right at my hand.

Newly pissed off, I tackled him and cracked my elbow across his face. Blood began pouring out of his own nose now, and I sat on his chest long enough to laugh at him as he coughed on it.

"You can have the whore," he gurgled.

His friends came up from behind, but I turned, knocked them both onto their asses, and turned back to Alex before he'd had a moment to take a deep breath.

A sharp piece of a pole sat in the muddy snow beside me. I picked it up and held it to Alex's throat. With the sharp tip, I drew a thin pink line across it, from one collarbone to the other. "Watch how you speak about Emberly Markos." He nodded pathetically. Finally, fear entered his eyes. I dropped the stick to the ground and leaned in close to his face. "I'm watching you."

Whimpering, he nodded again.

Then, since Emberly was too far away to hear, I leaned in and whispered a threat in his ear. A threat that I meant with all my mutated self.

As a general rule, I only terrorized others out of necessity. I never thought of myself as twisted or wicked. While Alex lay there in the snow, face bloodied, I watched sheer horror crawl across his features, and smirked.

Few things had ever given me as much satisfaction as that moment.

Maybe some people do deserve to live in fear.

CHAPTER 28
MY VICTOR

I JUMPED UP, leaving Alex on the cold, dirty road. The crowd that saw us through the other dancing and brawling teens erupted in applause. Emberly looked at my hand and the smattering of fresh blood beneath it in the dirty snow.

She rushed over and embraced me. I didn't hug her back, despite how desperately I wanted to make sure she felt safe after having been attacked. But she was wearing white, and though her clothes already streaked with mud, adding blood to the mix would have made Markos question me. *What would I tell him if he asked if I'd had my hand on her back?*

Aneta lay on the ground, actually injured or not, I had no idea, but she didn't dare get up. I don't believe I'd have struck her, even if she'd proven to be foul in the most personal way possible.

"Is your hand okay?" Emberly asked.

I felt nothing. Already, in a short amount of time, my body had learned and adjusted. It had blocked the pain without me giving it the direction to.

"Let's get out of here," she said, taking my good hand and guiding me to the edge of the crowd.

The parade continued without us, and though the people

who'd been watching didn't seem pleased as we left, their looks of irritation or disapproval weren't enough to stop us.

Emberly went ahead of me down the road, and I stopped, looking back at the boys I'd left on the ground, making sure none of them rose up to follow us.

Emberly guided me down the streets until I was hopelessly lost. She led us to the front steps of a pointed cathedral with eight ornate spires that reached up like arms, holding up the lower portion of the roof that extended over a small sitting area. A few benches surrounded a firepit which had burned down to the embers and now sat abandoned. Those who'd started it and enjoyed the flames were gone, either home or to watch the parade we'd deserted.

"Thank you," Ember finally said as she climbed the last step. "For all that."

"It was nothing." I smiled at her as she took a seat on the bench facing out to the road.

"You know, from anyone else, I wouldn't believe that. But you made it look as easy as walking and breathing."

"It comes naturally to me."

Out here, Emberly and I were completely alone. I listened closely, only barely able to hear the music in the distance. The glowing embers in the pit at our feet crackled and hummed.

"I hope you don't usually wander the streets at night," I said. "It's not safe."

"I'm safe with you," she said.

I laughed, relieved that I hadn't scared her away. That certainly wasn't the reaction I'd become accustomed to from others.

"Did you mean what you said to him?" she asked, adjusting the white scarf around her neck.

"What?" I asked in return.

"The graphic threat on his life if he ever talked to me again. The specific way you'd kill him if he called me that again."

If I'd been standing, I might have slipped on the ice at her comment. Instead, I just stared at her. There was no way she should have heard what I'd said to Alex. No way she *could* have heard it. I'd barely said it loud enough for him to hear me. The temptation to deny that I'd said anything like that to him was strong, but she wasn't asking what I'd said. She was asking if I'd meant it.

"How did you…" I began but stopped. "Did you really…"

She smiled, but I couldn't believe anyone could smile at what I'd said. Anyone besides me.

"I guess it's true what they say about lurpers having a, well, *colorful* vocabulary."

My face grew warm. I wouldn't have phrased it quite the way to him I had if I'd had any idea she'd hear me. I must have said it louder than I'd meant to in my moment of wrath.

"I have good ears," she said, and then, likely taking stock of my concern, she reached out and playfully pushed me. "I just wanted to say thank you. I'm not one to ask for help, and I've been managing him fine, but it was, well, it was really nice to have someone stand up for me like that. He's been getting more…pushy lately, and I…I just get…" I thought she might say scared, but instead, she said, "tired."

"I didn't intend for you to hear that," I confessed, though it had already been obvious from my alarmed reaction. "You shouldn't have to put up with him. Or anyone like that."

"Well, your threat was convincing. I'm pretty sure he slagged his pants." She laughed, and I joined her. The music became more distant, only a high note or two making its way to us, and while I'd loved hearing it up close and seeing the celebration, I preferred sitting here alone with Emberly.

"Will your parents be looking for us?"

"Yes, but they won't be expecting us until after the parade ends. We'll be back in time to burn the yule log." She looked down at my hand. It had stopped bleeding but now had thick scabs forming.

"That was really something back there." Emberly reached up and removed her mask, setting it gently beside us.

"Oh," I replied as my face grew warm. "Well, I'd hate to lose my job as your bodyguard."

"You really know how to fight."

"Yeah, well, you know my secret." I found myself covering my left wrist with my right hand. "It wasn't my first. Won't be my last."

"We're lucky to have you," she said, adjusting her position on the bench.

"Well, I hope I make Khizmit proud."

"You impressed me."

I looked quizzically at her. "By beating them up?"

"No, by standing up for me. By standing up for yourself. By showing mercy when you could have broken them all into pieces."

Mercy. I chuckled. "In Rhosivi, we just called that weakness."

"You're not weak," Emberly said, scooting closer to me on the hard bench. Instinct told me to put an arm around her, but I didn't want to misinterpret the situation. She reached up and untied my mask. I felt exposed somehow as she stared at me, and I stared back at her.

"Do you want to return?" I asked, knowing that if I stayed here with her for much longer, I wouldn't be able to keep my hands to myself. "I'm fine, really. I've been through worse."

The wind had picked up and found a way to slice between the ornate columns, carrying fat flakes in with it. I wished for a log to put on the dying embers in front of us. I looked up at some of the drifting flakes just as Emberly scooted even closer and cuddled into me. I must have gone rigid at her touch because she sat up immediately and asked, "Is this okay?"

I nodded and lifted my arm to make room for her. She nestled underneath my arm to lay on my chest. I was surprised she could rest there at all without her head bumping up and down from my pounding heart.

"You're going to The Outskirts tomorrow," she said, her voice getting quieter.

"Yeah. Early." I kept my words monosyllabic lest they reveal how my whole body was reacting to her affection.

"How do you feel?"

"Mostly excited." *Was I saying it about going to The Outskirts or my current condition?*

"Excited?"

"Is that wrong? What should I feel?" I asked.

"Um, scared. I'd be scared. Or I'd expect you to be apprehensive. Nervous. Anxious. I didn't expect you to be excited."

I took a deep breath and pulled Emberly a little closer to me, the flowery scent of her hair helping me to relax. "I've waited my whole life to prove that I'm not a monster. That I'm not a liability or a walking powder keg waiting to go off."

"You don't have to prove anything to anyone," she said, removing her right glove. She took her bare hand and wiggled it beneath my right sleeve, trying to get it into my glove. Her touch sent my heart racing.

"Unfortunately, you're wrong. I have to prove quite a lot." My gloves weren't really wide enough for both our hands. Instead, I reached around her, hugging her for a moment, while I pulled the glove off. She slid her fingers around mine and then brought our clasped hands to rest on her lap.

"People shouldn't have to prove they're good. You should never have had to earn your freedom," she said, her breath warm on the right side of my face.

"Well, if only more of Khizmit felt the same way."

"They will. In time, they will." For a brief moment, a look crossed her face like she was hatching a plan, and then the look was replaced by something else. Something that made my heart hammer harder inside my chest.

"Luka," Emberly whispered, turning to me. "I'm going to miss having you around."

"Thanks," I said. "I've never been missed before." All those transfers and roommates and none of them ever said they'd miss me. Then again, I couldn't even remember all their names. *I suppose they didn't have names though, did they?*

"I'll miss you too," I whispered, not even meaning to. I held her closer, breathed in her scent, and relaxed into the backrest of the bench.

Markos trusted me. *Did he trust me to not do this? Was I destined to betray him?*

I wanted to prove him right. Prove that I could be trusted.

But I wanted this more.

Emberly and I sat like that together, her hand warming mine, her touch distracting me from everything and anything else as the world seemed to spin around us. I could have sat like that with her all night, even if the night froze us into statues. I never would have wanted to leave.

"Luka," Emberly said gently. "What does your tattoo really say?"

"What do you mean?"

"I don't think you're a Charlie like my dad said," Emberly whispered.

"Oh yeah? Why's that?"

"Because he asked you to stay away from me, right?"

"He did," I said, beginning to pull away.

She grabbed my hand and held my arm around her. "But you're not obeying him."

She knew that Charlies were compliant? How? "I'm sorry—"

"I'm not." She began gently looking at my burned wrist again. "If you're a Charlie, do what I ask and don't leave."

I chuckled. "I don't think that's how it works. But, I should leave. We should go back. You dad would be—"

"Let's not talk about my dad right now," she said, leaning into my chest.

"Do you want to go back to the parade?"

"No," she said simply. "For me, it was never about the parade. I just wanted…some time…alone together."

We were very much alone, and the moment felt as fragile as a snowflake.

"I don't want to go back to the parade either," I confessed.

With her next to me, I felt her body move as she spoke. "I don't think you're a Charlie because they can't do what you did back there to Alex. Or what you did to Erik. Charlie's aren't dangerous. What you did was…"

"Terrifying?" I asked, finishing her sentence for her.

"No," she said adamantly. "What you did was incredible. It was mesmerizing. What you did was beautiful." She reached a hand up and placed it on my cheek for a moment. It left me desperate to hold her closer and never let go. "A Charlie could never have fought them off the way you did."

"That's true," I said. "I didn't think you knew what the different designations meant." When I'd arrived in Khizmit I wasn't sure any of the youth knew about TPI. I'd assumed it was a policy passed and enforced behind closed doors. Maybe her peers all but forgot the lurpers and resented or feared the vaznov, but Embrerly was different. She cared and had learned enough to know which characteristics suited a Charlie.

What did she know about Victors?

Emberly leaned in to warm her face by the embers for a moment before leaning back onto me. "Word travels fast around Khizmit. With the rapid tests right around the corner, I think most people know what to expect from a Hotel versus a Romeo." Her eyes lit up. "Is that what your wrist says? Are you a Romeo?"

"No," I said softly.

"You don't have to tell me I just…I just wondered."

My identity needed to be a secret for my safety, but there was a certain closeness that could come if I told her. And before I let myself feel any more of what I felt for her, I had to know if she'd care. I had to know now if what I was would get in the way of what she and I could be.

"My wrist says V-27," I said softly, preparing myself for her reaction. She sat up, creating distance between us as she stared at my face. Her eyes were wide. My hopes were higher than ever. She could kill me with rejection now. "I'm a Victor."

"Are you really?" She stared into my eyes.

I nodded. My heart pounded dramatically. *What was it about her that made me crave her validation and acceptance? What was it about her that left me feeling hungry and comfortable all at once?*

She stared on, intrigued.

"Do you know what it means?" I asked.

"I know it means you've got more than one mutation in your DNA. And now I know that you definitely went easy on Alex tonight. You could have killed him, couldn't you? You could have killed them all and never even broken a sweat."

I didn't want to admit it, but she might have seen an admission on my face.

The seconds drew longer, and I was ever aware of how she'd moved away. And then, just when I thought she'd stand up and walk away, she leaned back into me, even closer than before. I exhaled slowly.

"Do you want to see something else I can do?" I asked.

She nodded.

I held out my hand. "Look there," I said, directing her attention to one of the darker scars Then, careful not to heal too much, I erased the mark. She gasped, and I flipped my hand over, healing another one of the deep ones.

"Could you heal the whole thing?" she asked.

"Yes," I said, willing my body to stop and leave the rest of the burn as it was.

"But you can't let anyone see how they've marked you."

I nodded.

She continued, "Khizmit is so worried about keeping the world safe *from* you when what they need is to make it safe *for* you."

I held her closer. She understood.

"A Victor," she said, rubbing my arm. "Those are rare."

"Yes," I said, not wanting to complicate it by telling her I was also an X-ray. "I guess I'm one in a thousand."

"No," she corrected. "You're one of a kind, Luka."

She sat like that for a moment. The wind blew again, and the music in the distance continued. Her father would come looking for us once the parade ended.

"Are you…nervous?" I asked. "Knowing what I am?"

She scowled at me, her nose wrinkling with the expression. "Knowing what they marked you as doesn't make me feel nervous. Actually, it makes me feel safer with you. After seeing what you did to Alex and his friends tonight, I already knew that you were dangerous." She stared at me, her face closer to mine than it had ever been. "But you're not a threat to me."

"No," I said emphatically. "I'd never hurt you." I tucked a stray strand of her hair behind her ear, careful not to let it catch on any of her many earrings.

She smiled and bit her lip for a moment, as if trying to keep from saying something. "I know." Her face hovered in front of mine while she studied me. "You're not just a Victor," she said breathlessly. "You're *my* Victor."

I noticed the distant light from the lanterns at the edge of the alley reflected in her dark eyes just before she leaned in and put her lips on mine.

The kiss was quick. Before I even had time to realize what happened, she'd pulled away. In the dim light, I found her gaze searching my face, checking my expression.

Her mouth asked a question. *Did I want her? Did I want this?*

My answer was direct. I slid my hand up her arm and placed the palm of my burned left hand on the base of her jaw. I leaned in and kissed the edge of her mouth on one side. Gently, I turned her face and kissed the other side before the heat in my cheeks made me second-guess myself. This was Markos's daughter.

It would be too easy to lose perspective here. To cave. To give in to the craving I had for her.

I'd gone without food. I'd gone without water. I'd resisted breaking Bolest or killing Velky back at Rhosivi when he spat in my face.

Because of my practice, I could resist her. I was stronger than my desire.

I dipped the tip of my nose to her neck. She was warm. Warm like a lantern in the cold upper levels of the mine. Warm like sveetin still sending spirals of steam up into the air. I nuzzled into her, my breath catching. My chest was tight as I dragged my lips across the smooth skin of her neck up to the base of her jaw.

I could hardly breathe.

"Please," she whispered.

I glanced up to her glossy eyes. She wanted me to kiss her. Maybe she'd always wanted this as much as I had.

Her cold fingers pressed into my arm as she climbed her hand beneath my sleeve.

"Luka," she said my name, her breath warm against my lips.

I let go of restraint. Let the way she said my name unravel me. My mouth found her sweet lips. Kissing her was as instinctive as fighting to me. She tasted like peppermint. Soft and warm. I could drown in her. She wrapped one of her hands around my head, twisting her fingers into my hair.

The world drifted out of my grasp and for a moment she was the only other person who existed.

Bang!

A distant crash from a nearby alley brought the rest of the world back within my reach.

I moved away from her, breathing heavily. Neither of us said anything as we caught our breath. I sighed, trying to steady myself. I could kiss her for the rest of my life and never get enough. We had to stop though. I had to be strong enough to stop.

I leaned my forehead against her cheek, still cradling her face in my right hand.

"Your dad will kill me for that," I said. If I died right then, I'd have no regrets at all. I'd die happy.

Emberly leaned into me, her hand finding mine again. "He never has to know. Besides, rumor has it, Victors don't go down that easily."

CHAPTER 29
THE HEAD WARDEN

THE MUSIC GREW MORE distant as I floated on bliss. The kiss made me more drunk than I imagined any amount of rakia could. But she and I both knew that as much as we wanted to stay there cuddling one another, we had to get back for the rest of the festival. Imagining if Markos came looking for us and found her in my arms, with my hands tangled in her silky black hair made me quiver inside.

We scooted apart and re-secured our masks before getting up.

The night, silent and private, seemed calm now. Emberly and I didn't speak to one another as we walked back, this time in no rush. *Was she reliving the moment as I was?*

Though we were more than a couple blocks from the jumping, flickering light of the gigantic bonfire near the largest decorated tree, I dropped Ember's hand.

"You lead the way, and I'll follow a little bit behind," I said, not wanting to spread any more rumors than already plagued this block. Ember nodded and began walking ahead of me. I followed, staring at her while my cheeks grew sore from smiling so widely.

My gaze followed the reddish fur of Emberly's crown,

when suddenly my view was blocked by a man who stepped out of a small side street to face me.

"I've been looking for you," said a familiar cold voice. A fruity aroma hit me. Instantly, I became nauseated.

I looked at his boots.

My gaze traveled up his uniform as it passed the ribbons and rank. A silver double headed eagle with a crown. He was now a High Warden and Head Warden of Rhosivi. No wonder he was smiling.

The familiar sneer made my blood turn to ice. A tickle, like pins and needles, began in my fingertips and scurried up my skin clear to the hairs on the back of my neck.

The way the man smiled at me surely made my heart stop, at least for a moment. Even the notes of the music froze in the air as I stared at him.

Head Warden Velky.

He'd found me.

He reached out, clapped me on the shoulder, and I knew by how he'd touched me that he didn't know who I was. Somehow, miraculously, he didn't recognize me.

Had he known, the blade at his waist would have been buried in my chest with a laugh so joyful it could have rivaled the musicians' song.

"I saw what you did back there," Head Warden Velky said, his voice full of admiration. "With the performance. You're quite skilled."

I stood up straighter, to my full height, something I'd never done with Velky. I stared into his dark eyes, unflinching. He wanted me to say something, and I fought every instinct to duck and say, "Mr. Chief Preemptive Officer."

"Thank you." I made my voice deep.

"If you can play like that with your peers, I'd love to see what you could do with a weapon in your hands." His goatee was longer than it had been last time I'd seen him. His eyes still glistened with the same malice they always held, but this time, it wasn't directed at me. It was just there. Hatred, always behind his eyes, no matter the circumstance. The pins and needles continued to tickle my arms and hands.

I stared on, too scared to even look behind him to see where Emberly had gone. When he figured out who I was, and he would, he couldn't know I was here with Markos's daughter.

"Do you know who I am?" he asked.

I could have asked the same question. I looked back to the rank on his shoulder and hat. Based on how the men in this enclave behaved, they'd know who Head Warden Velky was.

"Yes," I replied. "You're Andrei Velky. Head Warden at Rhosivi Prison."

His mouth slithered into a hateful smile. "That's right."

Hatred, stronger than steel, threatened to spill out of me. I clenched my fists, praying he didn't notice.

"You should consider coming to Rhosivi. Help me keep some of the skrags there in line." He paused.

I clenched my fists. They wouldn't loosen even though I tried to relax. "I'll consider it," I said, though I'd never return to that hellhole, no matter the circumstances.

Velky surveyed me, looking closer at my face, and I feared he'd recognize me if he stared for too long. "You were in the parade, which makes me believe you're seventeen. Is that correct?"

"Yes," I said.

"In less than a year, you could be a private. We'd get you trained up right away. If you thought the parade tonight was fun, you'd absolutely love working at Rhosivi." His gaze went to my hands, where half-dried blood shone from my left glove. "Are you injured?" he asked, and it was the first time he'd ever voiced concern for me.

"I don't think so," I said, not moving. I checked to make sure I wasn't blocking any pain. My hand should have hurt, but it didn't. Not even the quietest whisper of pain responded when I twisted my hand around.

"Take off your glove," the demanding voice returned. I knew I had no choice. *What would be beneath the burn?*

With my right hand, I tugged off my glove and knew before it had even come all the way off that I was skudged.

Something had triggered complete healing. *Was it the fear of seeing Velky again?* No. I thought back to running my hands through Emberly's hair. It had been healed then. When all my walls were down and I'd lost myself in the kiss, I'd healed.

My hand was as whole as it had been before I'd left Predvoi. My fingers trembled as I removed the rest of the glove. I kept my palm down as sweat trickled along my back and the side of my neck. It was hot. Too hot. Too dark. In the distance, I heard Emberly's footsteps approaching again.

"It must not have been mine," I said, preparing to put the glove back on. "It's not my blood."

"How remarkable." Velky reached for my hand. I pulled it back out of his reach.

"Really," I insisted. "I'm fine."

His look became dangerous as his right hand went to the knife at his waist. "Show me your wrist."

With well-practiced hands, he pulled the blade. *What choice did I have? There had to be something I could do or say?* Velky forcibly flipped my left hand over.

The mark was faint. Extremely faint, especially in the darkness of the alley and the mixture of dried blood on my hands. If I'd kept my hand in the flames longer, I would have burned out all the ink.

I began to pull my hand away from Velky.

"What's this?" Velky asked, leaning closer. He rubbed his glove across my wrist, and though indistinct, the letter V still marked me.

Velky threw my wrist down with a gasp. "You skudging skrag," Velky said, his voice equal parts fear and disgust.

With his dagger, he reached forward and cut off my mask, freezing at the sight of me. It was as if I could read his mind. He noticed my healed face. He knew that I knew what I could do. If he'd feared me when I was twelve, it was nothing compared to his terror and revulsion of me now. "You're supposed to be dead."

"I'm nothing if not a constant disappointment to you."

"Luka," Emberly called. She'd come back. *Skudge it all, why had she come back?*

The fear in her eyes told me she knew she'd made a mistake.

Warden Velky turned to face her, recognition dawning on him as his mouth opened slightly before he clamped it shut. He'd pieced it together. He knew Markos's daughter. He knew me.

As if in slow motion, he stepped forward with the sharp steel aimed toward me. I knew exactly how to end this as fast as possible and what it required. He stepped in, driving the blade through my skin and stomach. As he twisted it, hot blood gushed out. Emberly screamed at the sight. With the majority of the blade in my body, I controlled it. With it still buried inside me, I twisted, wrenching it free from Velky's grip.

I gasped. Wanted to fall. Wanted to cry. But Emberly was still screaming. Velky bared his teeth, and his hand went for his revolver.

Though I saw the world move around me slowly, I moved just as slowly, which allowed me the precision I needed. Velky turned and pulled the trigger of his revolver just as a huge man jumped out from the alleyway and blocked Emberly.

Commander Markos took a bullet to his arm. Blood stained the sleeve of his uniform in a blotch that covered his shoulder. Behind him, Emberly was fine. Safe.

"You traitor!" Velky screamed at Markos. *Where was*

Markos's revolver? His attention stayed on Emberly. Keeping her safe. Markos had Velky distracted.

Taking the knife out of my gut didn't hurt. I felt no pain. No joy. No fear. Only rage and a need to protect.

Velky heard me coming and turned to face me, his hand too slow for mine.

I wouldn't mourn him.

No one should mourn him, I thought, and I drove the knife directly into Warden Velky's heart. His back bit the rough brick as the blade punched through bone. He gasped.

With my senses enhanced, I heard the crunch of his sternum and the sudden stop of his heart. His boots scraped against the ice, squeaking twice as he fell to the ground.

Emberly was still screaming until Markos slipped his hand over her mouth, cradling her.

"Sir," I said, breathless. "Warden Velky, he—"

"I know," Markos said, before turning Emberly around to embrace her. Her eyes brimmed with tears.

She opened her mouth, but only a stifled sob came out. Her gaze went to the blood on her father's arm and the sticky blade in my hand. Her face, rigid with fear, turned back to her father. *Was she scared of me?* She'd seen me kill Velky. *Should I pretend remorse?*

Another figure stepped out of the alley, silhouetted by the distant bonfire. I prepared myself for a fight.

But it was Roman who came out of the shadows, holding Markos's revolver.

"You did it," Roman said. His tone didn't carry pride but weight. He understood the burden of taking a life.

I tried not to look back at Velky's still body. "I killed him," I said, my voice smaller than I wanted it to be.

"You healed already." Roman stared at my stomach. Then, and only then, I remembered that I'd been stabbed. Frantically, I searched my side, but the wound was already gone.

I was fine, but what about Markos? I moved tentatively in

their direction, wanting to comfort Emberly. She wiped at her eyes and took some deep breaths as she leaned into her father. Then the two of them stood. Markos moved closer, his arms around Emberly.

"Your hand," he said. I held it out. The V was faint, but it wasn't gone.

"I didn't mean to heal it." I flexed it, my fingers grateful to have full mobility back.

"You can't stop your body from performing its normal functions. Now that it knows how to heal, it will. Every time, whether you intend for it to or not. It would take more work to keep it injured at this point."

"How are you?" I asked, looking at the large blood stain on his shoulder.

"I'm fine. It just grazed me." He didn't even look under the sleeve to check his skin or the wound.

"But Velky..." I said, turning toward the dark heap on the floor of the alley.

Markos turned to Emberly. "Get back to the parade. Tell your mother I had something urgent come up and took Luka with me. Don't give her any more information. Say nothing about Velky. Someone will find him soon, and we can't be here when that happens."

Ember had streaks down her face from tears. "Luka." She reached out for me. Her outstretched fingers brushed against mine.

"I'm sorry, hun," Markos said "There's not really time for goodbyes."

Obediently, Ember nodded, gave my hand a final squeeze, and then dashed away down the streets toward the festival.

Watching her go pained me. She was everything I wanted. Being with her made me feel peaceful and happy, and without her I knew my life would become dark again. Dangerous again.

Would *I* become dangerous again?

She ran out of my sight, and I realized that I had something to fight for. Someone to come back to when this was all over.

Once Emberly had disappeared, I glared at Velky's corpse. He'd ruined everything.

"Come, Luka. We have a car ready. Lockbox is in the back. I was planning to take just him tonight, but I guess it'll be all of us now," Roman said.

"We must move quickly," Markos said, his voice stern again. He pointed down a side street and then began to run.

Mechanically, I followed Roman and Markos, too heartbroken to worry about anything else. I had to leave Emberly. I didn't know when I'd be back. Each step took me further from her. Each step took me away from the life I thought I'd wanted.

Was this path my fate? Did some greater power demand that I fight? If so, for what purpose? I had to believe that what I had to face next would require a different sort of strength than the past had.

I would face the trials head-on. I would accept them, and overcome them, and I'd be back. Arms pumping, I caught up to Markos.

"Sir," I began, blinking as we stepped through some flickering streetlights onto a more narrow alley. "Where are we going?"

"We have to get some distance from Khizmit so they can't link any of us to Andrei's death."

Markos didn't even pant as he sprinted. We passed through three more blocks, avoiding the busy parts where they held their own festivals with large, dancing bonfires.

I knew we were going to the Outskirts. To war. To the legion. It was too far to walk or run. What had Roman said about a truck? My thoughts refocused as we arrived at a warehouse.

The dirty red bricks stretched along the sides of the building, their pattern broken by the large metal doors wide enough for four mine carts to sit side by side. Markos gripped the handle of the second door and pulled it up. With a rattle and a grinding sound the door opened and rolled onto the tracks above us. Inside sat a truck, the back heavy with supplies. Most of the boxes and barrels in the back were big enough to hide Lockbox. *Which was he in? Was he warm enough?*

Markos opened the door and jumped behind the steering wheel, and I climbed into the small, fold-down bucket seat in the back. Roman settled into the front seat, and for a moment my heavy breath was visible in the cold air. Markos dug in his pocket for a second, then jabbed the key into the ignition. The engine sputtered to life.

We were leaving Khizmit. Leaving Emberly. At the thought of her, a worry nudged me to ask Markos a question as he shifted the truck into drive.

"How did you know where we were?" I asked. Somehow afraid that I was going to be in more trouble for kissing Emberly than I was for murdering Head Warden Velky. *Did he know what we'd been doing during the parade?*

Markos pulled out of the garage, the headlights on the truck illuminating a small path through the snowy streets as we barreled down the street. At this speed, I worried we might lose traction and smash into one of the many buildings that blurred past us.

"Stay silent until we leave the Enclave," Markos replied, and I swallowed my questions. If he intended to scold me, I was sure he'd want to do it once we were away from danger..

With a deep sigh, Markos slowed and took a sharp right turn. We drove slowly. Had someone already found Velky's body? I hoped it wouldn't be a child. If anything could ruin the joy of the celebrations, it would be stumbling across a bloody body in the street.

Markos continued to take the wide roads through

Khizmit, and I sat silently until we reached a thick metal gate. Three guards waited on each side. In the dim light from the few sconces set into the stone towers, I made out their rank patches. A captain approached the car.

The beady black eyes belonged to Captain Crease.

"Evening, Commander," Crease said, saluting. "Happy Koliada."

Markos saluted back. From the shadows, I hoped Crease wouldn't notice the blood on Markos's shoulder.

"Captain Kral," Crease said. "Didn't you just get back from Predvoi?"

Roman nodded to him. "Yes, but you know how it is. When you work with skrags, there's no time to rest."

I cringed at the term.

"Where are you going tonight?" Crease asked.

Markos answered with a hint of irritation in his voice, "Urgent news from The Outskirts. I'd really hoped to spend Koliada with the family, but war doesn't wait."

"But, Sir," Crease said, narrowing his beady eyes. "Latvani swore they wouldn't attack us during the week of Koliada."

"Well, it isn't Latvani. It's the skudging Lurper Legion. They don't follow rules too well."

Understanding seemed to reach Crease's eyes, even as he found me in the back seat of the truck. Crease saluted again and then shouted to his soldiers to open the gate. They pushed it with their gloved hands, chunks of ice breaking off at the hinges as they screeched into the night sky. Markos returned Crease's salute with his injured arm. He gave no sign of pain. No small expression of discomfort at the quick movement.

Markos gave the car some gas, and with a final salute, Crease disappeared behind us. I couldn't help but wonder if I'd ever come back. If I'd ever see Emberly again or taste the food which was nearly as sweet as the freedom. But nostalgia would get me nowhere. And now that my burn was completely healed, there was no way for me to reenter the city as a free man.

We drove for only a few more minutes before I started asking questions. I repeated the one that worried me most. "How did you know where we were?" I ran a finger along the faint tattoo on my wrist. I was a Victor. She was Markos' daughter. Maybe he'd followed us all along.

"We heard you," Roman said, a sly smile spreading across his face.

I wanted to ask, *"How much did you hear?"*

Perhaps only Roman had heard. He had remarkable eyesight. Maybe his hearing was as good as mine, but the night was quiet. My voice had carried as I'd spoken to her. The night had been quiet with most of the people at the parade. What I'd done was reckless but I didn't regret it. I hated to leave Emberly, especially under the circumstances. If we'd parted after kissing that would have been one thing, but instead, the final image had been me as a murderer. *Had I looked remorseful? Relieved? What had she seen?*

"Sir, your family...will they be okay?"

"We'll be back," Markos said, a certainty in his tone that couldn't be questioned. "We'll be back with an army, and we'll end this war."

The darkness pressed around us, and I could almost believe we were the only three living souls in the world. The passion in his voice lit a fire in my chest. "How?" I asked.

"I'm the Commander over the most dangerous battalion in the history of the Enclaves. I have Victors, Whiskeys, X-rays, and Yankees training with weapons. I have soldiers with unregistered abilities studying strategy and practicing warfare against Latvani soldiers until we're ready to fight our real enemies."

Other Victors. More boys like me. *But he'd said Latvani wasn't our real enemy?* "Our real enemies?" I asked.

"Khizmit." He said it as though it should have been

obvious to me from the get-go. "Our real enemies are those who put children in prison and force them to slave their lives away. Our enemies are those who stand and shoot 18-year-old boys because of their supposed proclivities for crime. Because of their abilities. Because of their parents."

My enemies were his enemies. Excitement ran through me like a jolt of lightning, electrifying my nerves, sending my head spinning.

"What are you going to do?" I found myself whispering.

Markos's face looked half-crazed in the light reflecting off the snowy road in front of us. The crazed look was something that invigorated me. He was hungry, hungry for change and revenge. That's why he'd said nothing, not a single word, about what I'd done to Velky. His voice was low and conspiratorial. "We're going to take over the government and dissolve the Preemptive Initiative."

"How?"

"A coup. A military coup."

"Led by…"

He grinned, slapped Roman on the shoulder, and then gripped the steering wheel again. "Us, Luka. Us."

Now that we had some distance from the Enclave, I leaned over to look at Markos's injured arm.

"Do you need me to wrap it or anything?"

"No," he said stiffly.

I leaned over and reached out, poking my finger through the big hole in the dark brown fabric.

"Luka," Markos protested, but I turned his arm over. On the other side of his bicep, his uniform had an identical hole.

Dried blood flaked on his skin at the prod of my finger but the skin beneath it showed nothing. No injury at all. My breath caught as I stared at his arm again, looking for the source of the bleeding.

Markos exhaled slowly, glancing at me from the side while driving.

"But Sir…" I didn't dare ask.

Roman leaned forward, taking stock of the lack of injury himself. "Commander," Roman said. "How?"

"But this means," I said, sitting back up as Markos pulled his arm away from both of us.

He'd healed.

He'd been shot by Velky, and based on the amount of blood and placement of the holes in his uniform, the bullet had done much more than simply graze him.

I knew what this meant, but I needed to hear him say it. I needed to hear him confess it to me.

"What are you?" I asked, my voice barely louder than the whine of the engine.

The vehicle slowed and then stopped. Markos pressed the brake and turned to look at me and Roman.

Outside the stars and moon reflected on the snow, bringing enough light in through the windows for me to see his expression. Resignation and apprehension crossed his face.

"I was a Test Criminal," Markos confessed, shooting a glance at my wrist before looking back to my face. "I'm… skudge it, I'm Victor-1."

ACKNOWLEDGMENTS

I owe a debt of gratitude to many more than I'll remember to mention, and I apologize for anyone I've forgotten. The following people come to mind as I write this:

-Matt, my husband and best friend. Thank you for the life of adventure, your gentle manner, and the endless encouragement.

-My girls for their enthusiastic support. Adi especially for reading every word and letting me know when too much was too much.

-Natalie for coloring and listening, and caring about my boy.

-Caleb Hafen, who did so much more than just narrate the book. Thank you for the edits, the support, the life you breathed into the story, and your patience with my proclivity to add so many characters with a wide range of accents.

-The Stag Beetle Books team: Chey and Dannie for edits, and Kevin for the energy and encouragement when I needed it most.

-Ilse, for her edits and suggestions. All the Vaznov owe you a debt of gratitude.

- Jenny Autry, you have been unwaveringly supportive. Your early read of the first draft shaped a lot!

And please, reader, wherever you are, know that I am so grateful to you for joining me in Khizmit and caring about Luka, Roman, Lockbox, and Emberly.

Warmly,
L. Blaise Hues

FROM THE PUBLISHER

Thank you so much for reading The Masked Victor!

We hope you enjoyed the journey and characters as much as we loved bringing them to you. **Please leave a review on Amazon** and Goodreads while the story is fresh in your mind. Reviews are writing fuel for authors and help their books get into the hands of other hungry readers. If you're a big fan of speculative young adult and middle-grade fiction, we invite you to join our street team. Get copies of our books in advance, early access to covers, and other freebies!

Stag Beetle Books

www.stagbeetlebooks.com

ALSO BY L. BLAISE HUES

Legacy of Debris: A Gritty Young Adult Dystopian

Republic of Ruin

Shattered State

Crimson Nation

*

The Eden Compound

*

Kids of Cybercity: A Middle-Grade Trilogy

The Search for Silence

A Voice in the Noise

The Thundering Echo